The Origin of the Fays
and Other Stories

The Origin of the Fays
and Other Stories

Edited, introduced and translated by
Brian Stableford

A Black Coat Press Book

ISBN 978-1-61227-821-6. First Printing. January 2019. Published by Black Coat Press, an imprint of Hollywood Comics.com, LLC, P.O. Box 17270, Encino, CA 91416. All rights reserved.
Printed in the United States of America.

TABLE OF CONTENTS

Introduction

When Charles-Joseph Mayer attempted to compile his massive collection of *contes de fées* and other *contes merveilleux, Le Cabinet des fées* in 1786, initially in 37 volumes, although it was subsequently expanded to 41—combining the contents of more than a hundred volumes issued between 1697 and 1755—he found it difficult for several reasons, stemming from the fact that, with exception of little more than a dozen volumes, all of the original publications had been issued without the royal privilege required for licit publication in Paris.

In the latter part of the relevant period the privilege in question was regarded by some writers as an unnecessary superfluity, given that so many books were published without the benefit of approval by the royal censors that their wholesale suppression would have been impossible; only a limited number of texts considered dangerous or offensive were actively pursued and persecuted. Nevertheless, the fact that unprivileged volumes existed outside the formal protection of the law meant that the books were almost always issued anonymously, with title pages bearing false places of publication, often omitting or falsifying the name of the publisher. Many such publications were fugitive, and although copies of many of them eventually made their way. one way or another, into the Royal Library—which became the Bibliothèque Nationale after the 1789 Revolution—many did not, ensuring that Mayer's problems would be perpetuated for generations of subsequent researchers, all the way to the present day.

Mayer made assiduous attempts to discover the identities of the authors of many of the anonymous works he reprinted. Often, he succeeded, because the authors were often only reluctantly anonymous, and the secret was allowed to leak out, once they were dead and thus immune to prosecution, if not while they were alive. In many cases, however, he was reduced to guesswork and supposition, and because bibliography, like proverbial nature, abhors a void, he was by no means a reluctant guesser. He routinely strove to correct inaccurate guesses made by previous bibliographers, as well as correcting his own mistakes when he became aware of them, but his endeavor was and remains haunted by inevitable clouds of uncertainty. His efforts were undoubtedly heroic, and his labors left an enormously valuable heritage for later commentators interested in the evolution of fantastic fiction, but he was working in very difficult and somewhat hostile conditions; the *Cabinet* was itself unprivileged, and although that could be reckoned almost irrelevant by 1786, it still involved inconveniences, rapidly compounded by the social and economic turmoil of the Revolution. His uncertainties and occasional tendency to error, although understandable, have to be taken into account in any attempt to follow in his footsteps.

The stories in the present anthology all illustrate, in various ways, the difficulties that writers of *contes de fées* had in publishing their work and the occasional problems that Mayer and other bibliographers had in identifying their authors. The three stories by Catherine Durand can only be reliably assigned to her because the volumes in which they first appeared were reprinted in 1737, after her death, in a five-volume set of *Oeuvres de Madame Durand*, not only bearing a signature but issued with the aid of a royal privilege that their original anonymous publication had not been able to obtain, their satirical content having become innocuous in the interim. Modern bibliographers take the view that Durand was actually the author's maiden name, identifying her as Catherine Durand Bédacier (1670-1736), although the eighteenth century bibliographer Jacques de Long reversed the order of the surnames in his *Bibliothèque historique de la France* (1719), and several subsequent commentators did likewise. If Bédacier was, in fact, her husband's name, he might have been the Jacques Bédacier born in 1648—it was common practice at the time for young women to be married off by arrangement to much older men—and if so, she would almost certainly have been widowed before she died, and perhaps before she began publishing, but all of that is uncertain.

The two portmanteau works in which Madame Durand's *contes de fées* were interpolated, as tales told by the characters, were *La Comtesse de Mortane* (1700), which includes "La Fée Lubantine" (tr. as "The Fay Lubantine") and *Les Petits soupers de l'été de l'année 1699, ou Galantes aventures, avec L'Origine des fées* [The Little Suppers of Summer 1699; or, Gallant Adventures, with "The Origin of the Fays"] (1702), which includes "Le Prodige d'amour" (tr. as "The Prodigy of Amour") as well as the tale identified in the extended title. Although they belong to the "first wave" of *contes de fées*, and the author might well have attended one or more of the Parisian salons in which the vogue for such tales began and from with it spread, the first and last off Durand's tales differ sharply from the pattern of such salon tales established by Mademoiselle de La Force, the Comtesse de Murat and Madame d'Aulnoy, and can be seen as reactions against it.

The downbeat quality of "La Fée Lubantine" bears some resemblance to the two anomalous tales included in Catherine Bernard's portmanteau *Ines de Cordoue* (1697; tr. as "Ines de Cordova")—both of which are translated in a previous Black Coat Press anthology, *The Queen of the Fays and Other Marvelous Tales*—but it is more violently tragic than Bernard's couplet. The similarity prompts one to wonder whether it is entirely a coincidence that Bernard and Durand, the authors of the most bitterly pessimistic *contes de fées* in the original set, were the only two not of aristocratic heritage. "Le Prodige d'amour" is a much more orthodox tale in its optimism, but "L'Origine des fées" broke the mold of the "fay mythos" devised by the inventors of the 1690s genre decisively and flamboyantly. It not only offers a highly idiosyncratic account for the origin of the fays, but also of the apparent extinction of the species, after a period of allegedly-inevitable decadence. The removal of "the time of the fays" from Medieval times to a vague period of prehistory is featured in several other works

9

of the "contraband renaissance" of *contes de fées* that began in the 1730s, most notably in Pierre-François Beauchamps' *Funestine* (1737; tr. in the Black Coat Press anthology *Funestine and Other Adventures in Romancia*), which acknowledges Durand's influence on its own idiosyncratic account of the origin and extinction of the fay species.

The next story in the present anthology is one of two novelettes published as *Le Prince des Aigues-marines et Le Prince invisible* [The Prince of Aquamarines and The Invisible Prince] in 1722 by Louise Cavelier (1703-1745), who became Madame Levêque (or Levesque) a year after its publication, when she married one of the king's men-at-arms. Although published anonymously, the volume had the very unusual distinction of a royal privilege. The work of a writer not even born during the first wave of *contes de fées*, and still in her teens when she produced it, the two stories are among the first new publications of the "second wave" of *contes de fées*. It is something of a mystery how a youthful commoner from Rouen was able to acquire a privilege for publication at a time when it seems to have been almost impossible even for highly-placed courtiers, and one can only speculate as to how she did it. It was, however, not unknown for highly placed individuals at the court, including the princes of the blood, to arrange marriages with servants of the court for their mistresses, for the sake of convenience. At any rate, the volume was reprinted posthumously in 1744, when the renaissance was more fully under way, and a demand had been clearly demonstrated for such works.

As might be expected of a work by such a young author, Cavelier's stories are a trifle crude in their narrative construction, and flamboyant in their plotting. Although by no means as cruel as "La Fée Lubantine," the relentlessly violent "Le Prince des Aigues-marines" does make one highly unusual narrative move in marrying its heroine, albeit briefly, to the wicked fay's loathsome son—a "fate worse than death" that most heroines contrived scrupulously to avoid—and although its final narrative twist is not without analogues, it has a telling measure of disenchantment that reflects a certain ideological kinship with the author's fellow commoners Bernard and Durand. The author went on to publish several more books of poetry and drama, and two novels, including *Célenie, histoire allégorique* (1738), which is not a *conte de fées*, although the eponymous heroine is temporarily metamorphosed into a dog by the magic of her governess.

The writer of the 1730s renaissance who followed most evidently and most scrupulously in the footsteps of the Comtesse de Murat and Madame d'Aulnoy appears to have been baptized Marie-Madeleine de Lubert, although she was also known as Marguerite de Lubert; she became one of the most prolific writers of eighteenth-century *contes de fées*, publishing several long novellas in the form of booklets, although the precise extent of her work is difficult to ascertain, because of difficulties of attribution, and some of the stories retrospectively credited to her are probably by other hands. The four novellas translated in the Black Coat Press collection *Princess Camion and Other Tales of Enchantment*—*Tecserion, ou Le Princes des autruches* (1737; reprinted in 1743 as *Sec-et-Noir*; tr. as "Tecserion"), *La Princesse Lionnette et the prince Coquerico* (1743; tr. as "Princess Lionnette and Prince Coquerico"), *Le Prince Glacé et la princesse Étincelante* (1743; tr. as "Prince Frozen and Princess Sparkling"), *La Princesse Camion* (1743; tr. as "Princess Camion")—are definitely her work, but the attribution of the three included herein is a trifle dubious.

La Princesse Couleur de rose et le prince Celadon (tr. as "Princess Roseate and Prince Celadon") and *La Princesse Sensible et le prince Typhon* (tr. as "Princess Sensitive and Prince Typhon") were both published in 1743, allegedly in The Hague by an unnamed publisher, as part of a set of six booklets, along with the four items cited in the previous paragraph, and the similar format of the six led to their all being attributed to Mademoiselle de Lubert. That attribution is reasonably convincing in the case of the former item, which has a good deal in common with the other four and is set in a similar milieu, but it is far less convincing in the case of *La Princesse Sensible et le prince Typhon*, which is considerably shorter, far less subtle in its satire and equipped with a brutally eccentric moral distinct from the tacit morality of the novellas making up the rest of the set.

The supposition that the last-named item might have been added arbitrarily to the set by the publisher, rather than the author, seems more plausible because another booklet issued in the same format in 1752, also allegedly in the Hague but with the publisher named as "Pierre de Hondt," a satirical *conte philosophique* entitled *Cornichon et Toupette, histoire fée* (tr. herein as "Cornichon and Toupette"), was also attributed to Mademoiselle de Lubert by Mayer when he reprinted it, presumably on the basis of that similarity of format. It is very difficult indeed, however, to believe that it is her work; it gives every appearance of having been written by a male *philosophe* with an agenda very different from hers. On the other hand, writers often do want to vary their work, adopting seemingly different personas in order to follow different agendas, and there is no doubt that Mademoiselle de Lubert had the intelligence, the philosophical acumen and literary ability necessary to have written *La Princesse Sensible et le prince Typhon* and *Cornichon et Toupette* had she had the inclination to do so.

It is worth noting—and the later stories in the present anthology illustrate the point very well—that the authors active in the contraband renaissance of *contes de fées* were all well aware that they were working in an "Age of Enlightenment" whose ideological context was markedly different from the one in which the first wave writers had been active. Many of them were *philosophes* themselves, and all of the rest, seemingly without exception, were acquainted with *philosophes*. Mademoiselle de Lubert knew Voltaire—he dedicated a poem to her, addressing her as "Muse et Grace—and seems to have known Montesquieu as well. Both of those writers were active participants in Parisian salons at the time when writing *contes de fées* came back briefly into fashion there, along with

Beauchamps and the other prolific writer who flourished at the same time as Lubert, the Comte de Caylus.

Although Mademoiselle de Lubert was the writer who paid the most overt homage to the first wave tales in her works, her works nevertheless have a particular sardonic flippancy and calculatedly surreal absurdity that places her very solidly in the context of her own era. She was certainly not incapable, therefore, of writing biting satirical works set in the milieu of Faerie, or of varying that milieu to the particular purposes of a satirical tale. Nevertheless, having translated the three stories included in the present story in swift succession, the sensation I obtained from them suggests very strongly to me that the second is probably not Lubert's work, and that the third is almost certainly due to another hand.

Indeed, I suspect that *La Princesse Couleur de rose et le prince Celadon* might have been Lubert's last *conte de fées*: a suspicion endorsed by the wry acknowledgement, in the final line of the story, that the author had completely lost control of a plot that had developed too many complications as it evolved, and had felt forced to bring it to a cursory and highly unsatisfactory conclusion—an experience that might have deterred a sensitive writer from further experiments in the genre. Most of the subsequent literary work that is definitely hers is editorial rather than primarily creative, including a four-volume edition of *Amadis de Gaule* (1750), and new versions of two first wave portmanteaux: a 1754 edition of *La Tyrannie des fées détruite* (1703; signed "Comtesse D.L" and tr. under that name in the Black Coat Press collection *The Tyranny of the Fays Abolished and Other Stories*) and a 1756 edition of the Comtesse de Murat's *Les Lutins du château de Kernosy* (1710; tr. as "The Goblins of Kernosy Castle" in the Black Coat Press collection *The Palace of Vengeance and Other Tales of Enchantment*).

No indication seems to be currently available as to where Mademoiselle de Lubert met Voltaire, or which literary salons she attended in the 1730s and 1740s, but it is known that one of the salons where the writing and reading of *contes de fées* was actively encouraged and practiced was the one hosted by Françoise Le Marchand, whose two attributed tales are translated in the Black Coat Press volume *Florine and Boca*. Although the story by the renowned artist and writer Charles-Antoine Coypel (1694-1792) translated herein was not published until much later, it was certainly written in the late 1730s and read aloud in Madame Le Marchand's salon, as the story itself, and the footnote that Mayer attached to it when he reprinted it in the *Cabinet*, make clear. The story and the note also make it evident that, after publishing "Boca," Madame le Marchand—or "Thémire," as she nicknamed herself after a character is Montesquieu's *Le Temple de Gnide* (1725)—gave up reproducing her work in print, contenting herself with the private acclamation of the select audience of her salon. Coypel, following her example, left "Aglaé ou Nabotine" (tr. as Aglaé or Nabotine") unpublished for thirty years. How many other contributors to the genre, one wonders, never got around to publishing work done in that environment at all?

Among the well-known *philosophes* who made a contribution to the genre was Charles Pinot Duclos (1704-1772), author of *Acajou et Zirphile* (1744; tr. as "Acajou and Zirphile"), allegedly written as a result of a wager, around a set of illustrations by the artist François Boucher. Duclos, a close friend of the Comte de Caylus—who had helped to facilitate his early publications in the genre of libertine fiction—was already a member of the Académie des inscriptions et belles-lettres when the story was published, and was subsequently elected to the Académie française; he was a significant contributor to the *Encyclopédie*, but was regarded by his fellow *philosophes* as something of a lightweight, more adept at *bon mots* than serious endeavors; Voltaire, Diderot and d'Alembert all disapproved of him. Even so, he replaced Voltaire as France's official historiographer in 1750 when the latter gave up the post. His *Mémoires secrets sur les règnes de Louis XIV de Louis XV* [Secret Memoirs of the Reigns of Louis XIV and Louis XV], however—derived from and supplementing the authentic but controversial memoirs of the Duc de

Saint-Simon—could not be published until after the Revolution, although they enjoyed great success then, in English translation as well as in French.

François Boucher's illustrations had earlier played a crucial role in the production of *Faunillane, ou l'infante jaune* (1741; reprinted 1743; tr. as "Faunillane; or, The Yellow Child"), the imagery of which—unsurprisingly—has several significant similarities to the Duclos story. Although written in French and very much in the French tradition, it was the work of a famous Swedish diplomat, Count Carl Gustaf Tessin (1695-1770), who allegedly wrote it in haste specifically in order to be able to commission illustrations for it from Boucher, who had recently painted his portrait and whose wife he wanted to seduce; the first edition allegedly consisted of only three copies, one of which is in the Bibliothèque Nationale and is reproduced on *gallica*. Whether that legend is true or not, the story is remarkable for its exaggerated bizarrerie, which might have taken its lead from Beauchamps and Caylus but outstripped them with deliberately casual effrontery, becoming the most surreal work of its period. Although it is unlikely to have influenced other writers, even via the 1743 "commercial edition," it is not improbable that it was read aloud, as a joke, in aristocratic salons where the Count was reckoned to be a prestigious visitor.

Charles Duclos was the most prestigious of the French dabblers in the genre during the 1740s, and his example might have been significant in prompting Jean-Jacques Rousseau (1712-1778) to try his hand at it, Rousseau having appreciated him a little more kindly than other leading *philosophes*, probably because of his similar reputation at the time. Although "Acajou et Ziphile" does have inclinations in the direction of a *conte philosophique*, it is primarily a colorful joke, but the author does seem to have progressed from a spirit of pure parody to being caught up by the fascination of the genre's toils, and the story's elaboration surely exceeds the necessity of its original impulse.

Rousseau's own contribution to the genre, "La Reine Fantasque" (tr. as "Queen Fantasque," which is thought to have been written in 1752, long before such classics as *Julie, ou La Nouvelle Héloïse* (1761) and *Émile* (1762), although it was not published until 1769, is one of numerous second wave *contes de fées* that revolve around a series of exemplary moral dilemmas, provided with fanciful magically-aided resolutions, all resolutely comical, although reflecting real philosophical debates that their authors were undoubtedly sharply aware.

It might not be a coincidence that 1752 also saw the publication of *Cornichon et Toupette*, which has a similar focus and tone to "La Reine fantasque," and it is not improbable that Rousseau read it. The references in *Cornichon et Toupette* to Montesquieu's *L'Esprit des lois* and Alexander Pope's "Essay on Man"—both fairly recent when the novella was published—are strongly suggestive of an author with his or her finger firmly on the pulse of contemporary thought, and although the Abbé de Saint-Pierre belonged to an earlier era (he had been a participant in Madame de Lambert's salon, alongside the inventors of the *contes de fées*) the sympathetic citation of his endeavors in the story is also significant. If the probably-male author of *Cornichon et Toupette* was not a notable *philosophe* himself, he was surely acquainted with some of them, and both Duclos and Rousseau might well have been among his friends.

The position of official historiographer of France, inherited by Duclos from Voltaire, was also held for a while by François-Augustin de Paradis de Moncrif (1687-1770), like Duclos a member of the Académie française, whose first publication, in 1717, was *Les Aventures de Zeloïde et d'Amaznaridine, contes indiens*, one of many pastiches of Galland's *Mille et une nuits*, in a genre of *contes merveilleux* that Mayer conflated with that of *contes de fées* in his *Cabinet*. There is a strong element of the *merveilleux* in many of Moncrif's prolific works for the theater, but the handful of *contes de fées* that Mayer reprinted, the most substantial of which is "Les Dons des fées, ou Le Pouvoir de l'éducation"

(tr. as "The Gifts of the Fays; or, The Power of Education"),
are more earnestly didactic and moralistic, set very firmly in
the tradition of *contes philosophiques*. It was probably one of
the first such tales to be written, almost certainly predating the
previous three items, although it does not appear to have been
published until 1751, and it is probably one of the first tales to
fuse the two genres combined by Mayer—a practice that became increasingly commonplace in the 1750s as *contes de fées*
suffered a drastic decline in fashionability, while Oriental fantasies resisted eclipse somewhat more robustly.

That tendency to hybridization can also be seen very
clearly and equally artificially in "Durboulour," allegedly by
Marianne-Agnès Pillement de Falques (c1720-1785?), first
published in a collection entitled *Contes du serrail, traduits du
turc* [Tales from the Seraglio, translated from the Turkish]
(1753), more for reasons of temptation than accurate description. In spite of a tokenistic mention of "the prophet," the attribution of the sword that becomes the object of a quest to
Solomon, and the brief appearance of a caravan, the story is a
pure *conte de fées*, set in the same fictional milieu as the para-
digms of the genre, replete with fays, ogres and other standard
motifs, and written in much the same tributary spirit as Mademoiselle de Lubert's stories. Falques, however, certainly was
the author a much more robust Arabian fantasy, the short nov-
el *Abbassai* (2 vols., 1753), aided by her real knowledge of
Oriental languages, as well as a long satirical account of *La
dernière guerre des bêtes, pour servir à l'histoire du XVIII
siècle* [The Last War of the Beasts, a useful contribution to the
History of the Eighteenth Century] (2 vols., 1758), which reflects very ostentatiously to the stormy intellectual climate
established by the *philosophes*.

A defrocked nun who was eventually forced by scandal
to flee to England—where she is said to have assisted William
Beckford with his translations from the Arabic and might have
made a significant contribution to his classic *Vathek*, initially
written in French in 1782—the exiled Mademoiselle de
Falques (which might not have been her real name, and even if

17

it was, the *particule* was certainly a fake) can be seen in retrospect as a significant loss to French literature, because rather than in spite of the excessive nature of her contributions to the genre of fake "secret memoirs," in which many of the original inventors of *contes de fées* and several of the second wave writers made their initial literary reputations. As the author of "Durboulour," she is entitled to be hailed as the author who carried forward their rebellious spirit into the era of the genre's final decadence more robustly than anyone else. At any rate, "Durboulour," certainly seems to have been written purely for the fun of it, as a kind of homage to the inventions of the Comtesse de Murat and Madame d'Aulnoy, and thus seems an entirely apt conclusion to the present sampler, as well as yet another illustration of the kinds of bibliographical uncertainty that haunted the genre at the time, and still do.

The three stories by Catherine Durand, the three attributed to Mademoiselle de Lubert and the story by Mademoiselle de Falques were translated from versions of the relevant texts available on Google Books. The translation of "Le Prince des Aigues-marines" was made from the copy of *Le Prince des Aigues-marines et Le Prince invisible* reproduced on the Bibliothèque Nationale's *gallica* website, from which the translation of *Faunillane* was also made. The remaining stories were translated from various volumes of Charles-Joseph Mayer's 1786 *Cabinet des fées*, from versions available on Google Books.

Brian Stableford

Catherine Durand: *The Fay Lubantine*

There was once a fay in Asia whose power had no limits; the likes of Circe and Armida did not come up to her waist. She loved her husband infinitely; destiny, which has always gone its own way, took him away from her in her early youth; nothing remained of him but a daughter so beautiful and so charming that her graces were infinite even in the cradle.

The young princess was seen from a very tender age to have an inclination for pleasure that astonished all those who approached her; no tears ever emerged from her eyes; her little mouth did not open to cries, its only usage being a gracious smile that inspired joy; games were invented for her; her little arms opened to embrace and thank the women who contributed to her amusement; violins, oboes, dances and spectacles made her delights; she showed a marked distaste for symphonies whose tones were melancholy, and anyone in the court who was sad did not appear before her with impunity; a delicate but piquant mockery made them sense the antipathy she had for them. Her mother, the fay, who had never seen anything like it, although she had seen everything, gave her a name that suited her character; she called her Lubantine, and that is how the ancients made their goddess Lubantine, known in their theology as the goddess of joy and liberty.

In fact, young Lubantine could not abide anything that constrained her; when her mother tried to moderate that violent love of liberty slightly, she sulked as prettily as anything in the world, but soon resumed a serene face, employing supplicant badinage to beg the fay not to exclude her from the only wealth one has in this life.

When she was fourteen years old and her person was formed, her mother consulted her books regarding the destiny of such an extraordinary young woman. She found that she would always live happily and amid pleasures, if she could avoid seeing a foreigner. That fatality appeared easy enough to deflect; we shall soon see what order her powerful mother brought to it.

Lubantine's stature was mediocre and slender; her arms were placed by the Graces, her feet were small and well-turned; her hair was a bright brown, her eyes had a dazzlingly brilliant finesse; her nose was small and made for the rest of her features her face was round, her full, delicate and vivid cheeks each had a little dimple formed by the very hand of Amour; there was also one in her chin; her mouth was one of those that it has never been possible to depict, small, fashioned, red, laughing, ornamented by two rows of perfect teeth; her breasts were full, white and youthful.

She had intelligence; her imagination was sparkling, if one can speak thus, and one sensed a secret charm in her conversation, but she was libertine; she gave in to all her desires. Lubantine's mother, however, no sooner saw that she was at an age to be established than she proposed a very advantageous marriage to her. As you can imagine, that was not calculated to please her; she manifested such a strong opposition to it that her mother, who thought her the prettiest person in the world—as, in fact, she was—and who only thought of making her happy, established her with cheerful young people made to please her in a palace that has never had an equal. It was built of precious stones; the doors were never closed; there were magnificent baths, aviaries filled with birds, halls for spectacles; a regulated Opera whose inimitable actors never caught a cold; actors who never grew old; players of all sorts of instruments; gaming tables where the women became more beautiful and the men more gracious.

The general order of that court was to surprise Lubantine every day, and not to have any sad thought; malady and mortality were banished from that beautiful abode, amour made its pleasure felt, absolutely separated from its pain—for no one there believed that its pains were pleasures.

Four different gardens were seen from the four facades of the palace. In one of them there were swings of a particular form; Lubantine often availed herself of that amusement, and for the rest of the day her retinue performed plays. There were stakes planted with rings attached, and those who used the swings were obliged to carry away the rings; when they did not succeed, a penalty was ordered, which went no further the making up a garland of flowers for Lubantine or composing a madrigal in her honor. When hazard caused people to fall, one could laugh in safety, for then the previously beaten and solid terrain softened and became a padded mattress.

In the second garden there were acrobats, rope-dancers and jumpers, all so sure of their skill that no one was afflicted by the anxious attention caused by the fear of seeing them fall, even though they performed surprising feats.

The third garden was occupied by female bathers who worked in shifts incessantly. One pool of Cordovan water had, as well as the odor, the faculty of rendering skin whiter. Lubantine had a separate one in the palace, but she often went to amuse herself by pestering the bathers; teasingly, she tugged their bathing costumes, which were woven from nettle-cloth garnished with Malines lace; those women played countless different instruments on the edges of the pools; neat and elegant beds extended under magnificent tents served them for repose after that pleasant exercise. Men were excluded from the enclosure of that garden, but the walls were so low and people knew so little restraint in the place that they often violated the refuge with their gaze.

The fourth area was a park rather than a garden; it was filled with beautiful, clean and gentle wild beasts, which allowed themselves to be hunted by Lubantine and her court, and which enjoyed themselves afterwards with the same dogs that ran after them without doing them any harm; the hunting equipages were superb, and Lubantine's livery crimson and gold.

At the center of the palace there was a large courtyard surrounded by four facades. It was there that the ladies watched tourneys, jousts, ring-races and carousels, which the young princes admitted to Lubantine's court often put on in order to amuse her. Their skill was astonishing, and they received prizes from the hand of their sovereign when they merited them. She always had some new petty intrigue, but her heart was only engaged to the exact extent required to amuse her.

The three gardens I mentioned were, in any case, so beautiful, and everything that could render them delightful was so unsparing, that they were a spectacle themselves; as for the park designed for hunting, there were woods, streams, plains and a hill that was often preferred by arrangement to other places. Lubantine did not have to take the trouble to express a wish; her desires were always anticipated; but as she had a exquisite taste in everything, she treasured delicate cheer; never has there been anything to compare with what she was served at every meal; the wine wines were chosen carefully, and I have even heard it said that champagne was often served, even though no mention of it in that century is known.

When the fay put her daughter in that place she made her this speech, or very nearly: "My age and my cares, my dear Lubantine, no longer permit me to savor the pleasures that suit you. I don't envy you them; on the contrary, I'm lavishing them upon you. Live happily, since I don't anticipate that your destiny can change, I'm going to retire to my manor in the words; come to visit me there occasionally. Remember me and be a fay like your mother, since I've been able to allow you to participate in my art."

The savant fay refrained from prescribing to Lubantine never to receive any foreigner and not to leave the enclosure of her palace—that would have given birth to the desire to do so—but she extended that enclosure prodigiously. It did not have any appearance of a prison; one would have searched in vain elsewhere for what was found in that delightful abode, but there were stakes planted on all the roads that ended there on which the following inscription could be read:

Refrain from having the desire
To see the lovely Lubantine;

Death would follow closely the dangerous pleasure
Of contemplating her divine person.

Travelers, frightened by that warning, turned away from such a terrible path immediately, and Lubantine remained in the midst of delights for six years without ever experiencing any dolor or chagrin.

She sometimes went to see her mother. One day she found her bathed in tears; the young fay's first impulse was to flee an apparition so contrary to her humor; she had already taken a few backward steps when the afflicted mother said to her: "Come closer, Lubantine; your fate causes me compassion; you will soon be delivered to great misfortunes. I don't know yet what form they will take; it only depends on you to avoid them; it's necessary to deprive you of some pleasure; I can see that the fatal point is there, but as I can't disentangle which one will be deadly to you, deprive yourself of all those you take for a while; you'll discover more taste for them afterwards."

"Me, Madame," said Lubantine, "deprive myself of joy and liberty? I might as well be deprived of daylight. You're naturally sad," she added, "the situation of your humor might have made you dread imaginary perils, and should I deprive myself of real and imaginary possessions for that? No, no, rather..."

"Well, my daughter," said the sage fay, "The future is developing a little to my eyes; I can see that a hunt is going to cause you horrible misfortunes; don't go hunting for three months."

"Oh, Madame," said Lubantine, "you know that it's to liberty in particular that I attach my happiness. I might well have no desire to go hunting for ten years in succession, but the necessity of depriving myself of it would inconvenience me. I'll quit you, Madame," she added, "for fear of participating momentarily in the melancholy that I see in your eyes."

In fact, the free Lubantine went to leap into a carriage harnessed to six lions, which were meeker than lambs, and raced to the Palace of Pleasures.

She was embarrassed by a dream all that night. Until then the god of sleep, respectful of her repose, had only presented agreeable images to her, but this time she thought she saw an unknown individual whose appearance pleased her greatly; he had a little dart in his hand with which he teased her; she acquired a taste for that teasing; the dart had already inflicted a wound in the middle of her heart; she sensed her pleasures redoubling, but soon afterwards a beautiful woman whose features she did not know plunged it in so cruelly that she thought that she was falling, bathed in her own blood, and all that she could do was to kill the people who had just taken away her life.

She uttered a cry that woke her up and attracted her women; the agitation of the dream did not permit her to pull herself together until she had been awake for some time; then she started to laugh at her fear, and got up as quickly as possible, in order to dissipate that baleful imagination.

The pleasure she chose for that day was hunting; she even released the deer herself, which hurtled out of the park where the hunt usually concluded. It was the first time that had happened, for her journeys to see her mother were made by air; but destiny was conducting her, with the aid of her love of liberty.

Lubantine found herself somewhat fatigued; she suspended the hunt and dismounted from her horse. She sat down in a forest at the foot of a large tree that she chose.

"Go away," she said to the hunters. "I need repose; let me sleep."

Immediately, a bed of moss and flowers rose up beneath her; cushions of magnificent fabric were placed under her head, and an elegant awning was attached to the branches of the tree.

She had not yet savored the charms of slumber when she heard a man who was saying in a very agreeable tone of voice:

"Is it possible that you can repent of having made me happy? Yes, divine Melisene, I am happy, since you have been good enough to confide yourself to my faith and have quit your father's kingdom to follow me. What my happiness lacks is essential enough, but I await your kindness with a respect with which you ought to be content. Don't be afflicted, then, and don't tarnish what you have done for me by an appearance of repentance."

"No," said a woman to whom the speech was addressed, "that isn't the subject of my tears. The fatal time is approaching when you are to endure proofs that frighten me. I only know you; will my feeble charms hold out against those of a..."

"Oh," interrupted the man who had spoken first, "don't alarm yourself ahead of time; the obscurity that encloses predictions might be hiding an agreeable verity from you, and whatever might happen, I shall belong as long as I live to my dear Melisene."

Lubantine thought that the man's promises were reckless, and that the woman to whom they were addressed was very imprudent to have followed a lover into such a solitary place: a severity that an unfamiliar impulse caused her.

Have these lovers come to spread the poison of amour in this locale? she wondered. *We only know its pleasures*, she added, *let them leave the places of my dependence.*

With those words she got up and soon found what she was seeking. A young blonde woman, pale and possessed of a perfect beauty, clad in an elegant but neglected costume, was sitting on the grass; a man was at her feet in a tender and respectful attitude. He was tall and handsome, with large dark eyes.

"Who are you," said Lubantine, "who come on to my land to talk about amour?"

The voice of the fay, her charms and her magnificence, attracted the gaze and the veneration of the lovers. The stood up diligently, and the man spoke. "We are, Madame, an unfor-

25

tunate brother and sister seeking a refuge against the fury of a cruel and implacable family."

"A brother and a sister!" said the fay. "Who, then, said the passionate things that I have just heard you saying to one another?"

The young woman blushed; her lover threw himself at Lubantine's feet.

"It's necessary to admit to you, Madame," he said, "that I love the beautiful Melisene, whom you see here, passionately. Cruel relatives have forbidden us to see one another; a mutual love had made us seek means of never being apart, and we beg you, Madame," he added, "to suffer us in this place, where you apparently command."

The good looks and noble appearance of the man did not permit the fay to refuse his plea. I know not what impulse even gave her response a tender softness different from the joy that normally shone in her eyes. The beautiful young woman had no part in that mild welcome; on the contrary, the fay looked at her disdainfully. Then, turning back to the agreeable stranger, she said to him: "After having granted you what you request," she said to him, "don't refuse me your name. As for your birth, it would be difficult to hide it; the appearance you have is not encountered in ordinary people, and the title of king struck my ears when you were talking to this person." She pointed at Melisene.

"My name is Ciridor, Madame," he replied, "and my father is King Absolute, a name that has been imposed on him because he never yields to anyone, and everyone has always done his will. The princess you see is the daughter of the King of the Gentle Isle, and her mildness does not belie her origin."

"That's sufficient," Lubantine interrupted. "You can tell me the rest of your adventures at your leisure; not only will I receive you in my lands, but I'll take you to my palace; we'll seek there the means of rendering you happy, and prescribe for Princess Melisene a life a little less vagabond than she is leading at present."

With those words she sounded a small enameled gold hunting horn garnished with diamonds that she wore at her side, and the whole of her brilliant court soon gathered around her. Prince Ciridor's squire and Princess Melisene's governess came to mingle with that elegant troop. Ciridor aided Lubantine and his princess to mount their horses, and mounted his own with such grace that he attracted the attention of all the spectators. The deer that had rested in company with the pack gave a further hour of pleasure to the hunt, after which everyone returned to the palace.

The magnificence and the pleasures that were savored there gave Ciridor a sort of agreeable distraction, which cost the tender Melisene sighs. Lubantine allotted her an apartment whose views only overlooked the hunting park. She conducted her there personally and told her as she quit her that she would send ambassadors to her father's court to inform him that she had her in her power and was taking her under her protection; and that while awaiting his response she was obliged to keep her in a kind of solitude more appropriate to the estate of her destiny. With those words she embraced her and left her with her governess, in a kind of dolor that had something so piquant that tears soon covered her beautiful cheeks.

"Has anything ever been seen comparable to my misfortune, my dear Celinte?" she cried, as soon as she was alone with her. "What a bizarrerie of my star! You know everything that I have done for Ciridor; the virtue of which I make a profession ought to give him an eternal gratitude for the excess of my tenderness, and yet I see in him the deadly penchant of which a cruel prediction had warned me."

Celinte interrupted the dolorous reflections of the princess, and asked her what one could dread of a lover like Ciridor.

"What can I dread?" said Melisene. "Lubantine is charming; Lubantine is a fay; her power, her beauty, the pleasures that follow her everywhere and the fickleness of men all give me a mortal apprehension. And have I not seen Ciridor looking at her, admiring her and forgetting me momentarily?" she added, redoubling her sighs.

Celinte employed all her eloquence in consoling the princess, and promised to report to her faithfully what she knew, but the means were forbidden to her; she was not permitted to leave the apartment, where they were given in abundance, however, everything that might satisfy the senses.

Meanwhile, the prince, who was young, gallant and who loved pleasures, had an admiration for Lubantine that could already be called a liking; he spent the first days in a transport that made him forget Melisene. The fay had an inexplicable charm in all her actions; her fêtes were very extensive; the sighs that a commencement of amour was causing her to utter had a grace from which it was not possible for him to defend himself, and, as her sighs only marked the passion that gave birth to them, without having the sadness appropriate to them, her lovely smile followed close behind them.

Ciridor, heaped with joy by the effect of his merit, was more handsome and wittier than usual; Lubantine and he gave themselves gradually to amour and joy. The spectacles multiplied, the Palace of Pleasures finished new ones continually.

Lubantine went out on her own one day in order to stroll in the hunting park; her heart was already sensing the more impetuous movements of amour, but until then everything had passed in gazes. She plunged into the wood in order to dream at her ease. Ciridor, driven by the same desire, encountered her in that remote location.

"How I have wanted this moment," he said to the fay, "and how I have dreaded that it might not be favorable to me! You only like pleasures," he added, "I am not their enemy, but I am so jealous of them and I am audacious enough to wish that you only loved me."

That declaration was rather bold, but Lubantine was naturally too distant from the furious impulses of anger to invoke them on this occasion, and the tenderness that she felt added its effect to her temperament.

"Thus far, Prince," she replied, "you have no reason to complain of my rigors. I have not hidden the penchant I feel for you; I find pleasure in seeing you, I have an infinite one in hearing you. Let us love one another with ardor," she added, "since we are summoned to it. Is it not necessary to seize the opportunities that are presented to savor new felicities?"

That morality pleased Ciridor infinitely. He added further impetus to it in his fashion. They had a very long and very agreeable conversation. Lubantine agreed on emerging from the wood that only Ciridor could bring her pleasures to a culmination, and they plunged into sensual pleasures.

The fay's example gave birth the countless new amours in her court; everyone was in love; everyone abandoned themselves to its delights, while the unhappy Melisene was dying of dolor and jealousy. She had seen her lover and her rival from her window emerging from the hunting park; their appearance was so contented and so amorous that she had no reason to doubt her misfortune. She abandoned herself to everything that a delicate soul is capable of suffering.

One day, losing the little patience that remained to her, she tried to force her way past her guards in order to go and reckon with the fay for her detention and her lover for his infidelity. Her emergence was opposed, but that action caused rumor; Ciridor was informed of it; a slight return to the past caused him to lament the situation of the princess. He tried to say something in her favor, but Lubantine, who did not want to be troubled by anything, replied that she would release her from her prison and that she even wanted to render her witness to their amusements.

"I have no fear," she added, "that she would dare to dispute anything with me, nor that you might return to her."

In fact, the fay went to fetch Melisene, in a gracious and mild manner. "Come, Princess," she said to her. "It is time that you had your part in our fêtes."

The sad Melisene left with her. But what a change! She no longer had the perfect beauty that might have been able to generate amour in the most insensible; her figure and the sound of her voice remained to her, but her face became so frightful, her features so irregular and her sort of ugliness so bizarre, that when Lubantine presented her to Ciridor he took several steps back, and even let an exclamation of disgust escape. The princess turned toward a large mirror, in which she saw herself as beautiful as usual, and became more indignant against her infidel lover; for the fay. in taking away her beauty and making her ugly for everyone else, had left her the slight satisfaction of appearing beautiful in her own eyes, and that was the origin of a self-esteem unknown before.

Celinte saw with astonishment the prodigious ugliness of the princess and forgave the prince his inconstancy. "Let us flee, Princess," she said to her. "let us flee a court whose voluptuous mores cannot fail to corrupt; no one will try to stop us."

"Why flee?" replied Melisene, sadly. "Could I resolve myself to do it? Ciridor is fickle, but his fickleness will bring him back to me."

Then Celinte could not hide from her the degree to which she had become horrible; she was not sparing in the portrait she made of her. The princess, who still found herself beautiful, nearly became angry with her confidante, and flattered herself that her displeasures had only brought a sight change to her charms.

On the other hand, Ciridor, whose ingratitude was confirmed by Melisene's appearance, told Lubantine, laughing, that she had taken a strange path to make sure of his heart, and that even if she had changed nothing in the person of the princess, he would not have broken his new chains.

"I assure you," she said, "that that vengeance is not excessive; it is always necessary to take precautions against reversions. And then," she added, "what harm have I done her? She still believes herself to be beautiful; her imagination will always be satisfied."

"Good, Madame," said Ciridor. "Not content with having made her ugly, you also want to render her ridiculous, and the security she has regarding her attractions will make her play the part of a pretty woman."

They had the inhumanity to mock her for a long time because of a misfortune that she only had because of them, and when they wanted to enjoy their malevolence they made her appear, pompously adorned, to see the spectacles that were prepared for them.

The prince, intoxicated by amour, decided that he wanted to render an effective worship to the fay. You are too charming," he told her, "only to merit adoration by virtue of your face. It's necessary to set up an altar to you, to burn incense to you, to immolate victims to you."

"Oh, as for bloody victims," Lubantine interjected, "I don't want any. People can offer them to me, but I shall give them liberty with my own hands."

That same day, an altar was constructed in a great hall of crystal; two thousand candles burned there incessantly before the figure of the fay, which was a single pearl with draperies of brilliant rose-colored diamonds. Behind the transparent walls of the hall, large hollow figures had been disposed, painted in perfection, which represented the peoples of all the continents of the world, adoring the beautiful Lubantine. Inextinguishable candles always made those bodies appear luminous. Each of them held an offering, which related to the character of the fay. There were pocket mirrors, diamonds, snuffboxes, boxes of beauty-spots, ribbons and all the rest of the elegant equipment of ladies.

The interior of the hall, which had become a temple, was full of players of instruments and singers; sarabands and chaconnes were danced there in favor of tenderness or libertinage, and a perpetual commerce of love letters, gazes and pretty amorous larcenies was seen; a continual distribution was made of the most exquisite dishes and the most delectable liqueurs; the ice creams and chocolate there surpassed ambrosia, and if no one acquired immortality, at least the women there were always young and beautiful, and the men always well made and elegant.

A sofa with a golden back enriched with rubies was beside the altar, destined for the pretended goddess, when she wanted to receive her incense in person; a cushion of the same kind was below the sofa for the amorous Ciridor. The superb awning that covered the area descended in a curtain when it pleased Lubantine to disappear from the eyes of her subjects. Perfumes were lavished there. In sum, everything that luxury and adulation could invent was put to use in favor of the fay.

She had the cruelty of wanting the unfortunate Melisene to witness the consecration of the temple; she nearly died of dolor there. Her rival was as beautiful as Venus. Ciridor picked up a censer himself in order to be the first to adore her, and as he had the most beautiful voice in the world, he began this hymn, to which the chorus responded:

> *Alone you know the fine sensual pleasure,*
> *Before you there were only feeble images;*
> *Sweet joy with liberty*
> *Are your gifts; receive our homages,*
> *Queen of hearts, games and pleasures,*
> *Who can drive away the ridiculous censors*
> *And, braving remorse and scruples*
> *Accord everything to your desires;*
> *Goddess Lubantine, may our incense always*
> *Rise above your altars;*
> *Can we envy the fate of the immortals*
> *When we contemplate your divine grace?*
>
> *Alone you know the fine sensual pleasure,*
> *Before you there were only feeble images;*
> *Sweet joy with liberty*
> *Are your gifts; receive our homages...*

The hymn went on for a long time, but it is so pleasant to be praised, Ciridor's voice was so harmonious, and the choir so marvelous, that Lubantine sensed what expression cannot

32

represent; there was even something tragic in the ceremony, which did not spoil its savor at all.

The princess could not bear the bitterness of her affliction; she fainted in Celinte's arms. Ciridor turned his head in her direction, allowed himself to be carried away without admitting pain into his life and ran to throw himself at Lubantine's feet.

"Let everything perish, my goddess," he said, kissing one of her hands, which she held out to him, "provided that I adore you all my life."

That transport caused others in the fay.

When the ceremony had finished everyone went to occupy themselves with the customary pleasures. No one enquired about Melisene. She was suffering woes that would have given rise to pity in cruelty itself, but the fay only felt precisely what was necessary to make her suffer more—which is to say, that her life should be preserved and that she should be prevented from harming herself.

Several days passed in the worship of the new goddess. Amid that vaunted sensual pleasure the princess recovered in spite of herself, and, impelled by an unknown emotion, she ran once again to the fatal temple where all the objects renewed her dolor.

The high priest Ciridor was brilliant with gems and even more brilliant by virtue of his beauty; the fay was contemplating him with eyes in which amour was painted. Even the princess had more passion for him than when he was faithful. Those sentiments furnished Melisene with courage; her voice was heard in the middle of the ceremony, rising up to pronounce these words:

Charming Queen of Cythera,
Whose wrath Psyche once ignited,
Beautiful Venus, will you suffer
The offense that a prince dares to make you in this place?
It is little that he violates his oath,

That crime only injures me,
But that ingrate, that reckless fool
Profanes his incense for another than you;
Render him forever the usage of his senses,
Charming Queen of Cythera.

When Melisene commenced that prayer to Venus every-one attempted to interrupt her, but no one was able to succeed in that; tongues were tied. Ciridor, the infidel Ciridor, opened his mouth in vain in order to impose silence; he could not articulate anything. Lubantine felt the same prodigy in herself, and that silence, which had a mysterious cause, was only broken after the princess had been seen to resume her original beauty.

Then the fay uttered a dolorous scream, and the assembly murmured a few words in praise of Melisene. As if recovering from an enchantment, Ciridor quit the worship of the false goddess and returned submissively to the feet of his first mistress.

Venus was recognized in those changes.

The temple was not destroyed; the statue of Lubantine remained standing; but the veritable Lubantine appeared ugly, with the same ugliness that she had previously given her rival, without the same consolation remaining to her. She found herself so frightful that, her love of pleasure changing into fury, and the goddess not having taken away her power of faerie, she no longer thought about anything but avenging herself on the innocent causes of her misfortune.

She had the princess imprisoned again, with terrible menaces. Ciridor, who wanted to repair his faults, opposed that with all his courage, but what could he do, alone against an absolute and sovereign fay?

Venus, the jealous Venus, had avenged her outrage; that alone was interesting for her; what did the success of the amours of Ciridor and Melisene matter to her? Lubantine went every day into a horrible prison where she had locked her up; there, with an unparalleled inhumanity, she disfigured her beautiful face with a diamond that wore expressly; then she labored on her incomparable breasts, and did not quit that mortal exercise until the force of dolors had caused her death.

Celinte implored her at least to send her body back to the sovereign of the Gentle Isle; the fay granted her that.

The poor king had no sooner seen that sad spectacle than he died of affliction; before his death he ordered that a magnificent sepulcher be built for his daughter, for himself and for Ciridor.

The fay attempted in vain to make Ciridor return to her; her ugliness and the repentance he felt excluded her from his heart. She applied herself to making him take a dose of poison every day, which weakened him gradually and often caused him furious pains; they only finished with his life, and the prediction of which Melisene had made mention was verified. No one has ever known the wording of it, but in essence, the prince was menaced with being unable to resist terrible ordeals, and then being exposed to a tragic end.

After that, Lubantine was tormented by remorse; she discovered too late that excessive sensual pleasure leads into profound abysms, and that, if one cannot have perfect happiness without amour, amour that is not regulated by virtue causes all the woes of life.

However, as the commencement of Lubantine's life presented a cheerful image, and the pagans sacrificed to much stranger divinities than Liberty and Joy, they erected temples to them under the name of the goddess Lubantine. But as no one was ever able to prescribe just limits to those two things, people only had imperfect ideas of them and always went beyond or fell short of joy and liberty.

The Prodigy of Amour

There was once a king who became a widower shortly after his wife, the queen, had given him a son whose beauty was so surprising and his health so perfect that the king, who was already old, resolved not to remarry and to give all his application to such a pretty child.

The king had reason to be content with his resolution for as long as the child was unable to talk, but as soon as he began to produce a few words it was evident that he never put one in the right place. It was thought at first that it was an infantile grace, and the good king took great pleasure in the petty derangement of his speech; he lost that confidence somewhat when he noticed in the young prince a dullness of mind that prevented him from acquiring a taste for anything. The curiosity so natural to children—the questions that Nature inspires them to ask so frequently, which make instruction so easy—and the vivacity of action that the blood causes at that age, were dead in him. His features were charming, his stature perfect, but it was evident that no soul animated such a beautiful body, and his father reached the point of having difficulty supporting it.

Always dull, somnolent and somber, the masters who were given to him were futile, although the king spared no effort in his regard, more in order not to fail in his duty than in the hope of success. He sent in vain to all parts of the world in search of the most skillful men, in order to try to cultivate such a savage nature. They assembled one day and came to declare to the king that, having employed all their study with the prince, they no longer had any hope for his education, and asked to be dismissed.

The king saw only too clearly that they were right. The prince, who was commonly known as Brutalis, was then seventeen years old. No nature is so ingrate that it has not taken on some form at that age, but his had remained in its raw material, and the more marvelous his person became, the more his extreme stupidity gave rise to aversion for him. His father could see no other course of action than sending away the masters, heaped with presents as a reward for the trouble they had taken, and to marry Brutalis, in order to have a grandson who might compensate for his chagrin.

The matter was not without difficulties; the neighboring kings were aware of the monstrous stupidity of Brutalis, and refused his alliance for their daughters. On the other hand, Brutalis, when shown the most beautiful women in the realm, looked at them with wide eyes and did not say a word to them. If he was asked whether he found them beautiful he replied, in an impatient manner: "Beautiful? I don't know," and then went to the king's stables, mounted a horse, and spent all day hunting.

That was the only thing he liked, and even that he did with an ill grace. Although he was firmly mounted, because he was vigorous, he conducted the horse so stupidly that one only had to see him pass by to divine that he had never thought like other people.

One day, after having gone hunting, he wanted to dismount in order to rest. He sat down on the moss at the foot of a large oak tree in the most beautiful forest in the world, but instead of leaning against the trunk he allowed his head to slump on to his chest, and his air of imbecility caused a man of quality who was with him to pass a flame-colored ribbon around his neck, with which he tied him to the tree. Then, no longer being the master of his attitude, he appeared quite graceful; zephyrs agitated the long blond hair that covered his shoulders, forming a thousand broad curls, which mingled with the flame-colored ribbon to cover part of the bark of the oak to which he was attached.

The nobleman found him so handsome in that state that he deplored in the depths of his heart the destiny of a man who would have been so perfect if Nature had only wanted to finish her work. Mulling over his thoughts, he plunged into the densest part of the wood, and the remainder of the hunters gradually turned their steps in different directions, not knowing what to say to a prince who did not know boredom or amusement.

Near the forest lived a fay named Mademoiselle Coquete, fairly young, very pretty, subject to the passions, not very severe in her morals and always on the lookout for handsome fellows. Once, when the infidelity of her latest lover caused her great anxieties, she took them into the most solitary places in the environs, and she found herself in the very place where Brutalis happened to be. At first she only saw him from behind; that prodigious quantity of blond hair attracted her gaze. The prince's clothing was magnificent.

That had the air of an adventure, and she was disposed to attempt it, as a person seeking less to nourish her dolor than to soothe it. Her pocket mirror was consulted; she reapplied a little rouge and a few beauty spots, and, soon drying up the tears that were flowing from her eyes, nothing more remained except to make them shine advantageously.

When she was fully assured of her charms, she went past the prince, and suddenly appeared before him in the costume of a nymph, with the most gallant air in the world. Anyone but him would at least have taken pleasure in such a pretty apparition, but he scarcely glanced at her. Mademoiselle Coquete thought then that he was prejudiced by some unlucky passion or depressed by tragic misfortunes.

"What's wrong?" she said, sitting down next to him. "Should a man like you abandon himself to dolor?"

"I don't know what you mean," said Brutalis, without raising his eyes.

The manner in which he pronounced those few words surprised the lively fay infinitely. "Why are you tied up like that?" she said. "If you like, I'll commence by rendering you a service."

"Oh," he said, "they'll untie me when I mount up again."

"I see," she replied, surprised by such a perfect resignation and unable to help laughing. "I don't suppose anyone will climb the oak behind you."

"I don't know," said the prince, again.

As you can imagine, after such a conversation Mademoiselle Coquete did not require all the finesse of her art to know what the situation was.

"But who are you?" she asked him.

"I'm the king's son," he said.

At those words, she remembered what was said in the realm about the young prince, and flattered herself at that moment that her charms might give him, if not intelligence, at least a few sentiments. She said the nicest things to him, which he did not understand at all, and to which he made even less reply. But ladies flatter themselves, and she left the place when she saw the hunters returning, with a good deal of passion and a little hope.

As soon as she was in her palace she ordered a bath composed of a thousand things that augmented beauty; she commanded magnificent garments, others that were simply gallant, and an incomparable equipage. All that was done in less than no time, and one fine day Mademoiselle Coquette was seen to depart, without telling anyone where her journey would terminate. Her followers were very surprised by so many trappings. Sylphs were under her orders, who transported her through the air whenever she wished, and she had a thousand other means of traveling promptly, but this time her progress was more reminiscent of a triumph than a journey.

She was alone in a carriage of pearls, the awning of which was a single ruby; eight beautiful blue elephants drew it gravely; there was a beautiful young woman on each of them, playing lutes, theorbos and the other instruments in perfect harmony while they walked. Two hundred guards superbly dressed in a Moorish manner and as adroit as the Moors of Granada were mounted on horses that ceded nothing to Bucephalus; the pages and the rest of the assorted livery, like the elephants carrying the baggage, had costumes each worth as much as a small kingdom.

Mademoiselle Coquette had no need to issue instructions regarding the place where she wanted to go. The elephants of her carriage, who were fays, took her directly to the realm of Paraminosara, where the father of Brutalis reigned. As soon as the set foot in the capital she passed the word to her retinue that she did not want to appear under her veritable name; they replied therefore to anyone who asked that she was Princess Azindara, who was undertaking a voyage.

The king was informed. Nothing so beautiful had ever appeared in his estates; he emerged from his palace in order to receive such a great princess. They made one another very gracious compliments, and the good king, who already loved Azindara like his own daughter, knowing that she was not married, desired passionately that she would not disdain his son, but he dared not promise himself that without a great generosity on the part of the princess.

However, Mademoiselle Coquete, who had only one goal, asked the king of what his family consisted. He replied, dissolving in tears, that he only had one son.

"Is that any reason to despair," she said, "if he has merit?"

"Alas, Madame," he replied, "that is my grief; his person is agreeable, but he has a stupidity that all the education I have been able to give him could not vanquish."

"Have him appear before us," said Mademoiselle Coquete. "I'll judge whether the problem is without remedy."

Delighted by such impatience, the delighted king asked one of his officers to inform Brutalis and to have him ornamented as if to go to a ball.

He was brought a short time later in all the magnificence that could heighten his beauty, but he was marching heavily, his head was inclined and his gaze fixed on the ground.

"Raise your head, Prince," the false Azindara said to him.

Brutalis did, in fact, raise it momentarily.

"It's also necessary to raise your eyes," she said.

He had the docility to do so, but it was without looking at anything.

The king was in despair; he could see clearly that so much care on Azindara's part was not without some design; what would he not have given for the honor of her alliance! He touched on it in a few little remarks; she replied as he could have wished.

"But," she added, "it's necessary that I see some hope of being able to render him similar to other men."

The king paid her great compliments, and gave orders for fêtes for the next few days.

Mademoiselle Coquete retired early in order to appear beautiful early the following day. She shone costumed as a nymph, which added a great deal to the gallantry of her appearance. First there was a carousel, where it was believed that the prince would appear, because he only liked riding horses, but it is one thing to chase a deer and another to mingle adroitly in the various courses of such a spectacle; all his adornment and all his beauty only made him seem more ridiculous to everyone except Mademoiselle Coquete, whose passion was visibly augmented, and her hopes with it. Her eyes seemed to be great enough enchanters to operate a change in Brutalis, and if that happened, what glory it would be for them, and how far her companions, the fays, who employed their art to make themselves loved, would remain below a power so natural and so gentle!

She resolved, however to make use of her métier in the firework display that terminated the day's pleasures; when everyone was at their most attentive in seeing them fired, a small rocket went up that snaked in the prettiest fashion in the world, pronouncing words instead of making the little sounds that the effect of gunpowder causes:

"Destiny has fixed the fate of Brutalis: he shall have intelligence; he shall have courage; you shall see him shine among the most polished; but Amour alone can do that work."

The king listened to that edict as if Jupiter himself had dictated it. He regarded Coquete as the surest object that Amour could make use. Turning to Brutalis, he said: "Did you hear, my son, what that rocket has just said?"

"I heard something," he said, "but I don't know what it was."

"What!" said Mademoiselle Coquete, biting her lips. "You didn't pay attention to a prediction that promises you such a fine fate?"

"I don't know what you want me to say," he said, and then turned toward the beautiful young women in the fay's retinue, but without saying a word to them.

Mademoiselle Coquete, however, fearful of division and believing herself very subtle, imagined at that moment that the certain means of subjugating the prince's heart was to get him into some solitude, where she would appear the only beautiful person.

As soon as she had decided what she ought to do, her greatest care was to leave the realm of Paraminosara. Before then, however, she wanted to attend the following day's fête, knowing that it was to be a ball, and that by dancing better than all the women she might perhaps attract the desires of Brutalis.

She appeared the next day, therefore, in a ball gown so laden with gems that all the riches of India did not come close to it. The ladies who danced appeared dull and vulgar by comparison; she had a lightness and a grace that made the good king weep with joy. As for Brutalis, however, he sang along to the violins loudly, and although he had a fine baritone voice, he annoyed everyone because he sang so badly and took no pleasure in anything; no matter what anyone could do, he never looked at Azindara. That was as many dagger-thrusts for the king, who had the dolor after that of receiving the fay's adieu.

"I'm leaving, Sire," she said to him, "but not because I no longer have the same sentiments; one sometimes arrives at the goal by a different route. I've thought of one that might succeed for us, and it's necessary for me to leave in order to put it into operation. If you don't hear any mention of the prince for some time, don't worry about him."

The king kissed her hand at those words, begged her to remember what she had promised, and assured her that only that hope would prevented him from dying after her departure.

Early the next morning Mademoiselle Coquete was preparing to leave when the king, who had given orders to alert him at the fatal moment, came to remind her of her promises; she reiterated them, and after having embraced him, she climbed into her carriage and departed in the same order in which she had arrived.

As soon as she reached her palace, her women had no other concern that to repair the fatigues of the journey; three whole days were spent in those occupations, after which she had herself transported by a sylph to the same forest where she had seen Brutalis for the first time.

That was a place where she could not fail to encounter him. He was hunting there one day, and the ardor of the hunt carried him away; he had soon outdistanced the beaters, but his horse cast a shoe and he dismounted in order to await the arrival of the other hunters. That would not have taken long if he had not felt himself drawn away into the depths of the wood by something invisible, which had no intention of letting him escape.

He cried out, but no hunter appeared; even his horse did not follow him. Who could have done that, except Mademoiselle Coquete? She emerged from behind a bush, took him by the hand, in an urgent and flirtatious manner, and obliged him to sit down next to her.

"Are you very annoyed," she said to him, "that I've taken you away from the hunt in order to bring you here?"

"Why," he replied, "are you preventing me from seeing the stag at bay? It's the most beautiful thing..."

"But I'm more beautiful than a stag," said Coquete. "If it's his tears that please you, you'll soon see me weep as much as him, if you only deign to look at me and your heart isn't determined in my favor."

During that little declaration, Brutalis was looking as a magpie that had come to perch in the tree under which the fay was sitting, and had no other application.

"Look at me, then," she said to him. "It isn't polite to be so distracted when someone is talking to you."

The poor prince allowed himself to be drawn, and showed two rows of pearls, laughing innocently.

Enraged by an imbecility that left her no hope, Coquete cried: "Oh, I'm a lot further forward! Would Amour take the trouble to launch one of his arrows into a heart so unworthy of sensing his pleasures? And even if that happened, would it extract anything other than what it operates on wild beasts?"

"What's that you're saying?" said Brutalis, whose sole passion was hunting. "It seems to me that you mentioned beasts?"

"Yes," she said. "Aren't you weary of bearing that name, and will your beauty never be accompanied by a rational quality?"

"I don't know what you mean," he replied, "but I'd like to hunt."

Meanwhile, Mademoiselle Coquete had resolved not to remain on such a fine path. She ordered a sylph to transport her, with Brutalis, to a small palace that she had constructed for her amorous design. They were there in an instant.

"Well," said Mademoiselle Coquete to Brutalis when the sylph has set them down, "did you enjoy traveling through the air?"

"I'd have liked me horse better," he said, "for I'd have gone to the hunt."

"Is it possible," Coquete said to him then, "that you don't remember having seen me before?"

"I don't know whether I've seen you," he said.

Mademoiselle Coquete took Brutalis by the hand, and tried to make him savor the beauties of her abode. It was a castle whose walls could not be seen because they were covered in honeysuckle and jasmine; instead of a roof there was a platform with an elbow-high palisade of the same flowers. There were fountains there, two delightful lawns and a wood in the form of an extraordinarily dark labyrinth filled with water jets, the coolness of which prevented the ardors of midday from being felt. The four faces of that admirable garden were all different and agreeably diversified; the famous gardens of Semiramis might have been larger, but did not approach the delights of that one.

The interior of the house was designed to inspire amour: little apartments always strewn with flowers and tiled with porcelain; furniture upholstered in gauze of various colors; beds heightened by festoons of orange-blossom, sustained by amours; mirrors that rendered objects more beautiful than nature; aviaries full of birds whose songs went to the heart; and a thousand other delights invented by Mademoiselle Coquete, which were very extensive. They would infallibly have inspired at least some desire in anyone but Brutalis, but after walking everywhere, because he could not do otherwise, he threw himself into a large armchair, and, without even looking at the fay, he began whistling through his nose.

She nearly lost patience, but she made it a point of honor to bring her enterprise to a conclusion, in addition to which, her heart was veritably touched; a meal was served in which all the dishes surpassed ambrosia; nectar did not come close to the wines that were drunk there. The prince had a good appetite; he sat down at table without being begged and ate marvelously.

Coquete did what she could to make him talk; she asked him whether he was sorry to be with her, and whether he was impatient to see his father again

"If I had a horse," he said, "I could go to see him right away."

"No, if you please," she said. "You're going to stay with me for a while; I want to try to give you intelligence."

"Well," he said, "give."

It was a great deal when a few words could be extracted from him in an entire evening.

He spent a few days thus; he was given magnificent and agreeable clothes; his long hair was done. Coquete put beauty spots on him. He was as beautiful as Amour, but his stupidity was still unparalleled. The fay took every imaginable care to appear beautiful and the entertain him. She made him hear tender symphonies. Moorish women—she had cleverly exiled all others—danced ballets before him, all of whose steps and movements would have made rocks quiver; they were wasted pleasures and prodigal delicacy. When she asked him whether he was bored he replied, yawning: "I don't get bored, but I'd rather go hunting."

Mademoiselle Coquete's shoulders drooped, and she made no reply.

She often took him into the labyrinth I mentioned, and made him look at its embellishments.

"It's nice," he said, "but what use is it?"

"What us is it?" retorted the fay, promptly. "First of all, the eyes are satisfied by it; but there's another usage to which it can be put, about which it wouldn't be necessary to inform you if you loved me."

"I like you," he said, "but I don't like you any better here than elsewhere."

"Oh, Prince," she said, "if you knew Amour and he had wounded your heart for me, you'd be delighted to be in a solitary place, where no one could see you or hear you."

Far from Brutalis glimpsing the passion there was in those words, he said: "Oh, I don't like being wounded, and I like you as much with your women as in this place." Then he got up in order to go to look at the view—or, rather, not to look at anything.

Often, after such responses, Mademoiselle Coquete stayed in the wood weeping; often, too, she followed him, unable to resolve to give up hope.

One day, when he was amusing himself parading his bewildered gaze over a beautiful meadow irrigated by a little stream, he perceived a shepherdess guarding a little flock; her air was noble and she seemed to be rather new at that exercise. Brutalis turned to Coquete and said: "Have that shepherdess come closer; I'd like to see her."

"What!" she replied. "Do you think she's more beautiful than me?"

"How do I know?" he said. "I never see anyone but you; it'll be a change."

"Cruel man!" said the fay. "Will you always give me new chagrins?"

"Oh well," he said, interrupting. "I'll call her then." At the same time he started shouting to the shepherdess with all his might to come closer. It was in the same tone that he used when hunting, if his dogs went astray.

The astonished shepherdess turned round and saw a charming face, so far as the distance would permit. Remarking that it was a man who was calling to her, she took her flock elsewhere.

"Oho!" said the prince. "She's very proud. I'd still like to see her, for she seems very pretty to me."

There was a naivety in the manners of Brutalis that often forced the fay to laugh; this time, she could not help it, although she was piqued by some jealousy. She took him down into the apartments, where she tried to make him forget the shepherdess with a thousand pleasant remarks and tender caresses, and although he seemed more distracted than usual, he nevertheless said as many stupid things.

The next day he went back to the garden early, and did not fail to see the shepherdess again. No matter how modest one is, one is not sorry to show oneself when one is beautiful. He gazed at her at his ease; she did not flee as she had the day before. He bowed to her in a sufficiently polite fashion, and she returned the gesture with a very good grace. If he had not heard Mademoiselle Coquete's women coming he would have remained in that pleasant contemplation for a long time.

He did not find an opportunity to return to the place that had become so dear to him for the rest of the day; he was even sufficiently shrewd not to testify any impatience to do so, but he felt a violent one the following day to see the beautiful shepherdess again. He therefore got up even earlier than the previous day and went to station himself at his post, from which he soon saw the arrival of the person for whom he was waiting.

She came singing a country ditty in a soft little voice, which completed inflaming Brutalis. He remembered then a song that someone had once tried to teach him, and as he had a marvelous voice, he sang it rather agreeably. After that, instead of calling to the shepherdess impolitely, he made a sign begging her to approach. She took a few steps and, pretending to stroke her dog, she showed the young prince a face in which laughter and grace were playing. He looked at her with an ardor and a pleasure that began to take away from his gaze the somber and stupid expression that obliterated all of its beauty.

He was only turned away from that pleasant occupation by the arrival of Mademoiselle Coquete. She had got up at the same time as him, and, having searched for him in vain in all the apartments, she went to see whether he was in the garden. He was fortunate enough to hear her and to have time to make a sign to the shepherdess to go back. He left the fatal place himself, and began to use the intelligence that Amour had already given him to hide from the fay the pleasure he had just savored. He manifested his usual mentality, and Coquete, who wanted to make a further attempt that day, only encountered repellant naiveties.

The next day, however, he returned to the place of his delights; he found the shepherdess there earlier than the day before; he completed acquiring all the amour necessary gradually to disentangle the chaos of his thoughts. For her part, the shepherdess did more than allow herself to be seen; from time to time she turned her lovely eyes toward the prince with an implication of giving him hope.

As everyone agrees, nothing opens the intelligence as much as Amour; he makes even the most brutal individuals polite, and no matter how stupid a heart is, when it is in the hands of an excellent workman like Amour, it does not take long to acquire polish. That general rule was more than proven in the person of the prince; not only did the tender sentiments inspired in him by the beautiful shepherdess render his humor milder, but his intelligence shone with the brightest fire as soon as his passion reached its peak.

By virtue of an admirable effect of the desire he had to please and to render himself lovable to the person he adored, all the instruction that his masters had given him, which had evidently been stored in his memory, gave him a facility of speech and an eloquence that would have surprised all those who had seen him before. He even had the glory of multiplying, if one can put it thus, the precepts that were believed to have been sown in ingrate ground, and everything within him grew miraculously.

I left the prince gazing at his mistress, and at the commencement of the effects of which I have just made a brief sketch. He realized that the fay would soon come to find him, and, not unaware of her power, he tore himself away by means of reason from a place where he always found new charms. He went to meet Mademoiselle Coquete, and bowed to her in a better manner than usual.

He had difficulty not allowing a few reasonable words to escape, but the fear of giving hopes or suspicions to such a redoubtable individual caused him to remain silent or to respond without wit to the fay's various interrogations. He even pretended to feel ill in order to retire to his apartment.

Already, Brutalis, the stupid Brutalis, was pretending, and doing more; he was thinking about means of being able to talk to his shepherdess. The nub of the difficulty was that he was not permitted to leave the palace unless the fay accompanied him. It was not a sure means of expecting his design, but he nevertheless hazarded to write a note to the shepherdess:

I am dying of the desire to see you and talk to you, but I can only get out of this place with the fay Coquete, who is keeping me prisoner here. I cannot see very clearly how I might succeeded in conversing with you, but it seems to me that if you would like to take your flock into the nearby forest, it might not be impossible for me to be there; it would only cost you a little extra distance, and you could, by means of that complaisance, render me the happiest of all men.

The amorous prince had no sooner written that letter than he went to bed; he slept very little, and not until after he had thought of a means of enabling her to receive it. As soon as he got up he took up a bow. He was an excellent shot; he put the letter in the fletchings of an arrow and directed it very adroitly to within a few paces of the shepherdess. She could not doubt that the piece of paper was for her; a slight shame, however, made her sit down before picking it up.

She called to one of her ewes, she sang, she stroked her dog, and finally took the note and read what you have just seen. Her gaze remained attached to the grass then; she did not dare raise her eyes; but by means of a movement of which she was not the mistress, she turned them toward the prince, and with a slight nod of the head, she made him understand that she granted his request.

At that moment he found himself at the summit of happiness; he tried to resume his customary countenance for the rest of the day, but the brilliance of his eyes spoke instead of his mouth. Mademoiselle Coquete, who believed herself to be very lovely—and, in fact, was—applauded the progress that she believed herself to be making in the heart of young Brutalis. He needed her in the plan that he had made, and, letting her enjoy her error, he pronounced a few words that finished convincing her of the power of her beauty.

That evening, more touched than usual by the charms of the prince, she asked him what he wanted to do to amuse himself. He begged her to take him hunting; she wanted to give him that satisfaction, and only put it off until the following day.

Mademoiselle Coquete had her beautiful bright chestnut hair powdered and curled; she donned a hunting costume embroidered with diamonds, and, mounting a superb dappled gray horse with a flame-colored mane, she seemed a veritable Bradamante. Brutalis had also been equipped magnificently for the hunt; the rest of the equipage matched him, and a fire was seen shining in the prince's eyes that she assumed to be caused by the sight of a pack, every dog of which merited a panegyric.

Coquete who was a excellent rider—she was everything she wished—matched the stride of her horse to that of Brutalis; she found him so handsome that day that, more stubborn than ever in looking at him and talking to him, it was a supreme felicity for her. The deer that was set running did not last long; the rest of the day still remained when the spoils had been divided. Coquete told Brutalis to urge his horse to a certain place she designated to him, where he would see great beauties. Alas, she did not know how truly she spoke; there is no science that is not the frequent dupe of destiny.

Brutalis was complaisant, in the hope of encountering his shepherdess, and plunged into the wood with Mademoiselle Coquete; she knew all the secret paths, and chose a place where a silvery spring emerging from a huge rock made a soft murmur and maintained a green moss. She dismounted and obliged the prince to do the same. They sat down beside one another on the edge of the stream formed by the spring.

"Well," she said, pulling the prince toward her and placing his head on her knees, "what do you think of such a solitary place? Don't you feel a certain languor that I'm trying to inspire in you?"

"I think," said Brutalis, looking at her with eyes more intelligent than usual, "that this is a likeable solitude." He added: "And I feel better here than elsewhere."

"Ah!" exclaimed the fay, who found his words sufficiently reasonable and thought that she had wrought that miracle, "You'll no longer bear the disagreeable name of Brutalis; in future you'll have the fine one of Polidamour. And in marrying me," she added, arranging the beautiful curls of the prince's hair around his brow, "you'll enjoy a felicity that will have no limits."

Polidamour was very occupied while Coquete was flattering herself with that deceptive idea. Hazard—or, to put it better, the blind god who sees clearly when he wants to—had brought the shepherdess to the other side of the rock of the spring; he had seen her pass behind it; the ardor of his desire to see her no longer permitted him any restraint; it was necessary to profit from the opportunity. He stood up abruptly and told the fay that he would be very glad to take a look around.

The fay, surprised to the highest degree by the manner in which he had pronounced those few words, saw him depart with an assured grace. Never had he been so lovable, and never had she feared losing him so much. She began to suspect that Amour had prepared some fatal trouble for her. The reflections that she made on that subject gave the prince time to execute his project, but in the end, no longer able to resist her impatience, she went in search of him tremulously.

How astonished she was to see him at the knees of the shepherdess she had seen from the platform! Her despair is indescribable, and her first impulse was to make her ingrate a thousand reproaches. A second thought stopped her; she wanted to see the end of the adventure and give her jealousy time to augment her fury.

A bush by which she was covered facilitated the means of seeing and hearing what was about to bring her dolor to its peak. The shepherdess had all the flower of youth and everything that makes for perfect beauty: ash-blonde hair whose curls were mingled with pomegranate flowers gave her the brilliance that is only seen in blondes; the kind of eyes of which one cannot distinguish the color allowed a vivid and tender gaze to pass through long dark eyelids; her complexion was dazzling in its splendor; her red lips fashioned a gracious smile that formed countless little charms around her mouth; her face was almost round, a little dimple in the chin giving it a proud and delicate appearance; and her nose was slightly turned up. It was a young face, the youth of which seemed to be assured for a long time. Her breasts were formed by the Graces and her white and delicately shaped hands, because they often served to hide a blush that the sight and speech of the prince caused her, enabled the desolate Coquete to see all too clearly.

She was wearing a dress of fine gauze trimmed with lace; her belt was woven from flowers, and her figure, seated as she was, appeared so neat and so beautiful that Mademoiselle Coquete, after an overly exact examination of so many marvels, cried dolorously: "Pitiless Heaven, what rival have you created for me?"

The lovers were too intent on their conversation to hear the fay's sad tones. As soon as he was at the feet of the shepherdess, Polidamour had commenced by giving her thanks for having been kind enough to come into the forest. Those thanks gave her a pleasant shame; she replied to him without looking at him that she took her flock into the forest and the meadow indifferently.

"Oh," the impetuous prince interjected, "don't repent of an innocent favor which renders me the happiest of men." He added: "We don't have time to observe decorum; I adore you; there's nothing I wouldn't do to prove it to you. Only tell me whether my person and my amour might make some impression on your heart."

"Alas," she said, blushing, "I dread giving you a poor opinion of me by making a confession that might be agreeable to you; perhaps it's going too fast, but you've made me envisage that we have no time to waste and I'd be in despair if you left without having learned that, by virtue of a sympathy beyond my control..."

The young shepherdess stopped at those words, and the handsome Polidamour cried, with an unparalleled joy: "Fortunate sympathy! Charming speech! Why can I not die at your feet, to thank you as I ought to do?"

At that point, Mademoiselle Coquete no longer had the strength to constrain herself; many people might even be surprised that she had delayed so long in emerging from her bush. She ran forward impetuously and demanded of the prince in a thunderous voice who had taught him so much.

He stood up, and aided his shepherdess to do likewise.

"Amour, Madame," he relied to the fay, "has enabled this prodigy; you pronounced the edict yourself; I'm sorry that it was not the work of your features. But he is a capricious god," he added, smiling "who made me neglect to respond to the generosity of a great fay, while constraining me to render to a simple shepherdess the same worship that one renders to the most powerful divinities."

The ironic tone with which the prince seasoned his words made Mademoiselle Coquete sense so sharply the superiority of the charms of that shepherdess over her own that, transported by rage and launching furious glances at her rival, she said to Polidamour: "You're not where you think; your amorous eloquence might die down, or change object; you're only talking like another, and better than another, to drive me to despair. Fear my just resentment, or cease to adore a petty shepherdess, whom I'll teach whether it's her who can trouble a fay."

The timid shepherdess, whose name was Brillante and who had been brought up in dread of those terrible women, whose very vices were respected, fell to her knees and, shedding a torrent of tears, asked her to pardon an offense that she had caused innocently.

"Go on, go on." said Coquete. "No rival is ever innocent." And, seizing her rudely by the arm, she took possession of her.

"Where is your generosity, Madame?" said the prince. "You have rendered an oracle; it has been fulfilled; that is honorable to your knowledge; the rest depended on the eyes of my shepherdess." Then he tried to extract his mistress from her dangerous hands; but human strength was futile in that circumstance.

"Well," he said, in his despair, "exercise on this divine young woman and me all the cruelties you can invent; you will never force my heart to change its chains."

Those are terrible words for a lover to hear; the fay felt their full force; but she was in love, and one is scarcely in control of oneself when one is agitated by that passion, to which she also added temperament.

"Ingrate," she said to Polidamour. "I have loved you, then, and told you so, only to see an unworthy rival triumph! I love you," she continued, weeping, "in a place where I thought to see you less inflexible, and it's to cover me with shame that

I brought you here. Follow me without resistance, unfortunate shepherdess, and refrain from turning your eyes toward your barbaric lover."

That order was poorly executed; Brillante had learned since falling in love to avoid the eyes of a rival, and she often encountered Polidamour's.

Her eyes glinting with wrath, Mademoiselle Coquete had no sooner spoken a few words than an obscure lair rose up, guarded by two frightful Furies, who took away the lovely Brillante in spite of the efforts of the prince, although his courage equaled his amour.

"How unfortunate I am!" he cried. "I have no sooner savored the sweetness of amour than the charming object I adore has been snatched away from me; I can only make use of the advantage of thinking reasonably to regret for as long as I live the person before whom my stupidity had disappeared. No, cruel woman," he added, addressing Mademoiselle Coquete, "you rage will not be exercised upon me for long, and this iron will deliver me from a long sequence of woes."

He drew his sword as he spoke; if the fay had not had power over the aerial spirits, it would have been all over for the handsome Polidamour, but three or four of them disarmed him and took him to the palace of the enemy of his repose.

No one would have thought, in that harsh constraint, that the prince was no longer the somber man of old; he sensed the misfortune of his situation keenly. Mademoiselle Coquete treated him only too well; Polidamour's intelligence, and the jealousy that it gave her, augmented her passion infinitely. She did everything to bend him, and the insults he made her by way of response irritated the fay without detaching her.

One day, he decided to resume his stupid countenance. At first she suspected the truth, but its continuation caused her some alarm; she feared that the excess of his affliction had caused him to fall back into his original state, and, her tenderness obscuring her reason, she could not refuse the remedy to an excessively beloved ingrate.

What a remedy! There could not be any other, however, than allowing him to see Brillante. It was dangerous, and it took time for her to resolve to do it, but the desire to render a great service to her lover gave her the strength to go through with it.

The nub of the difficulty was knowing whether she ought to conduct him herself or put him in the hands of zealous emissaries who could render her a good account of it. If the first course was the surer, there was also something very cruel about it; is there anything comparable to the dolor of seeing in a beloved person a joy that one has not excited? That thought determined her to put him under the guard of two sylphs, whose subtle and intelligent minds seemed appropriate to such an employment.

Mademoiselle Coquete made the two sylphs adopt the form of two formidable tigers; they bound Polidamour with chains of flowers stronger than metal chains; they set forth with that equipage toward the lair where young Brillante was being held. Polidamour had heard all the orders with which they were charged; he resolved to move them to compassion. His eloquence, augmented by dolor, made incredible efforts, but he arrived at the entrance to the cavern without having been able to extract a single word from the taciturn tigers. When they arrived they called to the two Furies and ordered them to let the prince enter.

Anticipation seemed sufficiently advantageous, and that frightful abode, more appropriate to wild beasts than an unfortunate beauty, appeared as a delightful palace where all pleasures were about to accompany him.

"I finally see you again," he said to the shepherdess. "I can tell you without witnesses what I feel for you."

Brillante, who was in a dark corner, lying on a bed of leaves that she had made, and who was perhaps weeping at that moment as much because of the absence of her lover as the captivity she was in, raised her beautiful eyes toward him. Sensible to that unexpected joy, she said: "It's you Sire! What fortunate adventure brings you to this place, where the cruelties that are exercised upon me have not distracted me for a moment from thinking about you?"

Such a favorable welcome soon put the lovers in a situation full of confidence, which is one of the great pleasures of amour.

The prince told her his story, and had a delicate pleasure in rendering thanks to her for having given him a passion whose violence, far from constraining his reason had enabled him to find his own. Brillante wanted to instruct him in her own regard, which she did in these terms:

"It's necessary, Sire, that I justify the liking that you have acquired for me. I am a princess, the daughter of the sovereign of the Gallant Isle; it is a very agreeable country, where one no sooner has the use of reason than one commences to love; but it is held as a maxim there that, if changeability is not a virtue, it is at least such a great pleasure that it would be very inconvenient to be deprived of it.

"The prince, my father, practices that maxim to the letter; never was anyone more inconstant than he is. He had already rendered his cares to all the beauties of the court when I left; he was even starting on the ugly ones, and sustained that rather than not change, he would attach himself to ladies who, by virtue of their old age, no longer attracted sighs. 'Is it not a laudable curiosity,' he said, 'to discover different fashions of loving, to examine the diversity of characters and to retrogress, so to speak, toward past centuries by means of the commerce of a venerable woman, to whom age has given experience?'

"I was untouched by that depiction; on the contrary, I imagined a great pleasure in engaging myself for life. It was in vain that I saw myself served and adored by several princes of my father's estates; their dangerous maxims frightened me, and not having the heart to employ reprisals, I avoided as much as possible finding myself at the continual fêtes held in the Gallant Isle.

"'How do I know,' I said to myself one day, when I was walking alone in a wood, 'whether one of those lovers might touch me in the end? What a misfortune, to be sensible to a fickle individual who will soon quit me for another?' Then I heard a nightingale, which was singing these words distinctly:

> To follow the order of the gods,
> Princess, flee this place,
> Receive the help of an invisible hand,
> And come to test the power of your eyes
> On the heart of a sensible lover;
> You alone can make him a precious gift,
> He alone can give you a sweet and placid fate.

"Surprised by that prediction, I looked in all directions, but I only saw a light vapor, which slid beneath my feet and carried me away, all the way to this country; gemstones that I had on my clothing served to acquire a sheepfold and to live with the inhabitants of these villages. Hope amused me there, and you can see, Sire, that if I have justified you by my story, I am also disculpated by my oracle for the sentiments that I acquired for you. I cannot doubt that you are the lover who ought to render me happy, and the gift that I have made you is precious enough. It is true, however, that I have only dispelled the chaos that was obscuring your ideas; you had the intelligence and reason you are enjoying within you, which was not shining as it is today for lack of a certain fire; Amour is a grandmaster; he disentangled the chaos of the vast universe; how could he fail that which he found in a heart ready to submit to his power?"

Transported by joy, Polidamour kissed the beautiful hands of his beautiful princess a thousand times; neither of them was thinking any longer about their situation; they had forgotten the fay's power; but one of the tigers came to tell them that it was time to separate. They protested dolorously against that fatal order, and their plaints found grace before the aerial spirit.

"Go on," he said to them, smiling, to the extent that a tiger can smile. "I want to aid you in your amours; we sometimes mingle in the sights of our light empire, and in order not to keep you in suspense any longer," he added, addressing the princess and taking the form of a handsome boy, "it was me who transported you from the Gallant Isle to this place. As a minister of destiny in your regard, Mademoiselle Coquete could never have chosen worse; she has some power over us, but we evade it when it pleases us."

He called his comrade then, who adopted the same form as him, similar to such a degree that they could no longer be distinguished.

They made the air surrounding them taken on substance, formed a very agreeable little chariot therefrom, and while the immobile Furies no longer had the strength to oppose their design, one of the sylphs said: "Let's crown our triumph and our deceit, and let Mademoiselle Coquete be informed of your adventure."

At that moment a porphyry column rose up, on which the mischievous spirits engraved the words:

Choose better in future
The ministers of your vengeance,
And of our two lovers lose the memory;
They will no longer have any other suffering
Than that of amorous hearts
They will not see you again, and will be only too glad.

All four of them departed then, and in a very short time they reached the realm of Paraminosara; God knows how perfect the king's joy was on seeing his dear son again, as the most amiable of all men.

No circumstance of his story was omitted, and the aerial spirits, who were able to listen like oracles, put Mademoiselle Coquete, whom they declared also to be Azindara, in such bad odor with the king that he would not have wanted to see her married to Polidamour for anything in the world. As for Brillante, her alliance appeared very honorable to him. One of the sylphs went to make the request, and brought back a favorable response. The King of Paraminosara only put one condition on it, which was that after the death of the sovereign of the Gallant Isle, the abuses that had crept in there would be reformed.

The celebrations of that marriage were marvelous. It is true that after the spouses, the Princes of the Air were its finest ornament; they gave amour to several amiable young women touched by the glory of immortalizing their lovers, but those fickle lovers departed when they were well furnished with immortality, and their mistresses, not knowing what to do about it, sought less agreeable but more solid conquests.

As for Mademoiselle Coquete, the inscription on the pyramid caused her such a rage that she was ill for some time; however, the hope of soon reestablishing herself, and fortified by the protection of the King of Paraminosara, of which she believed herself to be sure, she departed on a hippogriff to go to his court; but the prince was married; he still adored his life; she could not do anything about that, and after many actions and adventures of which she ought to have been ashamed, she was obliged to resume the route to her old palace. As for the one about which I have spoken. It was then in imaginary space.

The Origin of the Fays

Whatever discoveries poets have made concerning the gods, they have not penetrated all their secrets; human intelligence is not sufficient to develop the profound mysteries of their pleasures.

Amour having made at all times the delights of Jupiter, and secrecy being an essential part of that passion, some of his mistresses have escaped the knowledge of mortals, and only revelation has been able to substitute for that default.

Some time ago, a woman who flatters herself with being one of the favorites of Apollo was meditating profoundly about the tales of the fays that pass for chimeras. Only able to think that there was no veritable foundation to traditions so ancient, however, she remained in vision and falsity so long as she only had her own intelligence for a guide, and her application guided her insensibly to slumber. Shortly thereafter, she thought she had been woken up by the harmonies of an instrument, the sounds of which caused her sweet and extraordinary transports.

She opened her eyes, or thought she opened them, and saw that she was in a pleasant woodland, through which a stream ran over brilliant diamonds. A blond young man clad in antique drapery was playing a lyre on the bank. He had graces so spiritual and so uncommon that she recognized him as the god of verses.

She tried to throw herself at his feet, prejudiced by her erroneous belief that she was his protégée.

"Stop!" he cried to her. "Stop! Do you believe that for a few rondeaux and petty songs you are worthy to approach me and penetrate into the secrets of the gods? That's how mortals are; their self-esteem always renders them dupes; proud of a slight talent that I tolerate in them, they behave as if I had enabled them to savor the precious waters that I reserve for my favorites."

Apollo's discourse astonished the dreamer greatly; she reconsidered herself, and confessed with a profound humility that her ignorance had caused her temerity until now, but that in future she would not attempt anything that surpassed her range.

"That's how I desire you to be," the god said to her, smiling, "and to recompense such submissive dispositions, approach; I'll grant you a favor with which I have rarely honored your sex."

She went on her knees to the feet of the handsome Apollo. He put a drop of the mysterious water on her lips.

"Go," he said. "Return to mortals, and since they are unjust enough to treat fays as imaginary, I give you the ability to disabuse them; you will no sooner take up the quill than the majestic origin of those admirable women will be revealed clearly to your eyes."

She did, indeed, wake up, very surprised to find herself in her bed, but so filled with what had just happened that she immediately started to write, and did not hesitate for a moment to compose the following story.

A few centuries after Jupiter had organized chaos he acquired a passion for a nymph, the most beautiful that there has ever been. Nothing was lacking in the regularity of her features; her figure was divine, her manner gallant and majestic; her complexion surpassed the most beautiful flowers, her laughter was gracious and her intelligence had a sublimity and a charm that it was impossible to resist.

Doubtless Nature, in order to render thanks to Jupiter for the ornaments with which he had embellished her, had made her utmost efforts to accomplish a masterpiece in the person of Ogilire, in whom the god found the recompense for his labors. He had already had several mistresses; all had succumbed to his first attacks. The conquest of Ogilire was attempted in the same fashion, but the result was different.

She would not accept the rapidity with which Jupiter wanted to take the places to which he laid siege. Although sensible to the glory of submitting to such a great god, her heart rebelled against the means of which he made use, and, sure of not succumbing unless he made use of other ways, she did not do him the honor of avoiding him.

"Great god," she said to him one day, "I can neither dread you nor love you so long as I only see you as overwhelming Jupiter. You believe that you have only to appear in order to be victorious; learn that a young person who has virtue and who only fears the weakness of her heart is always shielded from the enterprises of the power that you value so highly, and which, after all, is worth far less than a faithful amour.

Jupiter was not accustomed to find so much resistance; he tried to make use of his power to subjugate her, like the others, but, with the eloquence and the majestic mildness that was natural to her, she was so well able to suppress the audacity of the master of the gods that he had recourse a few days later to his ordinary disguises, under which he had stolen so many favors. The amiable Ogilire was never deceived, however; always attentive to her duty, she rendered his enterprises vain, but without deterring him.

"What!" he said, finally. "A girl, a simple girl will be more powerful than me? It will not be said that, master of everything, I can surrender to her will. Let us employ other weapons, since my ruses are as futile as my grandeur."

At that moment, he perceived Amour hidden in the foliage of a large myrtle, laughing wholeheartedly at seeing the Thunderer beside himself.

"Cruel Amour," he cried, "lend me your aid; you know the matter in hand better than I do."

"You'll know as much about it," Cupid replied, "when your heart is veritably touched. Until now, you have only had desires; you have satisfied them without delicacy, and without the sensible pleasure that one savors in the pursuit of a heart. Go," he added, unleashing an arrow at him; "learn what sentiments are, and treat a mortal woman as if you were mortal; that is the means of savoring delights that you have not yet experienced."

Jupiter did, in fact, feel a pleasant languor; the desire to be loved made itself sensed sharply at that fatal moment. He asked Amour to give him dispositions favorable to the beautiful Ogilire.

"I'll take care of that," replied Amour, "but it's up to you now to make your destiny."

The god thought then that he had changed his nature, that he was no longer the reckless Jupiter who only wanted possession, that he was a tender lover who wanted to please.

IIc went into a meadow where Ogilire was taking the air as the daylight declined. She was lying on the green grass bordering a spring. Jupiter was very handsome when he was disarmed of his thunderbolts and his eyes only wanted to emit the flashes that cause tender passion. That evening he had all the grandeur of divinity, all the charms of an amiable mortal, and all the youth that solicits amour. His costume was elegant; it is necessary to neglect nothing when one wants to succeed. He threw himself at Ogilire's feet; he said things to her capable of surprising a heart, things of which one only thinks when one is in love, and that have their effect sooner or later when one is not dealing with a prejudiced soul.

The nymph got up when he arrived, and then sat down next to him; she listened without difficulty; for the first time, it was not without emotion. She feared the surprise of the senses, but, mistress of herself, she only allowed to escape precisely what was necessary to nourish a little hope. The god was charmed by the slight progress he had made, content with so little because he hoped for more and because he was very much in love. He returned to the heavens enchanted with his lot. Juno found him so mild toward her that she did not suspect anything, being an ignorant goddess who did not know that passions mollify the mind.

The master of the gods left the universe in repose during that amorous pursuit; he was only capable of tender cares, mild ideas and cheerful designs. At Ogilire's feet every day, he assured her of an eternal fidelity; she had often had recourse to flight in order not to abandon herself to the penchant that was already so strong within her.

Let us hide, she said to herself, sometimes. *Jupiter is amiable; he treats me with all the application of a passionate lover, but I know him only too well, and the charms of his person and those of his amour; I would no sooner be favorable to him than his delicacy would diminish; perhaps he would give me a rival, and what would my consolation be then?*

Her reflections bore her footsteps to remote places, but nothing was hidden from Jupiter. "You are fleeing, cruel nymph," he said to her one day in the depths of a wood. "You are fleeing me; do you hate me?"

At those words she turned her gaze in his direction, and he saw a delightful mixture of amour and modesty there. "Cease making vain efforts to avoid my research," he added. "I would find you everywhere, even if I were not a god. The little blind person who is guiding me would not leave me ignorant of your whereabouts for long, and you will never have anything to combat but my amour."

That discourse reassured the nymph; she abandoned herself to the limitless pleasure of seeing the person one loves, and her lover's respect gradually disarmed her virtue.

At that time Briareus and his monstrous brethren made their escalade, as well as all the nations.[1] The desire to please by means of evidence of valor extracted Jupiter from the agreeable languor in which he had been living for a long time. He crushed those audacious individuals with an intrepidity worthy of his power; as for his flight into Egypt, that is a horrible slander, the authors of which have been punished with the utmost severity, although that has not been able to interrupt the course of the tradition.

Meanwhile, Ogilire sensed movements in her heart augmenting, which sometimes rendered her the happiest person in the world, and sometimes the most unfortunate. The absences that Jupiter was obliged to make in the interests of mortals caused her the most piquant woe, but his return soon calmed such cherished alarms.

For six months, already, he had been the perfect lover without having been able to obtain the slightest favor; he complained of that tenderly, but with a submission that, in leaving the power to be rigorous, gradually took away the desire.

---

[1] In Homer and Hesiod the giant with fifty heads and a hundred hands named Briareus aided Zeus against the Titans, but in Callimachus and Virgil (the latter being the author's likely source) he became an enemy of Zeus and one of the rebels who tried to storm Olympus. The allegation that the gods of Olympus took refuge in Egypt during the war with the Titans, where Jupiter became a ram, is found in Ovid's *Metamorphoses*, a favorite text of the first wave writers of *contes de fées*; it is most aptly construed as an allegory, and is devoid of previous mythological foundation.

During that time, Ogilire exercised mastery over the master of Olympus. Comus took care of her table, Momus of her amusements, Plutus of her wealth, and the Graces of her attire, but the nymph only found pleasure in the cares of her lover; because they assured her of his amour, all the rest was indifferent to her.

One day when she was with him and they were talking to one another with the confidence that creates the most touching pleasures of the union of hearts, while her lover was making her party to all the secrets of nature and pouring his heart out confidently with such a lovable mistress, they suddenly found themselves in a kind of cavern of clouds that exhaled the most delectable odors; they saw little streaks of fire that traced, in clearly legible characters: *Profit from the moment, great god; it is the time that Amour ordains.*

Jupiter and Ogilire read that precise order at the same time.

"You see," said the god; "my submission is finally too great."

The nymph lowered her eyes, and pretended not to have read anything; an instant later, the words disappeared and others took their place.

Recompense your divine lover, nymph; when it is time, modesty pardons you.

"Will you resist such a sacred edict?" cried the amorous Jupiter. "Is there a means to defy it?"

Immediately, the new cavern, which had previously had an opening guarded by two Amours, closed, and, its luminous obscurity—if one can speak thus—giving a little boldness to Ogilire, she extended her hand to Jupiter and allowed him to kiss it, with the transport that a first favor causes. She withdrew it afterwards, ashamed of having done so much, and called Jupiter temeritous when he complained of her rigor.

That lover, confused by such a reproach, begged her pardon, and ceased his insistence. Then they heard one of the Amours burst out laughing. "Behold the god become a shepherd," he said to his comrade. "That's how he'll be used one day."

Ogilire called the Amour a libertine and a corrupter of morals, and begged Jupiter to put another in his place.

"I consent to that," replied the little mischief-maker, "but you won't be any better guarded for it."

In fact, it is known that the nymph surrendered shortly thereafter, not without being able to increase the purchase price of the most precious gifts of all.

The delight of Jupiter was such that it was sensed throughout the heavens, without any inhabitant of the celestial vault being able to penetrate the mysterious case, except for Phoebus and his sister, Diana, from whom it is impossible to conceal amorous larcenies. As for the Amours and the gods employed in Ogilire's service, they had sworn by the Styx never to reveal what they knew.

The perfect happiness of Jupiter made him more eager; his mistress had forbidden herself for so long, ambition had had no part in her defeat; amour alone, the amour that nothing can resist, had gradually engaged her in its web, and his passion was so long, so happy and so faithful that it could hardly be criticized.

"No," Jupiter said to her one day, "until now I have only had a false idea of perfect pleasure; my unregulated desires were veritably satisfied with famous beauties, but, contented as soon as amorous, I only encountered a vulgar resistance soon vanquished by an equally vulgar ruse or an insipid abandonment to my divinity, with no regard to my person. They were not felicities worthy of me, but you have guided me to the supreme felicity, charming Ogilire. What can I do to recompense you for such a great benefit?"

"Love me forever," said Ogilire. "That alone can render me more fortunate than you are; loved by a simple mortal, you cannot savor what I feel in the greater amour of the gods."

It was thus that the lovers spent their days, in hiding, or in the obscurity of a forest, or in valleys irrigated by streams; amour has always sought solitude.

Eventually, the nymph became pregnant. She had difficulty declaring it to Jupiter; her modesty was alarmed by having such a speech to make; the tears that it caused her to shed, paralyzed her with dread.

"You're weeping," he said to her, "although I love you and I swear that I love no one but you."

"Alas," she replied, I cannot doubt that, but if you knew that fatal condition that I am in, you would understand that it is that very love which is causing my tears."

He took some time to divine the reason for such a touching affliction, but by virtue of interrogation, she revealed the important secret to him.

"You can see the state I'm in," she said to him. "If you don't take care to hide me and console me, I'll become the most unfortunate person in the world."

"As for hiding you," said the god, "you can trust me, but as for your consolation, either my power will fail or I'll do things in your favor that will render your fate very different from other mortals.

"You will have a daughter by me whose destiny will be beautiful and brilliant, and her knowledge so extensive, that she will be called a fay, a name that will be honored for centuries, and which will only fall into a kind of debasement because everything has a period, after which decadence comes; the most powerful empires experience the same fate. But a day will come when illustrious women will celebrate the fays and renew their deeds with a great deal of intelligence and art. At first those works will be regarded as the effects of a vivid and fecund imagination; then a simple mortal will learn from the god of Parnassus the veritable origin of what people would like to pass off as fables.

"I cannot hide from you that among your descendants, some will have supreme virtues and other great vices, but all of them will have a redoubtable or marvelous power. As for you, charming Ogilire, you will be the first of the sibyls, known throughout the vast universe by that famous name, and you will participate in immortality."

Thus spoke Jupiter; his mistress rendered him thanks for a prediction that flattered the nobility of her heart and was appropriate to her virtue.

She did, in fact, give birth to a divine daughter endowed with all graces and all enlightenments; she had an amiable husband, and several daughters as beautiful and enlightened as her. Everyone felt their benefits and for several centuries their posterity only applied themselves to rendering mortals happy, but, something audacious perhaps having interrupted the course of their ancestors, some were accused of crimes, others of moral libertinism. Often, their absolute power gave them the desire to use it badly. Several impulses motivated them; avarice, ambition, amour and vengeance bore them to cruel extremities.

There were a few, however, who conserved the purity of their ancestors, and in those virtue seemed to be hereditary; not only did the women of their posterity not belie it for a long time, but even the men of that lineage were favored by those precious heavenly gifts; several of them had the art of faerie, and thus were as many sage enchanters and protectors of oppressed merit. From them the eleven sibyls were born, who, with Ogilire, made up the number twelve, which has never been surpassed.

What glory to have ornamented the earth with those marvelous women, whose penetration discovered the most hidden recesses of the somber future! The purity of their life, their independence, their authority, and, above all, the precious chastity praised by all peoples, all conserved their stainless reputation until our own day. It is true that Ogilire had placed a serious crack in that last virtue, but what cannot be pardoned in a violent amour caused by the master of the gods? She soon repaired that fault by means of her harshness of her mortifications, and that famous sibyl has always been known until today as the divine Ogilire.

That digression was unavoidable, in order to accord to the reputation of those extraordinary women what is legitimately owed to them; their relatives, the good fays, did not all exercise such austere virtues, but they shone for a long time amid the darkness of the most uncouth centuries; knowledge resided in them alone, while the rest of the world languished in profound ignorance. Several of those worthy daughters of Jupiter only wanted the power to do good, and refused the gift of doing harm.

Meanwhile, they lived together in a sufficiently perfect union, the most malevolent hiding themselves from the others in order to exercise their cruelties, and as they often had great secrets to communicate to one another, they resolved to construct a superb edifice in order to be able to hold their council there on certain appointed days, to which they rendered from the four continents of the world, permitting those who were judged worthy of it to reside there. That place, so beautiful and so singular, merits description.

The Council of Fays was a fortress built in the middle of a vast plain; a large river that ran over mother-of-pearl served its moats; the surrounding area was shaded by fruit trees of every species, always laden with exquisite fruits, which travelers could pick in complete assurance because they were always replaced more abundantly as soon as they were detached.

The river could be crossed by four different bridges, which led to the gates by which the fortress was entered; those bridges were constructed of incorruptible wood, and had a delectable odor that could be sensed ten leagues around; appropriate golden figures ornamented the arches and the parapets; countless little vessels, painted and gilded, were everready to set sail whenever it pleased the fays to make an excursion on the water.

The gates were emerald and their hinges gold; each of them was guarded by four animals, which allowed mortals to pass whose intentions had nothing criminal, but if any reckless individuals appeared whose desires might harm the fays, the four elephants that stood guard at one of the gates would lift them with their trunks above the edifice and hurl them on to the horn of one of the unicorns at another gate; with an inconceivable skill, she would throw them with a similar dexterity in order to deliver them to the wild boars guarding the third gate, who would plunge their tusks into their hands in such a way as to mark them for life; then the excessive pain would force them to flee such a dangerous place, but, wanting to avoid the road they had initially taken, they would go to the end of the bridge, which four lions would immediately traverse with impetuosity, in order to imprint their formidable claws on the foreheads of the unfortunate criminals; thus, without making those audacious individuals die, they were put in a state to remember their misfortunate enterprise eternally.

That vengeance was so terrible that few people risked becoming an example of it. As for honest people, we have already said that they were permitted entry, and the furious animals did not make mistakes.

When one had entered the fortress, the eye, already surprised by so much beauty, could scarcely sustain the splendor and majesty of the incomparable place. Each of its facades was composed of a hundred pavilions made of gold and enabled in green; the casements, open all the way to the floor, were crystal, more transparent than glass, which never broke; their secret has been absolutely lost since a cruel emperor put to death the excellent artisan who had renewed it under his reign.

The balusters of those windows where alternately made of turquoise, ruby, emerald, amethyst, topaz and sapphire, cut with the greatest artistry. The pavilions were covered with burnished gold and crowned with figures of white cornelian, which represented the most beautiful fays of antiquity. As for the arcades, in which it was possible to walk under cover, they were sustained by wide gold columns enriched with brilliant diamonds. In the bas-reliefs above the arches one saw the most memorable actions of heroes, until the present century. The terrain on which one walked was of similar workmanship, which only represented flowers; the eyes were often deceived thereby, and one bent down to pick them, as if from a flower-bed.

On emerging from the arcades one found an area separated by a balustrade, behind which was the garden; that space was paved with compartments of aventurine and lapis; the grille was excellently wrought with porcelain of various colors and strings of unwitherable flowers, if one can speak thus. A thousand porcelain vases filled with similar flowers ornamented the top of the elegant grille; nothing so bright and so fresh had ever appeared to the eyes; one could have believed that one was in the palace of Flora.

That grille had no gates; it enclosed what might be called the fays' sanctuary; it was a delightful garden in which they amused themselves together; they were only imperfectly visible through the balustrade, the gaps in which were very narrow, and the power of the inhabitants of that charming abode even took away the natural penetration of eyes. Enough of the beauty and their pleasures was visible to create the desire to enter it, but it was with a kind of veil that partly hid the mysteries into which they never initiated anyone.

There, after having decided the duration of empires of felicity or the misfortune of mortals, the youngest and the most beautiful amused themselves, while the old went to repose in their rich apartments; they all reserved the faculty of seeing those whose curious eyes wanted to pierce the slight obscurity of the grille, and, their hearts not being insensible, they often found objects worthy of their affection.

Above the garden that enclosed so many marvels, by virtue of an astonishing prodigy, the sky always appeared the color of flame. The ardor of the sun never made itself felt there, but somber night never deployed its veils there either; the stars, brighter than everywhere else, cast a light in that beautiful place gentler than that of broad daylight and much more luminous than four thousand candles. It was a clarity that rendered beauty; a few of the fays needed that aid; there were others for whom it was unnecessary. The flame-colored sky was never obscured by clouds; the air there was pure and the rain that sometimes refreshed the external gardens never made itself felt there.

Jupiter was invited to the consecration of that place, the most beautiful in the world; his daughters celebrated his glory with games, with which he was content, and the odor of their sacrifices often made itself sensible all the way to the heights of Olympus.

Several centuries went by, during which, although there was disorder in the conduct of a large number of fays, order nevertheless reigned in their Council, and among them; but Amour, that tyrant of souls, accompanied by deadly jealousy, inspired terrible furies in those omnipotent women.

Everyone knows that amour acts differently in accordance with the various temperaments it encounters; a virtuous people mourns its disgraces, but what can be worse is being consoled and hoping that a new passion will be more fortunate; that need not offend anyone, but a soul that has within it the seeds of cruelty imagines that having a lover other than oneself is a crime, all the more so if it is exclusive. When power is combined with the transports of jealous amour, there are no errors to which it is incapable of committing.

Several fays, having found themselves in those situations, exercised such horrible cruelties that their crimes, their murders and their prescriptions, the consequence of their fatal aberrations, astonished the tremulous world to such an extent that those among them whose virtue was unshakable by such dire examples concluded that there was no other means of stemming the flow of so many horrors than destroying their Council, which served them as a shelter, where they came to enjoy the fruits of their pernicious conduct with impunity.

The master of the gods was begged to blast it with a mighty thunderbolt. He had difficulty resolving himself to destroy the most superb of edifices, where nothing had been able to trouble the harmony and concord of his daughters for so many centuries, but it was represented to him that all was lost if he deferred that execution. The Council was smashed mercilessly, and the lightning fell upon it with so much fury that the most curious individuals of antiquity were never able to find the slightest trace of it, no one even knows in which part of the world it was built.

The causes of such a great loss were relegated to obscure lairs, and their power was so limited that it could only extend over a few wretched animals, which they amused themselves persecuting, for want of more beautiful victims.

Such was the end of the Council of Fays, and those proud women whose fatal power had made itself felt only too well. As for the other fays, whose virtue did not belie their origin, they lived peacefully in agreeable or magnificent abodes, with more or less lovable husbands. Such was the famous and knowledgeable Melusine, one of the best known; she possessed the beauty, the grace and the intelligence of the amiable Ogilire. Nowadays, it is simply known that she was responsible for the commencement of an illustrious house, but her origin is unknown; at least, what is said about it is very uncertain or quite fabulous.

That is how everything worked out in the end, and that is what could only be known by virtue of a formal revelation. Melusine had wealth proportionate to her birth, and twelve sons, all crowned sovereigns; if they each had a natural defect, that was to expiate the harshness of one of their ancestors, who had devoted the least beautiful of her daughters to the service of the gods without consulting their will. Thus, everything has a mysterious cause, and children often bear the iniquity of their forebears.

In those days there were still fays in the world, a few of their deeds have been passed down to us; they were held in veneration and people fortunately learned to fear and respect them, but in the end, their race dwindled away, like the majority of families; their power diminished, their reputation was destroyed, their intelligence evaporated.

Nothing under the sun is stable; tradition appears to the eyes as a distant perspective that one suspects of illusion. No one any longer has dread or admiration for the fays; their very names, which had made crowned heads tremble, are no longer pronounced except by the mouths of children, whose governesses relate their deeds very imperfectly.

As soon as one crosses the brief interval that leads from infancy to youth, people make fun of the faith they had added to them, and the first tales that appeared under the title of tales of the fays were narrated with the puerility that is the only language of such a tender age; but beautiful hands have not disdained to work with the same material, and have nobly extracted from forgetfulness those women worthy of an eternal memory, of whom they have rendered adventures so agreeable and so interesting that they are owed a profound meditation on our part.

Otherwise, they would still be enveloped in the darkness of ignorance.

Louise Cavelier: *The Prince of Aquamarines*

The isle of savages resounded with cries of joy, and the frightful rocks with which the isle is surrounded responded to the sound of instruments of war and the clamors of the barbarians. The sea, which came to break violently against the rocks, mingled its roars with all those cries and further augmented their horror.

Those monsters, who took pleasure in murdering all the luckless individuals that the fury of the winds forced to set foot on their islands had assembled to choose a king. Already, floods of human blood had flowed over the altars of their gods; the shore was soaked in it, and the bodies of the unfortunate victims, heaped on a pyre, would soon be reduced to ashes; the savages were beginning to dance around the pyre when they perceived the debris of a ship. The broken masts, the shattered spars, the scattered rigging and the ripped sails were floating at the whim of the waves. They also perceived, further away, several swimmers who were trying desperately to reach the shore of their island. The hope of an imminent salvation reanimated their strength, which long fatigue and redoubled efforts had almost exhausted.

Alas, they were running to death in approaching that deadly shore, and the fate that appeared to be snatching them from the waves and desirous of saving them, as preparing a death a thousand times crueler by pushing them toward that strand.

Scarcely had they reached the coast than the savages seized them, bound them, and dragged them by the foot of their altars. There, their throats were cut and their blood, still fuming, was collected in cups that the barbarians emptied in honor of their gods.

They only reserved one of the foreigners, whose beauty, grace and youth would have excited the compassion of anyone but those ferocious people, nourished on blood and carnage. His stature, above average, was noble, without constraint; the most beautiful blond hair in the world floated in long curls over his shoulders; his broad forehead shone with a mild majesty; his eyes were dark and glittered with a piercing fire, and something mysterious, more seductive than beauty, rendered him the most lovable of mortals. He was destined by those barbarians to serve as nourishment for the king that fate was about to give them.

Their manner of electing a king was no less cruel than the rest of their mores. Six of the most considerable and most renowned for their barbarity were chosen and whichever of those six pierced with an arrow the heart of the widow or nearest relative of the deceased king was the one who would be elected. Already they had attached their queen to a rock, and five of the barbarians had struck her with their arrows in the thighs and arms, when the sixth advanced to the mark and flexed his blow. The arrow flew through the air and transfixed the heart of the unfortunate queen.

A thousand confused cries were immediately heard. All the people prostrated themselves at the feet of the new king, and then carried him as if in triumph around the island. The women and girls, their hair scattered and daggers in hand, marched ahead. Their song resembled the cries of furious Bacchantes. Old men curbed beneath the weight of their crimes even more than by the years, followed them at a slow pace, and the king, surrounded by the young men of the island, closed the march.

The foreigner who had been reserved, gripped by horror, followed with lowered eyes that funereal pomp. Two savages held him, tied up, and led him like a young victim being conducted to the altar.

After having made a circuit of the island the people finally stopped in the middle of a forest. That was the place destined for their feasts. A thousand savage beasts were laid out on the grass, and large vases full of blood were arranged at intervals. The most exquisite wine, even nectar, would have appeared less sweet to them than that beverage.

The new king was set on a throne covered with the skin of a lion, and, ready to commence the feast, he seized the foreigner, dagger in hand. He was about to cut his throat when the dagger suddenly fell and the king was laid out at the feet of the foreigner, dead himself. All the people, surprised, directed their eyes at the foreigner, but all those barbarians experienced the same fate, and fell, swimming in the blood that was running from the vases that they had overturned as they expired.

The astonishment of the young stranger, at the sight of all the people whom a divine and invisible hand had exterminated in an instant, was indescribable. The barbarians were lying on the ground, the horror of death painted on their faces, their eyes turned toward the heavens, seemingly accusing the gods of their demise; their open mouths seemed to be blaspheming against them, and their arms, which the chill of death had frozen while held aloft, seemed still to be menacing them.

The stranger promptly armed himself with the spoils of the king and, passing through the middle of the cadavers, plunged into the forest. He reached a rock from which a spring emerged, which, falling from rock to rock, further augmented with its noise the horror of the wilderness. It was there that the foreigner, reflecting on his misfortunes, abandoned himself entirely to his dolor.

He could not think without shuddering about everything that he had suffered since leaving the Brilliant Isle. That was an isle where his father reigned as king. Crystal rocks and emeralds surrounded its shores; the hills were strewn with precious stones; the trees were laden with fruits the color of rubies, and the superb diamond towers that closed the gates of the capital city dazzled the eyes. It was an entire year since he had departed from there and had gone wandering over the seas.

Everything that had happened to him was painted in his memory at that moment. He could not retain his tears in thinking that he might be separated forever from his father. He remembered then that the king, as they parted, had given him a box, which he had ordered him not to open until a year after his departure.

The year having ended, the prince opened it and found a piece of paper that he had read eagerly. It was written in the king's hand, and it was in these terms that the unfortunate father in question instructed him as to the source of his misfortunes:

It would be in vain, my dear son, that I tried to hide from you the misfortunes that menace you. The gods are my witnesses to everything I have done to calm their wrath, but the fay Noirjabarbe, an enemy of this isle, condemned you to the most frightful torture at the moment of your birth. Why did she not take your life? I would have been happier and it would have meant less pain for you.

That cruel fay arrived in my empire at the moment when the other fays had just made you a gift of everything that can render a prince accomplished. They had wanted by those gifts to take away all the means that the fay Noirjabarbe had to harm you, but who could have imagined the cruelty and barbarity of her vengeance? The fay, unable to take away all the gifts that you have been made, elected to render you the horror of the world and to condemn to instant death all those who looked at you, as soon as you had attained the age of twenty years.

Imagine my dolor when she pronounced those terrible words. I did what I could to bend her, but it was in vain; she even forbade me to reveal it to anyone but you, and before your twentieth year, hoping that I and all my people would perish in gazing at you, and that you would be their executioner. Alas, although I offered her my life, she was insensible to my tears, and she flew away in the midst of a black whirlwind of flaming bitumen and pitch. You know the care that I took of you in your childhood, and you know the tears that you have cost me, the funereal price of my tenderness. I shall not see you again; you have already made the sad proof of the

*misfortunes to which the fay Noirjabarbe has condemned you.
Seek a desert, my son, where you can spare mortals by hiding
yourself forever from their eyes, and think sometimes about
your father.*

Scarcely had the prince, who was named the Prince of
Aquamarines, finished reading than his eyes filled with tears.
"Oh gods!" he cried. "Have I merited such a cruel punishment? What places sufficiently deserted will I find on the
earth in order to hide myself from the eyes of mortals? Still, I
am fortunate in my woes that fate pushed me to this barbaric
shore, and that those monsters were the first victims that I
have immolated."

The unhappy prince stood up then and emerged from the
forest. He found himself at one of the gates of the savages'
city, built in a valley surrounded by high mountains entirely
covered by woods. A torrent that was precipitated from the
height of rocks with a horrible sound divided the city in two.
The houses were very low, all stained with blood and almost
covered with dread bodies and scattered limbs. The air of the
island had the property of conserving bodies, and they never
rotted. The prince was horrified by such a frightful place. He
emerged from it and consoled himself slightly for his troubles
with the thought that he had purged nature of such cruel monsters. He resolved to stay on the island and to live there on the
fruits that the earth produced.

He chose for his dwelling a grotto hollowed out in the
rock, from which the sea was visible. The horror of being
alone on that unknown shore was diminished slightly by the
necessity he was in of living far from mortals. The cruel penalty that the fay Noirjabarbe had imposed on him at birth banished him forever from the commerce of humans. He had just
made the sad experiment, and his solitude seemed to him to be
less frightful when he thought that at least the sight of him
would not be fatal to anyone.

He would have consoled himself for his woes with the
pleasures of a mild and tranquil life if amour had not com-

bined with Noirjabarbe's cruelty to overwhelm him; but he was in love, devoured by a burning fire; he sighed night and day, and to add further to his woes, he did not even know the name of the person he loved. He only had her portrait. Occupied incessantly with the pleasure of considering it, his fire and his regrets were augmented continually.

"I'm in love," he cried. "Amour has sharpened for me what is most violent in his empire. I don't know the person I love, and I can never hope to see her without it costing her life. My sight, fatal to all mortals, would cause to perish that which I would adore if I saw it. O gods, to what horrible torture have you condemned me?"

Such were the cruel reflections of the unfortunate prince.

He often went to walk on an isle planted with orange trees that almost joined the one where he lived. One day he went to sleep there, and was only woken up by the noise of thunderclaps. The sea was already beginning to swell, and to rise on the coast; everything announced an imminent tempest.

The Prince of Aquamarines thought, however, that he could get back to his island. He climbed into his boat, and had almost reached land when a gust of wind pushed him out into the open sea. The tempest suddenly increased, and the prince's boat, which was only made from a hollow tree trunk, was soon carried to the far extremity of the sea. He was waiting for death tranquilly, believing that he could not avoid it, when the boat struck a rock and was broken.

He swam for some time, but the night that arrived threw him into new dangers. He could no longer see to guide himself; he feared drawing away from the shore while thinking that he was approaching it. He swam on, however, and was ready to succumb, his strength being exhausted, when he felt an iron ring that was attached to a tower. He held on to it, suspended, resolved to wait until dawn, when the returning dawn would reveal the nearest shore to him.

He was lamenting and sighing at the destiny that was persecuting him when he heard a woman's voice, which said to him: "Unfortunate stranger, whom the sea and the winds have pushed to this shore, cease lamenting your fate. Alas that you cannot end my woes, as I can end yours by saving your life. Seize this rope; the gods have not yet ordered your death."

The Prince of Aquamarines hesitated for some time. He reproached himself for exposing to the risk of death someone who wanted to save his life. His forces were so enfeebled that he nearly resolved to perish, no longer able to resist. The reigning darkness emboldened him; he grasped the rope, climbed up into the tower and found himself in a room where he could not distinguish anything, so great was the obscurity there.

He had decided to throw himself back into the sea as soon as he saw dawn reappear and to swim to the nearest island, not wanting to cause the person who had just extracted him from such an urgent danger to perish.

"What do I not owe you?" he said to the woman who had just saved his life. "And how can I ever recognize the benefit that I have just receive from you? But what can an unfortunate prince persecuted by destiny do for you? Your pity, in saving my life, might perhaps engage me to further misfortunes, from which death would have delivered me. Don't leave me ignorant, however, of the climes to which the sea's waves have brought me,"

"This tower is near the Isle of Night, where my father reigns," the woman replied. "It is known as the Dark Tower; it was built by the hand of a fay. Neither the sun's rays nor the gentle light of the moon ever illuminate it; an eternal obscurity surrounds it, and the nearest objects cannot be distinguished here."

That discourse consoled the Prince of Aquamarines. He no longer feared that the sight of him might cause the death of the princess, since people only had to die on seeing him. The profound and eternal darkness that surrounded the tower reassured him.

"But what climes have given birth to you," the princess continued, "and how has the tempest cast you up on this shore? Don't refuse me the story of your adventures."

After a few sighs, which the memory of his misfortunes extracted from the Prince of Aquamarines, he began his story.

"I was born on the Brilliant Isle, and my father, who had reigned there for a long time, saw dolorously the sterility of my mother, the queen. Finally, she became pregnant. Several fays witnessed my birth and gave me all the virtues for which a prince could wish. My father, to honor them better, had prepared a magnificent feast in one of the halls of his palace. Everyone was ready to commence the feast when the air suddenly darkened. A black vapor spread through the banqueting hall and my father felt himself lifted up by an invisible hand. All the other fays recognized that it was the fay Noirjabarbe who had played that trick, but they had no power over her. They only felt sorry for my father, knowing that fay's cruelty.

"My father came back some time later, so afflicted and dejected that he was no longer recognizable. The fays had pressed him to tell them what the fay Noirjabarbe had said to him, but he could not or dared not speak. Dolor had gripped him and drew a torrent of tears from him. The fay Noirjabarbe had forbidden him, under threat of the most frightful penalties to reveal to anyone but me what she had just told him.

"My father had me brought up with all possible care, but what gave pleasure to other fathers overwhelmed him with dolor. They saw my age increasing with chagrin. The more I appeared to respond to the education he gave me, the more he felt pity for me, and the more tears I cost him. Finally, I was already in my nineteenth year when my father took me to the sea shore. He maintained a profound silence; I followed him tremulously; he had never seemed so downcast.

"He stopped on the edge of a wood and embraced me tenderly. 'Flee,' my son, 'he said. Flee this unfortunate land where you have received the light of day. The time has come when it is necessary for us to separate. I have hidden your departure from my people; they might have opposed it, and

83

would perhaps have perished in trying to save you. Go, then, my son; on the far side of this wood you will find a ship that I have equipped expressly. I will even hide from the people I have give you to accompany you; my dolor might perhaps make them suspect something. Hasten to depart and let the winds guide you. Above all, my son,' he said, 'do not open this box until a year after you have left his fatal shore.'

"He told me all that while embracing me and bathing me with his tears. I was so emotional that I scarcely had the strength to put my arms around him. 'What do I have to fear?' I cried. 'Can it cost me more than life? No, my father, if it's necessary for me to die, at least let me die embracing you.'

"'Flee,' he replied, 'and, sensible to a father's prayers, go far from this abode.' Then he escaped me and plunged into the forest. I remained motionless and it was impossible for me to take a step to follow him. I came back to myself a few moments later but I searched the forest in vain; I did not find my father there. I saw the ship he had prepared for me. It was only waiting for me. He had told those who were accompanying me that I was going to the Blessed Isles, which are not far from the Brilliant Isle. I embarked, therefore, after having prayed to the gods to preserve my father's days. We had taken the route to those islands when the wind suddenly turned and pushed us toward an isle where it was necessary to lay over.

"We disembarked in order to recaulk our vessel, which the tempest had damaged slightly. I advanced into the island, which seemed an enchanted abode. No rocks defended the shore; it was surrounded by a smooth coast where one breathed a mild and agreeable air; groves of orange trees, planted everywhere, led to a city that could be perceived from the edge of the sea; broad channels cut across the avenues, and beds of jonquils, ranunculi and tulips bordered the channels.

"Such a charming abode made me curious. I advanced further, and saw in the distance a man coming toward me whose clothing surprised me. I approached him. A long robe open at the front and trailing along the ground was covered by a jacket of the most magnificent cloth in the world; broad sleeves surrounded his arms; his head was covered by a bonnet ornamented with gems. He was holding a book in one hand and a golden wand in the other.

"He stopped when he saw me, and, after considering me for some time he said: 'Young stranger whom the tempest has cast up on these shores, follow me, and take advantage of the moments that you have to spend on this isle.' At those words I felt as if I were being drawn away involuntarily. I followed him. He turned in the direction of the city that was visible at the end of the avenue.

"While we walked he talked to me about their customs and way of life. 'This island,' he told me, 'where everything there is of the rarest in nature is assembled, is the Isle of White Magic. The number of its inhabitants is fixed. There is no jealousy between us; our power is equal; we all live as friends, because neither envy nor interest troubles us. We are all the same age and we all die on the same day. We do not keep our wives here and we only ever have one son. At the age of twenty-five we all marry the princesses who please us most in all the world. Genii that we command bring us portraits of them, and everyone chooses his own. They all give birth to a son on the same day, whom they keep with them until he age of twenty-five; for then, as we are fifty and that age is no longer appropriate to pleasures, it is the one at which we all die. We bring our wives back to the island with our sons, to whom we hand over our books and our wands, and we are buried in out tombs with our wives, who are drawn along with us, by the tenderness they have for us, into the black empire. It is today that we are all to die; soon the sky, the sun and the daylight will disappear from my eyes; I shall be plunged into an eternal night and will cease to be forever.'

"We had reached the city when he finished speaking to me. It was built entirely in marble, of magnificent architecture. He took me through it and then took me to the top of a rock, from which I could see the entire island. There, after having embraced me he said: 'I want to reveal to you, by means of my art, a part of what will happen to you. It will be fortunate if this can preserve you from the misfortunes that menace you.'

"Then he made a circle with his wand and set me in the middle of it. He opened his book and raised his wand three times; at the last stroke I saw a black vapor rise up around me; as it increased, I could no longer see; the sky was hidden from my eyes, the earth disappeared; and when the vapor had dissipated I was surprised no longer to see the magician who accompanied me, or the rock on which I was standing, or the island, or anything else I had seen before, and I found myself on a vessel beaten by a tempest.

"After having struggled for some time against the waves it struck a rock, and I plunged to the bottom of the sea. There I saw horrible monsters, which disappeared from my sight, and left in my arms a princess of unparalleled beauty. Fear had effaced the features of her beautiful complexion, and her eyes could scarcely tolerate the light, but the color returned as soon as she had envisaged me. I had never seen anything so beautiful. It seemed that she thanked me for having rendered her life, but she was taken away from me at that moment by a monster of frightful form. I was trying to snatch her from its claws when everything disappeared from my sight.

"The vapor that had surrounded me at first dissipated gradually, and I found myself on the same rock with the magician. I regretted not having been seduced for longer. The agreeable idea that remained to me of the charming princess occupied my mind completely. I would have liked the enchantment to last forever. Amour had already slid into my heart. I cherished the arrow that has since given me more sensible pains. I remained motionless. I tried to retrace the charming features that I had just seen vanish. Amour had already painted them in the depths of my soul, alas.

"I asked the magician, for mercy's sake, to tell me whether the lovely princess was an illusion, or whether it was possible that the gods had made a mortal who could steal from them honors that ought only belong to a divinity. He replied: 'The object that is igniting a new fire in your heart, whose portrait alone forges chains, reigns on the edge of humid plains, but you will only see her at the foot of your tomb.'

"'Will the gods prolong my life very long?' I cried 'Can I not cut short its course, since my wandering shade will enjoy the pleasure of seeing such a charming object? What will it serve me to live, if it is on the condition of never seeing the one I adore?' Nascent amour had troubled me so much that I did not perceive that the magician had already quit me and was advancing toward a wood, into which I followed him. It was a forest of myrtles, the sweet and charming odor of which rise up all the away to the heavens. All the pathways were the same width and they all intersected. Alternating with the myrtles were tombs of black marble ornamented with white marble statues of a superb magnificence.

"'Here, said the magician,' is the sepulcher of our ancestors. There are as many tombs in each pathway as we are persons; thus, each generation is counted by the pathway and the row of tombs.' I walked along the pathways where the first magicians were buried. The profound silence that reigned in the wood, the myrtles that were never agitated by the slightest zephyr, and the tombs arranged at equal distances, inspired a faint horror.

"We arrived in a path where the tombs were covered. I asked the magician for the reason; he told me that these were the ones destined for the present generation, and that I would soon see the entire island renewed. Immediately, I heard a horrible noise; the sky was covered with darkness; thunder rumbled in the air; the earth trembled under my feet; but all that died down gradually and the daylight returned by degrees. I saw the sky covered by an infinite number of chariots, which descended into the pathway where I was standing.

"I saw a princess emerge from each one, each of whom was holding a young man by the hand. They all advanced toward the magicians, who were all sitting on the edge of their tombs. They embraced, and after having put their books and their wands in the hands of their sons—for the princesses were their wives—each one entered into his tomb with his wife, and a moment later, all the tombs closed.

"The son of the magician who had taken me under his protection then advanced toward me and told me that it was no longer permitted to me to remain on the island; that profane eyes could not see the mysteries that they were about to celebrate for the shades of their fathers; and that it was necessary for me to leave.

"He embraced me, and gave me as he quit me the portrait of the princess that I had seen at the bottom of the sea. I recognized there the same features that I had remarked, and my wound was reopened by that fatal sight. Charmed by such a precious pledge, I went back to the sea shore, keeping my eyes attached to the charming portrait that I had just been given. I embarked again, still occupied by the pleasure of admiring it; I could not weary of considering it; I kissed it thousands of times a day; every moment augmented my desire further. I had resolved to visit all the courts in the world in order to try to find the original.

"We had been sailing for a week when another tempest caused us to wander for a long time in the immense space of the seas. Beaten by the waves, our vessel sank to the bottom, and we tried to swim to an island that we perceived in the distance; but, O gods, it would have been a thousand times better if the sea had swallowed us than to land on that deadly shore.

"All my companions were murdered there by the savages that inhabited that coast. I saw their blood put in cups to serve those barbarians as a beverage. I was reserved to serve as fodder for their infamous king. All the people had already assembled in the middle of a forest, in the place destined for their feasts and the king's arm was already raised, armed with a dagger, about to cut my throat, when he suddenly fell dead at my feet.

"The savages saw that prodigy with astonishment, but they all experienced the same fate. I saw them expire instantly. I armed myself diligently, fearing that others might come, and I plunged into the forest. It was there that, reflecting on my misfortunes, I remembered the box my father had recommended me to open a year after my departure. I had counted every day, and the year had just ended; I took out the box and opened it."

The princess of the Isle of Night, hearing the sound of trumpets, fifes and drums, interrupted the Prince of Aquamarines at that point. "Sensible to your misfortunes," she said, "I await with impatience the continuation of your adventures, but my father the king, whose boat I can hear cleaving the waves, forces me to postpone such a pleasant conversation. Enter this cabinet, Prince, and allow me to flatter myself that as soon as the king has gone, you will not refuse me the detail of a life to which pity renders me sensible."

The princess advanced on to the esplanade of the dark tower to meet her father.

"Come, my daughter," he said to her, "your misfortunes are over. The gods, whom I consult every day, have finally declared to me that there is nothing more to fear for you. Come and embrace a father who has been waiting for this moment for such a long time."

The princess descended from the dark tower then, and entered her father's boat. They embraced tenderly, but without being able to see one another, for an eternal obscurity surrounded the tower. They immediately set forth in the direction of the island, to the sound of instruments and the acclamations of the people who were lining the shore, and who made the air resound with cries and songs.

The princess would have liked to be able to stay longer, in order to learn the rest of the adventures of the Prince of Aquamarines, but there was no means of revealing him to her father, because the oracle had threatened her with the most terrible misfortunes if she ever received anyone in her tower.

She drew nearer to the Isle of Night; her eyes saw the light for the first time; huge bronze vases filled with a liquid that burned perpetually without being consumed, illuminated the shore of the island; they were placed on tall columns of the most beautiful marble, placed at intervals all around the island. Without those fires, and eternal obscurity would reign there.

The princess disembarked, and was conducted to the capital city along an avenue of fir trees, the branches of which were charged with the same lamps, which never went out. She arrived at the gate, which was illuminated in the same fashion, and went into her father's palace. Its architecture was the most beautiful in the world. Firepots ornamented and illuminated the roof of the palace, which was entirely illuminated. All the gardens were perpetually illuminated too.

The princess was taken up on to a terrace that was above the palace. The entire island was visible from there. The art of a fay, the protectress of the realm, had corrected the defect of nature, which had refused sunlight to the island, by means of those lamps.

The princess was astonished to see a city so large and so magnificently constructed. The high walls by which she was surrounded were distinguishable by means of those lamps. Every tree in the countryside was illuminated in the same way, and the hills and the forests resembled brilliant stars, the gentle light of which was supportable to the eyes. That spectacle amazed the princess, but her heart was even more troubled than her eyes. The idea of the Prince of Aquamarines returned incessantly to her mind. She was in despair at not having been able to know the rest of his adventures.

Although she had not been able to see him, she was nevertheless already interested in him. She thought that a prince, to whom the fays had made a gift of all the qualities that could render him accomplished, must be a very lovable prince. She would have liked so much to have seen him. Doubtless that desire would have been much diminished, if she had known the peril there was in seeing him, at the cost of her life.

She did not know how to slip away from her father in order to return to the dark tower, and in any case, what good would that journey have done her? It was absolutely forbidden to take the smallest light off the island. Thus, she would not have been able to converse with the Prince of Aquamarines; however, that prince was continually represented to her.

While walking one day in a large forest that at was at the end of her father's gardens, she was thinking about everything that the Prince of Aquamarines had told her; and as she had been condemned by a fay to spend her life alone in the dark tower until a monster that killed with its sight came to deliver her, she imagined that the prince might be her liberator. Her father, who consulted the gods every day in order to know the time when his daughter's misfortunes were to end, did not understand any more than she did what the fay had meant to imply by that monster, which killed by sight alone, but in the end, the oracle had replied that the time had come. That was what alarmed her strangely.

What! she said to herself. *That prince, whom I imagine as being so handsome, is the monster by which I am menaced? Why should I want to see him? Can I doubt that he is one, after what the oracle has just said?*

It was thus that she debated with herself, and she had already lost the desire to return to the dark tower when she found herself at the door of a temple. It was that of Morpheus, to whom it was consecrated. A magnificent portico led to a vestibule of marble and porphyry; from there one entered the temple.

The sweetest perfumes burned incessantly before the statue of the god, who appeared in the depths, recumbent, leaning his head on one arm. Beds of grass dotted with the most beautiful flowers invited repose; poppies, the only presents offered to the god, covered a table that was n the middle of the temple. It was sufficient to offer them to him immediately to sense a languor that was impossible to resist flowing through the veins. One yielded insensibly to the slumber that spread over the eyelids, and then, what one most desired to know was depicted in a dream.

The princess presented poppies to Morpheus, and immediately, feeling her knees buckling beneath her, she lay down on a bed of grass sown with violets, and went to sleep, wishing to see the Prince of Aquamarines.

Scarcely had sleep closed her eyes than the god of dreams, taking on the face of the Prince of Aquamarines, presented himself to her. The surprise of seeing that prince, so different from the monster she had imagined, woke her up instantly.

"O gods!" she cried. "Can it be that a mortal is even lovelier than the gods are depicted to us?" She thought she was still dreaming.

She searched for the prince in the temple, but he was only the light shadow, which the slightest wind and the slightest agitation dissipates. She was in despair that the dream had passed with such rapidity. She offered further poppies to Morpheus. Her languid gaze attached itself to his statue fixedly, begging him to render her such a sweet slumber, but that favor was only granted once; it was in vain that her heart flattered itself that she might obtain it. Morpheus, insensible to her prayers, went to sleep himself listening to them.

She left the temple, burning with the desire to see the prince again. Amour had already entered into her heart. She was no longer in control of herself; she was no longer thinking about anything but the Prince of Aquamarines. She was not following any definite route in the forest; full of the charming idea that she bore in her heart, she let hazard guide her steps.

Without thinking about it, she found herself on the edge of the sea, at the same place where she had left the boat that had brought her from the dark tower. Her first impulse was to embark in order to go and engage the Prince of Aquamarines to come to her father's court. She therefore climbed into the boat, and, following a cable that extended from the shore to the dark tower she arrived at the foot of the tower. She heard the voice of the Prince of Aquamarines, which caused the rocks to resound with these songs:

O sea, whose tranquil waves
Come to die, moaning on this shore,

The slightest wind, the slightest storm
Suffices to trouble you repose.
In the midst of lightning and the sound of thunder,
Suddenly your furious waves
Seem intent on opening the earth,
And soon to inundate the skies.

Thus when one least expects it
Amour comes to trouble the peace of our hearts.
The cruel god with a single arrow,
Banishes happy innocence therefrom.
But your roars, which make the air tremble,
The fury of which the wind stirs,
O sea, make slight portraits
Of the troubles that amour excites.

"What harm has love done you, then, Prince?" replied
the Princess of the Isle of Night. "And what remains for me to
learn of the adventures of your life? I have come here to hear
the continuation; speak, then. The silent winds are no longer
agitating the air, and the calm and tranquil sea seems to want,
like me, to listen to your woes."

The Prince of Aquamarines was charmed by the return of
the Princess of the Isle of Night, for something in the depths of
his heart suggested to him that she was the same princess that
the magician had enabled him to see, the idea of whom had
not quit him for a single moment. He therefore continued his
story.

"I was on that frightful rock when I opened, tremulously,
the box that my father had given me. I found a piece of paper
there on which I read the cruel words that my father had written with his own hand."

The Prince of Aquamarines repeated then to the princess
everything there was in the letter is father had written to him;
he revealed to her that the fay Noirjabarbe, to avenge herself

on his father, had condemned him pitilessly to kill all those who gazed at him.

"I cannot express to you," he continued, "what passed within me when I had finished reading that paper. My first impulse was to throw myself from the rock where I was into the abysmal depths. But alas, to add to my misfortune, an invisible hand retained me, and I sensed that I was condemned to live. I was no longer astonished that the savages had expired on seeing me; I even thanked the gods for having permitted my sight to purge the earth of such inhuman monsters. I explored the whole island, which I found full of horror.

"For my dwelling I chose a grotto carved into the rock. There I lived on animals that I killed by hunting; I fished with a line; I strolled along the sea shore; of moments of pleasure I only had those I spent gazing at the portrait that I loved more and more. I was not separated from it by day or by night. When I slept I held it in my arms, and only woke up in order to look at it again.

"Sometimes I went to a neighboring island that was planted with orange trees. I went to sleep there one day, and, a tempest having blown up while I was asleep, I had the imprudence to try to get back to my island. The winds, which suddenly increased, pushed me out to sea, and after having been their plaything for a long time, I was pushed into the tower into which you pulled me."

"Oh, Prince!" cried the Princess of the Isle of Night. "I can never see you, then, without it costing me my life?"

"I would give mine to see you for a moment," the prince replied. "The charming idea of the object I saw at the bottom of the sea is engraved on my heart, with features that time can never efface. I love it, and something tells me in secret that you are that amiable princess. O gods, to what woes I am condemned! I am in love, and I cannot see the person I love without causing her death."

"You are not the only person in the world to lament," replied the princess, "and to know the torture of not being able to approach the person one loves, to love him without being able to see him."

Those words were an enigma for the Prince of Aquamarines. He could not penetrate the heart of the princess, and the words that had escaped her seemed to him to have been spoken at hazard. He begged her to tell him why she had spent her life in hat tower.

The princess told him that a fay, the protectress of her father's island, had been summoned at the time of her birth, and that, having foreseen that she was threatened by frightful misfortunes, she had condemned her to remain in the tower until a monster that killed with its sight came to deliver her from it. The princess refrained from telling the prince about the curiosity that had caused her to go to the temple of Morpheus, and, fearing that amour might eventually betray the secret of her heart, she returned to her island.

The princess revealed to her father what the fay had meant by a monster that killed with its sight, and told him the story of the Prince of Aquamarines. The king, moved to compassion by the woes of the unfortunate prince, had everything that might be necessary to him taken to the dark tower. He sometimes went himself with his daughter to converse with him, and both of them tried to alleviate the rigor of his imprisonment.

But alas, in trying to render him repose, the Princess of the Isle of Night lost her own. She was in love with a violence that she could no longer retain; she hid in the depths of the woods in order to be able to talk to the echoes; her words were halting, and sometimes made no sense; her eyes were full of a somber fire; her complexion no longer had a vivid and brilliant sheen; her beauty was almost effaced; she was hardly recognizable as the Princess of the Isle of Night.

Finally, she could no longer resist. It was necessary to confess to her conqueror that she loved him. She embarked for the dark tower. Her heart trembled as she approached it. She had no sooner arrived there than she called to the Prince of Aquamarines.

The prince, who was accustomed to respond the slightest signal, did not reply, and the princess began to shiver. She called to him several times, but in vain. As one could not climb up to the tower without a ladder, she returned to the island, and, having commanded one of her slaves to bring one, she returned to the tower, and climbed up herself, because she knew the slightest detail of it.

Alas, she did not search for long. Scarcely had she gone up on to the esplanade than she felt something at her feet. She bent down, and found a motionless body, colder than marble. She had no doubt that it was the Prince of Aquamarines.

"O gods!" she cried. "My lover is dead!" A torrent of tears immediately emerged from her eyes, and her sighs took away the power of speech entirely.

It was, however, necessary to tear herself away from the cadaver, which she had her slaves carry away. She had a magnificent tomb built in the middle of a cypress wood that overlooked the sea shore. She had a pyre of cedar-wood constructed, on which the body was consumed.

She collected the ashes herself, which she put into an urn made from a single emerald, and the urn was enclosed in the tomb. The tomb was black marble; four bronze statues ornamented the four corners, and on its front these words were engraved in golden letters:

Here lies the unfortunate Prince of Aquamarines

Prince that an enemy fay
Condemned forever to the most frightful torment,
From whoever saw you for a moment
The Light of the heavens was suddenly stolen,
But in order to see you, dear lover,
Alas, I would give me life.

It was at the foot of that tomb that the Princess of the Isle of Night spent all the moments than she was able to seal from the homage of her court. She no longer had any fear of admitting the amour that she had for the Prince of Aquamarines; she told the springs and the fountains about it; her sighs and regrets troubled the silence of the woods.

She believed that the prince was no more. Unnecessary tears, superfluous sighs! The prince was still alive.

Pirates, who knew that the King of the Isle of Night had imprisoned his daughter in a tower in the middle of the sea, attracted by the hope of a considerable ransom, had come to kidnap her, but instead of the princess they had found the Prince of Aquamarines, who, in spite of his resistance, was constrained to cede to the efforts and the number of the barbarians. He had killed the first one who had dared to attack him, but when they had all thrown themselves upon him they seized him and bound him to the mast of their ship, and immediately set sail. It was thus that he was constrained to quit the place where he had had the pleasure of conversing frequently with his princess.

It was not long before the pirates were punished for their temerity, for scarcely had they passed through the obscure zone that surrounded the Isle of Night than, at the first rays of the sun, they all fell dead on perceiving the Prince of Aquamarines. The prince had no less reason to lament for that. He was tied to the mast of the ship, and sure of perishing of hunger, unable to hope for the aid of any mortal, since anyone who saw him would die as a result.

The winds and the waves conducted his vessel at their whim. Finally, it encountered a sandbank, where it ran aground. A frightful rock rose up on that bank, raising its face to the skies. There he waited for the death he believed to be no longer avoidable.

The memory of the Princess of the Isle of Night always occupied him, in spite of the horrors of death, which he felt approaching continually. Already, his extreme languor had robbed him of the light; he could no longer see, and, his weakness still increasing, he remained motionless.

His unconsciousness lasted for a long time, but he nevertheless came round. What was his surprise, however, when he found himself, on awakening in a meadow! He was still so weak that he did not have the strength to get up. He was seeking in vain to penetrate the mystery of how he had come to be in that place when he saw a woman coming toward him carrying a basket of fruits.

She approached him and said: "Try, unfortunate Prince, to prolong the days that the gods are protecting in spite of the cruelty of the fay Noirjabarbe."

At that fatal name, the Prince of Aquamarines nearly fell back into a faint, but the unknown woman continued speaking to him. "I am a fay," she told him, "and I make my abode in the rock near to which your vessel ran aground. I perceived you from the top of the rock, where I was walking that day, and, taking pity on the state you were in, I took you from the ship in order to bring you to this place. My art of faerie informed me of all your misfortunes. I know your most secret thoughts. I know that you love a princess of whom fate forbids you the sight, for fear of giving her death, but I also know that a day will come when your troubles will end."

That hope completed reanimating the strength of the Prince of Aquamarines. He got up, and threw himself at the knees of his liberator.

"Get up, Prince," the fay said to him. "You cannot stay here for more than a day, and I have many things to show you."

Immediately, they went together into a large wood that bordered the meadow, and which led them to a bronze door of prodigious thickness. As the Prince of Aquamarines advanced he heard horrible screams and howls. When he reached the bronze door, he read this inscription:

THE PALACE OF AMOUR'S VENGEANCE

The fay touched the door with her wand, and it opened of its own accord. The prince entered into a large area completely closed by iron grilles and entirely surrounded by springs as clear as crystal. There, a infinite number of princes and princesses, who appeared to be looking into the water attentively, were uttering frightful screams, but nevertheless could not tear themselves away from the springs that seemed to be the source of their woes.

The Prince of Aquamarines asked the fay what the reason was. "It is here," she replied, "that Amour punishes lovers. The infidel incessantly see the new object of their amour in the arms of another; they incessantly appear to them to be happy, and always insult their woes. The regret that they have for having quit their lovers, with whom they lived in a happiness that reciprocal amour augments, and of which one can be assured, and the despair of seeing themselves scorned by those same lovers for whom they quit everything, is and will eternally be their torture. The jealous incessantly see everything there that can augment their jealousy. The inconstant cease to be, but they see themselves unworthily betrayed. In sum, every lover finds a penalty here proportionate to his crimes, and those punishments are eternal."

Among that great number of unfortunates the Prince of Aquamarines remarked one princess who seemed more afflicted than all the others. She was tearing her hair, which was the most beautiful blonde in the world; she was bruising her cheeks, colored more brightly than a morning rose; she was beating her breast which would have put the whiteness of alabaster and the hardness of marble to shame. In sum, her dolor was so great that the prince asked the fay to tell him who that princess was.

"She is the Princess of the Isle of Graces," the fay replied. "She loved a prince she had engaged in her chains by means of her attractions and her false promises. Her seductive gaze and flattering speech had ignited the most violent passion in the prince's heart. He had abandoned himself entirely to that deadly poison. Charmed by his new amour, he spent all his time in the arms of the princess. They lived contentedly then because they loved one another with an equal tenderness, but in the time that she swore a sincere and eternal fidelity to that prince, and her tender oaths augmented the unfortunate prince's amour further, the perfidious woman listened to another lover and gave him her heart. The tears, plaints, sighs, reproaches, despair and, in sum, the tenderness of the prince having been unable to win her back, he died of dolor after having these verses engraved on his tomb as an eternal mark of his tenderness and the perfidy of the princes:

> *Betraying me utterly, my infidel princess,*
> *In spite of all her oaths, changed me in less than a day,*
> *Gods, to what choice had she reduced me?*
> *To lose, alas, life or my amour.*
>
> *Ah, it is all over, her perfidy bursts forth.*
> *Time changes her heart without changing her charms.*
> *But I still love the ingrate enough,*
> *To avenge myself by a noble death.*

"In dying, that prince left Amour the care of avenging him, and that redoubtable god, touched by his misfortunes, delivered that princess to the most sensible dolor."

The Prince of Aquamarines felt sorry nevertheless for the Princess of the Isle of Graces, for she was beautiful, and only lacked a faithful heart in order to be worthy of the love of the gods themselves.

"I have no fear of all these torments," the prince said to the fay who was guiding him, "since I will love the Princess of the Isle of Night until death."

He left that terrible place then. The fay conducted him back to the rock near which his ship had run aground.

"It is to me," she told him, "that Amour had confided the care of recompensing faithful lovers and punishing the inconstant. I cannot free you from the penalty to which the fay Noirjabarbe has condemned you, but this wand that I am giving you will be able to deliver you from many of the misfortunes to which you would succumb without it. It has the power to put those it touches to sleep. You have only to turn it round three times, and slumber, attentive to your order, will immediately close the eyes of those you want to put to sleep. When it is rotated in the opposite direction, sleep will flee their eyes with as much promptitude as it took possession of them. By that means, your sight, so fatal to the rest of humans, will cease to be whenever you wish, since they will not perish in looking at you. But that is not all; this vessel, on which you have run aground, submissive to your orders, will take you anywhere that you command it to go. Depart, Prince, and, faithful to Amour, remember that that god never abandons hearts truly attached to his empire."

As the Prince of Aquamarines was only occupied with the Princess of the Isle of Night, he commanded his vessel to take him back to the dark tower, where, in spite of the horror of the eternal darkness that surrounded it, he had at least had the pleasure of conversing with the princess. He approached that tower, and, immediately throwing himself into the sea, he swam to a forest that overlooked the shore of the Isle of Night. He slipped from bush to bush, as far as a place where he perceived a tomb, on which he read the inscription:

Here lies the unfortunate Prince of Aquamarines

He did not know what to think about what he saw, and he had plunged into a profound reverie when a noise that he heard obliged him to hide in a place where he could not be seen by anyone. The noise grew louder as the chariot, in which the princess herself was sitting, drew nearer. He recognized her as the same person whose portrait he had. She stepped down and, approaching the tomb, she embraced it with her beautiful arms and bathed it with her tears.

The Prince of Aquamarines attributed to his absence the idea that had been formed of his death. Hidden in the densest part of the forest, he observed the Princess of the Isle of Night.

His joy was extreme in seeing that she resembled, to the slightest feature, the model that he carried.

He remembered then what the magician had told him, that he would only see the princess whose portrait he had the foot of the tomb that she had erected for him. Not only could he see her, but he was convinced of being loved by her. He had never been so sensible to the penalty to which the fay Noirjabarbe had condemned him. He would gladly have thrown himself at the knees of the princess if the frightful peril to which he would have exposed her had not prevented him from doing so. He feared that the slightest sigh might oblige her to turn her head.

What a situation for a lover! To see that he was loved, to find what he had been seeking for such a long time, and to tremble with the dread of being perceived: what torture! He did not know how to announce his return to her. In addition, the dolor of the princess further augmented his own. He saw her dissolving in tears, unable to tear herself away from his tomb.

Then he remembered the wand that the fay had given him. He did not miss such a fine occasion for making use of it to put the princess to sleep, and, profiting from that moment, he wrote these verses on the base of the tomb:

Ever faithful and ever unfortunate,
My shade comes to share your grief again.
Go to the dark tower.
I shall put an end to your woes there.

The Prince of Aquamarines, charmed by the pleasure of seeing the princess he adored, contemplated her charms; but his heart trembled, because he was not yet entirely sure of the virtue of the wand. That is why he tore himself away from the vicinity of the princess, after having taken her out of her enchantment. Immediately returning to the sea shore, he returned to the dark tower, agitated by the sharpest torments of amour.

Scarcely had dawn commenced to illuminate the rest of the world when the Princess of the Isle of Night emerged from her palace and went to the supposed tomb of the Prince of Aquamarines. She read what he had written there. Her heart was stirred by joy in thinking that she might converse with her dear lover again. Full of impatience, she flew rapidly to the edge of the sea, embarked and arrived at the foot of the dark tower.

With joy, the Prince of Aquamarines heard that boat cleaving the waters and coming gradually closer to him. When it arrived, they conversed with one another for a long time. The Princess of the Isle of Night, who thought she was talking to a shade, had no fear of letting him see the depths of her heart. She revealed all her tenderness to him, and made him know the extreme dolor that she had felt at his death.

The Prince of Aquamarines could not dissimulate much longer. He related his adventures to her, telling her how he had been abducted from the dark tower by pirates, to the efforts and the multitude of whom he had been obliged to cede, after killing the one whose cadaver she had honored with such a magnificent tomb. He told her about the risk he had run of dying of hunger while he was tied to the mast of the ship, and how a fay had extracted him from that dangerous state.

He was even dearer to the Princess of the Isle of Night for that. It was for her that he had run so many dangers. Could she pay less for them than all the tenderness of which her heart was capable? Thus, as they separated, they swore an eternal fidelity.

In the end, the princess tore herself away from that abode and returned to her palace, charmed to have recovered her lover. Not a day passed when she did not return to the dark tower. They were both as happy as one can be. They loved one another with an equal tenderness. They spend days talking together. The hope that the fay had given the Prince of Aquamarines that his misfortunes would end one day, softened the cruel chagrin of not seeing the person he loved. His tenderness and that of the Princess of the Isle of Night took the place of everything; but destiny, too jealous of human happiness, could not leave them happy for long and had more frightful woes in store for them.

One day, when the Princess of the Isle of Night had embarked in the little boat that she used to go to the dark tower, the sea swelled in such a short time that the princess could not regain her island or land at the tower. A wave that crashed against her boat overturned it. She uttered a horrible scream, which was heard by the Prince of Aquamarines, who, not doubting that the princess had been shipwrecked, immediately dived into the sea; but he forgot his enchanted wand, because at that moment, his mind was only occupied by the danger that the unique object of his amour was in.

He swam for a long time toward the cries of the princess, who was being pushed out to sea by the waves and the wind. Finally, no longer hearing them, he thought that she had perished. Imagine the dolor of the unhappy lover. He strove to swim, and was almost exhausted, when he saw her returning over the surface, but motionless, like a corpse.

He seized her, and tried to reach the nearer of two islands that he perceived. He trembled that she might recover consciousness. She would have been doomed without recourse if she had come round, and to add a surplus of dolor, scarcely had he thrown her on to the shore than he was obliged to move away from her because he feared that she might open her eyes.

He dared not help her himself; she would have perished if he had extracted her from that state, but at least he could hope that someone would be able to give her aid. He therefore retired to a grotto that overlooked the shore, from which he could see without being seen.

Scarcely had he entered it than he saw an enormous giant emerge from a wood, who, approaching the edge of the sea, perceived the unconscious Princess of the Isle of Night. He considered her for some time, and then, drawing a scimitar that hung from his belt and seizing her long hair, which he twisted around his arm, he was about to cut off her head when the cry that the Prince of Aquamarines uttered as he advanced toward the giant arrested his arm and made him turn his head. As soon as the giant perceived him, he dropped dead.

That island was called the Isle of Giants, a terrible place in which it was absolutely ordered to massacre all those whom shipwreck cast up there. The Prince of Aquamarines picked up the princess again then and, throwing himself back into the sea, he contrived to reach another island that was not far away. He laid her down on the grass that covered the shore and withdrew into a nearby forest.

Scarcely was he there than the king of the island, who was diverting himself hunting, was guided by hazard to the same place where the Prince of Aquamarines had set the princess down. Her beauty, which her unconsciousness had only diminished slightly, struck him. He immediately dismounted, called his men, and had the princess transported to his palace immediately. The Prince of Aquamarines followed her for a long time with his eyes, but he dared not appear. He only emerged from the forest when he had lost sight of them completely.

He deplored his fate, in being force to flee the person he loved with as much care as other lovers take to seek out the person they love.

The sight of him was too dangerous for him to remain for long on that island. He went back to the dark tower, resolved to return with the enchanted wand and deliver the princess.

Scarcely had he arrived at his usual abode than a frightful tempest blew up that lasted for several days, during which it was absolutely impossible to put to sea. Finally, it ceased, and he immediately manned the ship that the fay had given him. He commanded it to sail to the island where he had left the Princess of the Isle of Night.

He landed there and, turning his wand around three times, he put the entire island to sleep. Then, advancing with confidence, he explored the whole of the king's palace without finding the princess.

He saw the king, who appeared to have been giving a few orders at the moment when he was enchanted. He descended into the gardens, traversed them, and reached the other sea shore, there he saw a tower. He approached it. It was surrounded by iron grilles.

A very obscure chamber, which only received daylight through one low barred window, occupied the entire base of the tower. There was another above it, and the top of the tower was destined for guards who watched there day and night.

The Prince of Aquamarines approached it; he looked though the window of that basal chamber. O gods, what was his surprise when he saw the princess! Her head was leaning negligently on her arm; her eyes were bathed with tears and she appeared to be plunged into the most frightful dolor.

A spectacle so sensible for the Prince of Aquamarines nearly took away his life. He did not know how to discover the reason why the princess was locked in that tower because he dared not wake her. He could not discover any other means of finding out than to get into the room above the one that the princess was in. It was open, so that was what he did.

Then, rotating the wand in the opposite direction, he woke up the Princess of the Isle of Night on her own, and called to her.

What was the joy of the princess when she heard her lover's voice! Great gods, what an awakening! She believed that it was another dream. Even so, she ran to the window of her cell, and soon realized that it was not an illusion, and that the Prince of Aquamarines was in the same tower as her. She could not understand, however, how he could have found the means of getting into it. She was about to ask him when the Prince of Aquamarines anticipated her.

"What barbarity, what sufficiently inhumane heart can retain my princess in this horrible captivity?" he cried.

"Alas, I don't know how I was pushed to his shore," the princess replied. "I was going to see you in the dark tower when the tempest broke my boat. I fainted, and only recovered consciousness by virtue of the cares of the king who reigns in this island. I found myself in his palace, without knowing how I had been transported here. He could not tell me anything except that he had found me on the shore."

The Prince of Aquamarines told the princess then that he was the one who had saved her, about the shipwreck and the fury of the giant. "But why this prison?" he continued. "Is my princess a criminal?"

"Alas," she cried, "my only crime is to love you too much; faithful to the oaths I made you to love you until death. I resisted the solicitations and menaces of the king of this island, who wanted to share his empire with me, if I would agree to respond to his amour. But as I did not want to consent to that, the cruel man thought he could force me to do it by taking away my liberty forever. He had me locked in this tower, which a fay has built, and which he alone has the power to open. Thus, all the powers in the universe cannot get me out of the hands of that barbarian; but I no longer fear anything, since I can still talk to my lover.

"I only fear for you," replied the prince, "the torments that you are going to suffer. How can I get you out of his horrible abode?"

The reciprocal tears of the two lovers finished that conversation, and the Prince of Aquamarines, not wanting to give suspicions to the king of the island, released him from his slumber.

Scarcely was he delivered than the king ran to the tower where the Princess of the Isle of Night was. Surprised by the sleep that had gripped him, he knew that a superior power was combating for her. However, when he saw her in the same place where he had left her, his suspicions calmed down. The pleasure of seeing the person he loved again took way any other reflection. He pressed her again to respond to his desires, and threatened in case of her refusal, to make her suffer a thousand times worse.

The Prince of Aquamarines heard all those excesses. Many a time he was tempted to appear and punish the cruel individual by death for the torments with which he was threatening the princess. But what would have become of them both then? The door of the tower could only be opened by the will of the king. It would be necessary, in abandoning himself to his vengeance, to renounce the deliverance of the princess.

Amour prevailed over anger, and he deferred his vengeance until he had extracted the princess from the slavery she was in.

As soon as the king had quit her, the Prince of Aquamarines put the guard to sleep and made arrangements with the Princess of the Isle of Night to save her.

He left the tower and returned to the dark tower, where the father of the princess, in despair at the loss of his daughter, had gone to console himself with the Prince of Aquamarines. It was during that time that he informed the king of everything that had happened. He told him that there was no other means to deliver her but to try to surprise the king who was holding her captive, to take him away and to hold him in a narrow prison until he had rendered liberty to the princess.

The King of the Isle of the Night embarked, therefore, with a small number of guards, on the enchanted ship, which took them to the island where the princess was. After having made use of the power of his wand, the Prince of Aquamarines ran to the tower where the princess was. He called to the Princess of the Isle of Night but it was in vain; she was no longer there. He went to the king's palace, which he found deserted. He searched the entire island, but fruitlessly.

In despair at the abduction of the princess he returned to his vessel, where the King of the Isle of Night and his guards were still asleep. He commanded his ship to take them to where the Princess of the Isle of Night was. The ship cleaved the waves and stopped on the shore of an island which appeared to be entirely forested. The Prince of Aquamarines did not fail make use of his wand. He enchanted all the inhabitants of the island and advanced with great strides toward a city that he could see at the end of an avenue traversing the forest.

He arrived in a large square, where he saw all the people gathered around a pyre that had been built in the center. What was the astonishment of the prince when he saw that his princess was attached to it, and that the flames were about to devour her, along with the king who had wanted to marry her!

How many times did he thank the gods for having conducted him to that place with enough time to deliver his princess from death. He untied her, and, immediately reanimating all the inhabitants of the island, he showed himself to them and caused them to perish as punishment for their crime.

Those barbarians had surprised the king of the island who was retaining the princess, and had captured both of them. If the Prince of Aquamarines had arrived a moment later, it would have been all over for the Princess of the Isle of Night.

He took her back to his ship and, after having disembarked the King of the Isle of Night and his daughter, he returned to the dark tower.

Scarcely had the king and the princess emerged from their slumber than they went to thank the Prince of Aquamarines. All the help that the princess had received from her lover had further augmented her tenderness. She forgot everything that she had suffered and all the dangers she had endured as soon as she could converse for a while with the Prince of Aquamarines.

But in amour, one is not happy for long.

Near the Isle of Night was another island, ruled by the son of the fay Noirjabarbe. He was a thousand times more malevolent than his mother. He was a monster. He was a dwarf; a hump in front and another behind rendered him even more deformed. His eyes were small, sunken and red-rimmed, his pug nose allowed the depths of his brain to be seen; his red, flat hair covered a wrinkled brow full of bumps and scars; his broad mouth only had the remains of rotten teeth; his pale lips covered half his chin; his legs were twisted and his heart was a thousand times more horrible than his face.

One day, while traversing the air in a chariot pulled by dragons, he perceived the Princess of the Isle of Night, who was walking in her father's garden. He became amorous, and immediately went to ask the king for her in marriage.

That unhappy father, who feared the fury and vengeance of such a powerful prince, sacrificed his daughter to the interests of his people. He knew the power of Noirjabarbe's son. He knew that he would have killed everyone on the island if he had refused him his daughter. The unfortunate princess was therefore delivered to that monster, who took her to his palace.

No princess ever had more to lament. She did not even have time to warn the prince, her lover. It was necessary to depart with that new husband.

To be distanced from a lover, to lose him without hope,
Gods, what an extreme pain that is!
I judge that be the despair
To which I would be reduced myself,
If I lost everything I love.

The distress of the unfortunate princess is unimaginable. The anxiety of the Prince of Aquamarines was no less. He dared not suspect the constancy of the Princess of the Isle of Night. He did not know what to think, however, about such a long absence. Death would have been a hundred times milder than the cruel state to which he was reduced; but what would he not have suffered had he known where the princess was?

She was locked up under a hundred keys and guarded day and night by her husband, in a palace whose walls were made of bronze. The monster only quit her in order to go into a cabinet that was not far from the chamber in which he had put her. It was in that cabinet, or with the princess, that he spent his days and nights. There was no window in the palace. It was only illuminated by a simple lamp, to which the fay prince had given the power to fly through the air by itself and light up as soon as it was commanded to do so.

The Princess of the Isle of Night spent entire days in tears, and as the Prince of Aquamarines still possessed her heart, she pitied him for the extreme anxiety that she rightly judged him to be in by virtue of her absence. But what could she do to relieve him of it? Her cruel husband never quit her. She scarcely had a moment of freedom to lament her misfortune.

One night, when the fay prince appeared to be more deeply asleep than usual, curiosity caused the princess to make the resolution to go into the cabinet into which her husband went so frequently and see what was inside it. To that effect she stole the key from him and, getting up without making a noise, she commanded the lamp to light her way.

She left the room, and opened the door of the cabinet, where she did not find anything but a simple table, on which there was a book, around which there was an infinite number of phials. In the first to which she directed her eyes there was a liquid of which a single drop poured on the eyes could put someone to sleep for a hundred years. She immediately seized that phial and, walking on tiptoe and holding her breath, she approached her husband's bed.

She did not waste time uncorking the phial; moments were precious. She broke it over the face of the monster, and by that means put him to sleep, not for a hundred years, but for a hundred million years.

Mistress from then on of the palace, she returned to the cabinet; she opened the book that was on the table; she saw that all the phials contained the spells that the fay Noirjabarbe had cast on the majority of the princes and princesses of the world, and that as long as they were not broken, the charms would last forever. She looked for that of her lover, found it, seized it, and, charmed by the thought that she was going to liberate the man she loved, she left the fay prince's palace after having broken all the other phials in the cabinet except one, which she was still holding. That was a liquid that rendered life, but with mild and tranquil mores.

She reached the edge of the sea and from there went to the dark tower. She dared not return to her father's isle because she feared his anger. Her amour drew her to where her lover was.

What was the joy of that unfortunate prince when he heard the voice of the Princess of the Isle of Night! She took him down to her boat and, after having recounted everything that had happened to her, she broke the phial containing the spell that the fay Noirjabarbe had cast on him, and, leaving the wind and the waves to conduct their boat, they drew away gradually from the dark tower. Already they were beginning to perceive the sun's rays, and, charmed by the pleasure of seeing one another and intoxicated, so to speak, by joy, they were not giving any thought to steering their boat when it hit a rock and broke in two.

The Prince of Aquamarines seized the princess then, and, swimming with one hand and sustaining her with the other, he landed on a shore that he recognized as that of the isle of savages, where he had once been cast up by the tempest. They found it deserted. He showed his princess all the people who had perished by virtue of looking at him.

The Prince of Aquamarines took pity on them and proposed to the Princess of the Isle of Night that she render life to those unfortunates by means of the power of resurrection. The princess consented to that gladly. They sprinkled all the bodies, which were immediately reanimated; but they lost their natural ferocity and recognized the prince and princess as their legitimate sovereigns. Thus, the island that had formerly been an isle of horror, became civilized in very little time and was named the Fortunate Isle.

Attributed to Mademoiselle de Lubert: *Princess Roseate and Prince Celadon*

There was once a king and a queen who loved one another passionately. All that their happiness lacked was to have pledges of their amour, but in the ten years that they had been married, Heaven, otherwise so mild for them, appeared insensible to the ardent prayers they formed of that sole benefit. In vain the princess went to the waters every spring and autumn; in vain the most knowledgeable fays were consulted; they were sent magnificent presents, and all of them responded that they were in despair at not being able to bring better news; that it was impossible for them to divine something so undivinable but that it was necessary not to give up hope.

The poor queen was desolate, and the king, as afflicted as she was, hid his dolor in order not to augment his wife's. His kingdom was called the Realm of Cedars. The queen had a sister in her court whom she married to the King of Aquamarines, a very powerful ally of her husband. The ceremony of the marriage amused her for a while, but what redoubled her affliction is that, having asked her brother-in-law to remain with her for a year, the Queen of Aquamarines gave birth after nine months to a prince as beautiful as the daylight. The fays were invited to the birth of the beautiful child; they endowed him with all the virtues and all the most brilliant qualities. They wanted him to be called Celadon.

The queen never ceased asking whether he was menaced by any misfortune. "Great queens," said the principal fay, "we do not foresee anything nasty in that beautiful life, except for the thorn of a rose, which might cause him great misfortunes. If Prince Celadon can avoid that, we can answer for his felicity and can assure you that he will live very happily."

After having embraced the good fays and heaped them with rich presents, the queens accompanied them as far as their chariots and remained charmed by what had just been predicted.

At the end of the year marked for the departure of young Celadon's mother she departed with her husband and her lovable son. On his faith in the word of the fays, the King of Aquamarines had sent an order to destroy every last rose-bush, and to forbid anyone to have any such flower, on pain of death.

The queen separated from them with many tears, but eventually, as everything fades away, after a few months of her sister's absence, the queen forgot her chagrin in order to deliver herself to the most vivid joy, because she perceived that she was pregnant.

How many prayers there were for the preservation of that fruit! How much incense burned to the gods! How many thanks to the good fays! The queen marked her joy and gratitude by means of perpetual sacrifices. What plans were made for the lovable child! The sex of the child did not matter; the king was transported; he thanked the queen a thousand times a day. The fays sent word that they would be present at the birth.

Finally, that moment so desired and so long-waited arrived. The queen brought into the world a daughter who made the admiration of the fays and all those who were in the chamber. If she had been a thousand times less pretty she would still have been thought marvelous, but she left nothing to desire: large dark eyes, a beautiful little mouth; a perfect nose; a complexion of lilies and roses; pretty blonde hair already curly; a body of alabaster—in sum, a delectable creature. The king no longer knew himself; he kissed the queen, his daughter, the fays, all those who complimented him and even those who did not dare. In sum, no one has ever felt so much joy.

"I want to call her Roseate," he said. "It's the name that suits her best. Doesn't she resemble it? She's charming, and I'm mad about her."

Everyone applauded the king's sentiment. the palace resounded with the beautiful name of Roseate, and the king sent in search of more than a thousand aunes of velvet of that color to give to the fays, who, in recompense, endowed the little princes with beauty, intelligence, charm and, above all, the gift of pleasing. Then, unwrapping their presents, they displayed things so rare that the whole court was in admiration. Among others, they showed a bouquet of six roses of roseate diamonds, which would only fade if the princess's lover was unfaithful.

"I want," said the Fay of the Green Oaks, who was the most apparent, "her never to experience that misfortune, which is the only one she has to dread."

"Oh, my sister," said the fay Sempiternelle, who was a rather redoubtable old fay, "She wouldn't be the first, and before being as fortunate as her horoscope predicts, it's good that she knows a little of what misfortune is. Yes, yes," added the cantankerous old fay, "Roseate will be unhappy, because she will fall in love..."

The other fays did not let her finish, because they feared that Sempiternelle might spread the bile of her humor over the pretty child.

"Yes, my sister," said the Fay of the Green Oaks, "What you have pronounced cannot be destroyed; but if Roseate does not fall in love before the age of fifteen, that misfortune will have no effect at all."

Sempiternelle, rather discontented with that restriction, went out shaking her head, by which the queen was very alarmed. But the other fays reassured her and promised her assistance. Then they embraced the beautiful little princess, whom they embellished further, and retired.

The queen had made reflections on what had happened; she communicated them to her husband; she agreed that, in order to avoid any inconvenience of tenderness that their daughter might acquire, it was necessary to marry her early, but that it was also necessary to avoid her knowing amour beforehand. Thus, ladies were chose to educate her whose severe virtue would not permit young Roseate any reading or conversation that could give her the slightest idea of it. The queen wanted to be her first teacher herself, quite sure that the cares of a tender and reasonable mother make more progress than ten years of lessons from the most assiduous governess.

The young princess delivered herself to everything with all her heart; her mildness, her naivety and the candor of her sentiments equaled her intelligence and her marvelous beauty; she grew in sagacity and in virtue, as in charms. The king and the queen loved her passionately; she had no suspicion of her beauty, and yet everything burned in her presence; one of her gazes or a word from her bore inevitable darts, for which there was no cure.

She was already nearly twelve years old when the queen thought that it was time to marry her. For a long time she had destined her for her cousin, Prince Celadon; she resolved to speak to the king about it; she would have done so immediately if that prince had not come to see her himself, to inform her that the fay Sempiternelle had just written to him to propose a husband for the princess, who was Prince Muguet, the son of a king with whom she was allied.

"You can believe, Madame," added the king, "that this proposal is an order, and that we ought to accept it, in order not to attract to Roseate the misfortunes that the cruel fay is preparing for her."

The queen, very surprised by that adventure, which disconcerted her projects, thought that it was appropriate to open her heart to the king at that moment, so she told him what her intention had been for her daughter and the desire she had to see the marriage of Prince Celadon with the young princess succeed.

"If you believe me," she added, "We won't give the exclusion yet to Sempiternelle's relative, but we can say that we think that the princess is too young to think of marrying her; by that means we'll gain time, and afterwards, we'll be in control of events."

The king approved strongly of the queen's opinion, and resolved to follow it punctually. The fay received a response in consequence, and the queen, delighted to see her husband in accord with her sentiments, wrote to her sister, and asked her for the favor of sending the young prince to the court promptly.

That letter was no sooner received and the request granted than a magnificent equipage was prepared for the young prince and his mother pressed him to depart. While they were awaiting him in the home of Roseate's father, and everyone in the courts was joyful that his arrival would not be long delayed, Sempiternelle arrived herself, with her relative Prince Muguet.

"I've come," she said to the king and queen, "to obtain your promise and to introduce you to your son-in-law. It's true that your daughter is still young, but the Prince is willing to wait, and I'll leave him with you, in order that he can become accustomed to her, but the moment he finds her worthy of her affection I advise you to conclude the matter, for neither he nor I are inclined to wait for your petty precautions."

The king, rather shocked by that fashion of talking, was about to respond haughtily to that beginning, when the queen, fearing some bad turn on the part of the fay for her daughter, spoke first.

"You're not unaware, Madame," she said, "that it is dangerous for my daughter to be able to love before the age of fifteen, so you won't find it bad that I hide her from the eyes of the Prince until that age. It's you who have shown me the consequences of that, and thus I believe it futile to make any engagement before that time. For her person, I admit that one could not have chosen better, but don't force us to do anything before we are sure that my daughter has nothing to fear. You have dictated that law yourself, so you won't think badly of us for executing it to the letter."

The fay, who had no response to make to the queen's speech, because she could not change destiny, merely appeared rather discontented, but she preferred to dissimulate for the time being.

"Prince," she said to Muguet, "it's now your affair to determine these obstinate individuals. Your face is dangerous to the darling that is being guarded so preciously, but when you're married, she'll become accustomed to it, and will be more fortunate that she deserves; if anyone takes it into their heads to quibble with you, I swear that I'll avenge you."

"Why the threats, Madame?" the queen interrupted. "Haven't you been cruel enough already? At least leave us time to determine my daughter's affection; and if she has no aversion..."

"Aversion!" the fay interrupted. "I'll hold it against you! In any case, it will be new, Adieu, Madame. I'll leave you. The day your Roseate reaches her fifteenth year, I'll be here, and I'll see what I have to do."

As she spoke, the fay, who was very angry, took the small broom from the corner of the queen's fireplace, and, sitting astride it, flew away up the chimney, bursting into laughter.

The queen went very red at that lack of respect, and Muguet, who had not yet said anything, started to make rather stupid apologies, which were received very coldly. His face would not have been bad if one had not observed a certain air of pretention that reigned from his head to his feet, and which instantly took away the desire to find him good. The insipidity of his speech, which always revolved around his perfections, completed making one succumb to the desire to find him insupportable. In a word, he was a child spoiled without resource, for he only had enough intelligence to make him an accomplished fop.

He asked to see the princess, but, the queen having told him that it was impossible, he no longer thought about it, and amused himself by making himself adored by all the scatterbrains of the court, who became mad about him. Among others he turned the head of a princess related to the king, who was neither young nor pretty but who, by way of compensation, was very coquettish, and so stupid that she was known as Transparent.

The king and queen, very uncertain as to what they could do to ward off the misfortune with which the cruel Sempiternelle was threatening them, resolved to send word to the Fay of the Green Oaks, who had always protected them. The queen even determined to go to see her, in order not to neglect anything that might put her in their interests. She departed secretly and went to find her.

The fay lived a long way away, but in the end, in spite of the hazards of the journey, the queen arrived there.

The name that she bore had not been plucked out of the air; it came from the agreeable solitude that she had chosen for her dwelling; it was a vast forest of oaks in the middle of which there was one so huge and so leafy that a thousand men holding hands would have had difficulty circling it; that was her palace; the trunk was hollow and it contained rooms, cabinets, wardrobes and marvelous galleries.

It was evening when the queen arrived; she was surprised to see the forest illuminated by large glow-worms distributed in all the trees; the oak in which the fay lived was covered with more of them than the others. The queen went in; their light illumined the interior of the marvelous tree, and the gallery in which the fay received her had a tapestry of them, which formed people, trees, porticos and fountains. In sum, it was a work as striking as it was marvelous.

The fay was beautiful and polite, so she received the queen with amity.

"I know what brings you here, Madame," she said, "and I ordered my subjects to illuminate your passage in order to enable you to arrive sooner. But let's not waste time in unnecessary discourse," she added, seeing that the queen wanted to respond to her compliment. "Sit down, Madame and listen to me. Our elder, the fay Sempiternelle, has nothing for which to reproach you except having a daughter more beautiful than her. That chagrin in unpardonable; her jealousy wants to punish you for having made her that affront, but although she is our elder, she has less power than me.

"In truth, I cannot undo what she has done and prevent that, if the charming Roseate takes a liking to someone before fifteen years of age, she will be very unhappy by virtue of the very person that she loves; but by taking great precautions to prevent it, we can deflect that misfortune. She is already twelve years old; send her to me, Madame; and in order not to give Sempiternelle reason to think that you have removed her from your court, have Prince Celadon guarded carefully, in the clothes of the young princess, and put about the rumor that your sister did not want to send him to you. I'll take charge of informing her of all that. Afterwards, we'll see what we can do, and I hope all will be well."

The fay had supper served to the queen, and they retired early, not without the fay having talked further about what she would do to amuse the pretty Roseate in her retreat, and the queen about the chagrin caused to her by old Sempiternelle. In the end, as she was to leave early the next morning, the fay left her in her room, after having wished her good night.

The next day, the queen, having taken her leave of the fay and recommended to her strongly the deposit that she was about to confide to her, set forth to return to her realm.

She told the king everything that the Fay of the Green Oaks had said to her. He approved of her idea and consented to deprive himself of her daughter during the three fatal years. He pretended to have received a letter from the father of young Celadon suspending for a few years the arrival of the prince in his court, and after receiving secret notification of his arrival, the queen also ordered the departure of her daughter; she confided her to a trusted woman who had been her first governess and whose name was Lucinette. After having embraced her tenderly, she begged her not to quit her dear Roseate and to send her news of her frequently.

The beautiful princess, who was irritated no longer to be appearing at the court and always being shut away, quit it with less regret than one would have thought, and although she wept at leaving the king and the queen, it was obvious that it was more by virtue of sensibility for them than the chagrin of seeing herself deprived of the privileges of her rank.

The Fay of the Green Oaks had recommended the queen, above all, to remove all the marks of her birth and to dress her very simply. People were occupied in making her elegant garments. On the day of her departure she had a white taffeta dress in the style of a shepherdess covered in garlands of blue flowers; her beautiful hair was sown with them; she had never looked so pretty. The whiteness of her skin, the brightness of her colors and the rose-red of her lovely mouth heightened her adornment. She wanted absolutely to put on her bouquet of diamond roses, and that small satisfaction was not refused to her. The queen embraced her a thousand times and, recommending her to her conductress, embarked them secretly in the carriage that was to take them to the abode of the Fay of the Green Oaks.

The queen never ceased to be anxious between the departure of her daughter and the arrival of Prince Celadon, whose mother, instructed by the Queen of the Green Oaks of the consequences there would be of sending him openly to his uncle's court, had taken the precaution of dressing him as a girl, and had also confided him to a clever and prudent woman of her court to take him to the one who was expecting him. He was nearing his fourteenth year and his beauty, although a little more masculine than that of Princess Roseate scarcely ceded anything to hers.

A few leagues from the capital, he wanted to walk for a little; it was the middle of the day, and as it was very hot, the governess had no difficulty in letting him get down in order to seek some fresh air. She advanced with him under trees that were rather leafy, the feet of which were washed by a little stream. Seeking out a place where the thicker grass might serve as a bed, she made him sit down and asked him to wait while she gave orders to his retinue to return to his father's realm and chose the ones to which her secret would be confided in order to take him to the mother of Roseate.

The prince promised not to go astray, and, his governess having gone away, he amused himself following the course of the stream. The extreme heat inviting him to bathe there, he had already chosen by eye a palace to sit down and undress when, through the trees, he saw a young woman lying on the grass, profoundly asleep. He soon abandoned his first deign in order follow the desire that gripped him to consider that object at closer range.

Nothing so beautiful had ever struck his eyes. It was young Roseate, who, with the same design of avoiding the heat of the day, had lain down under the trees with her governess, and, having no fear in such a solitary place, had gone to sleep like her.

Celadon approached quietly, and in order to contemplate her more at his ease, he set one knee on the ground and remained in admiration. A bush covered with wild roses shaded the head of the princess. Their beautiful color, unknown to the young prince, gave him the desire to pick some in order to strew them over the beautiful sleeper. He had already taken a few, and had placed them in her beautiful hair, when the bouquet of diamond roses that she had at her side came undone and was about to fall. He retained it, and tried to fasten it again, but a part of her breast being uncovered by the disturbance of the bouquet, the prince was dazzled by the whiteness and beauty of that object.

His hand trembled, he felt slightly queasy, and tried to get up, fearing that he might wound the young woman. He supported himself on the grass, but a wild rose on which he placed his hand pricked him with so much violence that he uttered a loud cry and fell next to the princess in a faint. She woke up at the sound, as did her governess, but their fear turned to compassion on seeing beside them such a young and lovely young woman in such a dire state—for Celadon was already in female attire.

The princess and the governess hastened to help him; they were astonished to see that a young woman so beautiful and so richly dressed was alone in that place. The princess took her hands and squeezed them in her own; she felt an insensible dolor in seeing her suffering for so long; she embraced her tenderly and implored her governess to go and fetch water in order to bring her round more promptly. She perceived that her hands were full of blood. "Oh gods!" she said. "She's dead; she hasn't fainted, her blood is flowing."

It would not have taken much after that for her to faint as well, so much did she feel her heart stirred by that discovery. She sat down next to the prince, and, raising his head, she placed it on her knees, while her governess went to draw water from the steam. The princess, whom a certain shame, the cause of which she was unaware, had prevented from weeping before a witness whom she feared might have reproached her for such a sudden amity, allowed her tears to flow, and watered the face of the prince with them. He opened his eyes then, and, surprised to find himself in such an agreeable situation, raised them toward the beautiful face of the princess.

"How beautiful you are!" he said "And how I..." At those words, gripped by an unknown pleasure, his heart was seized by a sentiment to powerful to resist and constricted by it, causing him to fall back into his faint.

It was then that the young princess no longer spared anything; she uttered piercing screams, and, embracing her new friend, she nearly died of dolor. Her governess, the prince's, and the people of his retinue came running. The latter were very astonished by the event and asked what had caused it.

The lady who was with the princess told them what she knew, and, seeing that those people were interested in the young woman who had fainted, that they no longer had any need of her help, and that it was absolutely necessary to reach the home of Fay of the Green Oaks and hide the name and rank of the person she was conducting, she made the princess understand that the young woman would be cared for without her. She pulled her away from the body of the prince, whom his governess and his men picked up and placed in his carriage, in order to take him to his aunt's court as night was falling, as they had been commanded to do, in order that no one would perceive the exchange that the fay and the queen had projected.

It had required all the eloquence of the governess and all the power that she had over the princess to convince her to quite the beautiful child that she had seen unconscious, and all the meekness and obedience of the young princess to convince her to do it. Never had anyone been so afflicted and never had her heart been so tenderly interested as it was then

"Perhaps they won't take enough care of that beautiful girl," she said to her governess. "It was necessary to take her with us since you absolutely insisted that we go. We should have taken care of her."

"Oh, my God, Madame," said the governess. That young person is in the hands of people who are as interested in her as you are. Your amity is troubled too easily. Apparently, she's a princess, like you, but she doesn't have the same reasons to hide, so it was necessary to avoid anyone recognizing you, and a longer delay might have been harmful to you."

"But at least it will be necessary to have news of her," said the princess, "for I'm in a mortal anxiety; I've never seen anyone who pleased me as much, and my father's entire court has no beauty that can compare to her."

"What are you saying, Madame?"

"Is it compassion for her condition or her veritable beauty that interests me in her? Do you feel the same amity?"

"Both are interesting, naturally," said the governess, "but I don't understand your anxiety or the excess of your amity. One ought to be cured by the care that will probably be given to her; as for the other, it's by long acquaintance and studies of a lovable character that one can deliver oneself to the amity that you have already reached. Something so violent can't last long, Madame, and I'll envisage with pleasure that you'll console yourself easily for perhaps never seeing that princess again, since you'd like so much to know her."

The princess, who was meek and timid, blushed and lowered her eyes at that little remonstration. "I assure you," she said, "that I believe her to be worthy of always being loved. I'd be very sorry," she added, sighing, "if you believed me capable of forgetting what I find lovable; I shall never forget, for example, the amity that you have in coming to shut yourself away with me in the abode of the Fay of the Green Oaks."

The governess kissed the princess's hand, moved by the goodness of her heart, and tried to console her until the moment when they arrived at the home of the fay. who received the pretty princess with the graces of which she was very capable.

As for the prince, the lady who was conducting him and the men who had stayed with him hastened to bring him round from his faint, and success soon responded to their efforts. He told them about his accident, at which they all shuddered, not because of the prick of the rose, which was not dangerous, but because their minds were filled by the prediction that had been made at his birth, about which his mother talked every day.

His hand was bandaged, and they hastened to bring the equipages in order to conduct him in the dead of night to his aunt's home. He was in no hurry to depart; he searched among the trees and ran along the length of the stream; finally, not seeing anyone, he said to his horsemen and the lady conducting him: "What has become of her, then? Tell me what you have done with the charming young woman who helped me and shed tears over my faint?"

"I have absolutely no idea where she is, Sire," said the lady. "We did, in fact, see two shepherdesses who had helped you, but they returned you to our hands and went away. We were so occupied with your condition that we didn't pay any heed to which way they went."

"It's necessary to search for them," said the prince. "I want to mark my gratitude to them." As she spoke he tried again and to follow a beaten path that appeared to lead to some habitation, but the lady, who had a great authority over him, made him see that it would be failing the queen, who was waiting for them, and that the daylight was scarcely sufficient for them to get out of that place, far from any help.

The prince dared not resist; he climbed into his carriage, not without looking to the right and the left so long as the daylight furnished him with the means.

A few miles from the capital, the queen came in her carriages on the pretext of going to meet Princess Roseate, who, she pretended, had gone to walk with her women at one of her father's houses of pleasure. The prince's carriage arrived alongside those that were waiting for it, and the cortege had already set forth to go into the city when Prince Muguet, elegantly harnessed, arrived at the door of the pretended princess's carriage and said to her everything that a fop can say in such an occasion; the most pompous commonplaces were displayed with all the art that can be put into them. "It's funny," he said "that they're afraid that I might not please you, and don't enquire as to whether you will please me—which I don't doubt, for I believe that you're very beautiful."

The queen, who had instructed the prince, begged him to let her reply; he submitted willingly to that. He would have laughed at that adventure of he had not been too occupied with his own, but, dreaming continually about the beautiful object that had struck him, and thinking that he might perhaps be drawing away from her forever, he could not enter into the pleasantry.

The queen spoke and answered on behalf of the princess.

Muguet begged the queen at least to let the princess speak. "I can't see her, Madame," he said, "her lowered veil and the obscurity of the night are denying both of us the pleasure of looking at one another; it has permitted us to aid ourselves with an unexpected encounter, so leave the beautiful princess, I beg you, the liberty of responding to my sentiments."

"The queen will permit me to tell you, then," said the false princess, "that I know so little of my sentiments yet that yours do not touch me. I don't know whether that comes from my indifference, or the scant faith one can add to what I'm told that men want to persuade us. Whatever it might be, Prince, I beg you to wait for the time when my credulity might render you justice. For the present, that isn't possible."

Those words having been said, they found themselves so close to the palace that the prince could not respond. After having embraced her nephew and pitting him in the hands of the women who were to conduct him to his apartment, the queen got down, from her carriage.

Muguet lent her a hand, not without darting a glance at the princess, of whom he could see nothing but her stature and her stride, which appeared to him to be a trifle free; but that only piqued him more, and all night long, he only talked to Transparent about the intelligence and grace of Roseate, which she thought very bad, in accordance with her praiseworthy custom of being unable to suffer anyone finding someone younger and prettier than her. She acquired a jealousy in consequence that augmented her ill humor, and the prince, naturally given to mockery, made jokes about it so offensive that he constrained her to retire earlier than usual.

As for the queen, she had a satisfaction that expanded over everyone that approached her; she had receive news the same evening of the arrival of her daughter at the home of the Fay of the Green Oaks, and although it was reported that she was very sad, as she imagined that that was only caused by her departure, she was not worried by it. Every day she went to spend two hours in Prince Celadon's apartment in the afternoon, as she had done since her daughter had been confined there. There, she instructed him as to everything that it was necessary to do in order to give Prince Muguet a natural distaste for Princess Roseate.

The young prince, who was also sad, promised the queen to do his best to aid her designs, but he seemed very annoyed that he was kept captive for such a long time.

"You can go out occasionally," said the queen, but it's necessary that we don't change our fashion of acting right away. Above all, I fear Transparent; hide from her eyes, my dear Celadon. I leave it to your intelligence and prudence only to show yourself to Muguet."

Delighted that he was permitted to go out sometimes, the prince seemed a little more cheerful, and the queen found him so handsome then that she feared the disruption of her projects; she begged him always to be somewhat neglectful, in order that adornment did not further augment his prodigious beauty.

Toward evening the next day he went into the palace gardens; he wanted to be alone and to meditate; his women moved away and he went into the heart of a large wood that was neatly maintained and full of charming little paths, one of which he chose in order to entertain his thoughts.

He was already recalling, delightfully, the encounter with the ravishing Roseate, whose name he did not know. "That was not a mortal," he exclaimed. "It was doubtless a goddess. How beautiful she was, and how stirred I still am by the memory! Where are you, charming object?" he went on. "Where can I find you?"

Prince Muguet, who was also walking nearby, overheard those last words. He advanced in order to see where they might be coming from, and was pleased to see the false princess through a palisade, lying on a grassy bank that bordered a beautiful pool, supporting her head with one hand and dreaming.

After the few words she had spoken, it was only necessary to have that prince's vanity in order to interpret them favorably, so he did not fail to do so. He stopped in order to continue listening and to enjoy the pleasure of hearing himself named, but that did not happen.

"Why have I seen you so briefly?" the pretended Roseate continued. "You were snatched away from me at the moment when I was about to seem sensitive to you; I would not have been able to hide it from you. Oh, why not allow me to enjoy a privilege without which I cannot live?"

Flattered by the prompt effect of his charms, Muguet did not want to leave the amorous beauty in despair any longer. "Here I am, my beautiful princess," he cried, emerging from behind the palisade and throwing himself at her feet, which she allowed him to embrace by virtue of the surprise caused by the unexpected event. "Here I am, filled with an ardor as keen as yours, and which will last as long as your charms."

The pretended princess had great difficulty not bursting out laughing after she had recalled what had caused the prince's error. Wanting a diversion, however, she adopted a serious expression and withdrew her feet modestly. "What do you want with me?" she said. "What has permitted you to disturb my solitude?"

"Oh, Madame," replied the prince, "Don't take amiss what makes my happiness. I heard you, my beautiful princess, and my heart is only anticipating you. But why does your modesty oppose such a sweet confession? The fay Sempiternelle wants to unite us, so you ought not to blush at your flame."

At those words the princess could no longer contain her laughter; it burst forth with so little restraint that Muguet was disconcerted by it.

"I don't see," he said, "what the motive for such extraordinary laughter could be. I shall even see something very disobliging about it if you continue not to say anything else to me."

"What do you want me to say?" said the princess. "What you said to me was so funny that I can't help laughing at it, and I'll quit you in order not to offend you further."

As she spoke, she replaced her veil and drew away, making the woods resound with bursts of laughter.

Muguet remained consternated by that adventure. He had never admitted with impunity that he was in love; this appeared to be a novelty; the foolish women that had loved him had never taught him what scorn is, but he could not dissimulate that it was one of the most violent that the princess had expressed for him. The only resource that he found in the despair that that conviction caused him was that no one had witnessed it; but the princess's bursts of laughter, which he could still hear in the distance, inspired a rage in him that he had difficulty mastering.

He was in that cruel situation when Transparent approached him. "So you're dreaming about the princess," she said to him, taking him by the arm, "fickle as you are, and you're not aware that she's telling her women about the ridiculous confession you've just made to her of your passion. Come and listen, Sire," she added, on seeing him go pale with anger. "Come and witness the progress you've made in her heart. I'm well avenged for your change, and I'm glad to have learned from her how it's necessary to treat you."

She tried to draw away as she spoke, but the prince stopped her. "You don't know me very well, Madame," he said, "or you render yourself very little justice if you believe that I was able to tell Roseate in good faith that I loved her. I swear to you that that much-vaunted and uselessly-exalted beauty is no great prize in my eyes. She's beautiful enough, but in good faith, I see nothing in her person that has moved me, and if you want to know what led me to talk to her about love it's because I'm not cruel, and a man who cannot doubt that he pleases makes no great scruple of saying that he loves someone, especially when a young princess..."

"Roseate loves you?" Transparent interrupted. "And you're certain of what you're telling me?"

"Unless you want to doubt the evidence of things," he said. "That can't be hidden; but as for me loving her, that's different."

"How do you expect me to be convinced, ingrate," said Transparent, "that you don't love her? What assures me that you aren't deceiving me? You'd be flattered to be loved; you already are, since you say so, and you're sacrificing me to a young scatterbrain who only has the merit of having been imprudent."

"Me!" he cried. "Me, love a woman who is due to be mine, and lets her head be turned by a quarter of an hour of

130

conversation I had with her before the queen! You don't know me very well, Madame, and my heart ought to be the guarantee of my constancy, although it pleased you to doubt it yesterday."

"Well," said Transparent, "I'd like to believe that you don't love her yet, but in order to remove all my scruples it's necessary for you to quarrel with the king and queen, depart from here and marry me."

Muguet, master of himself as he was, was astounded by that proposition; he pulled himself together, though.

"You want to test me, my beautiful princess," he said, "and you believe that your charms are not strong enough to combat Roseate's. Even when I'm her husband, do you think that I can forget you and descend to the cares of loving a young princess because she adores me? Let us allow time to act..."

"No, no," said the furious Transparent. "I don't want to hear anything more, and that discourse tells me what I ought to believe. You'll no longer enjoy my credulity, ingrate; I'll be able, without you, to rid myself of such a dangerous rival."

As she spoke, she escaped from the prince, who tried to retain her, and went back into the palace before he could overtake her.

The fury and jealousy of Transparent had risen to a peak; to begin with she made a thousand extravagant projects, but in the end she settled on the one that seemed to her to be the surest. She departed that night in order to go to find the fay Sempiternelle.

She arrived at daybreak, and found the other woman roasting three bats for her breakfast. Her dwelling was frightful; it was an old cavern so profound that it was necessary to walk for two hours underground in order to reach the place where she lived.

"I'm desperate, Madame," the jealous Transparent cried. "Your nephew loves and is loved by Princess Roseate; that ingrate has scorned and betrayed me; in sum, he's the most perfidious of all men."

The fay, attentive to her work, was struck by that declaration, turned round to see who was speaking, and was so surprised by the ugliness, the thinness and the bitterness of that person that she dropped her skewer and her bats into the fire, which consumed them in an instant. That put her in such a terrible wrath that Transparent would have felt its effect if the fay, finding in her discourse a means of harming the young princess, had not calmed herself in order to enable Transparent to recover from the fright her anger had just caused her.

"You're saying, then," she said, with a slightly less terrible expression "that Roseate already loves Muguet? Oh, I suspected it, and I'm delighted by it."

"Yes, Madame," said Transparent, "but do you know that he loved me first, and that the traitor has quit me for her? What has he not employed to seduce my overly credulous heart?"

The fay, fully occupied with her own objective, could not look at the ugly creature who confessed herself so sensitive without bursting out laughing, but having need for her for her projects, she stopped.

"But, tender darling," she said to her, "I've destined my nephew for the princess, and the confession you're making me would offend me if I didn't hate Roseate more than I love the prince. She can't love without risk before the age of fifteen; she's only thirteen, so I have the power to punish her. Try to see her, and make her accept this jewel," she added, taking a rich turquoise ring from an old chest in the corner of the cavern, on which talismanic figures were engraved. "As soon as she has that ring on her finger you'll be avenged; but be careful, and refrain from confiding this secret to Prince Muguet, for he'll prevent its effect if it's true that he loves the princess. Adieu, my dear Transparent; when you're content, don't fail to come and tell me so."

The malevolent princess embraced the fay wholeheartedly, and allowed a joy so vivid to burst forth that the fay was infinitely pleased, and promised to do her best to enable her to marry Prince Muguet.

Transparent departed, full of joy, and returned to the court that evening, where she had never appeared in such good humor. Prince Muguet was astonished by it, and although he flirted with the queen's maids in order to annoy her and make her jealous, she was so transported to have the wherewithal in her power to avenge herself on Roseate that she did not seem at all offended.

Muguet retired early, and that was what revived all her anger; she thought that he might well have a rendezvous with the princess, and that the pretext he employed for leaving was not the veritable one. In fact, he had put into that departure an air of mystery that could easily give rise to some such conjecture.

She retired soon after him, and, opening her windows, in spite of the obscurity of the night, she saw a man walking under those of the princess. Soon afterwards, someone spoke to him, but she could not distinguish who it was or what was said. Her fury was then borne to the ultimate excess. Not doubting that it was Roseate, she racked her brains in search of a means of making her take the fatal ring—for the princess's apartment was inaccessible to everyone except the queen.

What a night she passed! All that she said and thought is indescribable. Finally, the next day, as she was emerging from her dressing-room, the queen came to see her, and, seeing the beautiful turquoise on her finger, she asked to borrow it, so that she might have a search made for a similar one, in order to give to her daughter, who desired one.

Delighted by such a favorable and natural opportunity, Transparent urged the queen to accept it, and did so with such a good grace that the queen agreed. It was not the fake princess that had asked for it but the veritable one, and when she returned to her apartment the queen dispatched a courier to take the ring to her dear child.

Transparent, judging that the effect would be prompt, awaited news with impatience, but nothing transpired. She was in extreme anxiety; finally, she went to the queen's apartment, where people were conversing tranquilly. She had come back from the apartment of the fake princess, having spent her usual two hours there, but was not talking about it. Transparent feared that she might have forgotten the ring, but dared not remind her about it; that would have given to much evidence of wanting to be thanked for it again. She only had eyes for those who came in.

Evening arrived, and nothing happened. Nothing was said that could calm her down. She remained until the queen went to bed. The latter, while letting down her hair, took a diamond cluster therefrom, which she put into Transparent's hair.

"It is," she said, embracing her, "a feeble recognition of the pleasure that you gave me this morning."

Transparent, delighted by that opening, asked her whether that princess had been content.

"Charmed," said the queen—she could only suspect that, having not yet had news of her daughter.

Transparent withdrew, very discontented with Sempiternelle, but after all, she thought that the charm might act during the night. She went to bed with that fine hope, not without having looked once again through her window to see whether Muguet was under the princess's; but he did not appear.

The next day the queen received terrible news from the Fay of the Green Oaks, who sent word that Princess Roseate had disappeared at the moment when she had put the ring that the queen had sent on her finger; that it must have been a charm that had not been suspected; that it was necessary nevertheless to keep the affair secret; that she would travel the earth in search of news of the princess; and that she would send back the governess in order to give her more detailed information.

In despair at that cruel adventure, the queen sent word to the king, and shut herself away with him in order to tell him what had happened. They both understood very well that the charm was in Transparent's ring, but they could not accuse her of having wanted to cast it on the princess, inasmuch as the queen had request the ring herself, without her appearing to want to offer it. Thus, they decided that it was necessary not to say anything until the Fay of the Green Oaks gave them news.

The governess was introduced secretly thereafter; she tore out her hair and struck her breast on seeing the king and queen, throwing herself at their feet and bathing them with her tears. The queen, moved by that spectacle, lifted her up and embraced her, weeping even more bitterly, and the king, impatient to learn the truth of the matter, ordered her to call a truce in her dolor in order to tell him how the adventure had come about.

The poor governess obeyed, and, wiping away her tears, commenced.

"The wretched fay Sempiternelle, Sire," she said, "betrayed the princess as soon as she was born, and the Fay of the Green Oaks has no doubt that the misfortune is caused by her."

"If I remember correctly," the king interrupted, "she could not have any power over my daughter unless she loved someone before the age of fifteen years. She has only accomplished thirteen, and her heart is still in surety."

"The Fay and I can answer for that, Sire," said the governess, "unless old Sempiternelle has been able to punish her for a simple amity, acquired in truth very promptly, as if it were amour."

"What sudden amity?" said the queen.

Then the governess told Their Majesties about the encounter they had had in the wood with the young beauty, and added that the princess had been very occupied with it ever since; that the fay had even tried, by all sorts of cares, to makes her forget it, but that it had been futile; that in the end, in order to take her mind of that idea and extract her from her melancholy, she had had applied her to painting, but that the princess had only ornamented her apartment with paintings depicting her adventure; and that her imagination was so struck by the young woman that she had painted her very accurately.

"I even took away from her a little miniature portrait," added the governess, "in which she had dressed her as a man, which she hid carefully by night under her pillow."

At that story the king and the queen looked at one another, apparently confused to learn such things. The queen, more excited, was the first to speak. "Do you have the portrait, my dear Lucinette?" she said to the governess.

"I had it, Madame," she said, "but I put it in the hands of the fay, who urged me to leave it with her—but she appeared to me to know more than I told her, for when she received it she sighed, and let these words escape: 'Unfortunate princess, your destiny is stronger than me.'

"It was the same day, Madame," she went on, speaking to the queen, "that you sent the princess the fatal ring, which she received with transports of joy. She immediately brought it to the fay, and, putting it on her finger, she was advancing her hand in order to show it thus placed when she disappeared before our eyes. I uttered a frightful scream at that moment, but the fay, less astonished than me, said: 'Go, return to the queen, tell her about this adventure and tell her that it's necessary to remedy the misfortune, which couldn't be prevented, and to rely on my cares.'

"Right away, she made me mount a bronze elephant with her, which travels faster than the wind, and in passing, she made me get down here in order to tell Your Majesties the deplorable story."

"Oh, Sire," cried the queen, "there's no doubt about it, a power hostile to our happiness has caused Celadon to encounter the princess, and that's the cause of our woes."

"I judge it as you do, Madame," said the king. "What point is there now in keeping him shut up among us? Nevertheless," he added, "it's necessary to wait; the Fay of the

Green Oaks desires it. Go to see him; try to find out whether he remembers this adventure, and whether we can obtain some further enlightenment. I no longer expect anything but the catastrophic, but after the loss of my daughter I don't dread anything further."

With those words, he got up and left.

The queen, overwhelmed by her dolor and that which the king had allowed to appear, left with the princess's governess, whom she ordered to go with her to the apartment where Prince Celadon was being kept.

As the queen as very afflicted, the young prince had no difficulty in perceiving that when she came in; she dismissed his women and went into his cabinet with him. She closed the door, after having made Roseate's governess come in; the latter had recognized the prince at the first glance.

The prince, fully occupied by the tears that the queen was shedding, had not paid any attention to the individual that was with her, but the order she gave her to enter with her on her own caused her to look at the lady. Recalling an idea too deeply engraved in his heart to be mistaken, he cried, addressing the queen: "What do I see? Is this not, Madame, the mother of the young shepherdess that I encountered as I arrived at this court? O Heaven!" he added, on seeing the queen and the lady redoubling their tears. "What are you announcing to me? If she is no more, I cannot survive!"

With those words, young Celadon became very pale, and fell, devoid of strength, on the sofa where the queen had sat down. She hastened to help him.

"No, my dear Prince," she said to him, "No, she is still alive, and I'm confirmed, by your sentiments, in what I have just thought. She is my daughter, my dear Celadon, not Lucinette's; it is Roseate that you love, and whom I destined for you. I was hiding her from everyone in order to conserve her for you, but the barbaric Sempiternelle has stolen her from me, and I don't know where she has put her. Help us to recover her; I give her to you with all my heart, so don't waste any time in making your happiness and ours."

If the queen's first words had rendered life to the prince, the last animated sentiments so intense and so grateful that he threw himself at her feet and embraced them with transport.

"Yes, Madame," he said, "I swear that I will return Roseate to you, or that I will lose my life. I have no need to be animated by the charming prize that you are giving me for my troubles; the honor of serving you is sufficient recompense. And I dare say that if Roseate were a simple shepherdess, as I thought until now, she would merit all my tenderness and my cares; but what price does she not have in my eyes, being your daughter? Yes, Madame, I will render her to you, I swear it by the immortal gods; or, if their power does not second me, I will die for her, only to glad to end a life that would not be worthy of being offered to Roseate."

The queen embraced her dear nephew, and, lifting him up, she responded with very tender words to the obliging things he had said. Afterwards, telling him what Lucinette had said to her, she begged him to moderate his urgency and to await news of the Fay of the Green Oaks.

The prince had great difficulty resolving to do that, but she finally obtained his consent to it, granting him that at least the princess's governess would remain with him in order to console him by talking about her and to relieve his irritation by talking to him about her tenderness. He promised, therefore, to remain in the costume of the princess for a few more days, but it was a great effort of his complaisance for the queen to yield to what she asked of him.

When she had gone, what caresses did he not make Roseate's governess? "My dear Lucinette," he said, "Speak to me about my charming princess. You say that she liked me, that she remembered me, and that, in sum, her amity had all the features of amour? How glad I am, and how beautiful she must be! But tell me in detail her thoughts and her words; I can't hear them too much, or have them repeated too often."

The complaisant Lucinette searched with exactitude for everything that she had heard her mistress say or seen her do that might tend to prove to the prince that she had a sensitive heart, the occupation she had with that amity, the desire she had to see its object again, the dread of being forgotten thereby, and the pain caused to her by the contradictions brought to that attachment. All that delighted the young prince.

"And me," he said, "and me; what have I not thought, what have I not said? But does not the charming, the sensitive, Roseate merit it? Always occupied with her I have not wanted anyone to talk to me about her; I feared offending her by allowing myself to hear about her; I refused a happiness that I might have enjoyed, all the charm of which I have discovered too late; her women, who are serving me, tried a hundred times to talk to me about her perfections, but I did not want to listen to them, or I only applied them to the beautiful object that filled my soul; blind as I was, Roseate charmed me and I feared being infidel to her by filling myself too much with the idea of her! Pardon me, beautiful Princess, that crime was involuntary; I did not know you, and my heart will avenge you today for all the praises that I have refused you."

In the end, Lucinette perceived that he had remained shut away for too long. He returned to his women; he ate the midday meal, and after having put on his veil, he went down into the gardens with Lucinette and a few others—but he went into an arbor in order to be alone with her and to talk about Roseate again.

"Don't you admire my blindness?" he said. "I never asked the queen where the beautiful princess was; I never talked to her about her. Solely occupied with what had struck me, I neglected everything, including decorum. I think that she pardons me now for my impoliteness; fortunately, the depths of my heart justify me."

He was speaking actively at that moment to Lucinette, and did not perceive that the jealous Transparent was observing them. Lucinette was the first to perceive it, and remarked on it to the prince, who, annoyed to have witnesses, returned to his apartment.

What rage for Transparent! Her rival did not appear other than as she had always seen her; the charm was not working. She turned all her fury against the fay. "That old witch," she said, that pitiless fay, was laughing at my dolor and abusing my credulity. Oh, I'll be able to avenge myself without her, and her charms won't be able to prevent me doing so."

In her fury, she thought that it was necessary to observe whether Muguet, who had been avoiding her for several days, was still wandering under the princess's windows. *There*, she said to herself, *I'll be able to pierce the heart of that dangerous rival, perhaps after I pierce his. Doubtless he doesn't merit a better fate.*

Having made that resolution, she waited for night impatiently, and when it arrived, dark enough for her liking, she went down into the gardens and hid behind one of the statues that ornamented the terrace overlooked by the princess's apartment. She had not been there for an hour when she passed into transports of wrath, easier to imagine than to describe, as she saw someone arriving. She drew a dagger with which she was armed from her belt and, advancing slowly, she heard a woman saying:

"No, I'm not deceiving you; it costs me enough to serve you as I do, but even though you love the princess and no longer love me, I prefer your happiness to mine. I'll open her apartment for you, and if your horses are ready you can abduct her, for they believe that she's asleep, and I'm on guard in her chamber tonight."

"My dear Linda," said Prince Muguet, in a low voice, which Transparent recognized in spite of that precaution, as well as that of the princess's maid of honor. "I owe you my life, and will never forget it; but my love for Roseate is more an effect of my vanity than any other sentiment. I can no longer suffer that another might marry her. Come with me, with her, and you'll see which I love more. I fear Transparent's amour; I can't abide her; soon I'll no longer be able to constrain myself with her, so come with Roseate, and you'll take the first place in my heart, even if you don't hold it on my father's throne."

The young woman was weeping, and Transparent's fury and jealousy was holding her arm in suspense, in order to choose a victim, when Prince Muguet decided the matter by urging Linda to open the hidden door to the princess's apartment. "Hurry up and serve me," he said, "in order that dawn will find us far away from the jealous Transparent; let her die of rage, if she wants to, provided that I'm delivered from her wearisome tenderness."

"I won't die alone!" cried the furious woman, hurling herself upon him and plunging the dagger into his side. "You'll go to Hell before me to receive the price of your perfidy."

The prince fell, drowning in his blood, and the perfidious Linda uttered such loud screams that help arrived very quickly.

Transparent, judging correctly that the rumor she heard would enable her to be recognized, content with her crime, ran diligently to a garden gate, and found two horses and a squire there, waiting for Muguet.

"Your master has been wounded in the garden," she told him. "Run to his aid, and give me one of the horses in order to ride to the home of the fay, his cousin."

The poor squire, stunned by that news, did as he was asked and went in to help his master, leaving her the mistress of doing whatever she wished.

In response to Linda's screams, everyone—including the princess's maids, her governess Lucinette, and her—was soon out of bed. They came to the place where Linda, no longer hearing the prince speaking and believing him to be dead, had fainted.

The king, the queen and their entire household arrived in the garden with torches, and saw the prince losing his blood in the arms of his squire.

"Who has committed such a great crime?" said the king. "Who can have dared to assassinate Prince Muguet in my palace?"

"Princes Transparent came to inform me," said the squire, "but she didn't say anything else."

"Sire," said Muguet, whose blood flow had been stopped and who recovered a little strength, "only capture that cruel princess; it's her who has put me in the state in which you see me."

"O heaven!" cried the king. "What cruelty! What barbarity! Arrest her!"

"She's gone, Sire," said the squire. "She deceived me by sending me to my prince. She has taken one of his horses and is already far away."

"She's avoiding a cruel punishment," said the king. "But help the prince, and carry him to his apartment."

Several people helped the squire, and although no one at the court liked Muguet, his condition inspired pity, and the interest that the king was taking in him made everyone hurry to see to him.

The king and the queen went into Prince Celadon's apartment and found him occupied with his women in helping Linda. Celadon and Lucinette took the king and the queen into a cabinet, and the lady spoke,

"Sire, what you see here seems to me to be a sequel to my conjectures. I believe that Prince Muguet was trying to enter the prince's apartment by night, either because he is in love with Roseate or young Linda; the mystery is still unknown to me, but all I can tell Your Majesties is that Prince Muguet has sent several nights under the windows of this apartment, and that I judge from that things unfavorable to his innocence; so, if you are to examine everything carefully, you'll find Prince Muguet as culpable as, and perhaps more than, Transparent appears to be, for wanting to avenge herself so inhumanely for his perfidy."

Celadon, seeing the king and queen surprised by such tragic events, represented to them ardently the danger they

142

were running by leaving him any longer in the princess's garments.

"Have no doubt," he added, "that Sempiternelle will avenge herself on you swiftly for the murder of her son. Let me search for the beautiful Roseate, and in the meantime, take care of the prince; that will reduce the acrimony of the fay. You can say that I've been abducted by some fay, and at least Sempiternelle won't accuse you of having kept you daughter away from her cousin. Since the Fay of the Green Oaks won't take long to give you news of her, it's permissible for my impatience to search for her myself. I'm already reproaching myself for listening too patiently to all the arguments you've employed to prevent me doing so."

Convinced that he was right, the king and the queen allowed him to quite female attire immediately and he was equipped with the king's finest arms. They both embraced him tenderly, imploring him not to risk his life recklessly, but not to neglect anything to find Roseate. They renewed their promise to give her to him, and having had a horse brought to a secret door to the gardens, they escorted him there. The prince, full of gratitude, swore to them that he would die or return their lovable daughter to them.

That done, they gave Lucinette orders to keep the princess's apartment closed, even to her women, for several days, and then to come to inform them that a fay had abducted her. Then they ordered her to keep Linda locked away, without anyone other than her being able to see her in order to learn the secret of the prince's wound from her.

When he went back out, the king had Prince Muguet informed that he was not going to see him, because he had reason to complain of him.

He had no need to employ roundabout means with Linda to know the whole truth; believing Muguet to be dead, she confessed her crime to Lucinette, telling her about the prince's plans and Transparent's jealousy. The king and the queen did not have time to punish her or to pardon her; she died of the regret of her fault, and dolor at the extremity of Muguet—for

Lucinette had told her that he was not dead, but that there were no expectations; which was true. The harshness that the king showed to him, and the certainty that his projects had been discovered, reduced him to the brink of death; but it is time to return to Transparent.

Her bad luck conducted her through the obscurity of the night to the vicinity Sempiternelle's cavern. She was very astonished that, as she tried to recoil in order to flee by means of another path, the prince's horse, on which she was mounted, went into the cavern. When it neared the place where the fay lived, it threw the princess to the ground and whinnied in order to give notice that she was there.

Already troubled by the vengeance she had just exacted, and shaken by her fall, she remained on the ground without thinking of getting up. The fay Sempiternelle, who never slept, was far from having any such desire that night. Solely occupied with hiding Roseate, whom she had in her power, from the research of the Fay of the Green Oaks, she was consulting her books to see how she could achieve that when the whinnying of Prince Muguet's horse drew her away from her reading.

She shuddered; her spectacles fell off and broke, which put her in a very bad mood. She picked up her lamp, and in a furious temper she went to see who could be interrupting her. She found the horse at her door, which saluted her profoundly, and showed her Transparent on the ground.

The fay recognized her. "Truly," she said, "it's hardly worth the trouble of coming to tell me what I already know."

Transparent, in as bad a mood as the fay, got up, with some difficulty, and, looking at Sempiternelle with eyes in which rage and dolor were equally depicted, she said: "I haven't come to deny it. If I've attempted his life, it was to avenge myself for his horrible perfidy."

"What do you mean, attempted her life?"[2] said the fay. "She's in my power and you've had no rights over her person since; which I know because she's already been my prisoner for six days."

Transparent looked at the fay with a scorn mingled with astonishment. She shrugged her shoulders impatiently.

"What are you saying? Who has been your prisoner for six days? Not Roseate, whom your perfidious nephew was about to abduct tonight, if I hadn't killed him, in order to stop him."

It would be necessary to be able to express Sempiternelle's fury, and the horrible grinding of her teeth at that news, in order to render it in all its perfection, but that is impossible. She remained suspended for some time between the doubt and certainty of that story, but seeing Transparent mute and tranquil, awaiting her response, she seized her by the hair and dragged her into the depths of her cavern. There, without letting go of her, she said: "Go on, wretch! Finish confessing your crime. You've killed Muguet, my unique hope, and you have the effrontery to come here to boast about it? And you want to palliate your crime by saying that he was about to abduct Roseate, whom I have in my power? Look here, miserable creature, and don't join lies to your frightful cruelty."

At that moment, dragging her by her hair, she made her enter into a fissure in the cavern, and showed her a large bookcase, where several large folio volumes were arranged, magnificently bund in morocco leather of several colors. There, letting go of her and leaving her on the ground, more dead than alive, she took down one of the books, bound in roseate morocco.

---

[2] French pronouns do not work in the same way as English ones, corresponding with the gender of the noun that follows them rather than specifying the sex of the person to whom they refer, so Transparent's "*sa vie*" is ambiguous, permitting Sempiternelle's error.

"This," she said, "is the person you accuse of being loved by my nephew, and the ring that I gave you has rendered me mistress of her. I thought I had some obligation to you, and I was prepared to recompense you, but you'll only feel the effects of my vengeance, and after the entire confession of your crime, it will commence, be very sure of that."

Then, putting the volume back in its place, she seized Transparent by the hair again and took her back into the cavern.

"Speak now, wretched creature, speak, and finish piercing my heart."

Transparent, utterly distressed and in an indescribable state, told her in a very disorderly fashion what had happened, and swore by the fay herself that Roseate was still at the queen's court."

"You've only shown me a big book, Madame," she added, "and I saw the princess in the gardens yesterday with my own eyes. It's true that she was veiled, as she almost always has been since Prince Muguet has been at the court, but I can't doubt that it was her, in spite of your power and our enchantments."

"Ah! You're still talking nonsense," said the fay, who was slightly reassured regarding Muguet's life by the details she had been given. "Wait for me here and you'll see what I can do." So saying, she touched Transparent with her wand, and she became an ugly she-monkey, like the vile creature she was. Chaining her up in her library, the fay said to her: "Guard Roseate well; she won't escape you." And without looking at her, or saying anything further, she struck the vault of the library with her wand, which split, and Sempiternelle, astride her wand, which was transformed into a huge black dragon covered with yellow scales, launched herself through the opening and disappeared.

Transparent was in such a terrible state that she had not yet had time to become aware of her metamorphosis; the departure of the fay returned her to herself—which is to say that the horror of her situation was depicted in her soul in the blackest colors. She could not speak, which redoubled her dolor, for plaints at least soothe the unfortunate; she shed torrents of tears; but her naturally base and cruel soul did not lead her to repent of the woes she had caused; on the contrary, she only formed projects for the blackest vengeance, in case she ever resumed her form. That served to console her; she ate some walnuts and drank water courageously; that rendered force to her fury.

She gnawed her chain, but she could not contrive to detach herself. In the end, she went to sleep.

Transparent had already been in the cavern for twenty-four hours when, thinking about her sad adventure the following morning, supporting her head on her hand, she saw a young man enter the abode, fully armed, with only his head uncovered, allowing the sight of a face so handsome and so noble that the sentiments of fury by which she was agitated were suspended, to give way to those of the greatest admiration,

"Is there no one here," exclaimed the stranger, "who can tell me where I am?"

The great silence that reigned in the cavern augmented his astonishment. The she-monkey got up and bowed him, bumping her forehead on the ground; then, sitting down facing him, she gave indications of a great surprise.

Struck by that spectacle, the stranger bowed to the monkey, and, finding her amusing, gave her a few chestnuts that he had in his pocket. She took them very politely and make him understand that she was the sole mistress of the place. He caressed her, and she allowed herself to be stroked.

He scanned the bookcase, astonished to find such a beautiful and well-organized one in such a savage place; he imagined that it was the dwelling of a sage, and that the monkey was one of his amusements. As he was weary, he wanted to choose a book before going to sleep, of which he had great need. He searched, and the roseate folio struck his eyes, all the more so because he saw the title in capital letters, which traced the name of the person for whom he was searching.

As few people will have doubted, you will conclude from that urgency that it was the handsome Prince Celadon.

"Let's read this beautiful book," he said, aloud. Carried away by an unfamiliar impulse, he did indeed take it from its place, whereupon the monkey made excessive cries, rolling on the ground and bathing it with her tears.

The astonished prince turned round, and thought that the monkey had burned herself with the chestnuts he had give her. He approached her; she tugged at his coat and showed that she wanted the book he was holding. Being unable to take possession of it, though, she wept and sobbed. That astonished the prince; he gave her some sugared almonds, but she refused them and appeared to want the book. That combat lasted for some time.

In the end, the prince, no longer amused, freed himself from the monkey and went to sit down at the back of the library in spite of her cries, on a sofa facing a table, where he put the book down in order to open it. The monkey, in a suppliant posture, tried to stop him, but, as the prince was no longer paying any heed to her, she ceased her cries and set about examining what he was about to do.

Seeing her tranquil, he opened the book, and soon ceased to think about the wretched animal when he read the first words:

I am Princess Roseate, the daughter of the fortunate king and the beloved queen. I was born in the Realm of Cedars.

"O Heaven!" cried Celadon. "Is it my charming princess, then, who has written this story? What sweeter occupation can I have in this abode than to read things that will entertain me faithfully?"

Having said that, he scanned what followed avidly, curious to learn whether it might indicate where she was.

The smallest circumstances of her childhood were depicted there; he did not reproach her for puerility, so much are even the faults of those one loves veiled by amour. Eventually, he reached her departure for the dwelling of the Fay of the Green Oaks; that interested him more. The encounter she had had with a young woman in whom he could not help recognizing himself, the movements that were stimulated in her heart, the tender interest that she had taken in her, the faithful memory that she had retained of her, the desire to see her again, the torment of being apart from her, and the anxiety that she might never see her again, were all painted there in such naïve colors that the prince was dying of pleasure in finding her so sensitive, and of dolor and impatience at not yet being able to tell her that she had not found an ingrate. However, he was tormented by the fact that she still believed him to be a girl, like herself.

If some lover, he thought, could be fortunate enough to please her, *she would forget the girl she encountered by chance, and amity would give way to amour, for, judging by the tenderness of her style, I'm much mistaken if her soul isn't made to feel with all possible delicacy.*

"Oh woe!" he exclaimed. "Might she already be loved, and will these sentiments of which she made a trial for me, perhaps become more perfect for another?"

The prince fell silent then, and could not help shedding a few tears, while it seemed to him that someone nearby sighed, and that the sigh departed from the book. That surprised him. He lifted the book up, looked at the top and underneath the table. He saw nothing, was ashamed of his weakness, put it back on the table, and continued reading.

Another anxiety seized him; he feared that his reading might finish too soon. He scanned the book, and saw that almost all of the pages were blank, and that what had been written only filled ten or twelve pages. He had already seen half of them.

"Alas," he said, "I'm seeking urgently to read this work; am I soon going t repent of it? Perhaps her heart will change its object."

There was another sigh; he was alarmed by it, but the desire to read prevailed over a fear for which he reproached himself and which he soon mastered.

What pleasure did he not feel when he came to the war that the Fay of the Green Oaks and Lucinette had waged against the princess over her obstinacy in conserving too tender a memory of the unknown young woman? She had only soothed her ennui by depicting it with an infinite skill; but where he nearly died of joy was when he came to the place where she described in detail what happened in her heart when she imagined dressing him as a man in the little miniature that she had just finished.

Never, said the book at that point, *has anyone felt as much pleasure as I had in having grasped that imagination; it seemed to me, though, that I had to think of it; that is the only adornment that suits her perfectly. I said, and it seems to me that I have even more pleasure in gazing at her. How beautiful she was as I saw her! But how much more beautiful with her hair curling over her shoulders, floating over that light armor! Oh, if I ever see her again, I shall beg her to dress like that; it seems to me that I would love her more—but no, I believe that one can't love any more than I do; and that amity is forbidden to me! Oh, that's because they believe that I'm incapable of feeling it. What is it, then, to love very tenderly, if it isn't what I feel? For myself, I believe that the fay and Lucinette are mistaken in speaking to me thus; they believe me to be a child, but I sense clearly that when I'm fifteen I won't love any better, and that, for instance, I won't love like this the Prince Muguet that is destined for me.*

Celadon was dying, expiring of pleasure; he reread that passage a hundred times; he weighed every word; he always found new charms therein. He spoke aloud, and the monkey listened to him, and would have thought that his mind was somewhat troubled if she had not thought that Roseate might well have turned the young man's head, since she had already turned Muguet's.

"Adorable, charming and excessively lovable Roseate," he cried, in his transports. "Enjoy the amour with which you embellish your lover! What, you love me! What, my beautiful princess, you said it so tenderly, and I could not hear you when, burning with amour, I dreaded that you might be insensible? It's you who are informing me of my good fortune. O Fate, I defy you at present, and since my princess deigns to receive my tenderness...but alas, it's only as to a girl that she is addressing her discourse, and perhaps she won't love me any longer under my veritable form."

Ingenious in tormenting himself, he afflicted himself as immoderately with that dread as he had shown transports in his hope.

"Let's finish it," he said. "Let's see what I ought to expect, or where I ought to search for her."

He saw the taking of the portrait by the governess, the ring that she was given, and the story ended.

What dolor did he not feel at that moment!

"Where is she, then?" he said. "And how can I discover what has become of her?"

He left the book open on the table, walked around, came back, leafed through it, reread a few passages as if he were seeing them for the first time; his desire to sleep had passed very quickly, there was no longer anything but a question:

"Where are you?" he cried. "Where can I search for you?"

Finally, after racking his brains for a long time, he thought, on chancing to cast his eyes upon the she-monkey, that she was gazing at him tenderly.

His heart agitated, he was troubled; he approached her; she extended her hand to him; he fell to his knees and kissed that hand, which was abandoned to him, with transport.

Is that you?" he cried, in a feeble and tremulous voice. "Are you my dear princess, whom I see under this cruel form? Aid my heart to recognize you, receive the confession of my tenderness, and reassure my timid amour, which dare not appear to your eyes without being sure that you approve it?

The she-monkey, delighted to have found a means of forgetting the fickle Muguet and stealing another lover from Roseate, of whom she believed that she had a great deal to complain, left the prince in his error and tried by means of her facial expressions, sometimes embarrassed and sometimes caressant, to make him believe that she approved or disdained the amour of Prince Celadon.

"Oh, it's you, I no longer doubt it," he said to her. "How ungrateful I am not to have recognized you! Will you pardon me, my beautiful princess? At least you have been witness that I could only talk about you while I sought to penetrate the mystery of your metamorphosis. But let's quit this place; come on the faith of your lover and your husband, if you deign to accept him as such. Come to the home of the king, your father, who has already heaped my with the most flattering hopes if I were fortunate enough to find you. Come, beautiful princess; there you will be as free as you wish, and if your heart refuses me the charming prize that has been promised to me, I shall not reproach you, happy and only too happy to die in serving you."

At these words, the she-monkey adopted an expression of tenderness, which nearly made the amorous prince die of joy. She deigned to squeeze his hand, and showed him a box that was on the top of the bookcase. She made him understand that the key to her padlock was there. The prince flew and climbed with an infinite skill to aid in the liberation of his princess. In fact, he took a little golden key out of the box that the monkey had shown him and opened the padlock easily.

The delighted she-monkey performed leaps and bounds, which astonished the prince, who dared not approach for fear of lacking the respect that he believed that he owed her. He was surprised by that behavior, but he thought that the simian actions that she was making might originate from her metamorphosis rather than the aberration of her mind.

Finally, after having leapt abundantly, she went to the beautiful roseate morocco book, opened it, and tore out the first age. It emerged from the book with a scream of pain, and in a moment, it was covered with blood.

"What a prodigy!" cried the prince. "By what horror am I surprised?"

He took the book from the hands of the monkey and looked to see where what he had seen and heard could have come from. He even tried to replace the page, but he could not do it; the blood that was still dripping from it chilled him with a certain horror, the cause of which he could not divine. He occupied himself involuntarily with that event, and left the monkey, which was pestering him in order to turn him away from it.

Finally, pale and trembling, he turned toward her. "Don't be offended, my beautiful princess, if I give my pity to the object you see. I don't know what this frightful prodigy signifies, but I can't help interesting myself in it, and even if there's a power here that is hostile to me, I can't refuse it my compassion. It has told me who you are and what I owe you, even if it is contrary, I feel that I ought to serve it. Don't oppose the desire that I have to take it with me. You're no talking to me! And I can tell you in return for this aid…"

At those words the monkey threw herself on the ground and rolled around there with marks of excessive dolor; she filled the cavern with her screams.

The prince, surprised, quit the book in order to run to the aid of the pretended princess; he dared to take her in his arms; she became plaintive, and leaned her head negligently on his shoulder. He believed himself to be the most fortunate of all lovers; he would not have been moved if the most beautiful eyes in the world had gazed at him at that moment; he would not have traded them for the simian eyes that were looking at him askance.

"What have I done, then?" he said tenderly. "What have I done, what have I said that could displease you? Alas, it's in order to occupy myself eternally with you that I dare to desire to take away what speaks to me about that so obligingly. I won't take it away, I promise you."

The monkey passed her knavish arms around his neck at that promise. He was transported; he did not know what he was doing. He took the monkey and sat her down on the sofa; he knelt down before her, kissed her feet and, respectfully, the tip of her tail. He was beside himself.

Finally, the monkey leapt down and pulled him, to tell him to leave the cavern. He wanted before then to put the book back in its place; again, she thought that he wanted to take it with him and bit his leg so forcefully that he dropped the book on top of the little golden key that had just liberated the malevolent monkey.

He soon forgot his pain in order to direct all his attention to a faint and soft little voice that emerged from the book, and which said: "I am Princess Roseate, daughter of the fortunate king...," and everything that he had read thereafter.

The charm of that voice stopped him again, but the monkey, more furious than ever, threw herself upon the book in order to tear it to pieces. The prince dared to sop her, at the expense of his hands, which were bitten and scratched, but he saved it from the monkey's claws regardless, and the book, removed from the golden key, no longer spoke; it only uttered a little groan when the prince put it back on the shelf; and the evil monkey gamboled more excitedly, and tugged the prince so much that he finally left the cavern, and she leapt on the saddle of his horse before he could do so, to give him the example.

He mounted up after her, and, having picked her up gently, he placed her in front of him. She manifested a joy that compensated him for everything that he had just suffered; he believed himself to be perfectly happy at that moment, and his fate seemed to him to be worthy of envy.

He clasped the monkey in his arms; she returned his caresses, but he could not help finding his beautiful princess unjust for having prevented him from taking away that beautiful book. The soft and tender voice that had emerged from it pierced his heart with darts so touching that he did not dare approve them, nor seek the reasons for them. In the bosom of felicity he reproached himself for his ingratitude and in order to be in accord with himself he called the sentiment pity that was nothing less.

He searched his mind for what could have made his princess so angry against that unfortunate book. If it were the enchanter or the fay who had reduced her to the condition she was in, he said to himself, it seems to me that she could have avenged herself more nobly; and why, if it really is that persecutor, why take that form and borrow the name of Roseate?

He tried to ask the monkey a few questions, but she moved her head to signify yes or no. in accordance with the occasion, or appeared not to want to say anything. The prince, who feared offending her, no longer said anything, and contented himself with enjoying his present happiness, without daring to deliver himself to reflections that made him sense the harshness of which he accused himself in spite of his princess.

They traveled for several days; finally, they arrived in the vicinity of a river that separated the Realm of Cedars from that of Aquamarines, which was that of his father. When the monkey saw that he was allowing his horse to advance toward the bridge, she tugged the bridle and made it turn toward the Realm of Aquamarines.

"What are you doing, my beautiful princess?" he said. "Don't you want me to take you to your mother, the queen? What you rather go to the home of mine?" The monkey nodded affirmatively, and, without saying another word, the prince took that route.

The monkey, who had thus far only been occupied with her affairs, and who feared being taken to the queen of the Realm of Cedars, seeing herself about to be in repose, hidden in the home of the Queen of Aquamarines, recovered all her gaiety and began to find the prince sufficiently to her liking; his conduct, his respectful and tender protestations, the naïve character of his tenderness, and above all, his young and pretty face, tempted her to render to Prince Muguet, by means of a

155

good and veritable infidelity, the million coquetries that he had made her. She only found that Celadon was too sage for his age, and, enraged by being unable to talk, she decided in her tiny brain to make him enticements.

She did not reflect that that might cause him to fail to recognize Roseate, whose character he was convinced that she filled perfectly. But is an old coquette able to reflect? She began by making eyes at the prince, and, remembering that she had already put him beside himself by leaving her ugly head on his shoulder in the cavern, she tipped it back with all her might against his stomach in order to look at him.

The prince, as sensitive as one can be with a great deal of intelligence, found that attitude charming, but he dared not lend himself to what it appeared to signify, and was withdrawing gently for fear of wounding her, when, taking his hands in her furry paws, she squeezed them very tenderly. He thought that it might offend her to resist caresses so forceful, believing them to be merely tender; he marked his gratitude for them with words so passionate that the vile creature redoubled her efforts.

Celadon was surprised by that; he was astonished that the beautiful and virtuous Roseate could forget in a moment everything that he had seen of restraint in reading her history. He could not accord the combats that she had rendered for a simple amity for which she had been reproached with the indecent expressions that she was making to someone of whose sex she was now aware. What astonished him even more was the coldness with which he received all her advances.

Can it be, he said to himself, *that what I have been told is true, that the excess of happiness approaches distaste so closely? What, the charming Roseate, whom I desired so much, inspires nothing tender in me? As she senses it herself, I am drawing away; men are incomprehensible; can ideas alone render them perfectly happy? Is one never really happy, then?*

He was at that point in is reflections when a fully armed knight appeared before him, coming toward the place where

156

the prince was. The knight's face was hidden by the visor of his helmet, but the prince only had a small morion on his head, which left his face uncovered.

As he approached the prince and the monkey, the unknown knight threw his lance to the ground and, leaping down promptly himself, he stopped he bridle of Prince Celadon's horse respectfully, put one knee of the ground and cried: "Just gods, favorable gods, you are finally returning the beautiful, charming and beloved Roseate to me! Beautiful and adorable princess, suffer that your lover gives himself to you forever and that I guide your strayed steps to the cavern of my cousin, the fay Sempiternelle!"

By those words, Celadon recognized Prince Muguet, and knew in parallel that he was also in the error of mistaking him for Princes Roseate. He smiled scornfully, but finally he spoke.

"Prince Muguet," he said to him, "I know you, but you do not know me. Like you, I love Princess Roseate, and I have the advantage over you of being sure of the approval of the King and Queen of Cedars. However, if you want to combat before her eyes, in order to discover which of us merits the preference, I won't refuse to measure my sword against yours. You can take the field and we'll fight right away."

Muguet—for it really was him—had stood up, and listened with astonishment to the speech made by the divine person whom he still believed to be the princess.

"Do you believe, then, beautiful Princess, that my heart can be abused, as my eyes could be, by your attire? And have you not revealed yourself by proposing an immediate combat before Roseate's eyes? No, I won't consent to draw my sword against the person to whom I want to render it; dispose of my days and don't risk yours by a mockery of which a rival, and not my princess, might easily repent."

Prince Celadon, genuinely angered by Muguet's obstinacy, placed the she-monkey gently on the saddle of his horse and dismounted in order to fight his enemy. He approached him, sword in hand. "Defend yourself," he said, "and don't

157

make me waste time in vain discourse that we could employ better. I am not Roseate; there she is"—he indicated the monkey, who, sitting on the saddle, was looking with a malicious eye to see what might happen in that combat, only taking a rather mediocre interest in it. "Yes, Celadon went on, "that's her, whom a cruel fay has apparently metamorphosed this, and I am your rival, who adores that beautiful princess, and who wants to merit her by your defeat and that of all those who, like you, recklessly dare to pretend to her."

Muguet, astonished, looked at the young hero from head to toe; he did in fact, doubt that it was his princess, not by virtue of his extreme beauty, but by virtue of his tall stature and the sound of his voice, which was too strong and masculine for a young princess.

He lowered the point of his sword and approached the prince. "Since I'm mistaken," he said, "it's at least necessary that the princess assures me of what you say. Permit me to take her attachment in order to combat, and afterwards you'll see whether I can defend myself."

The prince was too frank and too generous to oppose a request that seemed just; he only replied by drawing away slightly, in order to allow the monkey the liberty to explain her sentiments, but he was quite astonished to see Muguet, who was as cowardly as he had thought him honest, mount his horse, embrace the monkey and depart like lightning.

Celadon could scarcely believe what he saw, but, not wasting time in complaints that the wind would have carried away, transported by a just fury, he went in search of Muguet's horse, which was grazing in the meadow where they were. Mounting it precipitately, he tried to run after the unworthy kidnapper, but, either because the fay Sempiternelle was protecting her cousin or because the horse really was too weary—which is more credible—whatever he did, after covering a distance of about a thousand paces, fell, and threw the prince into a deep river, where they both fell to the bottom.

If Celadon regretted the life that he believed that he was losing at that moment, it was not in regard to himself; the idea of not being able to deliver Princess Roseate from the hands of a cowardly rival who had snatched her from him so unworthily gave him such an excess of fury that he did not lose consciousness, and, ridding himself of his horse adroitly, he fell on to the sand.

The water, which was strong and rapid at that point, carried him all the way to the sea, where he continued descending, and found himself, after falling into a profound abyss, near to a huge rock, above which all the waters seemed to be suspended, forming a blue-green sky, slightly gloomy, but which allowed the assistance of a mild sunlight to penetrate, and yet was warm enough to be able to relieve the extreme cold by which he was gripped.

He sat down on a green moss that covered the sea-bed, and there he contemplated with astonishment the extraordinary sky that appeared above him. Several ships passed by; he even saw a naval combat. Occupied as he was with the misfortunes of his princess, he could not help taking pleasure in it; the sound of the artillery resembled a violent thunder; the dead and the dying did not fall as far as him; great marine monsters that were swimming in the fluid sky that surrounded the region into which he had fallen devoured the bodies. They appeared as brilliant comets, which, illuminated by the sunlight, allowed stars to be seen in broad daylight—and perhaps that is where the proverb comes from, for those living meteors astonished him greatly.

His clothes were dry, and when he had rested for a while he stood up, and directed his steps toward the rock that he saw a hundred paces away. He took it for the dwelling of Amphitrite, so elegant was it; the doors were made of coral inlaid with mother-of-pearl, and the entire rock was a single pearl, so huge, and hollowed out with such artistry that it contained a huge hall, a bedroom, and three cabinets large enough to make comfortable lodgings; but that magnificent habitation, ornamented with all the most precious rarities that the sea can furnish, and all that the most expert art and the most exquisite taste can enable the human mind invent and imagine, was nothing by comparison with the magnificent statue that was in the middle of the drawing rom. It was a representation of Thetis, in a single piece of rock crystal, set on a pedestal of gold and precious stones of all colors, in festoons that responded to the similar ornaments of the drawing room, the agreeable variety of which, combined with the most sublime art, formed festoons of natural flowers, and delighted the sight while surprising it.

The statue of Thetis represented that goddess at the moment when she was receiving the god of the day in her bosom; she was semi-recumbent; her beautiful arms were open, and her eyes were gazing amorously at the luminous god, whom a equal tenderness was forcing to descend into the depths of the water in order to enjoy his happiness. The god was made of the same crystal, so clear and so pure that he seemed to be illuminating that beautiful drawing room.

That masterpiece attracted the prince's gaze for a long time; he admired it as a connoisseur.

"Divinity of this beautiful place," he said, "receive my homage, and aid me against the frightful destiny that is pursuing me." He prostrated himself as he pronounced those words, and kissed the nacre of the pearls that served the drawing room as a parquet.

Three nymphs, all of whose skin was celestial blue, clad very lightly in silver gauze, and three marine gods as green as the nymphs were blue, with girdles of gladioli and pearls and breastplates of silver embroidery, came to take him, without him daring to defend himself, and took him into one of the cabinets of the grotto. Having lain him down gently on a little bed of moss ornamented by pebbles and pearls, they sat down in a circle around him, and listened in silence to what he was going to say.

The prince, naturally courageous, was not frightened by that ceremony, and finding himself sufficiently at ease on his bed, raised himself up slightly. Leaning on his elbow, he ran his eyes over the extraordinary assembly for some time. The three nymphs with blue faces were all beautiful, and the marine gods, although green, had charms in their stature and faces that made them look better than can be imagined.

"Beautiful nymphs," he said, "and gods, the unfortunate Celadon..."

At those words, the nymphs left without listening to him, and closed the doors on him. Surprised by their departure, the prince judged that his name had alarmed them, but as he had other things to think about than seeking a more plausible reason, he forgot it in order to deliver himself to the cruelty of his fate.

While we leave him prey to his bitter reflections, let us return to the land to see what the she-monkey, Princess Roseate and the fay Sempiternelle are ding, the fay having returned to her grotto an hour after Prince Celadon and the monkey had left.

To try to represent the astonishment of the old fay would be to presume too much of oneself. Her abducted monkey only occupied her at that moment because she had lost an object of vengeance. She ran to her bookcase and took down the beautiful book with the roseate morocco binding joyfully, having been fearful that it might have been taken away. She saw the torn page and the blood that was still leaking from it. With a spoken word the damage was repaired; it was only a corner. She leafed through it in order to see what had happened, and read with a malign joy the tender regrets of the beautiful princess regarding the prince's mistake and the pleasure that she had felt in spite of her metamorphosis, in seeing the charming object that had occupied her since her first encounter, and in knowing all the tenderness that she had for him, without being able to defend herself against the amour that she had felt under the name of amity. She described her sentiments with so much modesty that, for the first time in her life, the implacable Sempiternelle conceived the pity that unfortunate virtue inspires.

"Destiny," she proclaimed, in a hoarse voice, "is forcing me to punish you, but I hope that this sensibility, which is new to me, does not last, for in order to get out of it, it is only necessary for me to remember that you are the cause of my nephew's wounds."

The beautiful book sighed, and rendered a few plants punctuated by sobs.

"I give you," said the fay, moved again by what she had heard, "the gift of speech. Speak, and no longer write; that will also save me a good deal of difficulty."

Then the soft voice of the princess thanked her, and asked her how it was possible that she could be culpable of Prince Muguet's wounds, whom she did not know and had never seen."

The fay was happy to explain, and was finishing the story when the Fay of the Green Oaks arrived in the grotto and interrupted the conversation.

On seeing her, Sempiternelle resume her unjust anger against the princess. Closing the book abruptly, she went to meet the fay, who embraced her and came to sit down with her on the sofa from which she had got up, near the table where the beautiful roseate book as placed.

"I haven't come here, my sister," said the amiable fay, "to complain about the injustice that you did me in abducting Roseate, whom I was guarding with so much care; she has submitted to her destiny in yielding to an involuntary passion, and has been culpable in abandoning herself to it. You have doubtless punished her; she merits that; but I have come to ask you for mercy on her behalf and to see what we can do to restore calm to two realms that are overwhelmed by dolor, one by the loss of a unique heir and the other by that of Princes Roseate, whose destiny I don't know myself. As for Prince Celadon, you know that he has been drowned while pursuing your nephew, Prince Muguet."

At that news, the beautiful roseate book uttered a dolorous cry, and became as white as snow. The Fay of the Green Oaks was surprised by that and, less by her science than her sentiment, she divined that the princess for whom she had been searching with so much care was hidden under that appearance.

"Oh, my sister," she said, taking the book in her arms, "this, then, is the effect of your vengeance. I have no doubt that I'm holding Princess Roseate."

Sempiternelle smiled, showing teeth like the tusks of a wild boar. "Yes," she said to the fay, "I confess it to you now that the unfortunate Celadon is dead. That is your princess, and I even return her to you, since I no longer fear that she will resist the amour of my nephew. I'll restore her form, but take her with you, for I don't want to be witness to her wailing, and above all, render her pliable to my desires; if she resists them, I'll recapture her."

"Oh, my sister," said the Fay of the Green Oaks, "hurry up and return her form, in order that we can help her, for I believe that she's already ready to die, and in no state to oppose your will."

Sempiternelle touched the book with her wand; it immediately became the beautiful but dying Roseate, and her pallor was already imprinting the horror of death on her beautiful face.

The Fay of the Green Oaks hugged her tenderly in her arms, moved to compassion by that dolorous state, and without losing any more time, took her to her elephant, which was waiting at the door. Then, embracing Sempiternelle, she left, and arrived in very little time at her palace, where she hastened to help the princess.

After an hour she opened her eyes, and parading them languidly over the objects that presented themselves to her sight, she recognized the favorable Fay and her dwelling.

"Oh, Madame," she said, striving to kiss her hand, "how cruel your pity is to me! Why not let me die, since I have lost the object that rendered me woes so mild."

Her sobs and tears prevented her from saying any more. The fay embraced her and told her that the object who rendered her so sensitive was still alive, but that she was holding him captive herself in order to avoid greater misfortunes.

As the fay spoke, the beautiful eyes of the princess were animated by a new joy; they burned with a fire so bright that the fay, delighted to see her so beautiful, promised to render her happy if her lover merited so much amour.

The princess, who found herself cured of all her ills by what she had just heard had thrown herself at the fay's knees and was kissing her hands with the gratitude of which great hearts are capable.

"May I not see him, then, Madame?" she said to the fay. "Are you condemning me to the torture of knowing that he is a prisoner without being able to tell him that you permit me to love him?"

"No," said the fay, "I cannot show you to him before your fifteenth year; if, however, in that time, he conserves his tenderness for you, I will unite the two of you, but it is necessary to test him beforehand, and here. Is your bouquet of diamond roses, which I'm returning to you, in order that you can judge for yourself whether your lover merits your love; keep it carefully and remain here. I'll inform the queen, your mother, of your return here, and try to suspend the impatience she is in to have news of you. Don't leave this forest; walk in it, take care of my glow-worms and command them to do whatever you please; they will obey you."

After that, the fay embraced the princess and departed on her elephant to go and find the Queen of Cedars.

We left Prince Muguet some time ago. taking away the she-monkey whom he believed to be his divine princess. The cowardly and low trick that he thought he had played on his unfortunate rival delighted him, and the wicked monkey, delighted to be free of the irons of Sempiternelle, scarcely cared what it had cost Prince Celadon, amorous as she was, since she found herself within range of avenging herself on the infidel Muguet. She was only enraged by being unable to talk, in order to be even better able to deceive him, but she spared nothing in order to try to render him even more amorous.

They arrived in a large city that neither of them knew, whose inhabitants, astonished to see such a well-armed man alone with a monkey, took the horse by the bridle and led it to the palace of their king who was very sad, as was his wife, hoping that the stranger might be able to give them some news of the heir to the kingdom, who had been lost for some time. Prince Muguet did not oppose that ceremony, hearing it said that it was the custom of the land. He dismounted in the palace courtyard, and, holding the monkey by the hand, went into the Audience Hall, where the king and the queen arrived rapidly in order to discover what he could tell them.

"Well, sage stranger," said the king, "have you come to tell us what has become of the child, our only son? Or can you confirm for us a death that we are already mourning, and will mourn as long as we live?"

"Sire," said Prince Muguet, "I have no knowledge of the child about whom you do me the kindness of speaking. I do not know him, and I will not renew the dolor that you have by the confirmation of a death, which I hope is not certain."

During that august conversation, no one had noticed that the monkey had escaped, and, seizing the quill that he king's chancellor was holding in order to write whatever it pleased Their Majesties to order him, she had sat down facing him and was writing on a piece of paper.

Meanwhile, the king continued to interrogate the prince. When the monkey had finished writing, she returned the quill to the chancellor, who was swooning with laughter, but dared not but let it burst forth, in view of the serious things that his royal master was saying. She advanced to the foot of the throne and, making a reverence in the fashion of the country, which was to prostrate oneself, she climbed the three steps lightly and put the paper she was holding in the hands of the king.

Although very astonished, he took it, but he had no sooner read the first words than he threw himself to the base of his throne and embraced the monkey, which he took and placed on the knees of his wife, the queen.

"This is your niece, Madame," he said. "this is Princess Roseate. We shall learn, in consequence of what she has written, news of our son, Prince Celadon."

The queen made the monkey a thousand caresses, which were returned well. That had caused a great tumult in the hall. The king's ministers came to see the princess, and she gave them her paw to kiss, very seriously.

Finally, the king called for silence in order to read aloud what the monkey had written. She said that, having been enchanted in the cavern of old Sempiternelle, the handsome Prince Celadon had delivered her from captivity, and that, on the point of entering the Kingdom of Aquamarines, they had encountered Prince Muguet, here present, who, using a base and cruel trick, had stolen her from the arms of that prince and had fled with her all the way to this kingdom, to which destiny had bought him in order to punish him for his crime. She added that Prince Celadon must be still alive, and that she had left him wandering some twenty leagues from the capital.

The King of Aquamarines, inflamed by a just wrath against Prince Muguet, but not wanting to treat him as an ordinary prisoner, contented himself, after having made him admit the fact—except for denying that he had known the prince for that of Aquamarines—with having him taken to an apartment in the palace, where he would be kept under guard until Prince Celadon was found.

The she-monkey was served as a princess, praised, caressed and admired, and the queen did not want her to have any other apartment than her own. The nasty beast was triumphant in her malice; she had avenged herself on the prince who had betrayed her and she had deceived the king and the queen, who could not do enough for her. Meanwhile people were sent in all directions to search for the prince. Then a courier was sent to the Queen of Cedars to tell her not to be anxious about her daughter, who was safe.

The wicked monkey did not want any mention to be made of her metamorphosis, for fear of consequences; she made it understood that it was necessary to spare the Queen of

Cedars chagrin. She was praised for her good heart, and people loved her more for it, but her malice rebounded on her, as was only just.

The courier from the Queen of Aquamarines arrived at the court of Cedars as the Fay of the Green Oaks had just left, having informed the queen of her daughter's adventures and having told her that she was in her power. The queen thought at first that her sister had been correctly informed about her daughter's retreat, but, having found that idea implausible, she went to see the fay, in order make her party to the news she had received from the court of Aquamarines.

She found her occupied in consoling the young Roseate for the despair she was experiencing after seeing her roses so faded that they no longer conserved any color. During the absence of the Fay of the Green Oaks she had taken care of the glow-worms, but that occupation had not always been an amusement for her. They had had an order to obey her without question whatever she commanded them to do; she was so beautiful and so mild that they had taken pleasure in being submissive to her.

"Paint me," she had ordered one day, "the prince who loves me." She had not dared to say "the man I love," being too sage even to admit that to glow-worms. "Paint him for me, she said, therefore, "and show me what he is doing."

It is true that she already had some anxiety about that, because her bouquet was beginning to fade.

The glow-worms obeyed her immediately. First they amassed in a group of prodigious size; then they formed a luminous temple, in which some of them represented an altar, and on the steps of that altar, two individuals with crowns and royal mantles, who were holding hands; and it seemed, at that moment, that the one who received the hand of the one who represented the princess bent over to kiss it with a very eager and very tender action.

Then she saw the two individuals emerge from the temple, but, not being able to distinguish the features of the individuals, because the skill of the glow-worms had not gone as far as being able to depict them precisely, she concentrated on considering her rival, who appeared to her to be very small; she judged that it was the she-monkey she had seen in Sempiternelle's cavern.

She was already inclining toward excusing her lover, for she imagined that he might be deceived, as he had been deceived in the cavern, but she did not have that slight satisfaction for long; her eyes fixed upon her bouquet, she saw it so faded and so discolored that she could not doubt the inconstancy of her lover; she uttered dolorous cries, and, not being able to sustain the odious spectacle any longer, she left the place where the glow-worms has assembled in order to please her. They ceased immediately and ran after her to help her.

"Don't listen to me any longer," she said to them. "Stop obeying me; you're punishing my indiscreet curiosity too cruelly. What have I done to you for you to afflict me so dolorously?"

She wept bitterly in making them that reproach. They were all consternated by her dolor; they lost their light for an hour. The beautiful princess did not perceive it, so occupied was she with her chagrin.

"Ingrate! Infidel!" she cried. "He has forgotten me, and has not left my heart the pleasure of justifying him! Oh, why did I desire to see him? Why seek a woe that was nothing so long as I was able to be unaware of it? But rather, why are you feeble and unhappy, Roseate? Why occupy myself with him again when he merits it so little?"

The poor glow-worms sobbed with her, and despaired of being unable to give her any other evidence of sensibility. She finally perceived their dolor, for she knew that their obscurity was the great proof of their chagrin.

"My little friends," she said to them, "pardon me for my unjust reproaches. Alas, if you knew amour, you would excuse me easily. Console yourselves, and let me die of the shame of still being too sensitive to an ingrate whom I ought to hare. But can one love and hate at one's whim? Oh, barbaric

Sempiternelle, it's you who are the cause of all my woes. Perhaps, without you, that infidel lover would still be worthy of all that I have felt of torments while I was distant from him."

The Fay of the Green Oaks arrived at that moment, and the desolate princess told her the subject of her tears.

"If these are the woes that were predicted for me at my birth, Madame," she said, "that terrible prediction is accomplished in every point. I feel strongly that I shall die of it, and my shame is so cruel that it is sufficient to take my life, without combining it with the reproach of an unfortunate weakness that it is impossible for me to overcome."

The fay was very embarrassed. Whatever superiority she had over Sempiternelle, she could not verify that event, being unable to undo what another fay had done.

"My dear child," she said to the princess, "it is necessary to live to cure a malady that only has its source in your determination to conserve it. Rise above that weakness; to be able to do anything, it is only necessary to wish it. Live, my dear Roseate; it is adding to your shame to give in to it. Amour is not the stronger when one really wants to resist it; you want it, undoubtedly. Forget the person who has forgotten you; scorn is the only sentiment that ought to remain to you, and I expect a generous effort from you, worthy of you and of your courage. I will aid your heart to recover its virtue with all my power."

The beautiful princes lowered her eyes at that advice, and her cheeks, covered with a vivid blush, allowed the fay to comprehend all the disturbance that reigned in her heart.

Finally, she raised her beautiful eyes again, and posed their gaze timidly on the fay. "I sense, Madame, all the force of your arguments," she said to her, "but can a heart so long accustomed to the hope of being loved, and the certainty of being loved by an object one has believed to be solely worthy of pleasing, lose sentiments that have given it so much joy without a superhuman violence? I know that I ought not to think about that prince and longer. He has pledged his faith; I can no longer be his; but my virtue is very feeble against the despair that reflection inspires in me. His death, dare I say it, would seem less cruel to me; at least the consolation of following him, and having nothing for which to reproach him; but..."

At those words, the tender Roseate, seized by a surge of dolor of which she was not the mistress, fell almost unconscious at the feet of the fay, who could not refuse her help and her tears to the deplorable state of the young princess. She helped her, and was occupied for two days in consoling her and recalling her courage.

They were together when the Queen of Cedars arrives. Although she was delighted to see her daughter she was penetrated by dolor by her condition.

The princess suspended her dolor momentarily in order to deliver herself to the queen's caresses; the latter was informed of the subject of her plaints, and the queen and the fay were very embarrassed to disentangle the knot of that black treason.

While the princess was taking a little rest, the fay and the queen discussed the matter; they judged that it was a trick on the part of old Sempiternelle. "I am so irritated against the prince," the fay said to the queen, "that I do not want to clarify even the least of the facts regarding him. What! Without seeing me, without informing me of his designs, he marries the person given to him, and he remains tranquil?"

"But Madame," said the queen, "it seems to me to be very difficult for Celadon to have been able to escape from the prison of the sea where you confined him without help as powerful as yours, and I believe that he has been deceived in order to force him to marry someone other than my daughter. Before delivering yourself to the wrath he merits, let us please clarify this adventure, and if he is guilty, I consent to your punishing him thereafter with all your rigor; but let us not precipitate anything before having talked to him."

The Fay of the Green Oaks, who was very reasonable, agreed with what the queen said; she recommended her to remain with Roseate until she returned, and, mounting her bronze elephant, she departed like lightning to go to the sea shore.

Whatever diligence she made, she only arrived there at nightfall. She left the elephant on the shore and descended into the prince's profound abode.

When she arrived, the three blue nymphs and the three green marine gods lit torches and conducted her to the grotto of pearls, where the prince was already in bed. The nymphs drew the curtain of his alcove. He was profoundly asleep, and the frightful she-monkey was lying beside him, sleeping as soundly as him.

At that sight the fay uttered a cry of surprise, which woke the two spouses. The monkey, who was enjoying the fruits of her malice, reacted with sufficient arrogance to the noise that had been made, and demanded to know why she had been woken this. As for the prince, who recognized the fay, having seen her several times at his father's court, he sat up on his bed and begged the fay to end his torture by rendering his beautiful princess the form that she had previously had.

"Wretch," said the fay, "I've come, on the contrary, to augment it, by rendering her the form that you desire and to punish you for your inconstancy or your feeble credulity."

On hearing that, the monkey tried to escape from the bed in order to flee the fay's vengeance, but the amorous Celadon, still in his error, retained her tenderly.

"If it's necessary to die," he said to the fay, "Exercise all your vengeance on me and pardon this generous process, who, disdaining my crown, has been kind enough to accept my faith in this prison and to count for nothing the grandeurs for which she was destined."

Angered by that amorous scene, the fay touched the monkey with her wand in spite of her, and allowed the hideous Transparent to appear in her place. At the sight of that vile creature, the prince opened his arms and uttered a piercing scream. But for the respect he had for the queen he would have leapt out of his bed, but he contented himself with hiding under the bedclothes in order no longer to see that horrible princess.

"Well," said the impudent creature, "there's no reason for such alarm! And you, Madame," she said to the fay, "why have you taken it upon yourself to come and trouble our union? My husband, the prince, thought himself happy in possessing a princess of whom he had formed such a beautiful idea. Princess for princess, I'm worth as much as that one. Don't you know that men want to be deceived, and that they're more obliged to those who deceive them well that those who open their eyes to disagreeable verities."

"Her husband," said the prince, sticking his head out of the bedclothes, "I am not. I have pledged my faith to Princess Roseate, and I have never been able to love anyone but her."

Then the fay made a sign to the blue nymphs to dress Transparent and take her into one of the cabinets in the grotto of pearls. Then, leaving in order to give the marine gods time to dress the prince, she went to wait for him in the hall of Thetis. She had not been there long when she saw old Sempiternelle come in, who was not expecting to see the Fay of the Green Oaks there.

She recovered from her surprise, however, and, approaching her in a sufficiently open manner, she said to her: "I believe, my sister, "that after the little trick of which you made use in order to take Roseate out of my hands, you ought not to be annoyed that I've married her lover. It's me," she continued, seeing that the fay was not responding and allowing her to speak, "who, having discovered Celadon's prison, went to remove the she-monkey from the home of the Queen of Aquamarines and brought her here, where I married her, with sufficient pomp for a place like this."

"Do you believe, then," the Fay of the Green Oaks said to her, in a rather disdainful fashion, "that you are the mistress of these events, and do you not fear that I might finally make use of my power to make you repent of your cruelties?"

Fully determined as Sempiternelle was, she did not hear those words without being a little troubled; but as she had suc-

172

ceeded in her projects, and, similar to all people who do harm for the pleasure of doing it, it scarcely mattered to her what happened, as long as her passion for vengeance was satisfied, she said to the fay: "You can do what you please to Transparent, but you can't prevent the fact that she's your prince's wife. As regards my nephew, Prince Muguet, I consent to return the promise that was given to me, in order that he'll no longer marry your Princess Roseate; in any case, he'd be very unhappy with a little creature who has other ideas in her head. Only return him to me, and I won't involve myself any more, intimately or from afar, with this whole accursed adventure."

The Fay of the Green Oaks did not deign to respond; she merely made a sign to her to go away. Then, turning to Prince Celadon, who had just come in, she struck the floor with her wand and found herself with him on the sea shore, where she made him mount her elephant with her and took him back to her palace, where the queen was waiting for her, and trying to console the princess for the misfortunes of her destiny.

The fay did not want to expose him to the gazes of princesses that he had offended so cruelly; she had him enter a cabinet, and instructed him not to come out until she ordered him to do so. He was so afflicted and so unhappy that he found no difficulty in obeying the fay, who was removing him from the constraint of seeing anyone.

She went into the queen's room. The beautiful Roseate blushed on seeing her, and then lowered her eyes; she let torrents of tears flow therefrom.

"I have come," the fay said to her, "to take your orders regarding the punishment of culpable individuals that I have in my power. See, Madame, to what they wanted to condemn you, and be sure that my vengeance will follow your words."

"Oh, my mother!" cried the beautiful Roseate, addressing the fay and the queen, "Don't listen to your sentiments, and let the unfortunate spouses live, without wanting to augment the horror of their destiny any further. They are punished sufficiently, and I am sufficiently avenged if the ingrate Celadon knows the person that he has preferred to me."

The princess would have tried further to disarm the wrath of the queen and the fay if the fay Sempiternelle had not suddenly appeared.

"I have come," she said to the Fay of the Green Oaks, "to tell you that I am renouncing forever meddling in the affairs of mortals. I have just learned that my nephew, exceeded by rage against the monkey, whom he had always mistaken for Roseate, has run himself through with his sword, unable to sustain the triumph of his rival. In my fury, I've wrung the neck of Transparent. Thus, I shall no longer take any interest in all your affairs; I'm leaving forever and returning to the Realm of the Fays, never to emerge again."

With that, she disappeared

Delighted by that occurrence, the Fay of the Green Oaks looked at the queen in order to ask her permission to present Celadon to her. The princess understood to what she was about to be exposed; she asked for permission to retire to her bedroom. The queen permitted her to do so. Then the fay opened her cabinet and had the prince come out. He, fully occupied with his dolor, did not ask why he had been shut in, nor why he was being brought out. When he perceived the Queen of Cedars he wanted to withdraw, but she came toward him and embraced him.

Touched by a welcome that he hardly merited, he threw himself at her feet and washed her hands with tears, without being able to proffer a single word.

"It's not of us that it's necessary to beg pardon, Prince," said the fay. "A more redoubtable judge will sentence you, and it's from her that you're going to hear your condemnation."

"I don't merit being punished, Madame," said the prince, "by the orders of that divine person, and this is what will avenge her." Then he drew his sword and tried to pierce his heart with it.

The beautiful Roseate, too attentive to what was happening, although she had feared being a witness to it out of modesty, was listening at the door. She opened it soon enough to

174

be able to disarm her lover. He turned his head and recognized her.

"O Heaven!" he cried. "It's you who opposes my death! Do you believe that I can live after having offended you so cruelly? O, Madame, your pity is more deadly to me than your hatred; I merit it, and I can no longer live, since I am certain that you must no longer love me."

The princess bushed, smiling, and looked at the queen and the fay.

The latter finally spoke. "Live, Celadon. All three of us order you to do so; and live for this beautiful princess, whom the queen, in sum, accords to you." Then she told him what Sempiternelle had told them. That story caused him to throw himself at the knees of the queen, who embraced him, and who, making him approach the princess, took her hand and gave it to her lover, who received it with incredible transports of joy.

The fay, who wanted the wedding ceremony to take place in her abode, with a pomp worthy of the illustrious spouses, demanded twenty-four hours in order to arrange everything. The prince had great difficulty making his amorous impatience consent to that, but it was, after all, necessary to grant it. In the meantime, he told the queen and the fay how the cruel Sempiternelle, having rendered speech to the unworthy monkey, had secretly brought her to the rock under the sea, and had persuaded him only too well that she was the beautiful Roseate. He had given her his faith in the hope that she would resume her form after the marriage, as she has assured him that she would. The three blue nymphs and the three green gods had not ceased to weep during the ceremony, but that had only stuck him since he had emerged from that sad abode.

The fay told him that the destiny could not be avoided; that, on confining him in that palace she had instructed those divinities that he could only emerge again after having committed the most terrible infidelity to the princess. That was why the sea gods and the nymphs had never wanted to have any conversation with him, so afflicted were they by the necessity he was in of failing essentially in his honor and his duty in order to be happy.

Prince Celadon, who suffered impatiently anything that reminded him of his crime, begged the fay not to mention it to him again.

"Can I hold an involuntary crime against you?" said the beautiful Roseate, tenderly. "Does your repentance not tell me that I am no longer at risk from your inconstancy?"

Touched by the charming fashion in which the princess excused him, in spite of the pain that he had caused her, kissed her beautiful hand with transport, and swore a eternal amour thousands of times.

Finally, the time demanded by the fay having expired, they saw with surprise a magnificent palace built on a mountain near the beautiful tree, and the fay took the queen and the fortunate lovers there.

There, on a velveted hill stood an enchanted palace, the magnificent structure and the superb architecture of which suspended the astonished senses. Thousands of jets of water, which art and nature competed in causing to spring forth in that fortunate location augmented its rich adornment. The boscage, the birds, the flowers and the verdure engendered amour there and held it enchained in the bosom of leisure and sensual pleasure.

Youth follows, as well as beauty, where felicity, the worthy daughter of constancy, resides; and to complete the benefits of such an enchanted abode, time loses its omnipotence over mortals; old age and its weary and icy days are banished forever from its presence, and amiable fidelity gives fortunate spouses its sweet recompense.

The King of Cedars and the King of Aquamarines were found there; the joy was extreme on either part, Care had been taken to prepare a magnificence appropriate to a day so illustrious. Roseate and Celadon were finally united forever. The fêtes did not end for a fortnight, and were always new. As one might easily imagine, the glow-worms surpassed themselves;

they formed chandeliers, girandoles, fireworks and illuminations so beautiful and so varied that it created a taste for them, and it is to them that we owe the origin of Chinese lanterns.

The fays and all the divinities of the forests, with a hundred princes, each more amiable and more gallant than the next, witnessed that beautiful day, and the fay gave the newlyweds the beautiful palace, in order sometimes to come and relax from the tumult of the court. They loved one another with an unequaled constancy, and were always happy; they were the model of lovers and spouses; they lived for innumerable years, as happy as they were on the day of their wedding—something as difficult to believe as a tale of fays is to finish.

Princess Sensitive and Prince Typhon

There were once two fays, one of whom was named Prudalie and the other Champetre. The Sovereign Council of Fays charged them to supervise the education of a prince and a princess who were to be united one day, and in order not to leave them any pretext for negligence they were sent to the courts where the two children were due to be born a long time before they saw the light of day. The fay Capable, the doyenne of the College, recommended them above all always to have the union of the children in mind; that union was absolutely necessary for the happiness of the realms they were to possess; the provinces were so interlocked that the people would suffer too much if they were not governed by the same sovereign.

It is proven that the power of fays does not extend over hearts, and in the fortunate times of Faerie, Amour was left the care of forming alliances; politics was, at the most, a secondary cause in the marriages of crowned heads.

The two fays departed full of confidence, having no doubt of their success. Their characters being different, their conduct was too.

Prudalie went to the court of the king who was to be the father of the princess. The prince in question was the best of all men; he did not demand any kind of constraint of his subjects; his principal maxim was not to change anything in established customs any in all cases where he had to decide he always responded "as usual"; it was, we are assured, that prince who was the inventor of what is known as the *ordre du tableau*.[3]

---

[3] The original *ordre du tableau* was a protocol devised in 1675 by the Marquis de Louvois, the Secretary of State for War, to regulate the order of precedence between generals; the term

That fashion of governing, incontrovertibly the most facile, is subject to great inconveniences; it is often necessary to lead men with severity, and distinctions and praise have a great attraction even for the most virtuous of men; that good king, who did not know presumption, sensed very strongly the need he had of the aid of the fays, so he received Prudalie with the greatest pleasure. That fay had intellect, but she had the fault of loving it with too much complaisance, of preferring it to everything and wanting it everywhere. The most researched was incontrovertibly the item to which she gave preference, she desired it even in the things that were least susceptible to it. A poorly written dispatch, even if it was otherwise full of all the good sense imaginable, would have been sufficient to lose the fortune of its author.

Simple government was not to her taste; she only listened to theories, uniquely occupied with her principal object, she attached herself particularly to the detail of the court; that detail amused her; furthermore, she was convinced that it would be useful to the education of the princess. First she introduced the fashion of those assemblies known under the name of salons, which the Hôtel de Rambouillet has since rendered so famous. People began to prepare in the morning for the evening's conversation, and said, not what hazard or common sense presented but what had been meditated in advance. Then she established long dissertations on the sentiments, which, in reducing Amour to an art, had taken away all its charms. She invented madrigals, she formed preciosity, and finally succeeded, without believing it, in destroying Knowledge and Letters.

It was thus that she made the occupation of the entire court, and above all the queen, who became pregnant and died in bringing into the world, following the order of destiny, and as the fays had foreseen, a daughter who seemed charming. The dolor that the king felt in losing the queen would have

---

was sometimes broadened to take in other calculations of precedence.

been even more embarrassing for him if it had been necessary for him to hear talk of affairs, but, thanks to the fay, he had no other cares than those of being afflicted, consoling himself and dissipating himself at his whim.

The moment the princess came into the world, Prudalie endowed her; a charming face and a sublime intelligence were the fay's presents, but, following her taste, she thought that she could not add too great a degree of delicacy to two such precious gifts. In order to succeed in that she multiply the twirls of her wand and the necessary words. Sensitive was the name she gave her, finding her abundantly so.

The little princess was not at all easy to bring up; her little limbs were formed with difficulty, but they were formed, and their assemblage produced one of the prettiest persons in the world, although, in truth, always small for her age; at fifteen she was no more than three feet tall. Grace and proportion shone abundantly throughout her person; she had ash-blonde hair; her complexion was splendid, her blue eyes lively and burning, and her most indifferent glances made the greatest impression.

It was easy to perceive the accuracy and the extent of her ideas, in spite of the affectation and the preciosity to which the fay had accustomed her, but fibers as fine and delicate as hers, further weakened by a overly complaisant education, rendered her the impression of a very embarrassing delicacy; a slight sound that surprised her even during the day caused her a revolution that was always dangerous; the odor of the simplest flowers gave her insupportable headaches; velvet and satin were harsh to her touch, and her beautiful eyes far from being able to sustain the glare of the sun, could not look at bright colors for long without being dazzled.

The entire court, dressed in the softest shades, either out of habitude or flattery, only found beauty, following the example of the princess, in the dullest weather. Nothing equaled the exactitude with which her apartments were closed; her Academy of Sciences was uniquely occupied in finding means of always conserving the same degree of warmth there, by keeping out the exterior air, that redoubtable enemy of delicate individuals. The ever-attentive fay, however, had imagined and had constructed huge glass bell-jars into which she obliged the princess to retire every time the weather seemed uncertain.

Those bell-jars were of various sizes, in proportion to the rooms of her apartment. As soon as she felt, or thought she felt, the slightest alteration in the air, she shut herself in one; they also had the property of deadening sound and softening odors infinitely. It is true that the princess would have had difficulty making herself herd, but Prudalie invented, in order to spare her lungs, the art of speaking with the fingers, which has only been conserved in its perfection in Spain, because of the extreme need that lovers have for it during the night—which Sensitive had always preferred to the day, as much for her amusement as for the assembly of the court.

She incessantly had her back turned to the light, so she was only seen rarely; that was a great good fortune for the princes who were attracted to her abode by a liking for travel or the desire to see her; for, in spite of the ridicule with which she was heaped, as soon as anyone had been able to look her in the face or hear her speak, they fell in love with her; and that amour made the strongest impressions. Sensitive, however, whom nothing had been able to touch, was unaware of the effect of her charms. The extent of intelligence cannot lead to a knowledge of amour; it is necessary to have experienced it.

The works of fiction that had always been her most serious occupation were regarded by her as a game of the imagination, on which she loved to exercise herself. *L'Astrée*,[4] was the one that had always pleased her most, although she found it too concise. She had taken the trouble to develop all the

---

[4] Honoré d'Urfé's classic pastoral romance, published in four volumes—the last added completed by another hand after Urfé's death—between 1607 and 1625. Two further volumes were added by other hands, the portmanteau text being easy to supplement.

sentiments in it, and had composed twenty-four volumes. It is true that she had excluded from her library all the old romances of chivalry, the mere idea of which made her shudder.

When she had reached the age of reason, the age when the heart commences to make itself felt by way of amity, simple desires and inconsiderable attachments, it was easy to divine that the heart in question would one day know amour, and the most ardent amour. The loss of a little dog, or the death of a bird, became events by which her court was continually alarmed. In truth, those misfortunes never caused the princess any ill humor, but they brought her to the brink of death because of the extreme sensitivity to which she was susceptible.

It is time now to talk about the prince whom the fays destined as a husband for the princess. On arrival in the estates of his father, the king, charmed by the union of the king and the queen, content with the good order and simplicity that she saw reigning even in the court, and finding few abuses to repair, the fay Champetre resolved to follow her liking for retreat.

In order to satisfy her taste the established herself in the country several leagues from the city; the king had the liberty to come to consult her at any hour of the day. She had constructed a simple but subdued farm in one of the most beautiful situations on Nature; the fecundity of the soul, and the abundance of all the things necessary to life. rendered it a delightful abode; a fertile vegetable garden, orchards, countless espaliers, a neat and well-arranged milking shed, a population of animals of all useful species, and active servants whose order, wellbeing and neatness added to the charms of the habitation, all produced a perspective more capable of seducing than the brilliance of the most magnificent court. Humans always feel an attraction for the first occupations of humankind, and the most ambitious cannot contemplate a fertile field without envying the lot and the tranquility of those who cultivate it.

It was to that agreeable abode that the fay Champetre took the little prince a few moments after his birth. She named him Typhon, and endowed him with strength, elevation of stature, courage and good health, as the most precious of gifts that she could make him. The country air, simple food, perhaps a trifle coarse, combined with violent and continually repeated exercise would have sufficed to form an excellent temperament without the help of the fay, but all of it in combination rendered the prince one of the tallest and strongest men that had ever been seen. At seventeen he was seven feet tall; it is true that he did not go any further; his stature was perfect, his black hair was admirable, his facial features were very regular, but he had a gigantic appearance that was always displeasing, although, all things considered, one could say that he was a very pretty giant.

Satisfied with those gifts, Champetre had completely neglected to cultivate the prince's natural intelligence; the scantly-researched education that she had given him was always simply confined within the limits of what it is shameful not to know, but in recompense, he had profited perfectly from the exercises to which he applied himself uniquely. Running, playing the lute, acrobatics and skill with weapons rendered him in very little time the admiration of all those who saw him. Above all, he had an immeasurable passion for horses. That is a natural enough taste in young men, but he took it to excess; the stable that the fay maintained in her farm had been his most solid occupation and his most marked attachment; so the best equerries in the world, whom Champetre had brought from all parts, were soon obliged to agree that the prince outstripped them in all the aspects of their art.

In spite of the simplicity of the education that Typhon had received, he had been unable to avoid some of the snags and silliness inseparable from great youth. By virtue of a sentiment that was natural, but devoid of all reflection, he drew vanity from his strength and his size; he pleased himself so much in hearing the terrible sound of his voice that, far from seeking to soften it, he augmented its volume further. His frank and sincere character did not permit him to dissimulate the extent to which the advantages of the body seemed preferable to him to the charms of intelligence.

What a contrast, and what a difference there was between the form, character and way of thinking of the prince with everything that was admired incessantly in Princess Sensitive! They were, however, two people whose union the fays had resolved. Amour often delights in uniting things that seem the most opposed; he sees with pleasure the degree to which the heart is capable of blinding the intelligence, but it is necessary to agree that he had never yet produced such a great miracle.

Having reached the age of seventeen, the prince began to weary of rural occupations; he had a desire to see other objects than the farm on which he had been raised. The fay, who knew full well that curiosity is already a preparation for amour, had neglected nothing to inspire in him the desire to see Sensitive; she had engaged all the people surrounding him to talk about her incessantly. She had done more than that; dances and songs were among the principal amusements of the inhabitants of the delightful farm, and Champetre often had pleasure in watching that joy after work, so necessary and so true; wanting to make everything collaborate in the success of her projects, she had ordered that the princess should be celebrated in all the songs.

Typhon was convinced that exaggeration had a large part to play in all that praise, but he had the desire nevertheless to judge the truth for himself. He communicated his design to the fay; she approved it gladly, and charged him with obtaining the consent of the king, his father. She did not refuse him anything that could make up the most brilliant and magnificent cortege for that journey.

The prince wanted to have an equipage worthy of his vanity; he regarded those small advantages as the only means of pleasing, and was unfortunate enough not to know any others. The care of choosing his horses seemed to him to be the most essential matter; he thought that the success of the victories he intended to win in tourneys would depend on their strength and skill. He had no doubt that the princess made that her unique occupation; nothing appeared as beautiful to him as illustrious assemblies consecrated to the glory of women. He flattered himself that he would win all the prizes while sustaining the beauty of Sensitive; that was the only gallantry of which he had any idea.

Typhon is not the only lover who has been mistaken about the means of pleasing; in general, any means meditated from afar becomes futile with women; they demand that one lends oneself to the whim of the moment, and only an excess of submission is capable of touching them.

The prince, very content with his equipage and even more content with his person, soon arrived in the capital city that contained Sensitive's court. On the last day of his journey he showed the march considerably; he had planned not to make his entrance until midday. He had no doubt that he would find the princess up and dressed at that hour; he took a great pleasure in displaying before her eyes the excess of his magnificence.

In order to attract her gaze more surely, his first concern was to have the excellent trumpets that preceded his numerous cortege sounded. He was considering with an extreme satisfaction the well concerted march of his brilliant equipage, when he saw one of the princess's principal officers coming toward him. He arrived completely out of breath, making hand signals to the trumpeters to shut up, but they took no notice. They did not even understand him; a trumpeter sounding during a brilliant entrance is far from any distraction, concentrating on occupying an entire people.

The officer finally succeeded in reaching the prince. He had a great deal of difficulty making himself heard.

"How, Sire," he said, "do you dare to make such a terrible noise here? The Princess is still in her first sleep; what will become of her if, by misfortune, she is woken up? A long time ago, Prudalie proscribed that fatal instrument, which the delicacy of the princess makes it impossible for her to sustain."

"My drums won't have any effect if I silence my trumpets," replied the prince quite astonished.

"You will also have the goodness to impose silence on them," the officer replied. "Otherwise I can't let you advance any further."

"But no one has ever made an entrance," said Typhon, "without brilliant instruments and acclamations, or without cannons firing."

"Cannons!" interrupted the officer. "It's a long time since all those in the kingdom were melted down. It's cruel enough for the princess to be exposed to hearing thunder, without conserving an infernal machine that imitates the sound only too well."

"Your princess has no troops, then?" said Typhon.

"She has invincible ones," replied the officer, proudly. "Noise doesn't astonish them; they merely regard it as something unnecessary. But they are able to show their skill and courage with other arms that are no less redoubtable."

Finally, seeing that all his representations were ineffective, and fearing to lose the fruit of his journey, Typhon consented to what was desired of him. By a complaisance that cost him a great deal, he determined that he would make his entrance as he would have done to the room of an invalid. He allowed himself to be conducted sadly to the palace that Prudalie had carefully prepared for him—needless to say, she was aware of the prince's arrival.

Scarcely had he taken his boots off than he wanted to go to pay his court to the princess, but that proposal appeared so ridiculous that, in spite of the respect that was owed to him, no one deigned to respond to him; people contented themselves with shrugging their shoulders and looking at him with a scornful smile.

Typhon, who did not understand that mystery at all, reiterated his request; he was finally told that at eight o'clock in the evening, when she awoke, Sensitive would take her milky coffee; she would dine, as was customary, at midnight; at six o'clock in the morning she would be served orange blossom, which took the place of soup for her; and in consequence, he would only be able to have his first audience at four or five o'clock in the morning, or about eleven o'clock in the evening, before the princess dined. Only the disposition in which she found herself on awakening would determine whether she would be in a state to receive him before or after dinner.

Typhon, weary of all the ceremonies, repented of his curiosity a thousand times. He would gladly have abandoned the project of seeing Sensitive, but unfortunately, there was no longer time; such a prompt departure would surely appear ridiculous, and Champetre would not have approved.

In order to dissipate an impatience all the greater because he dared not express it, after having criticized everything that he had not seen in his own country, in accordance with the custom of foreigners, he spent some time considering the furniture of his apartment. He was astonished by all the comforts and all the refinements with which it seemed to him to be filled, for Prudalie had spared no reflection in leaving nothing to be desired. The sight of a dressing table surprised him infinitely; at first he could not imagine what its purpose might be; having no doubt, subsequently, that it must belong to the princess, he wanted to send it back to her. When he learned that it was destined for him, his anger was extreme. He complained loudly of the wrong that was being done to him in thinking him capable of such softness, and swore never to make use of it.

Then he tried to open a few books that had been carefully stacked on his night-stand, but he only found new novels and a few dissertations on the sentiments and means of pleasing; he threw them away indignantly, following the principles that had been given to him in his earliest childhood. A geographical map that he discovered in a corner of his room finally appeared to him to be a resource; he flattered himself that he could find thereon a shorter route than the one he had taken, in order to return to his father's estates. Unfortunately, the map was the *Carte du Tendre*,[5] and it became a further torture for him.

Racked by fury and a need for slumber engendered by the long habitude he had of getting up early, the prince spent the rest of the time that preceded his audience criticizing a way of life in such scant conformity with his own, half-asleep, yawning, pacing pack and forth, and looking at his watch a thousand times over. Finally, at three o'clock in the morning, someone came to inform him that the princess was waiting for him.

He found Sensitive surrounded by all the apparatus of delicacy and all the refined precautions that her weakness—or, to speak more accurately, her poor education—had rendered necessary to her. The moment he perceived her, however, admiration gave way to a very different sentiment. He was enchanted; he was dazzled.

As for the princess, she was frightened on seeing the enormous stature of the prince; however, her natural politeness engaged her to dissimulate her first impressions. She even strove to talk to him, and that was surely with grace, but the terrible sound of his voice completed disconcerting her to such an extent that she had to retire immediately to her bell-jar. Alarmed by her condition, of which he did not believe that he was the cause, Typhon tried to follow her; her maid of honor, dreading some fatal revolution, made the decision to break off the audience.

The petty flatterers of the court, the scourge of the most redoubtable strangers, joined forces with a few women and, wanting to amuse themselves at the expense of the prince, proposed a game of cards to him. He felt obliged to accept, but, sleep having overtaken him to the extent of making him

---

[5] An allegorical map illustrating the path to true love, drawn in jest by the female members of the literary salon at the Hôtel de Rambouillet and printed as a frontispiece in the first of the ten volumes of Mademoiselle de Scudéry's *Clélie* in 1650.

snore, he was escorted back to his apartment, where he found a magnificent supper that had been prepared for him. Unaccustomed to eating at such an hour, Typhon only asked for permission to go to bed; it was eventually granted to him, and the courtiers sat down at table. As one can imagine, the ridicule with which they heaped the prince was the unique subject of their conversation.

Sensitive had contented herself with complaining mildly about the terrible sound of his voice; the ladies of her court had not been so reserved; their little pleasantries were continual. One found him "exceedingly stupid," although he had not had time to say four words; another complained of the excess of his "surliness," and they were all in agreement in judging that he was a "provincial king" with whom nothing could ever be done, and that he was too foreign. It is the fate of all those who present themselves in a new society only to be seen as ridiculous. A court is even more redoubtable.

Meanwhile, Typhon was enjoying the greatest security, very content with himself; he believed that he had succeeded perfectly. He only woke up after having savored the sweetness of a long and tranquil slumber, further embellished by the agreeable dreams that had represented the princess to him, the idea of her charms more vividly retraced by his imagination. All the things that had astonished him the day before no longer made any impression on him. He even went as far as thinking that all princesses had the same etiquette.

He saw Sensitive again the next day, firmly resolved to conform to her tastes.

Prudalie, discontented with the first interview, having demanded that the prince lower his voice, had ordered the princess to receive him well. She had done more; she had said to the ladies and young men of the court, in a grave and composed manner: "I know that it is necessary to mock, otherwise one would die, but do what you can in order not to mock the prince to his face." They did not offer any guarantee, the thing being, they said, too difficult, but they promised to make an effort.

A simple and natural desire to please, somewhat poorly expressed, can only succeed with difficulty in a court full affectations, but as soon as Typhon was in love, for lack of familiarity with society, he persuaded himself easily that it would be easy for him to make himself loved. The simplest politeness on the part of the princess seemed to him to be a sentiment; the most mediocre attention became a favor that gave him rights.

It is thus that extreme youth is able to flatter itself and abuse itself; in brief, natural confidence, the reef of all men, and even more of princes, made him ridiculous—which he was far from realizing, since he did not even know the meaning of the word. In fact, how can one be ridiculous on a farm? One can judge without difficulty how a court uniquely occupied with the false brilliance of wit and details of the heart found pleasantries to make regarding a confident prince who did not disguise anything, who had nothing in his favor but common sense and a natural intelligence devoid of grace and cultivation.

By dint of persuading themselves that Typhon could not understand them, however, the courtiers abused their advantages. The prince became suspicious, suspicion increased to distrust, and from distrust to certainty the road is not long. The self-esteem that had blinded him thus far only served to wound his vanity more; his character, and his education even more so, took away the means of being able to avenge himself with the same weapons.

To begin with, the torch of war and projects of a striking vengeance occupied him uniquely, but amour soon destroyed those first impressions and he even blushed at having heeded them. It was already a great deal in his formation for him to begin to blush; that blush is the best of all lessons; however, the prince had a long way to go in order to become the sharp and light character who is ready for anything and is offended by nothing. One does not become amiable merely with the aid of reflection; it is the work of the care and the commerce of an enlightened woman, complaisant by sentiment. How could

Typhon be formed? He had never been loved; he had never even inspired coquetry. The timidity inseparable from amour had only served to render him more awkward and embarrassed.

All that Sensitive had been able to gain had been to suffer him, after having obtained—not without difficulty—that he lower his voice by fifteen tones. In spite of the extreme attention of the prince, however, laughter escaped him, or a word that eagerness engaged him to pronounce. In sum, the natural prevailed all too frequently; then he put the princess into a violent state. In general, though, he succeeded in having the voice of a little warbler, the most ridiculous falsetto in the world, for one ordinarily only corrects a fault by means of the contrary excess.

All the changes that the desire to please had brought into his character and manner, however, were scarcely noticed. It was thought that he expressed himself without grace; that he was too slow on the uptake; that wit was almost always utterly wasted on him; that he never pronounced epigrams, nor even wordplay; and, in sum, that he could only talk well about horses.

Meanwhile, the princess was sometimes surprised by his simple and natural responses. She could not help approving of them, for she was sensitive to everything; but prejudice soon prevailed, and Typhon was still very far from making any impression on her heart. Without Prudalie's orders, in all probability, no one would have paid any attention to him.

A lover who is merely tolerated has a great deal of which to complain; it is an even greater misfortune when he senses that he is importunate.

The opposition of character of the young prince and princess soon caused Champetre and Prudalie a great anxiety; they began to despair of being able to overcome the prodigious distance of Sensitive; it must be remember that the fay Capable, who knew how necessary their union was, had recommended the two fays, above all, to form them in order to love one another one day. They believed that they had taken the most reliable measures to succeed in that, without ever making the reflection that the excess of the best necessarily engenders revolt.

When they were convinced of their error, they commenced with the reproaches that one ordinarily puts in place of means of reparation; they said and repeated to one another a thousand times everything that could serve to excuse themselves personally.

"I've given my prince bodily strength, majesty of stature, health, dexterity and courage," said Champetre. "What more can one desire?"

"Charm," replied Prudalie, and added, with an expression of scorn and denigration: "In truth, my sister, I feel sorry for you. Your conduct, compared with mine, appears deadly dull; it will be thought execrable and frightful. For, in sum, I've rendered my princess charming to behold, I've filled her with sentiments, delicacy, intelligence and talents, and what proves more than anything else my advantages and the reproaches that you merit is that Typhon renders her justice, in spite of the savage and barbaric education you have given him."

Champetre responded, with the frankness of her character: "Typhon has a liking for Sensitive, I don't disagree, but he only loves her because he has never seen anything else. Do you think that, without that reason, he could have attached himself to a precious little creature frightened by the buzz of a fly, who catches a chill in the mildest open air, who spends her life in a bell-jar and speaks a language that no one understands?

"At any rate, my sister," she went on, "we've got it wrong, since we haven't been able to succeed. The doyenne will judge us; you know that she's severe. Believe me, let's not join ill humor to the division and embarrassment we're already in. let's go find Capable and beg her pardon; that deference will touch her, and perhaps engage her to give us her advice and the means we need."

Prudalie had a great deal of difficulty yielding to such a reasonable proposition; she repeated a hundred times over that she had done nothing wrong, that she defied the doyenne herself to do any better, but in the end she made her decision; it is the advantage of common sense always to prevail over preciosity and false brilliance. Furthermore, dread and authority lead easily to the confession of the sins one has committed, especially when it is only a matter of agreeing with someone who cannot be unaware of them.

The two fays departed immediately. Prudalie was mounted on her chariot constructed of madrigals, epigrams, quips, little tender romances and verses praising her; it was propelled by airs, prejudices and a host of sighs, which she had commanded. Champetre rode in her little cart; it had a charming neatness; two of the finest oxen from her farm hauled it easily. That conveyance would not naturally have made great diligence, but, difficult as it might be to believe, Champetre arrived before her companion, for nothing is as dubious as the reliability of sighs, even in the shortest journeys.

The two fays appeared together before the fay Capable, one with the confidence of success and the other with the simplicity that always mistrusts itself. The doyenne received them with the gravity of her age and her estate; she was informed of their procedures, but she wanted the confession of their faults to be their first punishment. When they had rendered an exact account of the lack of success of their efforts, she reproached them severely for the abuses they had made of her confidence and the excess to which they had abandoned themselves.

"What a perverse example you give to humans!" she said to them. "Should fays, who always ought to be guides by philosophy, yield to decided tastes and attempt to submit the children confided to their care to them? Would you dare to appear before me in such a tranquility if you had the slightest common sense?

"To punish you," she continued, "I condemn you, Prudalie, to maintain and make the most of Champetre's farm, and you, Champetre, will govern Sensitive's court. That isn't all; you will exchange forms with one another. For the honor of the corps it's necessary that your punishment be hidden from humans; it's sufficient for you to sense fully the ridiculousness of your faults when taken to such excess. Depart and obey; such is the sentence of the Council. I shall take care of the prince and the princess; the doyenne of the fays is not too good to correct two children that you have spoiled, and to bring together two characters born to love one another, which your efforts might have driven apart forever."

The fays were subjected instantly to the ordained transformation; the exchange of their vehicles became the first penalty of their metamorphosis. One rendered the oxen breathless and muddy, impeded everywhere by dint of wanting to go quickly and thinking of other things; the other, not knowing how to entertain or measure sighs, stalled or stumbled at every step, and continually broke her conveyance by virtue of her own weight.

In spite of so many obstacles, they arrived; their power of faerie sustained them; the interest they had obliged each of them to take on the reputation of the other, which further augmented the hatred and anger by which they were animated.

The new kind of life to which they found themselves subjected was, for them, a continual tissue of torments and troubles. The most considerable, without contradiction, was that of continually being someone other than themselves. What a misfortune it is for a woman, in fact, not only to lose a face that habitude and self-esteem have rendered so dear to her, but to be obliged to wear one that one has often criticized and whose slightest fault one has often taken pleasure in pointing out. Then again, what a torture is it to be bound to a body whose movements are almost always contrary to the mind that directs them.

Thus, the two fays appeared to themselves to be perfectly ridiculous, as much at the court as in the country. By virtue of a singular return of self-esteem, they often perceived one another and were charmed by it.

"That isn't me," they said, separately. "It's my sister, whom I often mocked, and that's all right; I want even more to turn her to ridicule."

Then they took pleasure in doing things that were even more singular, without thinking that they were supposed to be repairing them. It is true that they did not retain those initial ideas for long; character soon prevailed, and each one continued in good faith to yield to her inclination. The most rustic farm-workers and the least refined members of the court perceived the changes that they remarked every day, the cause of which they could not divine.

The agricultural laborers did not understand the questions they were asked or the orders they were given; Prudalie spoke to them in a new language; often, she even expressed herself in verse; she had put indentations in her cart, which rendered it incontrovertibly the most ridiculous in the world as well as the prettiest. She did not stop there; she had it ornamented with mirrors. The sight of her livestock not appearing sufficiently agreeable to her, she wanted to change their natural color; he had the goats dyed pale yellow, the cows blue and the sheep pink. The goats, seeming to have more intelligence and imagination than the other farm animals, became her favorites; she ordered that their horns be silvered and that they be exclusively nourished on biscuits and jam, which caused almost all of them to perish. Amber and perfumes were burned continually in all the animal sheds. In sum, there was no extravagance to which she did not devote herself.

The conduct of Champetre, although full of common sense, did not succeed any better in the court. The ladies and the flatterers court not get over her decisions regarding works of art, customs and ceremonies. Sensitive asked her for advice one day regarding the disposition of a fête that she wanted to give during the night; she responded that the night was made for sleeping and the day for working. If the princess invented some bizarre fashion, which had always been her principal occupation, or some new elegant and singular attire, the fay immediately asked her whether it was more comfortable than the one she wanted to quit.

A way of thinking so different from the one that she had understood thus far embarrassed the princess. However, she was sometimes touched by the simple and reasonable advice that she received from Champetre, although it was accompanied by the airs and manners of Prudalie, who, for her part, said polished and elaborate things on her farm with all the heaviness imaginative, which were absolutely wasted on peasants who could not understand them.

Let is leave the fays to extract themselves from their embarrassment and behaving quite inappropriately, each in her province, and see how the fay Capable set about repairing their bad conduct with regard to the princely young couple.

That prudent fay knew better than anyone that in order to bring someone who has gone astray back to verity, it is necessary to conform to their ideas. She therefore imagined taking the form of an equerry whom Typhon had known in his childhood, and whose liking for horses had rendered him the most intimate of friends. She presented herself to the prince, who was delighted to see a man whom a few affairs had taken away from the court, and to whom he could speak with confidence.

The fay, under the appearance of the equerry, soon represented the neglect that he was making of the exercises to which he owed his reputation, and reproaches for such negligence were inevitably attracted on his part to Champetre and his father, the king. She was careful, above all, to maintain the chagrin that Typhon could not help manifesting against the princess; no one knows whether she did not even give birth to it occasionally, but at least she sought to augment her wrongs and make him envisage the most piquant procedures in that regard. It is not necessary to be a fay to know how to take advantage of the discontentment of an amorous heart; even quite stupid women have a similar talent.

In the end, Capable was so well able to embitter his mind that she determined him to depart without even taking his leave. She took care along the road to maintain his chagrin. He wanted continually to return to Sensitive; the privation of the sight of her appeared to him impossible to sustain, but by flattering him with regard to his tastes, representing to him the idle life he was leading, reminding him of the scorn he had endured, retracing for him the nasty and vapid pleasantries of which he had been the eternal object, and, finally, by assuring him that only his absence was capable of piquing the princess and advancing his cause, the fay succeeded in making him continue his journey.

She even persuaded him that he might be regretted; the most common lover always flatters himself with that pretended regret—but what an error! Does the heart regret what does not touch it?

It was by similar means, and by all those that intelligence can employ, that she kept him at a distance. She took him to visit the most brilliant courts. The prince's self-esteem furnished him with dissipations, and sometimes even amusements: tourneys in which his strength or his skill ornamented him with splendor and actions in which his valor and cool head shone equally were means of consolation of which the fay was able to take advantage in order to deflect his ideas; at the same time she worked to form him, for she did not neglect anything that might contribute to giving him mildness and charm in his intellect.

She enabled him to spend time in courts very different from Sensitive's. The prince was often astonished to find that he had more wit than he had thought, to perceive that he understood everything, and that people sometimes listened to him with pleasure.

So many cares were not yet sufficient, in Capable's view, to complete the education of a prince in whom she was taking such a great interest. After having brought him to the point of reflecting and judging soundly, she wanted him to convince himself, and enable him to see by means of his own eyes the

197

source of all errors, the enemy of the veritable philosophy, the torment of society and the tomb of amour itself—I mean self-esteem, the scourge of the human race.

In order to succeed in that she gave birth in Typhon to the desire to examine a temple that the entire world fills in order to burn incense to a god continually adored but to whom no one wants to offer sacrifices.

That temple is open night and day; it always appears to be built on the design and in the taste in which the person regarding it would have constructed it. The statue of the god is alone in the temple, on which it occupies the depths; it represents with the utmost exactitude and in the most beautiful light the portrait of the person who is gazing at it, and that portrait, adorned by the amours and the graces appears to him to win the prize for beauty, or at least for merit.

That temple is only ornamented with pictures painted in the brightest colors, trophies and bas-reliefs. All of them represent in the greatest detail the actions and the attributes of the person who comes to worship the divinity. The procedures that might merit a few reproaches are borne on or accompanied by their excuses, which are perceived in the most favorable light; it is in there that one can admire the elegance and the keen expressions of the misunderstood generosity, false nobility, the supposedly necessary lie, the presumed duties of one's estate, false honor, and pretexts of vengeance.

All the objects that were presented to Typhon charmed and seduced him. As soon as he had entered the temple, his figure, his actions and his tastes appeared to him to be the idea of perfection: the horses he had tamed, the prizes he had won, and the proofs he had given of his courage were as many agreeable tableaux offered to his sight; he devoured them with his eyes and his heart was filled with joy and satisfaction.

In the midst of his enthusiasm he had an extreme pleasure in considering the tender and respectful worship that all those gathered there were rendering in general and in particular to the divinity. He felt in its full extent the complete delight with which they appeared to be considering the paintings and the bas-reliefs, and, unable to retain his enthusiasm, he cried: "Why can Sensitive not see me thus?"

Intoxicated by the spectacle, he did not pay attention to the notion that if everyone else was, in fact, worshiping the same god that he saw, they ought to have perceived his perfect resemblance thereto, and at least shared with him the adoration that they were offering to his image. Could the sentiment that was guiding him ever be enlightened? Self-esteem is even more blind than amour.

However, Typhon did not take long to be enlightened as to his error. The questions that he asked enabled him to discover that none of the observers was seeing the same things as him. When he wanted to talk about a horse he had tamed by making it cross a frightful precipice, and to point out the bas-relief in with that feat of boldness and temerity was perfectly represented, a pretty women who happened to be standing next to him said to him scornfully: "Where do you see horses in that bas-relief? There's nothing so vulgar. I only see a kind of basket that I've invented; it has had the most prodigious success; it's an effort of human intelligence."

The prince, not doubting her mental aberration, quit her abruptly and approached a man who seemed to him to be absorbed in the contemplation of the same subject, with the design of detailing that action and making himself known as its hero to a man who appeared to him to have intelligence. He was a geometer who, after having labored for a long time measuring the Earth, had found it to be square in form, and at that moment he could see his theory so clearly demonstrated that he had no doubt that everyone would yield to it. He wanted to make the prince agree to it as soon as he was approached, but the annoying Typhon began talking about cavalry, to which he responded with calculation and geometry, and addressed himself to a third party, who was a poet.

The latter, in the enthusiasm he was in, begged them to give him their opinion of a painting at the same instant that the prince was considering it. "You see that admirable situation," the poet said to him. "I agree that it's only a story but the story is well made, the verses have such a great energy that everyone is seized by horror; notice the different impressions of the audience, frightened and moved to compassion at the same time, at the slightest word from the actress. But the painting only renders those things imperfectly.

"That's not all," he continued, with the same urgency; "this temple only resounds with my glory, is only ornamented with my laurels; here you see the abstract sciences in which I write with the greatest facility, only ever having reflected on them for a few moments; you can remark a history written without a knowledge of the facts; everywhere the brilliant images and the fortunate turn of my expressions dazzle and easily cause the order and planning that my works lack to be forgotten; a bloody robe, a cannon shot, a night that I cause to appear and appear in accordance with the need I have of it, are strokes as bold as they are inimitable. Examine how I am cherished by Thalia, consider my comic scenes, always sustained by the epic. In a word, who has more right than me to say: My intelligence contains all intelligence? With such great talents, without being a philosopher, I'm very far from being a citizen."

"Where am I?" cried Typhon, drawing away rapidly.

"You are," said a woman who had passed her first youth, "in a place full of delights. Believe me," she went on, "I know; you'll only find people of good taste here."

The prince, convinced that he had finally encountered a reasonable person who would be able to render him justice, approached gladly in order to give her an audience that he had desired for a long time.

"I don't want to deceive anyone," she went on. "I agree that I'm past the age to please, but who, in truth, can perceive it? It's good to make a confession that nothing here can belie; for I don't see any date of years; but such is my character. I'm as sincere as I am beautiful. You see that painting," she continued, "which represents so naively the first triumph of my charms?"

"What has that painting to do with you?" Typhon replied.

"Doubtless you can see," she went on, "a child who promises all that nature will perfect in due course; I'm all the more astonished to find myself so well represented that no painter has never been able to make me resemble it. Examine, then..."

She spoke for a great deal longer, believing that someone was listening, but the impatient prince had drawn away in order to approach the statue.

At least no one can dispute that it's my image, he thought looking at it complacently. *How right people are to be content with its appearance, and always to have their eyes attached to that figure! It must surely please them! What pride there is in that gaze! What a martial attitude! What nobility in the stature! What a leg!*

He was occupied with those conceited ideas when a little hunchback approached, tugged the hem of his garment and said to him in a confidential manner: "Don't you find that that statue resembles me marvelously?"

The prince thought the joke so poor that he did not deign to respond to it, and contented himself with looking at him with a scorn that constrained the hunchback to quit him, doubtless in order to ask the same question of people he believed to be more enlightened.

Meanwhile, Typhon, still admiring the effort that Nature must have made to produce him, thanked her silently, and his gratitude would have lasted a long time, but it was interrupted by the arrival of a respectable old man whom he recognized without difficult by means of his costume as a high priest. In fact, he soon set about burning incense at the foot of the statue. A natural modesty, a sentiment of piety or perhaps a shame inspired by human respect made the prince exclaim: "What are you doing? I don't merit so much honor; I condemn this profanation of altars."

"What do you mean?" replied the high priest, indignantly. "Who is thinking of you here? It's me, and me alone who is revered here; these people that my examples and precepts have cured of errors and drawn back from the precipice, recognize my benefits and render me in this temple raised to me a worship that my merit and my virtues have justly acquired."

The austere and convinced manner in which the high priest pronounced those words astonished the prince and obliged him to withdraw. After mature reflection, however, he realized that all the members of the congregation only had themselves as an object, that they related everything to them and wanted incessantly to attract to themselves the admiration that each one deserved that he merited.

In spite of his reflections, and in spite of his astonishment regarding the prodigious ridicule with which the others were covering themselves, he surprised himself a few moments later in another corner of the temple putting his actions well above those of an old officer covered with wounds, who might perhaps, in truth, have been lauding his services a little too much, but with a sort of justice, since he had risked his life a hundred times over for the salvation of the State and the glory of the fatherland. That last feature completed making the prince retreat into himself and enabled him to perceive his aberration. He was ashamed of it, and imposed silence on himself; and, forgetting himself, he no longer did anything except listen. Thus, by means of a thousand examples, he was convinced of his error.

From then on, his eyes were opened, and, the enlightenment of amour combining with that of intelligence, he sensed how many reasons Sensitive had had for not loving him. He saw that he was too big, too heavy, too attached to his sentiment, and was fully convinced that everything that had occupied him until that was and ought to be indifferent to him to the people with whom he had lived. In a word, he succeeded in judging himself as he would have judged others.

Far from hiding his reflections from his faithful equerry, he gloried in confessing them. The fay, charmed by the impressions that a veritable and incontrovertibly more amiable philosophy were beginning to make in him, appeared to his eyes in her natural form, and assured him of an eternal protection. The prince testified the most ardent gratitude to her.

"To prove to you," she continued, "the interest that I am taking in what concerns you, ask me for whatever you wish and be sure of obtaining it."

After a few moment of reflection the prince said to her: "Render me lovable and permit me to return to Sensitive."

"You shall be satisfied," the fay replied. "Those wishes give me all the more pleasure because they are a convincing proof that your errors have struck you; you are lovable from the moment you think you lack something in order to be."

Instantly, his stature was reduced to four feet and he was transported to Sensitive's court by the fay Capable, who left Amour the care of finishing her work and returned to devote herself to her great and important affairs, which she had neglected for a long time.

Typhon soon experienced the anxieties mingled with joy and the transports inseparable from the idea of seeing once again a sovereignly beloved mistress; sentiment rendered him timid and embarrassed, unaccustomed to finding himself so lacking in strength. He walked like a man recovering from illness; he felt as light as a feather, but Amour scarcely left him time to notice and pay attention to changes of those sorts.

The first courtiers who perceived him were struck by his resemblance; they thought they recognized him, but they did not know who he was. In the uncertainty in which he found himself as to what to do, firmly resolved only to reveal his secret to the person who was its object, he took advantage of the impression of those who cried: "It's Prince Typhon's younger brother!"

He had himself announced to the princess under that name long before appearing in her presence; the eager individuals in a court do everything in order to be something, in order to have the sublime advantage of saying: "I'm the one who has seen her, I'm the one who spoke to her first."

The novelty of the little prince succeeded marvelously; all the women, occupying themselves with the comparison that they made incessantly between the big and the little Typhon, completed revealing to him the defects and inconveniences of his past conduct and confirming the sage and moderate ideas that he had newly but sincerely adopted. It was not without reason that he pleased people, even though he was still almost everything that he had been before—for it is not the work of a moment to correct the faults of habit—but a small stature almost always has a share of grace; thus, by a necessary consequence, the prince's strength was converted into dexterity, his ferocity into roguishness and his anger into petty impatience. A softer tone of voice rendered lively and pleasant a speech that a firmer and louder tone would once have caused to seem brutal.

The eulogies or criticisms of society are not ordinarily devoted to the most essential things; in sum, little Typhon became the darling of all the women. He was not touched by that, but he saw with an extreme pleasure that his face pleased the princess and that she could no longer do without him. That necessity does not take long to become amour, if it is not at its birth.

When he was convinced of Sensitive's sentiments, he made her the confession of everything that had happened to him, adding with the appearance of verity that is always convincing that he had only desired the diminution of his height in the hope of pleasing her. The princess applauded his metamorphosis; she was grateful to him for the sacrifice and touched by such an uncommon proof of amour.

She made so many efforts on herself that she corrected a thousand delicacies that she feared might importune her lover. She gradually accustomed herself to doing without her bell-jars, and under various pretexts she banished them from her apartment, even in winter. She did more than that; she wanted to ride a horse, and the sound of horns, dogs and beaters became agreeable to her, in the idea that her lover, having loved them, might love them still. Finally, that liking became so firmly hers that she arranged hunting parties herself, and they were only ever proposed by her.

The absence of Prudalie—or, to be more accurate, that of her mind—left her the liberty to agree with the verities that amour inspired in her every day. Simplicity and the natural appeared to her to be preferable to anything, and soon—for Amour moves rapidly—she reached the point of criticizing all the delicacies of which she had thus far been rendered the victim; she only conserved any longer that of the heart, which, becoming unique, was all the more vivid for it.

Such were the impressions of Sensitive while her lover, guided by the desire to please her, invented fêtes and amusements every day, in order to celebrate his good fortune and provide evidence of the occupation of his heart. Natural but embellished by amour, his intelligence continually produced new and charming things.

Meanwhile, the fay Capable, who was able not to neglect anything—which is a great ability—took advantage of the prince's violent exercises and those of the princess to enable them to grow. Who would ever have thought that Typhon would one day have need of it? In the end, however, from the four feet to which he had been reduced by the excess of his amour, he reverted to five and a half, and from the three that the princess possessed she reached four and a half, without either of them perceiving the changes that they had experienced and without their having desired them.

The princess conserved all her delicacy of intellect, the prince all his corporeal strength and the various graces; but the graces were always shared between them. Amour arranged everything, and everything as well arranged.

So much vivacity, so much sympathy and so much reciprocal desire naturally became sufficient to respond to their happiness, but what precaution sagacity ought to employ when it is a matter of consenting to a union that ought to be eternal! In order to have nothing for which to reproach herself, the fay Capable demanded yet another proof of the two lovers; she made them climb into her chariot of black varnish without telling them where she was going to take them.

They stopped at the door of a temple. They flattered themselves that they had finally arrived at that of Hymen, but it was that of self-esteem again. Typhon was carrying at that moment ideas so different that he was unrecognizable. The fay told them to get down and enter with her. They obeyed, and the young lovers were dazzled and intoxicated by what they perceived.

Capable questioned them separately and aid: "What can you see?"

The princess replied, blushing: "I can only see Typhon everywhere," and the prince exclaimed: "Everything here only respires Sensitive."

"Since you have emerged victorious from this proof," the fay said to them then, "I shall unite you."

They loved one another and lived happily, as did their subjects.

With regard to Champetre and Prudalie, the fay Capable, who had great projects for the education of a princess who was very difficult to marry, made only one fay out of the two, of whom it is claimed that there was nothing to desire. How many fused people would still compose a very imperfect whole!

Cornichon and Toupette

Advertisement

A manuscript in characters unknown to me fell into my hands a year ago, I ran to the libraries; my consultations were futile. I consulted scholars of ancient languages, equally fruitlessly. I imagined that it was magic. I am not a sorcerer; the fashionability of that passed a long time ago in France. What an embarrassment! Far from being discouraged, however, my curiosity was only more piqued.

"At least let's see the Cabalists," I said. I paled for six months over Paracelsus, Cornelius Agrippa, Raymond Lull, Albertus Magnus and the rest. If those authors did not provide me with complete enlightenment, at least they put me on the track. I found established there the existence of powers of the air, fays, genii, gnomes, sylphs, etc., and a relation of those intelligences with the Cabalists, the motive for which must, I judged, reside in the signs that they used. The acquaintance of a few Rosicrucians spared me a great deal of labor. I had myself initiated, but I was reduced to my own studies.

By dint of observing those signs and the letters of my manuscript, I thought that I was able to discern a few distant connections. I knew that the science of numbers is a principal branch of that of the Cabalist; I had recourse to the most profound algebra, and I eventually succeeded in discovering the unknown term. All the clouds that covered my work were dissipated, and I soon found myself in a state to compile a Cabalitico-Fayic Dictionary, with the aid of which I perceived that I possessed a precious fragment of the history of the fays.

The author, who appears to be contemporary, did not have it in mind to enlighten posterity as to the nature and the functions of fays, and the climes that they inhabited; that is a pity for the Republic of Letters. Faerie is a genre that is gaining favor every day; details of all those matters would have removed many doubts and enriched a foundation that produces so many fine tales.

I could dispense with talking about my translation; I am sheltered from the criticisms of confrontation; I want to say, however, that it is not literal. Fayicism in French would be more disagreeable than Germanism, or any other ism, for which translators are sometimes reproached. The facts, however, and everything that can be rendered into our language without torture are conserved there faithfully. I have been tempted, it is true, to suppress the greater part of a fragment that serves as an introduction to the book; that is the disaster of the islanders. That appears to me to be a little serious for a work that could be treated as a bagatelle, but I made the reflection that the fate of these puerile tales, with which children are amused, does not affect the entire horoscope of my book, which unites all the characteristics that one can reasonably demand for the confidence of a history, and that fragment also contains rather curious things, of which I dare not retrench any.

I confess that I have not been so reserved with regard to a large number of minor events detailed with a care as affected as it is futile, repetitions and reflections that a child might have made; I have excised all that, but I have taken care to note it in the relevant places. Although it is true that, while often suppressing the reflections of my author, I have permitted myself a few, that is because I thought them much better than his. That a translator can take the liberty of inserting a few of his own thoughts within those of his author is a small retribution for faithful, rather tedious labor, which it would be unjust to refuse him.

One might perhaps be astonished not to see in a work of this importance, either an index, or a privilege, or even a list of errata; that is because the urgency one has in producing a book of which one has a good opinion does not leave time to compile and index; I might provide one in subsequent editions, and even a list of errata, which will be all the better because one could then add one of afterthoughts. With regard to the privilege, there are so many good books that are published without one, that one is content with an approval; but it is so ample that, out of modesty, it has not been judged appropriate to print it. It will suffice to say that it relates principally to the words "the end."

That, I believe, is all I have to say about this work, and perhaps it will be too much, but I beg you to consider that it is necessary for an advertisement to advertise.

There was once a land a very long way from here, and in that land there was a spring that rejuvenated old people and aged young ones. That marvel was the work of the fay Dindonnette, also known as the Fay of the Island, and sometimes as the Fay of the Spring; she was a former protectress of the people of the country. That fay, the best creature in the world, but the most ill-advised, considering that youth almost always aspires to a more advanced age, while old people, on the contrary, incessantly praise and regret their youth, thought that she might procure their common happiness by procuring the accomplishment of both wishes.

If she had been acquainted with the works of Monsieur Pope,[6] she would have learned there that all is well; or if, at least, she had made her design public, perhaps someone would have been found with sufficient common sense to point out the

---

[6] The reference is to Alexander Pope's "An Essay on Man" (1733-34), which attempts to "vindicate the ways of God to Man," arguing that God's work—the Universe—is perfect, and that its apparent imperfections are due to the limitations of human intellectual capacity. Voltaire's characterization of Pangloss in *Candide* (1759) might well have had Pope in mind as well as Gottfried Leibniz.

inconveniences to her; but, having no suspicion of any, she wanted to add to that benefit the pleasure of surprise.

It was during the night that the sole source of fresh water in that land, which was small and surrounded by an immense sea, acquired by means of her power the quality that I have just said, to a degree in conformity with her zeal—which is to say, excessive. She did not fail, early in the morning, to go and station herself in a place near the spring, which was in the center of the city, in order to enjoy, without being perceived, the spectacle of the first metamorphoses that would occur there.

It did not take long to convince her that her intentions were fulfilled even beyond her hopes. Infants visibly acquired the stature and vigor of adolescents, and decrepit old people exchanged their caducity for the weakness and imbecility of early childhood. She believed that she had extracted them from the power of death. The joy that she felt did not permit her to follow any longer the design she had had of remaining unknown; recognition is such a legitimate price of benefits that she could no longer refuse the delicate pleasure of enjoying that which she thought she merited. She declared to all the people that such an astonishing marvel had assembled around the spring that it was owed to her.

It is not easy to represent the joy of those who gained from that exchange, the dread and disturbance of the others, and the general surprise of everyone. But the facility that the former had to spread out in all directions, or to let their common delight burst forth by coming together, caused it to prevail over the plaints of the latter, reduced by the weakness of the state into which they entered to moaning in isolation. The result was that the bulk of the nation, believing themselves to be fortunate, never ceased blessing the good fay Dindonnette, who had enabled them suddenly to find themselves in the state, or very nearly, in which everyone had desired to remain for life.

However, the effects of the enchanted water became ever more obvious as the use of it continued. Such rapid progress gave everyone fear for the future. It was not without suspicion that they approached the spring; they gave way easily to the most eager. Those who thought they still lacked the charms of the most beautiful youth were there at dawn.

They would have fortunate if they had been able to fix themselves, but every drop of water that they swallowed thereafter, acting in accordance with the irrevocable supernatural laws that had been given to it by the fay, soon made them surpass the imperceptible limits of the pleasant state that they had desired with so much ardor. Those who had been extracted from the infirmities of old age were seen, with astonishment, transported into infancy, and the prospect of an imminent caducity drove the young to despair.

The fay was alarmed herself, but it was too late; like gods, fays cannot destroy their work.

What was the desolation of that miserable people when the veil of a false joy had been lifted by the experience of a few days! They saw the full extent of their misfortune. Everyone set about digging wells in all the places they thought appropriate to it, but in vain. The bosom of the earth only offered in those climes masses of stone or arid sands. To increase the misfortune, the rainy season, the duration of which is brief and fixed, had just passed, and would not return for nine or ten months. People took advantage of the nocturnal dew, which was abundant, but far inferior to their needs, as well as animal milk and all the liquids that fruits and plants could produce when their juices were expressed.

The sea opposed invincible obstacles everywhere to the aid that a nation instructed in the art of navigation might have been able to obtain from elsewhere. The poor folk did not have the idea of a ship; content with the small portion of land that was their lot, they did not know that there was any elsewhere; or, if they suspected it, the one that they inhabited having thus far furnished all the things necessary to life, they had not envisaged anything beyond that could tempt their desires and which merited troubling the peaceful way of life that made their happiness.

In that extremity, a few, seduced by the hope of attaining more fortunate climes, dared to trust their strength in order to swim across vast seas. Their sudden loss, perceived from the shore, deterred the others. Several, seeing themselves constrained to draw the imbecility of infancy or the caducity of old age from the spring, avoided that cruel alternative by a voluntary death. A small number, more attached to their duties and the objects of their inclination, consecrated to the service of others the residue of vigor that they still enjoyed, until they were relegate themselves to the two extremities of life, and, equally incapable of procuring their needs, they were enveloped in the common doom.

It is true that the water did not contain any positively mortal cause, but the thread of the days of those who were obliged to drink it was nevertheless cut; the spindle merely turned more rapidly, bringing back the same individual several times over though the various ages, which had previously only been seen once in the course of human life. But such a prompt passage from one state to the other brought an indescribable disturbance to society. One arrived there without having had the leisure to prepare for it; nor were others, occupied with themselves, able to anticipate it and to dispose for every age what was necessary to its usage, and to constitute for every person his estate, his rank and his profession.

In order to regulate the general economy of the state and that of particular families it would have required the new ideas that such a great change can produce. It was necessary to put the views of the legislator in proportion with the sudden revolutions to which the life of the people had just been subject. What a task! Could the plan of a sage government, the belated work of the experience of several centuries, be born in such sad circumstances?

If those whose experience and reflections had acquired reliable notions of the things that form the bonds of society and ensure its consistency had been able to conserve them in the various states through which they passed so rapidly, everything would have evened out. No one would have been surprised to see a weak infant, provided with the enlightenment that he had once acquired, directing the difficult toil of a robust laborer who had not yet seen two harvests; and in the Senate, the advice of a man who had already given evidence of his merit and his talents would have imposed itself on young old men in spite of the mask of infancy. But that was not the way it was; every age was followed by its natural advantages and inconveniences; imbecility was the prerogative of both extremes, and the progress or decline of reason depended, as among us, on the state of the organs.

The man who fell into infancy on emerging from old age did not carry with him any memory of his past knowledge. A new world was offered to his astonished sight, and the apprenticeship that it was necessary for him to make in order to be useful to himself and to others was always forestalled by the fatal term in which decrepitude diminishes the exercise of reason, at the same time as it suspends or forbids the usage of corporeal faculties—hence the entire privation of any education, which entails that of the idea of the common good and the means of finding one's own. Sentiment was only an obscure instinct, which reason only enlightened for brief intervals, and only served to render those who enjoyed it more miserable, by revealing greater woes to them without allowing them to perceive the slightest remedy.

That situation, utterly deplorable as it was, might still have allowed those who experienced it to subsist physically for some time, but other misfortunes combined with it as a necessary consequence of the first. The child who is born finds an aid in the bosom of his mother that assures his life; the language of cries is always understood by maternal love. On the contrary, the old people did not find anyone to sustain their decline into infancy; the law had not substituted outside aid for the difference there is between maternal and filial love, since there was no law; it was only a small number of those wretches who found in their children cares capable of postponing their doom momentarily.

An even deadlier blow collaborated in the destruction of that unfortunate people. The fatal water operating more powerfully on those who drank it immediately, the growth of children in the maternal womb had almost its usual duration, and the term of childbirth usually surprised those unfortunates in a state of old age or infancy, which cost the lives of both.

In sum, the combination of so many fatal causes destroyed that people in a matter of months, and the desolate Dindonnette, their protectress—or, rather, their murderer—having not been able to render them any other service than the duties of the sepulcher, quit that place of horror never to return.

A few centuries after those events, the fay Selnozoura[7] who usually made a tour of the world twice a week, on medical advice, for a change of air and to find some relief for the restlessness in the limbs that tormented her, stopped off on the Island of the Spring. She never directed her route via the same places; that small part of the world was unknown to her. The beauty of the climate engaged her to explore it.

Cornichon and Toupette were accompanying her. The latter had been given to her at the most tender age by the geni-

---

[7] Author's note: "In the original language, this name contains the idea of grit and also that of agitation. The former was doubtless caused by the fay's character; the other, which appears contrary to it, was apparently combined with it by reason of her continual travels. It is noticeable that ancient names are appropriate to the qualities and occupations of the people to whom they were given." Naturally, the author does not bother to explain that in familiar French terminology, Cornichon refers to a stupid person and Toupette to an impudent one. nor does he point out other *double entendres*, arising from the fact that Cornichon is derived from *corne* [horn] and that a *toupette* is a tuft, although that etymology eventually become relevant to his plot

us Kristopo,[8] her uncle by marriage and her neighbor, who had taken her off the hands of poor and incapable parents and given her an education. Cornichon had been bought some time afterwards from a slave merchant; his family was unknown but he appeared to be a little older than Toupette, who was then fourteen years of age.

Their early childhood had made the amusement of the fay, who loved the children dearly, and the affection she had for them increased as age developed a thousand lovable qualities in them. None of Toupette's escaped Cornichon, who rendered her a sincere homage. Toupette mingled with a marvelous sagacity all of Cornichon's merit, and was too amiable not to love him madly; when Amour makes such good use of his power, he is sure of general applause. The fay gave him all of hers; the innocent expression of the sentiments of their hearts, which was given free expression in her presence, amused her.

Her design was to marry them eventually, but the status of wife might have rendered Toupette less appropriate to traveling, and the obligation of sometimes separating from her for long intervals, so she had contented herself with flattering them with their union without marking a precise time for it. That hope ameliorated the ennui of the ambulant life they led, and the fay diminished its fatigue by means of the power of her art.

She made use of a kind of little ship, which carried them through the air nine hundred and fifty times more rapidly than ours carry us over water. Her stables were full of extremely fast hippogriffs of great beauty, and the clouds that were at her orders would have furnished her with comfortable vehicles if she had wanted to make use of them , but she usually only

---

[8] Author's note: "In spite of the care that I have given to it, I have not been able to find any significance in this name relative to character. Kristopo was a good genius all round; perhaps there was nothing remarkable about him." The name could not, of course, be derived from the Greek cris- [separate, or decide] and topos [place]

made use of supernatural means in cases where art and industry could not do anything. The profound knowledge that she had of mechanics had given her the idea of the vehicle in question, and she made use of it with pleasure.

It was, as I have said, a small ship, whose port was on the platform of the highest tower in her palace. When she wanted to set sail, the vessel was released on a slide in the same manner as a ship is launched on to water. Then a large number of balloons attached around it sustained it in the air; she placed herself at a tiller that could be maneuvered with one hand, and the other operated a kind of keyboard, the keys of which corresponded to the various maneuvers of the sails and disposed them in a manner suitable to receive the wind that departed from a huge bellows operated by Toupette and Cornichon. It was fabricated in a manner to augment the impulsion of the air prodigiously, and yet to be handled with as much facility as winding a watch.

It was by that means that she traveled immense distances in such a short time, rising up into the clouds or skimming, so to speak, the surface of the sea. When she landed, a dragon that remained in the depths of the hull during the journey took up a position on the deck in order to guard the ship; once back aboard, when she wanted to rise up into the air, a trigger that she touched released springs embedded along the keel of the vessel, which, by their common effort, made it leap high enough to be sustained by the column of air established beneath it, and simultaneously enabled the bellows to act upon the sails and carry it even higher. In the same way, a bird rising into the air only employs the movement of its wings after having detached itself by means of a leap proportionate to its weight.

She usually communicated to her traveling companions the admirable subtlety that hid her from the most piercing eyes; it was only rarely that, slowing her progress, she consented to be perceived. A few of the most agreeable countries and favorite nations enjoy that advantage from time to time. One can imagine how our young people would feel about that:

to see the entire world and not to be seen by anyone is to lose half the pleasure.

Anyway, as I have said, struck by the beauty of the place, Selnozoura descended to the Isle of the Spring. She was surprised to find the countryside deserted, but her astonishment increased when, having entered the city, she found all its houses uninhabited, without any vestige of war or conflagration to which the cause of such a misfortune could be attributed. She wanted to discover it by means of her art.

While she was carrying out the operations for that on her own, Toupette and Cornichon wandered through the desolate city. The fatal spring, near to which hazard conducted them, offered them clear and fresh water. They were thirsty; they drank from it.

The art of faerie had just instructed Selnozoura of what she wanted to know. She hastened to rejoin her children—that was what her tenderness called them. At that moment, having slaked their thirst, they were considering the architecture of the spring.

"Oh, be careful not to drink that deadly poison," she shouted at them from a distance. "You'd be doomed!"

"What?" said Toupette. "What you call poison is the most delicious water I've ever drunk in my life, and Cornichon thinks the same."

"Oh, wretches," she said, "you've drunk some! Oh, you had to stay away from me!"

Then she told them about the destiny of the unfortunate islanders.

"You're going to experience a similar fate, my poor children," she added. "The power of fays operates when they wish for new marvels, but it doesn't go as far as destroying the work of another fay. You're soon going to pass into the state of the most decrepit old age. At least I can lessen its penalties by my efforts, and protect you from death, sustaining your misery by means of all the cares that the others lacked, but the charm is already operating. Cornichon's stature appears to be increasing, and a more masculine physiognomy is taking the place of his features."

While the fay was speaking, Cornichon, who was looking at Toupette, thought he was making similar discoveries in her regard. Far from his ideas leading to the sad consequences that could be drawn from the adventure, however, that present state filled him with joy. The fay had the custom of opposing to the desire he incessantly voiced to marry her with, among other reasons, the obstacle of their great youth; a moment had just removed that difficulty. He did not delay making use of that with regard to Selnozoura.

"Cease, divine fay," he said, "to complain of our fate. If the two termini of our lives must, as you say, follow one another closely, let us hasten to seize the brief interval that separates them in order to unite us. What does it matter that our old age is anticipated, if our happiness is too?"

At that speech Toupette found the profound sadness into which she had plunged diminishing. Her gaze, which she had just directed, while blushing, at Cornichon, settled on the fay, and marked the anxiety that her sentiments were in.

Selnozoura had sensed all the force of Cornichon's reasoning, and had been touched by the manner in which he had expressed them. "Yes, my children," she said, "you will be content. But this deadly place, the cause of your misfortunes, is inappropriate to celebrate the nuptials that my amity wants to render celebrated for you. Let us return to Bagota"—that was her ordinary place of her residence. "My entire court will be eager to contribute to your present amusements, and the hundred subaltern genii who are at my orders will be incessantly occupied thereafter in banishing the cares associated with old age."

The lovers would have preferred promptitude to splendor in the accomplishment of their wishes, but the experience they had of the rapidity of their journeys assured them that they would be in Bagota in a matter of hours, even though they were more than four thousand five hundred leagues away. They did not insist, and they departed.

On the way, Toupette begged the fay to maintain silence regarding the adventure of the spring; there was to need to become the topic of all conversations in advance, and give that purchase to the malignity of a hundred young women who only saw her nascent charms and her favor in the fay's eyes with jealousy. She promised that, and declared on arrival the marriage of the young lovers, which she fixed for the following night. They received compliments in consequence, and even endured speeches.

The advantageous change that had taken place in their persons in such a short time was easily remarked, and surprised everyone, but as no one divined its cause, it served to establish the proverb that travel forms young people. And with that, a thousand young persons of both sexes thought about seeking to obtain the two places that they foresaw that the marriage was about to make available.

In the meantime, the genius Kristopo arrived in Bagota. He was accustomed to making a few visits of amity to his nice from time to time, and she was glad that he had chosen the one when the establishment of Toupette would show him the value she placed on his presents.

Kristopo was surprised by the progress that the young woman had made, as much in terms of intelligence as grace. In his previous trips to Bagota, the child had amused him and occupied him. He began to be afflicted by Cornichon's good fortune; the idea of marrying Toupette himself came to mind. His passion, which was increasing with every passing moment, left very few for reflections on the disproportion between his age of three thousand years with Toupette's fourteen.

It was soon a firm decision, and there was no time to lose; she was about to pass into the power of Cornichon. He immediately went, therefore, to make his niece party to his intentions. He did not believe for an instant that his rival could hesitate over the preference that he was requesting. Imagine his astonishment when, after having employed, very gently, perfectly sensate representations, made in Kristopo's own interest, that he would soon repent of such an alliance. Selnozoura concluded with a formal refusal, which she then sustained with vivacity, against all the persistence that he renewed incessantly.

Finally seeing their futility, the genius appeared to yield to the fay's arguments, but he was only more confirmed in his initial design, and, taking advantage of the access to Toupette that he had, and a moment when she was alone, he carried her away via the chimney of her apartment a few moments before the one that was to accomplish her union with Cornichon, who was already waiting in the temple and complaining of her slowness.

As soon as he arrived in Ratibouf, the capital of his estates and his ordinary residence, Kristopo neglected nothing to justify with her the irregularity of his procedure, the blame for which he put on the fay. He had omitted nothing in order to obtain her consent; he had only endured a refusal that he had had no reason to expect; his passion was extreme, however, and time was pressing. Her marriage with Cornichon was preparing a misfortune for her all the more frightful because it would have no limits other than the duration of life, which was unknown. In those circumstances, was it natural that he should sacrifice himself to Selnozoura's caprice? And ought she even to have decided without his participation the fate of a child that she had from him? Toupette, therefore, instead of being afflicted, ought to give the greatest approval to his conduct and bless the moment that had just removed her from the tyranny of the fay and broken a marriage unworthy of her, in order to elevate her to the supreme honors that she was about to share with him.

Far from appreciating those reasons, Toupette was not even in a state to listen to them. Kristopo thought they would have more success when she had recovered from her initial astonishment, and ceased to importune her for several days.

Meanwhile, several ambassadors came successively on the part of the fay demanding Toupette's return, in the most pressing but the most futile manner. Even the threat of a cruel war did not shake the genius, who, far from changing his mind, often renewed his entreaties with regard to his captive, with as little result.

He thought that the authority of her parents might have more weight with her than arguments. He proposed to send for them. She consented to that, more in order to rid herself of his odious pursuits for while than in the design of subscribing to their will, which she foresaw would be in conformity with that of the genius. She only demanded of him that he suspend his solicitations until their arrival.

The courier who was dispatched to them found them both ill. They told him that their consent to such an honorable union could be presumed; that Kristopo's generosity toward their daughter would dispense him from the ordinary step if they alone could dispose of her; but that, since he had judged their consent necessary, they begged him also to obtain that of Selnozoura, without which they never regulated any matter of importance in their family, because of the infinite obligations that they had to the fay, and which, she being his relative and his friend, he would have no difficulty in obtaining.

The good people were unaware of the quarrel that had developed between Kristopo and Selnozoura; they were very surprised to learn from the messenger that their daughter's resistance could only be vanquished by their presence, but they asked for time to recover from their illness. The courier waited in vain for their cure; the malady only get worse. Anticipating the anxiety of his master, he asked them, in default of their presence, for their written consent, which they gave before a notary, to take effect as soon as it was ratified by Selnozoura, which they believed to be not in doubt.

The genius did not doubt that the document in question would be victorious; he ran to communicate it to Toupette, carefully refraining from mentioning the clause regarding Selnozoura's consent, which was not expressed therein. Her tears soon undeceived him; she begged him to defer the execution of his designs until her parents' recovery put them in a state to attend the wedding; the sight of them would augment her joy, if the reflections that she made in the meantime overcame her repugnance for the marriage, or would sustain her courage and at least serve as a consolation, if her heart still refused to accord with her duty.

Toupette would not have obtained that further delay from the passion of the genius if the alteration he remarked in her features had not persuaded him that her health was interested in it. In fact, the enchanted water, combined with chagrin, was beginning to produce a very considerable change in her. He believed her to be ill, and on her refusal to see any physicians, he occupied himself at least with diverting her by means of the variety of the fêtes that he prepared for her.

She wanted a change of air, and obtained permission for that. Not doubting that his presence was importunate to her, Kristopo had the generosity to leave her alone in the countryside.

I have said that Selnozoura had made the genius the most bitter complaints for the insult he had made her in the person of Toupette, and that those complaints had been followed by threats to extract a reckoning by way of arms. Cornichon, who sensed the importance there was for him and for Toupette in her prompt return, never ceased to press the fay to hasten the execution of her threats.

The interests of her dignity, combined with that of the poor lovers, determined her to march numerous troops to the frontier of Kristopo's estates; for his part, he prepared a defense proportionate to the excess of his passion for Toupette. They both commanded numerous and affectionate peoples, and, not content with their own forces, they had interested the neighboring powers in their quarrel by means of alliances. Their difference divided the fay nation.

The embarrassments inseparable from such a situation disrupted the voyages that Selnozoura was accustomed to make, which had no longer had the same charms for, her in any case, since her separation from Toupette. A change of air was, however, absolutely necessary to her, and the physicians did not relent on that article. What she imagined in order to procure it without her affairs suffering in consequence is curious enough to warrant reporting.

Every day she dispatched a large number of sylphs charged with empty containers, which they went to fill, in accordance with the choice she made, sometimes in one country and sometimes in another, with the air that was breathed there. As soon as they returned, all the air that her apartment contained was extracted carefully by means of pneumatic machines, and the new air was immediately substituted for it.

That was very ingenious, but what was even more remarkable is that the fay and all those who were allowed to enter her apartment took on the different mentalities every day of the peoples whose air they breathed. And if the interval of twenty-four hours was not sufficient to convince anyone that those differences extended into the utmost depths of the character, at least it indicated that a longer usage of the same air would infallibly produce that effect.

There were some days when that effect was more sensible, in proportion to the distinction of the character of the nation from which the air had been extracted. That of France, for example, although it ordinarily arrived in smaller quantities because it evaporates easily, nevertheless made itself noticeable, especially when it was taken from the capital.

At any rate, the verity of that singular fact was so fully recognized that the courtiers never failed to find themselves every morning at the Bureau where the couriers deposited their containers while waiting for daylight to reach the fay's apartment, in order to be informed of the country from which they were coming, and to regulate their daily conduct in consequence. There is every appearance that that is the origin of the phrase "the air of the bureau."[9]

---

[9] The French expression *prendre l'air du bureau* [take, or test, the air of the office] is used to mean seeking information as to

Now, it happened one day that young sylphs charged with going in search of the new air started larking about along the route; they threw containers at one another's heads, they played with them like balloons and indulged in abundant other mischief that gradually loosened the fastenings that sealed the containers, and even punctured the containers in several places, in such a way that the air that was initially trapped there gradually escaped. As it was immediately replaced, however, by that introduced through the opposite openings, the sylphs did not notice any voids and continued their route without suspicion.

It was only after they had arrived that they perceived the accident, but as it was too late to remedy it and they were too timid to make the confession, they kept the secret and contented themselves with blocking the openings in the containers as best they could until the time came to take them to the fay's apartment and to distribute it: no longer, as before, a unique air, but a composite of the air of almost all the nations of the world that they had traversed in their most recent journey.

Because the place that had been indicated to them that day was almost at the antipodes of Bagota, the day in question was marked by actions so full of sagacity on the fay's part, and so far from the extremes to which the usage of the unique air of certain countries had sometimes taken her, that she perceived it herself, and asked for the same air the following day. Then the sylphs made no difficulty about confessing their adventure.

That served to enlighten the fay, and to inform her that there is good everywhere; that the very excesses tempered one another; and that, in sum, from the collaboration of a host of the most opposed qualities, a median quality results that is good. Fixed in that opinion, she only wanted to use a composite air, and that is what is known as a good atmosphere.

---

what is happening in a workplace during a period of absence, or, more generally, spying.

I cannot help making a reflection here that would not have escaped my author if he had lived in our day, which is that this passage is so fundamentally in conformity with the opinion established n a few chapters of the book of *The Spirit of the Law* that one could suspect its author of plagiarism if one believed him to be versed in the history of the fays—but there is little likelihood of that.[10]

The fay had succeeded in procuring a suitable atmosphere, the restlessness in her legs still remained. A machine that set them in movement, and procured the necessary exercise without requiring her to leave her apartment, produced that effect. My author describes that machine, which is very similar to Abbé de Saint-Pierre's *trémoussoir*.[11]

---

[10] *L'Esprit des Lois* [The Spirit of the Law] (1748), one of the masterpieces of eighteenth-century political philosophy, is by the Baron de Montesquieu, although it was originally published anonymously, like most illicit texts. Montesquieu sometimes made use of fanciful tales in his writings, although Charles Mayer was stretching a point when he included him in annotated list of authors of *contes de fées* in volume 37 of his *Cabinet des fées*.

[11] Charles-Irénée Castel, abbé de Saint-Pierre (1658-1743) was an unorthodox *philosophe* now most famous for his *Projet de paix perpétuelle* [Plan for Perpetual Peace] (1713; abridged version 1729), which proposed the foundation of an international organization similar in many ways to the United Nations. He was a participant in Madame de Lambert's salon, along with François Fénelon and the coterie of female writers who invented *contes de fées*. He was notoriously expelled from the Académie française for criticizing Louis XIV, and in 1724 he was a founder-member of the Club d'Entresol, a discussion group of which Montesquieu was also a leading member; it was shut down by Louis XV in 1731. He invented his *trémousssoir*—a vibrating armchair (the word means "flutterer")—in order to agitate his muscles while he worked, so that he could keep fit in spite of his sedentary lifestyle.

Thus, the arts do not always have an epoch as recent as the one that is assigned to them. They often only emerge from the bosom of forgetfulness. The Chinese knew about gunpowder several centuries before the birth of those reputed in Europe to have invented it. But my reflections are straying from my subject and it is time to return to it.

Kristopo had given the command of his armies to a general of recognized capability, and those of the fay were under the command of Cornichon. The great interest that he had in the war had caused the judgment that no one was more capable than he of impelling operations with ardor. Already he was disposed to emerge from the retreat to which his chagrin had confined him since the abduction of Toupette, in which he was only visible to the fay. He went to obtain her final orders, and to promise to satisfy simultaneously, by means of a signal victory, amour, glory and vengeance.

Meanwhile, what was happening in Ratibouf distanced the genus even further from peaceful sentiments. Toupette's mother and father had finally arrived; Kristopo immediately took them to the country house where their daughter was. Imagine their surprise when, instead of the young and charming person they had expected to find, they only saw a woman, of pleasant appearance, in truth, but whose faded features only hinted at their former beauty.

In vain, the sweet names of *father* and *mother* were in her mouth, in vain she made them the most tender caresses; it was impossible for them to recognize as their daughter a person whose age surpassed theirs. For his part, Kristopo, offended by what he took to be a derision, having summoned all those who had been appointed to the service or the guard of Toupette, demanded of them angrily where she was, and who the person might be who dared to play such an indecent scene in his presence.

They replied to him that since Toupette had been in the house she had not shown herself to anyone, that she had only left her apartment—which they only had permission to enter while she was out walking—wearing a veil. It was then that she was taken, in accordance with his orders, what was necessary to her nourishment, which she ate alone. They had not had any occasion to see her, and had contented themselves with serving her carefully and guarding her with exactitude, and they had done their duty with a great deal of zeal and attention. They were as surprised as he was by what they saw, but they were firmly convinced that the person who was before their eyes was the same one that had been confided to them.

The simplicity of those responses was uniform, and the astonishment of those who made them dissipated the suspicions that the genius had conceived regarding their fidelity. He turned them on the fay, whose work that metamorphosis seemed to him to be, in order to avenge herself for the abduction of Toupette.

He was confirmed in that idea by a conversation he had with Toupette, which related to particularities of her childhood of which no one else could be informed. Then he fortified himself in the resolution of the war, no longer on a defensive footing, but accompanied by all the vigor and diligence necessary to anticipate on the fay's territory the hostilities that she was disposing to make on his. He flattered himself that he would soon constrain her by the effort of his arms to undo the magic by which he supposed that she had covered Toupette's charms. And, leaving her in her retreat with her parents, he ran to hasten the execution of his designs.

Selnozoura had not yet been informed of what had happened in Ratibouf; she had fully expected the surprise of the genius, but she was offended when she learned about his insulting imputation that she was the author of the metamorphosis. That dull and indirect manner of avenging herself was too distant from the elevation of her sentiments not to wound her sensibly. That circumstance aggravated her old resentments further; she delivered herself entirely to ideas of a striking vengeance. How the blood was going to flow!

However, her friends and the wisest heads of her Council, considering the disproportion there was between the cause of the war and the calamities that it was about to bring in its train, hazarded remonstrations on that subject. The amity with which she honored Toupette doubtless ought to have substituted for what was lacking on the side of birth and fortune and ought to have served her as an inviolable safeguard against anything whatsoever; but who was unaware of the aberrations to which a violent amour can cast a soul? The deference and past regard of the genius, her relative, which had not been belied for several centuries, proved well enough that he was no longer free at the fatal moment when he had been borne to such an extraordinary violence. Furthermore, the enchantment of the spring—for that fact was beginning to leak out in Bagota—in acting so promptly on Toupette, had forestalled the effects of the passion of the genius for her; nothing remained to him but the shame of such a blameworthy action.

These considerations were also sustained by the ministers of the powers allied to the fay, who only saw themselves engaged with regret in a war in which they had no direct interest. One of those princes—it was Zeprady, Prince of Mirliphipolia—offered his mediation. Although he had engagements with Selnozoura, former liaisons with the genius permitted a favorable opportunity to the negotiation for which he wanted to take responsibility to reach an accommodation.

The fay was fundamentally very reasonable; she understood that the advantages of war never compensate exactly for the woes that follow them, but, too proud to take the first step herself, she accepted Zeprady's proposal joyfully, and even consented to dissipate entirely the suspicions of the genius regarding the cause of Toupette's premature aging. That prince was informed in the greatest detail of the adventure of the Isle of the Spring, the state of which the definite condition of the two lovers rendered mystery futile henceforth. She demanded, however, appropriate reparations on the part of Kristopo, whose violence had evidently violated human rights and the respect due to sovereigns.

Zeprady therefore departed, furnished with the necessary passports, to go to the court of Ratibouf. One the way he saw Cornichon, who, entirely occupied with his vengeance, was only thinking of inspiring the same sentiments in the army of which he had just taken command. The order that he handed him on the part of the queen to suspend all hostile action until his return initially penetrated him with the sharpest dolor, but the hope of seeing Toupette again, which peace rendered far more certain than the events of a doubtful war, brought him back to milder sentiments, and even persuaded him to go to Ratibouf in order to be a decisive witness for the genius of the fay's good faith and the verity of the surprising adventure; he asked the prince to obtain permission for him to do that.

On arrival at the frontier of the genius's territory, Zeprady found troops assembled there ready to form a numerous army. He obtained from the general commanding them that he would not press his march until he had received further orders, and, continuing to follow his own with diligence, he soon arrived in Ratibouf.

The genius could not avoid recognizing himself as the author of the war that was about to flare up. The passion that had been the sole cause of it had ceased for lack of an object. Toupette, in the state she was in, no longer interested anything but pity. In such circumstances, it is usual that natural equity resumes it rights; he lent an ear to the overtures for peace that Zeprady made him. He insisted on the verity of the offense that he believed that the fay had committed in casting Toupette into the state she was in, in order to render her possession useless to him, and demanded that he be disabused in that regard, as if the verity of that supposition did not leave the insult made to the fay by the abduction of Toupette in subsistence.

Zeprady, seeing that his negotiation would only encounter that obstacle, which was easy for him to remove, did not take the trouble to destroy the prejudice of the genius by means of the maxims of law of which he could have made use, and hastened to say that he could furnish him with an irreproachable witness; that Cornichon was only waiting for passports to come to the court and convince him that what had happened to Toupette had no relevance to the present quarrel.

The genius consented to see him; he arrived, and the story he told of the adventure of the island, which he could not help mingling with his tears, drew some from the genius; however, he still demanded his confrontation with Toupette, and sent for her.

What a surprise for her, and what various sentiments agitated her by turns when she learned that she was going to see Cornichon again! Joy doubtless occupied al her heart at first, but how short its duration was! The most sensible humiliation soon took its place, and the certainty that she had that her lover was no better treated, far from giving her confidence, brought her chagrin all the way to despair. She succumbed to it for a few moments, and it was only with great difficulty that she was persuaded to climb into the carriage.

Cornichon's disturbance was scarcely less when it was announced that Toupette was approaching. Apparently more convinced, however, that their amour was of a higher order, and independent of the graces of appearance and youth, he promised himself an infinite and mutual joy from their conversation, and that sentiment left little room for regret for the losses they had both suffered.

In fact it was evident at the moment of recognition that Cornichon's amour was of a stronger caliber, so to speak; that it was more deprived of personal interest and more united with the beloved object; and Toupette, on the contrary, allowed to show in the effusion of tenderness that she could not refuse to Cornichon, reservations that uncovered all the wounds of her self-esteem.

Everything that the people of the court most versed in the metaphysics of the heart saw assured them that that was in conformity with the rules and experience. The physicists who were present also justified those various movements in their fashion, and all of them agreed that the scene was worthy of the best sentimental drama.

The genius, no longer able to refuse the evidence that he had already accorded to the enlightenments of reason, stripped of the clouds of passion, withdrew without saying anything, but disposed to be reconciled with the fay and to employ all sorts of means to make her forget his wrongdoing.

The lovers, having been the object of the importunate curiosity of the witnesses for some time, and having endured questions that were equally indiscreet and inappropriate, were finally left to themselves.

"Oh, Toupette, my dear Toupette," said Cornichon, then, "It's you that I see again. Let the memory of our past woes be put behind us forever."

"Of our past woes, you say!" cried Toupette, dolorously. "But what can destroy the cruel impression of our present woes, and dispel from our thoughts the frightful perspective of those to come—or rather, which are hurtling toward us so rapidly? What, Cornichon, are you insensible to that? You do not love me if my misfortunes do not penetrate to the depths of your heart."

"How unjust you are to doubt it," said Cornichon. "I feel them a thousand times more than my own—or rather, confounding your condition with my own, as our hearts are confounded, I would be overwhelmed by the double weight of misfortune if I did not enjoy..."

"Oh, what enjoyment?" interrupted Toupette. "What can we enjoy at present that can compensate us or what has been taken away from us? For, in sum, don't flatter yourself: the fatal water has already had the effect on you of more than half a century, and doubtless it has treated me no better."

"I confess," replied Cornichon, "that in recalling those nascent graces, the duration of which our common accident has so cruelly hastened the progress, I find you different today, but there are graces for all ages, and you, my dear Toupette, have those of the sexagenarian age. Yes, if our eyes had not lost the extreme vivacity that distinguished them, your faded complexion would reproach them for a gleam that they alone would have conserved. A few wrinkles that I perceive on your forehead justify the reasons that your cheeks have for flattening and descending, and your breasts, in withering, fall with much more decency. It's thus that all your features, aging in intelligence, do not cease to conserve between them a harmony that proves incontestably that you have been beautiful."

"Cruel man!" Toupette interrupted, sharply. "My breasts have withered, and it's you who tell me that?"

"But Toupette," said Cornichon, "don't you remember what scant value you once seemed to place on the fragile advantages of beauty? Was my heart not the unique object of all the wishes of yours?"

"Yes, Cornichon," she said, apparently a little calmer, "of course I remember; but can I not fear some diminution in your tenderness for me, when such monstrous changes have taken place in my face? For after all, we rely a great deal on external appearances; they are what strike the senses, and what power the senses have over our hearts, alas! Who will love me, if you cease to love me?"

"That anxiety is superfluous, my dear Toupette," replied Cornichon. "It relates to an impossibility; but even supposing it were possible, could the desire of strangers ever replace mine in your estimation? You can't even imagine it. You can see that you're forming phantoms in order to combat them."

"I can see," said Toupette, "that you take me for a visionary; it's very hard, at the culmination of disgrace, to see one's reason attacked as well."

"Oh, Toupette," he said, "how unjust you are. What, while my discourse, drawn from the purest springs of philosophy, only has your repose for an object, you can give it such an insulting meaning! But suffer that I support my arguments with a celebrated example. Are you unaware of the story of Baucis and Philemon, those two tender spouses who conserved without any alteration, into extreme old age, all the sentiments of the most perfect amour? Fortunate couple! They experienced with delight that the chains of marriage, and even the infirmities of old age, are very light when amour sustains their weight."

"A fine comparison, in truth," said Toupette, with chagrin, "a beautiful comparison. Baucis, in the course of a long life, had received thousands of times from Philemon the most sensible proofs of tenderness, while I...but seriously, either don't compare or find more accurate resemblances. That one doesn't do honor to your intelligence, or at least wrongs your memory; one might think that you had prepared a new proof for my patience, by stringing together the most singular, the most extraordinary words. How unfortunate I am!"

That conversation was not taking a mild tone when the Prince of Mirliphipolia came to tell them that the genius, full of regret for what had happened, was in the sentiments most appropriate to satisfy the fay; that he had asked him to return promptly to find her, in order to assure her of it, and to ask for passports for the ministers destined to go to Bagota as soon as possible, in order to subscribe to the conditions of a peace, of which he left her entirely the mistress; and that he would go to ratify them himself as soon as he could do so with security and decency. He had been charged with saying to Cornichon that he was the master of departing with him, and taking Toupette. The genius could not resolve to see them as yet, after causing them so much pain, but he hoped to render his presence more supportable to them in the future, and that he would explain himself more clearly when he was in Bagota.

"Prepare yourselves, then," added the Prince of Mirliphipolia, "by means of a little repose, to depart with me tomorrow, as soon as daylight begins to appear. I'll leave you now."

Cornichon and Toupette, anticipated the hour of their departure considerably; their misfortunes had deprived them for a long time of the sweetness of a long slumber, and the situation in which they found themselves was not conducive to sleep; they met up before dawn.

Joy was dominant in Cornichon's heart; Toupette was dejected. The pleasure of her liberty was poisoned by the idea of the usage that she was going to make of it. "Was not my prison preferable," she cried, "to the humiliation that awaits me in Bagota, where, instead of the charms that attracted the homage of men and the envy of women, I can now only offer subjects of scorn, or at least pity, for the former and a prideful triumph for the malignity of the latter?"

Cornichon tried to dissipate her chagrin by means of arguments similar to those he had used the day before; they were no better received. He persisted; Toupette had the vapors; he was embarrassed by that, but, still attached to the reasoning that the candor and ingenuity of his amour suggested to him, he only repeated them and did not vary them. The vapors were augmented; he was frightened that reason had no purchase on that malady, it being his only resource.

Finally, with the aid of smelling salts, Toupette recovered a passable tranquility, and the reflections that they both made on the mysterious promises that the genius had made them via the prince furnished them with a series of conjectures that, without producing anything certain, nevertheless occupied them agreeably enough until Bagota, where they arrived the same day.

It was late; Toupette was glad about that, she was far from desiring to see many people. The fay had retired, but having learned that the prince had arrived, she did not want to put off until the following day hearing his report, succinctly at least, on the success of his mission.

After having thanked him and put off until the next day a more extensive narration of his negotiations, she could not dispense with seeing Toupette, and even less with shedding tears for her fate. She consented to the plea that the unhappy lovers made her to keep a retreat in their apartments appropriate to their situation, and only to be visible to her.

The following days having been employed in the examination of the conditions of the peace, their ratification and the expedition of orders for the lieutenant of the troops, attention then turned to preparations for the celebration that would follow their publication.

In accordance with his promises, the genius did not fail to come to Bagota. His satisfactions were complete; he neglected nothing to recover the amity of the fay. Everyone experienced the most vivid joy, except for the lovers, delivered to dolor and only distracted therefrom in the moments when the charitable fay wanted to slip away from her occupations in order to go to their apartments.

Although the promises of the genius had flattered their hope for a time, they reproached themselves afterwards for their credulity. Several days after his arrival, he had not even enquired about them.

In his regard, they said to themselves, *we are in the most profound forgetfulness We serve on his part for a vain and impotent pity. Alas, not even the consolation of imagining that we are susceptible to it remains to us.*

Those sad thoughts were occupying them one morning—it was the day destined for the publication of the peace treaty—when they perceived the fay, accompanied by the genius, each followed by their court, advancing toward the place where they had the custom of meeting during the day. That visit surprised them; the occupations and trappings of that great day did not seem to permit the fay her usual attentions for them; the presence of the genius and his retinue surprised them even more. In fact, Selnozoura had prepared them not to see her that day, but the genius had implored her with such insistence to take him to see the unfortunate couple that the fay, who had emerged from her palace in order to see for herself the preparations for the fête that was to solemnize the day, was constrained to postpone that care, and could not refuse to satisfy an urgency that appeared mysterious in the circumstances.

When they drew near to the apartment where Cornichon and Toupette were, the former hastened to go to meet the illustrious company, while Toupette sought to hide her confusion in the darkest party of the room. Cornichon's strength did not respond to his urgency; he stumbled at the feet of the fay, and sustained a black eye.

The alarm that caused Toupette overcame the reluctance she had to show herself; she ran to him, utterly bewildered, but her debilitated feet tripped over Cornichon's legs as he was still sprawled on the ground, and she fell upon him rudely. Her mouth having encountered the forehead of the injured man, it cost her three teeth that had been meditating escaping from her mouth for some time.

That accident drew tears from the fay. She could not help saying to the genius that it had been imprudent to come and surprise the poor couple in that way. He responded with a confidence that enabled the fay to think that he had discovered a means of compensating them; she did not reply.

A few courtiers had difficulty hiding their joy. Cornichon and Toupette were favorites; several of them had experienced that at the expense of their self-esteem. Their imminent decrepitude ought, in truth, soon to distance those objects of jealousy. Decrepit favorites were rarely seen, and accidents like the one that had just occurred hastened the moment of their retreat, but they still saw all the indications of that with pleasure.

When they had been helped, Selnozoura proposed to the genius that they be left to take repose.

"It will not be in vain, Madame," he replied, "that I have engaged you to come here; a visit of consolation could have taken place in moments less crowded than today's. I chose it expressly in order to give more splendor to the reparation that I owe you for the violence that I exercised on a person who is dear to you, and more merit to the relief that I want to procure for the woes of these lovers.

"As soon as I was cured of the suspicions I had," he continued, "that the aging of Toupette was only an illusory effect of your chagrin against me, the sensible regret that I had of my procedure caused me to seek means of repairing it that would be sufficient for you and useful to the unfortunates whose union I had so unjustly prevented. The story that the Prince of

Mirliphipolia had told me of the circumstances of their adventure had convinced me. It is true that I could do nothing by myself to change their fundamental situation, which was the work of a fay, but I thought at least that good advice can sometimes take the place of a service. What I have to say might substitute in some manner for what I can do; this is it.

"You might remember, Madame, that at the last Estates General of Faerie, which were held before the Tribunal of Destinies to examine the works of each Intelligence, those of the Fay of the Spring were found so constantly full of good will that no one doubted that they were a naïve expression of her character. The harm that she was sometimes able to produce was attributed to an error on her part rather than the effect of a malign intention, and it was judged that, although it was contrary to the dignity of Faerie to allow any trace of the works of intelligences to subsist, it was nonetheless in conformity with the laws of justice to dispense a fay of seeing the entire execution of disastrous things that would only have given rise to scorn. It was therefore decided that without drawing consequences for others whose views were not so honest, the Fay of the Spring would have the liberty to diminish by half the harm that she had done in the aforesaid circumstances.

"She would then have made usage of that mercy in favor of some of the inhabitants of the isle, if death, which had anticipated that decree, had recognized any power superior to its own. How fortunate it would have been if she had at least destroyed the spring and precipitated the fatal waters at their source into the gulfs of the sea; she did not think of it, but, still disposed to do good for its own sake, she will doubtless seize the opportunity even more enthusiastically, if it is presented to her under the title of justice.

"I will take charge, therefore, of informing her that her presence is needed here, and although, as I have said, it is not permitted to her to repair in totality the harm she had done, at least she will be able to return one of these two lovers to the state in which they would presently be without this cruel adventure. It is up to you, Madame, to choose which of the two will enjoy that favor."

The last words spoken by the genius, which surprised the fay greatly, threw her into an irresolution that banished from her heart the joy that the first had commenced spreading there. The two lovers had an equal part in her affection; how could she resolve to pronounce to one of the two that he or she would continue to be the sad victim of a perpetual vicissitude, while the other would return to all the advantages of his or her age?

While she was making those reflections, the rest of the assembly was divided. "How," said the men, "can a fay as jealous of the brilliance of her court hesitate for a moment to render its most precious ornament to it by the rejuvenation of Toupette? Are beauty and grace so common here that she can neglect the opportunity to see them assembled in that charming person?"

"It is highly unlikely," said the women, on the contrary, "that it is uncertainty that is closing Selnozoura mouth regarding her choice; it is already made. Only the presence of the two persons who interest her so strongly prevents her from declaring it. It would be cruel to make it in the presence of Toupette; the delay cannot be interpreted otherwise. How, in fact, could the fay sacrifice to the temporary charms of the face of a little girl, the important services that she has a right to expect from a man like Cornichon, as many at the head of the army as in the Council? We have just seen the zeal with which he ran to expose himself to the hazards of a cruel war, in order to avenge the glory of the fay, and his premature intelligence announces that he will be no less appropriate to ministerial politics."

However, the fay's uncertainty not permitting her to make a choice, she took time to think about it, saying that it was necessary not to occupy herself that day with anything but the fêtes ad games that a fortunate peace warranted. She left the lovers, but she could not help saying in a low voice to her uncle that his discourse had prepared her for a more complete satisfaction; that furthermore, he had not put into it anything of his own, the advice regarding the Fay of the Spring could have been discovered without him; that she expected less common services from a genius like him; and that she hoped of his amity that he would think of something for which one could have a personal obligation.

With that, they arrived in the main square, where they applauded the preparations that had been made in order to give to the publication of the peace treaty and the renewal of alliance between the two States all the accompaniments of grandeur and magnificence that an event so advantageous to the two nations demanded.

Let us leave the fay, the genius and the court occupied with that grand ceremony, and go to find Toupette and Cornichon inside their apartment.

"Finally, my dear Toupette," he said, delightedly, as soon as they were free, "I am able to give you the most decisive proof of my amour for you, since you will see it disengaged from all the exterior circumstances that customarily sustain vulgar amours. Yes, while, reentering into all the advantages of my age, I shall be the object of the desires of the loveliest women of the court, I will only be seen to be sensible to the pleasure of sacrificing them for you.

"It will be at time when I am most convinced of the return of the graces with which I was once flattered that I shall take pleasure in making a striking homage to the wrinkles and infirmities of your old age. What attention, what tender cares will I not have for you? What a pure joy will you not experience yourself in recognizing then that the illusion of beauty counts for nothing in the homage that I will render you; it will only relate to your virtues, to the most beautiful soul in the world!"

"What!" Toupette interrupted, brusquely. "It's you who count on enjoying exclusively the favor with which the genius had just flattered us, while I remain...? I know," she continued, emotionally, "that the gifts of reason and virtue are pref-

239

erable to the fragile advantages of a seductive beauty; that the conquests procured by the former have a more solid glory than those of the latter; I know, finally, that a woman of merit is preferable in the eyes of reason to a pretty woman who is only that. But why not do me the honor of believing me capable of uniting that common advantage? Why, if your role would be more glorious, do you not even take the trouble to enquire as to whether I might have the ambition to pretend to it?

"Oh, Cornichon," she said, shedding tears, "what humiliation you make me experience! No, you don't merit the sentiments that I have for you; but the good fay is too equitable to share your opinion; I reproach myself for the pain it has caused me; it was as premature as your joy."

As she finished speaking she went into a neighboring cabinet abruptly, closing the door behind her. The entreaties that Cornichon made her for a long time to come back would have been futile if the time when the fay was accustomed to come to see them, which was approaching, had not determined he to emerge from her retreat, after having recovered from her disturbance somewhat, firmly resolved to make every effort to destroy Cornichon's project.

"Forget, my dear Toupette," he said, as soon as she returned, "the design that alarmed you; the delicacy of my passion had inspired it; yours is wounded by it; let us not talk about it anymore. Let us refuse, by virtue of a common scorn, an advantage that is not one for us, and which causes, on the contrary, such a diversity in our opinions. Let is submit to our original destiny, all the more willingly because it will match throughout the course of our life the different seasons through which we must pass.

"Our ages being almost similar, we shall experience the same winters and we shall see the same springs; the inconveniences that were capable of destroying an entire people who did not foresee them, and from which no one was exempt, will disappear here, where they will be foreseen and repaired successively by the cares of the best of fays. And if the bizarre nature of our fate forbids us to hope for a fortunate posterity from our union, the season of amours, as frequent for us as for the innocent birds, will have all of their ardor, and will only be distinguished by the purity of our flames."

That expedient of Cornichon's might have diminished somewhat the difficulty that Toupette envisaged in being the only one clad in all the charms of youth; doubtless she ought to have approved of it—but when one is prejudiced by an idea as agreeable as the one contained in the declaration of the genius and one applies oneself to profiting from it, it is difficult to let go of it, especially when one flatters oneself with seeing it realized. Far from applauding that opinion, therefore, she only occupied herself with casting ridicule on the terms in which it was conceived.

"Good God," she said, "what fine phrases! It's a pity that one can perceive all the travail that it cost you. Innocent birds, ardors, flames distinguished by their purity. How pretty! But wait; I'm obliged to tell you, my poor Cornichon, that the madrigal tone that is familiar to you does not suit our situation at all, and if you only have such things to say, be good enough to dispense me from listening to them."

Cornichon did not think it appropriate to continue a conversation that had engendered no much bitterness. They both commenced a mute scene, which as interrupted shortly by the arrival of Selnozoura, who, fatigued by the duration of the fête, had slipped away from it briefly and come to respire in her children's apartment.

She had anticipated a part of what had happened between them; the situation in which she found them made her understand that she was not mistaken. Toupette hastened to explain to her all the reasons she pretended to have for complaint against Cornichon. The author of these memoirs does not hesitate to list them, but as they are almost the same things that we have just reported, I shall spare the reader the repetition and content myself with saying that, in the hope of finding in association with the genius and the Fay of the Spring some means of improving their condition and perhaps extending to both of them the favor that was destined for one alone, Selnozoura excused herself from deciding their fate then, as they pressed her insistently to do. She founded her refusal on the futility there would be in announcing in advance a choice that would only take effect with the arrival of Dindonnette, who was the only one permitted to modify her work.

It was necessary, therefore, to be patient until the arrival of that fay, who made them wait for several days. I shall not say how they were employed; the reader's imagination will easily depict the fireworks, the balls, the carousels and all the other amusements that ought to celebrate the return of union to two people who had always enjoyed a constant peace and amity; it is only necessary to give each of those things the degree of perfection that is lacking among us, but which was doubtless not lacking among the fays.

Finally, Dindonnette arrived; she combined with the best intentions in the world a similar irresolution with regard to the decision she ought to make, which is usual when the murky vision of a limited mind can only discover inconvenience in a plan, without being enlightened regarding its advantages. One seeks the good with all one's heart, but gropingly, and often finds oneself so close to the bad that it is dangerous to make a false step. One knows that, one fears being criticized, and one makes the worst decision of all: that of not making any. That was exactly Dindonnette's situation.

All those who were interested in the lovers had successively taken possession of her. The fay Selnozoura, with an extreme delicacy regarding her reputation, fearing that a preference she gave to Cornichon would be interpreted maliciously, had fixed all her favor on Toupette. The genius, who feared acquiring new irons and was still shuddering at the catastrophic effects that his passion had been ready to cause, declared himself in favor of Cornichon. The divided court also gave Dindonnette various advice, founded on arguments that seemed to her to be of equal weight, and put her beyond a state to make any resolution. However, she had not been able to help indicating the day when she would make up her mind.

When it drew near, she finally settled on an inclination that she thought appropriate to satisfy everyone, because it gave everyone a part of what they wanted. Charmed by that marvelous idea, she abridged the delay that she had requested and wanted the lovers to appear before her immediately. She urged the fay and the genius to assemble the court and the people, in order to render more numerous the applause that she had no doubt that her plan would merit.

As soon as Toupette and Cornichon had arrived and everyone assembled in the great hall of the palace, the doors of which were left open, Dindonnette, having obtained silence, spoke as follows:

"Fortunate is the person who can repair the harm she has done; even more fortunate is the person who has not done any." That sentence not suffering any contradiction, she continued: "Far from enjoying the latter advantage, even the former is not accorded to me." Addressing Cornichon, she said: "I could render your beautiful youth, and," she said to Toupette, "I could also reestablish yours. I shall do both, and I shall do neither."

One can imagine the agitation that these words caused the lovers, particularly Toupette, but they only caused curiosity in the assembly, whose members did not understand them. A slight murmur rose up; then people reflected that fays ought not to talk like other people, and they shut up in order to hear what came next.

"No," Dindonnette continued, "I will not have the cruelty of abandoning one of you to the horrors of decrepitude, while I enable the other to reenter into all the rights of a flourishing youth. And since I cannot render them entirely to both of you at once, you shall at least each participate in it partially. I want half of your body to resume the vigor and graces of youth, while the other half will continue to experience the decadence to which the whole was destined. It is up to you to choose which part of you is dearer to you and ought to submit to that fortunate metamorphosis: whether it will operate by means of a perpendicular line, separating the body along its entire

243

length, or whether a horizontal line traced at the waist will be the common term of those two states, and in the latter case, to which of the two halves thus distinguished, the superior or the inferior, youth will be attached."

It was then that all the seriousness in which people naturally found themselves was overturned. A thousand bursts of immoderate laughter were unleashed at once; no one, except for the two lovers and Dindonnette, who were astounded, could resist it. Even Selnozoura, who felt obliged to restrain herself in order to restrain others, could not hold back at the excessive ridiculousness of such an idea.

Finally, after a few moments, she got a grip on herself, and those who believed that they ought to resume a decent air of gravity commenced to render it to others. Thereafter, Dindonnette recovered slightly.

Selnozoura thought then that she was obliged to offer an opinion that would terminate such a comical scene. "I believe," she said to Dindonnette, "that your benevolent intention and the extent of your power would be no less fulfilled if, instead of assembling such opposite states in a single individual, you enabled them to enjoy alternately the advantages and disgusts attached to old age and the prime of life, for a time of which you ought to fix the duration, just as you ought to choose which of the two will be rejuvenated first."

"That's marvelous," she said, "and in truth, that was my first idea; one should always stick to one's first impulse. I thought inappropriately, on the word of certain people who do not understand anything, that it was necessary to correct it by reflection, and see how one is deceived: would you believe that that happens to me every day? But I'm disabused. Now, to which of the two should we return youth first?"

Cornichon, ever ready to sacrifice his interests to Toupette's, hastened to fix her choice by begging her to let it fall on her.

"I am too sure of Toupette's heart," he said, "to fear that that change would rob me of the smallest fraction of it, and since she has that little whim, it's necessary, Madame, if you please, to satisfy it."

What joy did she not express at that moment? What gratitude did she not testify to her lover? Protestations of the most tender concerns, as was only just, were commencing to form a discourse full of pathos on her part, when Dindonnette, charmed no longer to have to exercise a liberty that fatigued her, hastened to touch her with her wand. Immediately, Toupette, like a snake shedding its old skin, found herself stripped of her wrinkles, and allowed to be seen in their place the features of a perfect beauty and the stature of a nymph.

The two fays and the genius were overjoyed, the men were charmed, the women confounded in their pretentions, and everyone was dazzled. Cornichon's surprise, although he was prepared for that event, was so great that he fell over, crying with all his might: "Help me, my dear Toupette." But the latter's joy scarcely left her enough presence of mind to give her liberators a part of the evidence of gratitude that she owed them, and Cornichon would have been at risk of not recovering his feet so soon if Selnozoura, who had been the first to perceive his fall, had not taken care to have him lifted up.

Then Toupette ran to him, slightly confused by having been deaf to his voice. She assured him that she would repair that distraction the next time he fell, and as the fay, who wanted to take her away, was calling to her, she promised Cornichon as she quit him to render him a faithful account of all the pleasures that the change was about to procure for her.

Selnozoura returned to her apartment via uncovered galleries, in order to let the people who had not been able to find room in the hall to see such a singular marvel, to which they gave a thousand blessings.

She had no sooner arrived than the genius approached her in order to bid her adieu.

"What, then, is the reason for such a precipitate departure?" she said. "Won't you flatter me with a longer sojourn?"

She was about to continue to express her astonishment when he interrupted her, saying: "Am I not unfortunate enough, Madame to have broken the ties that attach me to you by so many titles once? Do you want me to risk failing you again, and rendering myself utterly unforgivable? Is this not the same object whose charms cast me into the greatest aberrations? Alas, far from having lost their power over my heart, I sense only too clearly that, if they were capable of overturning my reason while they were only nascent, the degree of perfection that they have acquired will render them even more redoubtable. Suffer, then, Madame, that a longer sojourn with you be postponed until the time when, Cornichon enjoying the favors of destiny in his turn, I shall be able to see Toupette without danger."

"But in that regard," exclaimed Dindonnette, "we've forgotten to fix the epoch in which Toupette must cede her condition of youth to Cornichon. The poor fellow! Alas, I believe that there's no longer time. How stupid I am. But truly, no, there's no longer time; that condition ought to have been announced before Toupette was touched by the wand. Oh, fatal wand! But you, Madame," she added, addressing Selnozoura, "should have warned me."

Dindonnette's forgetfulness had not escaped Selnozoura, but the same motives of delicacy that had prevented her from appearing to be too interested in Cornichon had retained her again in that occasion; she had not dared to warn Dindonnette about her neglect.

"Your operations, Madame," she said to her, "were so prompt that I did not have time to enable you to perceive what was lacking therein. No, undoubtedly, our laws being formal in that regard, the conditions of a work of faerie cannot be substituted after the touch of the wand, which puts an inviolable seal on it. Cornichon can only expect the change of his state due to the enchanted water, which, in the decrepitude he is in, cannot fail to arrive soon; so the projected union can be concluded, and Toupette will fulfill successively in his regard the functions of wife, nurse and governess."

"How sorry I am," said Dindonnette, "that I cannot witness that wedding; I have infinite affairs at home, whereas, if had thought of it I would have marked a term to Toupette's metamorphosis short enough to enable me to attend the marriage—a week, for example; I couldn't spend any longer here."

"But Madame," said Selnozoura, "that would have made their condition worse instead of making it better, the enchanted water having much longer periods. Then again, what means are there of uniting people who trade conditions so frequently?"

"I agree," Dindonnette replied, "that the period of a week is a little short, and I hadn't thought about it. Let's not talk about it anymore, since it's no longer relevant; but as for the marriage, I sustain the possibility of it in the circumstances in question, and in the state of complete infancy. I know what I'm talking about; I'll explain myself: at the anticipated moment of the metamorphosis, they would be brought together, as is practiced between people who want to marry. When the moment came, Toupette, who would feel her strength abandoning her, would be retained by Cornichon, who would feel his own increasing proportionately and his stature straightening, and would recovering the free use of his tongue in order to pronounce the necessary words; they would then seize that moment of parity, and you would see married people! Oh, how pleasant that would have been!"

As it was evident that the good fay had resolved only to say and do absurd things, they dispensed with replying to her. Selnozoura gave all her attention to the genius, who, persisting in his resolution not to see Toupette any longer, took his leave of her and refused absolutely to offer she made, in order to retain him, to send that young person to one of her country houses for as long as it pleased him to remain in Bagota.

"You do not have enough obligation to me, Madame," he said, "to make that sacrifice; it is for me to depart and to remain far away from your court for as long as the common laws of human nature conserve for Toupette the charms that are so deadly to me; but I depart penetrated by the sentiments that you might desire of a good friend and relative, who will always regret having ceased to be one and will only occupy myself with giving you evidence of it."

Having said that, he launched himself into the air, where he was sustained all the way to his palace by two sylphs who held him by his ears; that was the mode of travel he fund most convenient—everyone has his own taste.

When a day so very full had passed, Toupette, on turning to her apartment, found Cornichon, who was waiting for her with the utmost impatience. Before quitting her, Selnozoura had not failed to recommend silence to her in Cornichon's regard as to Dindonnette's forgetfulness, which excluded him forever from the favor that Toupette alone would enjoy. There was no need for that; the sight of her delighted him so much that he forgot himself entirely. The pleasure he had driven out of his mind the thought that he might have been seen with an equal pleasure; he would not have traded one for the other.

"How beautiful you are, my dear Toupette," he said.

"It's true, she said, "that people have found me sufficiently so, and I'm not sorry that you share the common opinion in that regard; but how are you after your recent fall?"

"What kindness," he said, moving a little closer to her. "That's your usual amity, I'm sure of it. But beautiful Toupette, I won't limit to that sentiment my pretentions to your heart..."

"What?" she said, moving away. "You have more extensive pretentions? Oh, you have too much intelligence for that!"

At that moment, one of the genius guards commissioned to make a round of the palace every evening in order to maintain the order there that the fay had established, made audible at the door of Toupette's apartment the sound of his halberd, which served as a signal for retreat. Toupette informed Cornichon of that, and they terminated a conversation that was about to become embarrassing for both of them.

As he quit Toupette, Cornichon could not help saying to her that she was very exact. She excused herself on the basis of the day's fatigue, and they separated.

The following day and those that followed, until Dindonnette's departure, were employed in giving her less noisy, and hence more sociable, amusements than those with which she had found Selnozoura's could occupied on her arrival. Hunting, fishing, walking and several other pleasures particular to the fay species, were alternately brought into play; my author gives an exact description of them, which I believe I can pass over, at the risk of the reproach that translators often run of having truncated their author.

Finally, Dindonnette, after having asked for and given a thousand various items of advice on politics, finance, war and pompoms, and having sufficiently wearied everyone, departed, as she had promised.

Returned to herself then, Selnozoura did not forget, among the domestic cares to which she delivered herself, the consolation of Cornichon. She found him in the dispositions of indifference as to his fate in which we represented him just now, provided that he could enjoy the sight of Toupette. She believed that he was in a state to hear that it was, in fact, the only pleasure that was reserved to him, because of the stupidity of the Fay of the Island. Toupette, who was present, had new proofs in that occasion of the violence of his passion, which was entirely detached from his own interest.

Time passed, however, and while Toupette spent it with all the pleasure imaginable, a deluge of infirmities overwhelmed Cornichon; nothing remained to him of humanity but a heart that Toupette alone still animated, and thoughts that were incessantly directed toward her.

She was good and compassionate, it is true, but in the end, those most estimable of all virtues, which give activity to the aid of which one can expect some utility for those who receive it, become idle and as if stifled when their practice is evidently fruitless. That was the situation in which Toupette found herself with regard to Cornichon; the unfortunate fellow perceived it, and, the chagrin he felt collaborating with his infirmities, he fell into the final state of old age—by which I mean infancy.

Let us quit Selnozoura's court momentarily in order to pass to that of the genius. The affairs and amusements to which he devoted himself alternately, more in the design of distracting himself from his passion than by taste or necessity, did not produce the effect for which he hoped. Relentlessly occupied with an unfortunate amour, he could not enjoy any repose; all his art was useless to him; he thought of seeking elsewhere what it could not furnish him.

Genii have in regard to Destiny an access that is refused to mortals; he resolved to consult it. I shall not make the description of the palace of that supreme divinity, or the manner in which audiences are given there. It is sufficient to say that in the one that Kristopo obtained, he received the response that *it was only up to him to recover his tranquility in one of his horns.*

"My horns!" he cried, very surprised. "I know that the bold imagination of humans sometimes represents us in the most bizarre forms and those most distant from the truth, but..."

Destiny does not like replies; the triple veil that covers the redoubtable throne at the height from which its oracles are rendered was suddenly lowered, and Kristopo was reduced to seeking the meaning of that one in his own enlightenment. That did not furnish anything satisfactory. He wanted to consult that of his Council, and he assembled it as soon as he returned.

Of all the advice he received there, none struck him more than that of an old man who was the last to speak.

"You know, Sire," he said, "that when intelligences like yourself want to favor humankind with their precious caresses, the fruits of that temporary union do not fail to bear at birth few marks of the nobility of their origin; subject otherwise to all the infirmities of humans, it is not just that they are made in all regards like them. The particular signs of your illustrious house in that case are, for males, an almost imperceptible horn, just as a little tuft of black feathers distinguishes those who emerge female. Do you not have, Sire, any memory of having given rise to that mark?"

"It's true," replied the genius, "that some fifteen years ago, finding myself very thirsty while out hunting in an arid land, a young shepherdess of great beauty offered to guide me to a spring that she knew. That small service excited my gratitude; nine months later she gave birth to a son, but the memory of that event only increased my embarrassment by virtue of the consequences it had. I consulted my art with regard to the fate of that child and the relation it might have to mine, and discovered that he was destined to cause me violent chagrins by virtue of the competition he would have with me. The violent measures that the jealousy of the throne inspire in me all too often horrified me, but I thought that it was at least prudent to relegate that obstacle to my tranquility far away from me. I had him given to a slave merchant who was transporting several of them to another hemisphere, not doubting that such a great distance would put eternal boundaries between us. How, then, can I find that child, when I don't even know whether he's alive? And even if I could, what relation could that discovery have to my passion for Toupette?"

"If I had in hand," said the old man, "a power as great as the one that resides in you, Sire, I flatter myself that my research would not be in vain. But without having recourse yet to the supernatural means that are open to you, first consult the mother of the child, if she still exists; maternal tenderness is industrious and clear-sighted; one might obtain enlightenment from her, or at least a few clues."

The woman in question had retired to her hamlet, more sensible to the separation from her son than all the ease she might have enjoyed at the court. Someone went to fetch her. Firstly, the genius asked her whether her son did, in fact, have the horn that the old man had mentioned, which she confirmed. He then employed mildness and menaces by turns for a long time in order to determine the fearful woman to tell him what she knew about the child.

Finally, she admitted that, unable to resolve herself to be separated from him, she had followed the slave merchant for a long time when he left Ratibouf, that she had even resolved to give herself to him and travel all over the world rather than abandon her son, but that, touched by her tears, he had consented to sell him in the first city they came to, in order to conserve the hope for her of being informed of his fate, and even the means of seeing him sometimes; but that was on the express condition that she said nothing about it, for fear that he might attract the wrath of the genius, whom he had promised only to dispose of him three thousand leagues away from Ratibouf.

They were then in the territory of Selnozoura, and on arriving in the capital the following day, the merchant had sold her son to a lady of the fay's court, who had been struck by his beauty, and who made a present of him to her sovereign. The merchant had continued his route next day, and she, after having remained in Bagota for a few days incognito, partly consoled by knowing that her child was so well placed, instead of returning to the court, which abode no longer had any charms for her, she had fixed her residence in her cottage. From there she had gone to Bagota several times in order to have news of her dear son and to enjoy the pleasure, always incognito, of sometimes seeing him, but a horrible enchantment had finally taken him away forever from a place that could no longer offer her anything but a subject for tears.

"What is that subject, then" asked the genius.

"Alas, Sire," the poor woman replied, "at the age that you know he ought to have, he resembles a man a hundred years old, and perhaps at the present moment he had ceased to live."

All the circumstances of this story, in combination, left the genius no room to doubt that Cornichon was his son. He was glad about that. "This discovery does seem, it is true," he said, "to have some connection with Destiny's oracle. I have rediscovered one of my horns, but I don't yet see what relationship it can have to my tranquility."

"Sire," said the old man, "that first part of the oracle, grasped, is a feeble glimmer that ought to lead you to the light. The oracle, in saying that it only depends on you to discover the tranquility that you have lost, supposes on your part the collaboration of a few efforts, labors, or perhaps even sacrifices."

"Yes," said the genius, after having meditated a little, "yes Barmakaijou"—that was the wise old man's name—"your conjectures are accurate; sacrifices are doubtless necessary, and very sensible ones; but I shall not be reproached for having, for want of courage, raised obstacles to the edict of Destiny. Judge that by the resolution I have made, and to which I want to make you party.

"You know that my recent services have been of such importance for all the Supreme State of Faerie, that they have filled the measure to which favors of the first order are attached, in accordance with our customs. I was able, therefore, not long ago, to claim in my favor a fortunate uncertainty as to the object of my request, suspended thus far, and I postponed its determination until the time of our next general assembly.[12]

"My choice is made; it will neither be the Great Slipper, not the unworthy privilege of only shaving the half of my beard that forms my prayers; I shall not be seen to solicit from my peers with such ordinary entreaties the right to wipe my nose with my foot.[13] The rejuvenation of Cornichon, the anni-

---

[12] Author's note: "This is one of the articles on which one might have desired a few clarifications on the part of the author; one can only infer that, all the nations, being in accord on the general principle that it is desirable to recompense merit and services, only differed regarding the choice of the rewards proposed to them."

[13] Author's note: I am tempted to believe that there is a misprint in the text here, in view of the impossibility of this action, but genii are very extraordinary things." This is a joke; the French colloquialism "*il ne se mouche pas du pied*" [he

hilation of the bizarre law of which he is the victim; that is what ought to acquit the Republic toward me, as the sacrifice of my passion for Toupette in favor of my son will acquit me toward my niece."

That resolution was applauded, and the action appeared magnanimous. Kristopo, in separating from his Council, commanded a profound secrecy regarding the affair, as he did to Cornichon's mother, who was weeping with joy as she had just wept with sorrow.

A few punctilious readers might perhaps say that this incident is pillaged from Seleucus, father of Antiochus;[14] the value of that criticism depends on the times when the two events happened, which is a point of chronology whose discussion is not my subject.

The time of the General Assembly of Faerie was imminent; as soon as it arrived, the genius transported himself there. Selnozoura had also gone there. Imagine her surprise when, in the audience that was granted to Kristopo to make the exposition of his services and the requests that they merited, she heard that they were limited to the rejuvenation of Cornichon. Was it on the part of a rival that one ought to expect such an extraordinary mark of disinterest? But she was even more astonished when, on leaving the audience, the genius approached her and requested Toupette for Cornichon, in the capacity of his father.

Such a generous procedure completed effacing from the fay's heart all the nasty impression that the previous conduct of the genius might have left there. A mutual confidence succeeded it. The genius told Selnozoura about everything that he

---

doesn't wipe his nose with his foot] refers to someone who does things in grand style.

[14] Seleucus I Nicator, who took over most of the Alexandrian Empire in the third century B.C. after the death of Alexander the Great, allegedly permitted his son Antiochus to marry his stepmother, Stratonice, after being persuaded that Antiochus was in danger of dying of lovesickness.

had done since his departure from Bagota, Destiny's oracle, and the result of his Council; the description of such sage conduct received further applause on his part. They departed urgently for Bagota, where Kristopo wanted to go in order to hasten Cornichon's happiness.

"I shall take charge, Madame," he said to the fay, "of obtaining the consent of Toupette's parents."

"That will not be difficult," she replied. "It's necessary to confess to you that those who pass for such have only lent themselves to the necessity of hiding the origin of that young person, which is much more illustrious. Cornichon will not be making a misalliance, since Toupette is the fruit of the complaisance that one of our companions felt obliged to have for a young mortal who pleased her greatly; she did not think it appropriate to make her childbirth public; those sorts of adventures are not always well received. She confided her secret to me, and as soon as she had brought the child into the light, I took charge of her. You had occasion to see her in the hands of the pretended parent to whom I had given her in your estates; you can judge in consequence how capable she was of profiting from an education superior to the ne those poor folk could have given her; they abandoned her to you with joy when you told them that you had the design of placing her with me, and I received her from you as a stranger. You know the rest.

"If that is so," said the genius, "Toupette ought to bear a few marks for her origin."

"Yes," said the fay, "a little cluster of black feathers placed above her left breast distinguishes her without disfiguring her; that is why she was given the name Toupette, just as I gave that of Cornichon to your son because of the little horn that I discovered in his hair, of which it imitates the color so well that one might mistake it for a curl. The similar accident that heightens the whiteness of Toupette's breast has been mistaken thus far for an advantageous adornment. The absolute power over her given to me by her mother, who is a friend of mine, responds for her consent, but the laws of secrecy forbid me from revealing her to you; that is all I can tell you."

"Good, my niece," said the genius. "It's enough; at least I know in consequence that Toupette is my relative; that mark is precisely the one particular to fays of our house who desire to have contraband goods. I only love my daughter-in-law more for that, and my happiness would be complete if I could think that you were her mother."

"My uncle is always joking," the fay replied, blushing slightly. Then she changed the subject; they agreed that they would keep the secret of Cornichon's fate until the moment of his union with Toupette, which would be the epoch of his rejuvenation.

As soon as they arrived in Bagota the fay told Toupette that she had finally made the resolution to marry her, that the ceremony would only be deferred until the following day, and that she was to dispose herself for it.

"Your kindness, Madame, would answer to me for my happiness in the choice that you have made for me, if Cornichon's misfortune did not mingle regrets with an event that ordinarily only causes joy. If the unfortunate fellow enjoyed an estate similar to mine, I would not be reduced to asking you who the husband is that you have destined for me."

"Be tranquil as to your fate," the fay said, "but you will only be informed of that at the moment of your marriage."

Toupette withdrew in silence. Part of the night was employed by her in divining that future husband; a host of amiable men were presented to her imagination but her free heart did not settle her ideas on anyone; weary of thinking about it she abandoned herself to her destiny with sufficient tranquility.

Rumor of Toupette's marriage and the mystery that Selnozoura was making of the choice of her husband assembled in the fay's apartment, early the next day, all those who might pretend to it by virtue of various entitlements. The altar was already decorated and a crowd of people filled the temple, while the fay still maintained silence. Having entered, and not seeing Cornichon there, she commanded someone to fetch him.

""Madame," said Toupette then, "please spare that poor fellow the sight of a ceremony that is bound to fill him with dolor, if he is still susceptible to it, and to which his presence would only bring a sort of ridicule if he is not."

"I would like," said the fay, "not to raise the matter in this situation of a liberty that I criticize in you, and content myself with telling you that he will not be out of place."

Toupette made no reply. Cornichon was brought; the sight of the numerous assembly only excited in him an infantile laughter, and everyone was astonished that a fay so sage was acting out of character in that way.

When everything was arranged and the aspirants arranged in a semicircle were avidly seeking the fay's gaze, she said to Toupette: "Approach. And you," she added, addressing those supporting Cornichon, "place him beside her. This, my daughter," she said, "is a husband of whose tenderness, virtues and misfortunes you are aware; as many entitlements enough to render him dear to you; accomplish the decrees of Destiny in giving your hand to him without hesitation."

"Oh, Madame!" cried Toupette, seized by surprise and taking a backward step. "Yes, doubtless he has my compassion, but is that not all that one can give to the state he is in at present? Is it necessary…?"

The fay's gaze made her understand that all remonstration was vain. She took Cornichon's hand. The genius then touched all three of them with his wand.

"Enjoy, my son," he said, "the grace of Destiny, and know, simultaneously, your wife and your father."

It is not easy to describe the effect that the surprise produced on the spectators of that marvel. The hopes of the confounded aspirants, and the joy of a thousand women to whom that event rendered a lover about to escape them, cast an infinite variety into the scene; but in the dependency that all those people were in on the principal subject formed by the two spouses, they only appeared as accessories, as if lost in a vague background. It was from Toupette and Cornichon that all the light by which was illuminated departed: all that beauty can borrow from amour, and all that amour itself borrows from joy, was found combined so advantageously in the two lovers that it is impossible to give an accurate idea of it.

That is how my author expresses it, and it is necessary to believe it; he would not have lost such a beautiful opportunity to go into detail.

After the ceremony the spouses were escorted back to the palace by the fay and the genius, in the midst of the acclamations of an innumerable crowd.

Fêtes that ceded nothing in magnificence to those that had celebrated the return of peace filled the first days of the union of Toupette and Cornichon. The genius witnessed that with the liberty of mind that had been promised to him by Destiny, and only returned to his estates after having extracted a promise from the fay that the spouses would make occasional visits to his court.

They passed thus, in the continuation of their life, days that no adversity troubled, and to which a numerous posterity added a further degree of happiness.

Here our author, at the end of the career that he had proposed, seems to request of the reader the prize that he believes to be due to him. The merit of a translator does not give him the same rights; I do not request any, fortunate if the approval that I have procured in this work is not mingled with a few suspicions as to its utility; there are no genuinely useful works except those that have truth for an object, and all of this is perhaps not true.

Charles-Antoine Coypel: *Aglaé or Nabotine*

There was once a very ugly little girl, and so small, so very small, that her parents named her Nabotine. She had vivacity, intelligence and sentiments, and the bad treatment she endured in the parental home had engaged her to form a rather meek, humble character, in the hope of touching the compassion of a crotchety old princess who was her godmother and often came to visit her mother.

Nabotine succeeded in her project. The princess had a good mind, and reasonable people always like little children, however ugly they are, when they are very good and have a desire to please. The godmother asked for her goddaughter in order to take care of her herself; she was accorded to her with many thanks. So, Nabotine was overjoyed no longer to be exposed to the ill humor of a mother who could not stand the sight of such a small and ugly daughter.

She went with the old princess to her castle, which was also so very old that none had ever been seen that was as old. The furniture there had never been renewed. In spite of that, Aglaé, in the desire to please her godmother, wanted to pay a little compliment to the beauty and magnificence of her habitation. That sage person said smiling:

"My child, don't let the desire to oblige ever lead you to betray the truth, or the desire to tell the truth lead you to be disobliging. One passes for crafty in giving false praise and makes oneself hated by making true but disadvantageous judgments unnecessarily. There are occasions when silence is the only course one can take; that is what you ought to have done with regard to this castle; although you might not expect it, perhaps I can give you occasion to praise it with justice. Ancient as this habitation is, it is respectable for me, because it was the retreat of my ancestors, who were heroes. There is nothing here that does not speak to me about them, and that is the best conversation I can have.

"With regard to this furniture, independently of having the same merit for me, I could only renew it by incurring debts that I would never be in a state to repay; that would give me an air of grandeur founded on an unworthy baseness. It's true that a fay of my acquaintance has offered several times to enable me to have new furniture cheaply; but at my age, why should I risk reacquiring a taste for things of pure vanity, for which I have lost the desire, which might render me weak to the point of afflicting myself for having lived long enough not to have much longer to live? The antiquity of my furniture seems to me to console me for mine. In considering it, I see that everything must perish, like me...

"But that's too much moralizing, my child. Go ask Nursery maid Tonton to give you supper; it's late, you can come back afterwards to chat with me, or, if Tonton has finished her work she can come back with you and the three of us can play a little piquet before going to bed. Go, I tell you, go; for myself, I don't eat in the evening because it inconveniences me."

After having made a profound reverence to the princess, Nabotine went to find Nursery maid Tonton, who gave her supper, and then they came back to play a little piquet until ten o'clock, after which the governess sent Nabotine to bed. She woke her up early in the morning, so that she would be ready to go and pay her court to the princess when she got up. The good lady was touched by that attention, Aglaé perceived that she was succeeding; she redoubled the little cares that won the heart of the princess, to the point that she came to regard her as her own daughter, and the little person profited so well from the lessons she received from her that in very little time she became perfect with regard to the character of her intellect.

I have already mentioned a fay who was an intimate friend of the princess; scarcely a day went past without her coming to see her, or seeing her without making her new offers of services, but always in vain; the disinterest of the one equaled the generosity of the other. One evening, the fay could not prevent herself from making reproaches to her friend.

"Do you know" she said to her, "how much you offend me? I know that your way of thinking puts you above everything that I can offer you, but ought amity not to enable you let me enjoy at least once the pleasure of doing something for you? You bring me to the point of scorning my power when you make me feel that it is no use to you."

"Well, my divine," the princess interrupted—that is what she called the fay—"since you believe than you can only prove the generosity you have for me by putting your power to work, satisfy yourself by doing something for my little one."

"Now you're talking," said the fay. "Let's go; this very day, if you wish, I'll render her as beautiful as the finest day."

"No!" cried the princess. "Her character isn't yet sufficiently assured to make her such a dangerous present. What do we know, my divine? Perhaps, thus far, Nabotine might only owe her good mind to her ugliness?"

"Well, then," said the fay, "let's begin by testing her sentiments; let's see whether her heart is veritably good."

"I consent to that," said the princess.

The two friends separated, and the fay did not take long to carry out that project, but she decided to test, at the same time, how far the amity of the princess for her goddaughter could go.

The next day, she came back to see her, accompanied by one of her pupils, approximately the same age as Nabotine, but so admirably beautiful, polite and intelligent that no one had ever seen the like. Every time someone said that she was pretty she made a great reverence, blushed and lowered her eyes. At the age of six months she had acquired the habit of kissing the hand when she was offered a bonbon. When she was only eight years old she had already written twenty volumes of the history of the fays, which had been printed, a copy of which she presented to the princess. It is claimed—for this story is very recent—that the young person shines in Paris today under the name of Thémire,[15] and one is assured that the *Boca* that she has just brought to light and the *Javotte* that will

---

[15] In the version of the story printed in the *Cabinet des fées*, Charles Mayer adds a footnote that quotes a letter from M. Coypel to a friend: "The moderns say, then, that Thémire is the image of their Deshoulières? For myself I say that, by the grace of God, Thémire only resembles Thémire. Thémire has an imagination so prodigious that it requires nothing less than her prodigious reason to regulate it. Now, Mademoiselle Sapho had a great deal of imagination, but reason...zft! Madame Deshoulières perhaps had a great deal of reason, but would she have imagined *Boca*? I ask you. You can see that I'm right to tell you that Thémire only resembles Thémire. Besides which, Thémire is incomparable for sentiments. On great occasions Thémire's reason would be capable of loving the persons that her heart detested, and her mind arranges all that so well that the devil, or what is worse, a woman, could not tell whether it is the heart or the reason that loves. Finally, to complete the portrait of Thémire, her character is so mild that is all the petty bickering of society, she makes efforts to persuade herself that the wrong is on her side, and it is always the reason that dominates."

Mayer adds the observation that the author of *Boca* was Francoise Le Marchand, and that the story is question, also included in the 1786 *Cabinet des fées*, is the only work of hers still extant, although "Florine," the first story in Étienne Roger' 1717 *Cabinet des fées* was subsequently credited to her, probably having been written in her teens. "Mademoiselle Sapho" is Mademoiselle de Scudéry, whose protégée Mademoiselle de L'Héritier was probably the prime mover in the invention of *contes de fées*, and who wrote a spectacular feminist eulogy to the poet Madame Deshoulières. Thémire is the chaste heroine of a prose narrative by Montesquieu (although he denied authorship for a long time), "Le Temple de Gnide" (c1724), in which she is dedicated to a delicate cult of Venus soon appear can only be compared with Princess Violette, little Rosette and Prince Babillard, and a few other works by the same hand, whose excellence is known—but we are straying from our subject.

The amiable pupil of the fay charmed the princess. She recited fables, played comedy, danced and sang so well that there was reason to be transported by her. Aglaé was summoned to play with her. Tonton dressed her in her new dress—which is to say, a dress that had just been made from a piece of cloth from the train of her godmother's wedding-dress.

The poor little creature appeared to be very content at first to see such a pretty and well-adorned demoiselle, who had come, it was said, to render her a visit; she made her a profound reverence that the other returned with so much grace that Nabotine made a second one in order to try to do it as well as the beautiful demoiselle, who was too well brought-up to leave it there; she replied with another even better than the first. Our little one, who marveled at it, tried another; the third succeeded no better and the beautiful demoiselle went on, always augmenting their grace. There were a hundred reverences on either part, and they might have continued until nightfall if the good fay and the princess, after having laughed at the little combat of politeness, had not told them to sit down.

The little demoiselle placed herself in a nice low armchair, to the great pleasure of Nabotine, who asked Tonton to give her a stool, under the pretext of being more respectful before the fay, but I have a strong suspicion that it was because she had noticed that they were much higher than the armchairs—and, in truth, she ought to be pardoned for that little ruse, for the little demoiselle was so pretty and so brave that Nabotine needed for more help than that of stools. As

---

opposed to vulgar physical lust, as Madame Le Marchand seems to have been.

soon as she was perched on hers, she spread out her dress as best she could, to make the fabric appear to its full advantage.

The little demoiselle, who perceived that, and who had compassion for such an excusable weakness, smoothed her own dress without affectation, for well-born people are sometimes embarrassed, and, to tell the truth, ashamed of the great superiority that they have over others, either by virtue of the advantages of intelligence or the gifts of fortune, and they take as much care on those occasions to moderate the splendor that follows them as others take to borrow false brilliance.

Aglaé perceived such a delicate politeness only too clearly; she blushed at it, and her greatest chagrin was in sensing that the little demoiselle had beaten her again, in the matter of sentiment. The unfortunate child had not expected that; on the contrary, on seeing her so beautiful and adorned, she had imagined that she must be a spoiled child; and if she did not feel her heart swollen and overflowing, it was because she counted on having her revenge in the conversation, and, in sum, because she said to herself: "Perhaps she'll be as mortified in hearing me as I am in seeing her."

Their conversation was not very animated; Nabotine's embarrassment, always increasing, sufficed to render her more silent than usual, and the desire to overcome that embarrassment completed taking away the usage of speech, for it is sufficient to have the desire to speak well to be no longer able to say anything at all…one meditates for a long time in order to find something pretty; ashamed of having meditated, one meditates again on the means to repair the fault, and if it happens, by dint of meditation, that one finds something good, one is astonished that it has come too late and that the topic of the conversation has changed while one was meditating.

The beautiful demoiselle, who remarked Nabotine's embarrassment again, refrained from mortifying her by attacking the conversation, and made a semblance of also meditating.

Finally, the hour of separation arrived; the fay ended the session. Nabotine breathed again, but she did not know the full extent of her misfortune as yet. The fay said to the princess that she was about to go away for two days and begged the fay to keep her little friend in her house. The princess asked for nothing better. What a dagger blow! It was necessary to get over it, though, not without weeping abundantly. To complete the misfortune, as one can imagine, it was necessary to weep in secret, and to make a semblance of being perfectly content before the good godmother, who never ceased to praise the little demoiselle, and who took her so much in amity, in fact, that it was enough to choke the unfortunate Nabotine.

Finally, after two days, the fay came to see the princess again and to ask for the return of her dear pupil. What a joy for our poor thing! She recovered the use of speech, and set out to make the eulogy of her little rival with at least as much grace as an academician making that of the dead man he is replacing. Joking apart, she spoke so nicely that the princess and the fay were surprised; and the beautiful child had to take her little mirror out of her pocket in order not to be jealous of Aglaé at that moment.

Alas, the joy of the latter was as brief as it had been intense; she saw her godmother shed tears in embracing the little person! The fay told her friend that she was in despair at causing her chagrin by depriving her of the amiable child so soon, but that, unfortunately, she could only leave her on one condition, which might not be agreeable to her.

"Oh! What is that condition?" the princess interjected, eagerly. "There's nothing I wouldn't give to keep her with me. Speak, my divine, speak."

"Give me Nabotine in her stead," replied the fay.

"Adieu, my dear child," cried the good lady, embracing the pretty demoiselle and putting her back in her friend's hands.

At those words, Nabotine felt pressed by a surge of gratitude so violent that she lost the use of her senses and fell in a faint at her godmother's feet.

Tears came to the eyes of the fay, who departed immediately, not wanting to allow herself to become more emotional, in order to be free to follow her project. The princess summoned Tonton to come to Nabotine's aid; she carried her to her bed without her coming round from her faint.

As one can imagine, generosity alone had hastened the response of the princess, for in reality her amity was shared between the two little persons. The same generosity made her employ all her cares to help her goddaughter, who finally opened her eyes and recovered the use of her senses—but without recovering that of speech, so great had the shock been. She could not do anything but take the princess's hands, which she kissed a thousand times and moistened so much with the tears of gratitude that one loves to shed and excite that Tonton was obliged to go in search of a fine napkin to wipe them away.

However, Nabotine's speech did not return, and the princess was obliged to ask the fay to come and return it to her. She soon arrived, and, finding a mute little girl, she exclaimed: "By my wand, that's the most singular thing in the world!"

As an intelligent fay, she judged that the presence of her friend might be an obstacle to the invalid's cure by virtue of the emotion she caused her; she asked her to withdraw and remained alone with Aglaé, whom she made to swallow a dose of woman's milk, which she had bought in a little golden flask. The remedy had a prompt effect. Aglaé spoke: "Oh Madame," she cried, "what do I not owe you? What a penalty not to be able to speak and to have so many thanks to give!"

The fay was very satisfied with that beginning.

"Soothe yourself, my dear child," she said. "Talk as much as you please; I'll be charmed to hear you, if you continue in the same tone."

"Alas, Madame," the child interrupted, "I've recovered, thanks to you, the usage of my tongue, but where can I find the terms to express what I feel? For pity's sake, you who are so powerful, help me to say to you all that I would like you to have the goodness to repeat to the good princess, for I'll die if she's unaware of the sentiments of gratitude for which I don't know the words. No, I'll never be able to explain all that to you, and I'll be even more embarrassed with her, for I've noticed that the more she gives me reason to thank her, the more annoyed she is to hear me do it. She always says to me: 'Aglaé, that's enough; I hear you.' However, in truth, Madame, it isn't possible that it can be, although she has a great deal of intelligence, or, if she hears me, why doesn't she let me have the pleasure of speaking?"

At that point, sobs interrupted Nabotine for some time, and then, turning to the fay, she said: "Madame, divine me...divine me, Madame, if you want me to live."

The fay, moved, assured Nabotine that she divined her marvelously, and begged her to calm down, promising her to go immediately to render the princess an exact account of everything that she thought she could not explain.

She tried to leave, but the child called her back. "Madame, Madame, wait, wait...also tell the good princess that I'd like with all my heart to love something passionately, passionately, but absolutely passionately, to be able to prove to her that I love her even more than passionately, by detaching myself from it for love of her."

"Gently does it," said the fay, interrupting her. "Do you really think what you're saying? You don't know yet what it is to love passionately. Believe me, don't make that wish; perhaps you'd find it more difficult than you think."

"Me, Madame!" cried he little girl. "Oh, what do you take me for? How unhappy I am!"

She started to weep so bitterly that the fay promised to satisfy her, assuring the princess that she would not desire anything as much as to have the opportunity to make some great sacrifice.

A one can imagine, the good lady was very content to learn what Nabotine's sentiments were, and I think that I would eventually become tedious if I tried to report everything touching and pathetic that happened when they saw one another again.

The little person had soon recovered her strength. The fay, who was extremely satisfied with her, made her a present of the prettiest little dog in the world, whose name was Finfin.

His body was pink and silver, and his ears green; he danced several dances admirably well, but the one in which he surpassed himself was the figured minuet. In addition, he had all the other canine talents that can be desired.

It is easy to understand how Nabotine marveled at him; any other dog would have been dead the first day, so often did he repeat his dances and his other tricks. Sometimes it was to amuse the princess that she made him repeat them, then it was for Tonton, and then for herself alone; then she went to bed, and then she got up again; then she wanted to remake her little bed, which had never been so well made, and which she remade so often, over and over, that she was worn out.

Her lassitude hastened a desire to sleep that the joy of having a little dog had doubtless driven away. But who was awake as soon as it was daylight? It was Nabotine, and I leave you to guess whether Finfin slept any longer than her. He seemed even more amiable the next day, and to say everything, Aglaé discovered new perfections in him every day, and every day she loved him more.

One evening, when she was caressing him with all her heart in the presence of the princess, she cried with vivacity: "In truth, Finfin, I don't love anything as much as you; yes, my dog, yes, my little dog, I don't love anything as much as you, and you can believe me on that."

The princess, looking at her, smiled. Nabotine perceived that, reflected, blushed, lowered her eyes, and then let go of her little dog. She was pensive all evening, and did not have any supper.

The princess, who had not understood the effect of the smile that had escaped her, thought she was indisposed and ordered her to go to bed. She stood up, making a reverence deeper than usual, without daring to raise her eyes toward her good godmother, nor lower them toward her dog, which she left in the room. The astonished princess called her back, saying to her that she must be very indisposed to forget Finfin, whom she loved so much; she ordered her to take him with her.

The child took that speech for a further reproach, and was so confused that she did not have the strength to open her mouth. Trembling, she retraced her steps, made another reverence even more profound, still lowering her eyes, which were beginning to moisten; she picked Finfin up gently, without kissing him, and went to bed; but scarcely had Tonton closed her bedroom door than the poor child began to weep with all her might.

In vain she took herself as a witness that she had not had the intention of bringing the princess into play when she had told Finfin that she did not love anything as much as him; that terrible smile always presented itself to her imagination as a frightful reproach. She racked her brain in order to fathom whether, in fact, she did not love her dog enough for the princess to have reason to be jealous. The agitation she was in prevented her from being able to make any reasonable judgment.

The fear of being ingrate made her believe that, in fact, she was; and to complete her unhappiness she took it into her head to ask herself whether she would have the strength to give up her dog to please the princess. That idea made her shiver; she shuddered at having shivered, and regarded herself as a little monster of ingratitude. She started weeping again.

Finally, to complete turning her head, Finfin came to lick away her tears; she pushed him away; he came back; she put him on the floor; her jumped on to the bed; he made her a great many caresses, and, in spite of herself, she was so sensible to them that she made the resolution to lose him the next day, because she could not see any other means of preventing herself from loving him too much.

A petty vanity excited by that generous project tranquilized her for a few moments, sufficiently for slumber to take possession of her.

As she had only gone to sleep in the middle of the night, she only woke up at daybreak, and her first impulse was to call Finfin. But what a cruel reaction that first impulse had! And what became of her when she remembered that she had made the resolution to get rid of him! She started pacing back and forth in her room, with strides as long as the smallness of her legs would permit. She went to meditate in a little corner, and then came out of it in order to go in search of another.

Finally, after many combats, she made up her mind; she went very quietly to get the key to the garden door from Tonton's room and set forth with Finfin, on whom she dared not cast her eyes, and whom she led on a leash, because she was afraid even to touch him. Instead of following her, Finfin continually stopped and turned his head toward the castle, testifying in a thousand polite fashions that he wanted to go back. They were as many dagger-thrusts for Nabotine. It occurred to her that perhaps it was wrong of her to lose him without having asked the permission of the princess, whom the little dog sometimes amused. Wouldn't it be better, she thought, to keep him with that sole intention, and trying not to love him very much? For after all, if the poor little thing had the good fortune of amusing her...

Oh, she went on, *I'm only thinking that because I might not have the courage to lose him. But then, if the princess asks me why I lost him, what shall I say? Would I dare to say that I was afraid of loving him too much? What a frightful thought! Is it possible that a dog...? But why would I think that I'm an ingrate if in fact, I'm not? O Heaven, how unhappy I am! No, I can see that I'll only be assured of loving the princess as much as is necessary when I've got rid of the unfortunate Finfin.*

Then she started running in order to try to rid herself of an object of which she could no longer stand the sight; but she could not go very far; she fell, weakened by not having had any supper, much less breakfast.

Finfin, whom Nabotine's languor set at liberty, drew away without her perceiving it, and came back a short time afterwards, walking on his hind legs and holding the most beautiful peach in his forepaws, which he presented to her. That action, on the part of a dog from whom it was necessary to separate herself, nearly caused her to die of tenderness. She ate it for the sake of reason, because she felt that if she did not try to sustain herself, it would not be possible for her to go any further, or even to retrace her steps.

When she had recovered her strength somewhat, she found herself more embarrassed than ever. *What!* she said to herself. *Is this how I'm going to repay the service that Finfin has just rendered me? He's just saved my life and I'm going to abandon him! Is there any little girl more unfortunate than me? It's necessary for me to become ingrate in order to appear grateful. Well, my dear little friend, what if I put you in the hands of someone who'll take care of you…?*

While she was saying that, an old woman, who was very stooped, passed by. Aglaé thought she had found what she needed'

"Listen," she said, "listen my good mother."

"What?" replied the old woman. "what is it?"

"Would you like," Aglaé cried, "would you like..." She did not have the strength to finish—which made the old woman impatient.

"Go on, little girl," she said. "Would you like…? Would you like…? What?"

"My little dog," Nabotine replied, weeping

"Yes, truly," said the old woman, "all we need is a dog! One gets too attached to those little animals."

"That's only too true. Alas," cried the poor child.

"I've seen in my village," said the old woman, "a child unnatural enough not to want to let his mongrel to be skinned to save his father's life. a fay had said that if the skin of the wretched animal were applied to his breast, he'd be cured infallibly of a recurrent gout, of which he was dying."

"Just Heaven!" cried Nabotine. "Oh, Madame, take my dog, take him, lose him if you want, but save me from the dolor of losing him myself."

"No, truly," retorted the old woman, harshly, "you're very delicate. Look for your valets. Go on, little as you are, you're big enough to lose a dog."

The old woman said no more, and went on her way.

271

In truth, I don't know whether those who will read this resemble me, but for myself, my heart is so constricted by Nabotine's situation that it wouldn't take much for me to drop the pen. At least dispense me from reporting her further lamentations here, and find it good that I say right away that she encountered an old man who seemed more accommodating than the old woman, and to whom she made the same proposition.

She was not as badly received, and it was with a great deal of mildness that he refused to take charge of Finfin, representing to her that he already had two dogs, which were the source of his misfortunes: that one of them had caused the death of his wife by tripping her up during the time of her last pregnancy, and that the second had infected his children with a poisonous mange that had caused them all to perish.

"You can appreciate," said the old man, as he quit her, "that that doesn't give my any desire to have a third. Adieu, my poor child; believe me, lose your dog, lovable as it might be, for fear, if you keep him, that some sad adventure might befall those who interest you, or perhaps yourself."

With those words the old man disappeared, and Nabotine cried: "There's the sentence pronounced, then! Nothing ought any longer to retain me. Go, unfortunate Finfin, become what you can...but wait," she said, "we're not yet far enough away. You might go back to the castle."

Under that new pretext, which seduced her, she delayed for a further moment the cruel separation...

Finally, her courage got the upper hand. She saw a boat on the edge of a small river. She put Finfin into it, imagining that the boatman, who was perhaps not far away, might take care of him, or sell him to some great lady, who would be charmed to have such a fine dog.

What can I say? She did her best to stun herself, and then, suddenly, closing her eyes and plugging her ears, she started running as fast as she could, dreading that she might hear Finfin's voice, and see, without him, the route she had just traveled with him.

That precaution prevented her from seeing a large hole, into which she fell.

Having pulled herself out of it, she went home sadly, to get back into her bed. Did she sleep? The heart will respond to that question.

Tonton came to open her bedroom door eventually and told her that she had let her sleep for a long time, because of her slight indisposition. She asked her how she felt, on the part of the princess, adding that he had been very anxious about her health. That attention on the part of her good godmother touched Nabotine sensibly.

The nursery maid asked her what she had done with Finfin, whom she could not see. The little girl could not refuse her self-esteem and her dolor the flattering consolation of telling Tonton what she had done, begging her to keep the secret.

The governess, who had been greatly amused by the little dog, and who only had as much sentiment as is necessary not to be malevolent, told her that she was a little imbecile, and that she was going to tell the princess right away. She left the room in order to do that immediately, which did not distress Nabotine overmuch; she had only asked Tonton to keep the secret in the hope that she would not keep it.

The princess was no sooner informed of what had happened than she ran to Nabotine's room. She nearly stifled her with caresses. The most tender scene unfolded between them.

The princess saw the fay in the afternoon, whom she wanted to inform of what one might well imagine that she was not unaware, and for the first time, she made a request of her friend, to wit, toys for Nabotine, of which she soon had some of every species. Although the little person was very satisfied with herself, however, she could not forget Finfin, and the toys were indifferent to her; it was only to please her godmother that she made a semblance of playing with them.

One evening, when it rained heavily, a charming little voice was heard, which cried at the castle door: "Oh, for pity's sake, deign to open the door to me; I'm a poor child whose parents have just abandoned him, who has nowhere to lodge."

The good princess had the door opened promptly and ordered that the unfortunate child be brought to her. She was obeyed immediately, and she was dazzled; for in fact, it was Amour himself—or rather, Amour as he is depicted in operas was not as beautiful as that child was. He made the prettiest reverences in the world to the princess, who asked him by what hazard his parents had abandoned him.

"Because they became too poor to nourish me," the beautiful child replied. "If you're willing for just a few days to suffer me here, they'll surely come to find me, if they're able to amass something."

"Gladly," said the princess, "gladly, my little friend, let's get you something to eat; do the honors, Nabotine, and treat him like your little brother."

Nabotine did not have to be asked twice, for she had such a kind heart, and had always wanted a little brother. She made every effort to receive him well, and after half a hour they were already calling one another "my dear little brother" and "my dear little sister." The little girl, who had often heard people say "they love one another like brother and sister" thought that she could never love her little brother enough. When the meal was finished they played a thousand little games. The beautiful child taught her I don't know how many.

After supper, he asked the little girl whether she knew how to dance. She said, with a sigh, that he had had a little dog, which had taught her several dances, and that the one she like best as the figured minuet.

"Well, let's dance that," he said. "I know it too; it will amuse Madame la Princesse."

The little fellow acquitted himself so perfectly that Nabotine was obliged to agree that Finfin did not approach him. Bedtime arrived and Tonton took the newcomer to a small room near hers.

The next day, when she woke up, Nabotine thought, as usual, about the loss of Finfin, but she did not think about it for long, and the idea of the little brother chased away that of the little dog.

It's pleasant, she said to herself, *to have someone to call brother. I nearly died of chagrin when the princess retained the little demoiselle here, but I'm charmed that she took in the beautiful child, who is even more beautiful than her and no less intelligent. He must have a good heart to show me so much amity, for it seems to me that I'm very ugly to be his sister. Yes*, she added, with chagrin, looking at herself in the mirror—which she did not usually do—*yes, I'm getting uglier every day, and especially since yesterday morning, it's augmented by half. In truth, I can't be too grateful for the tenderness he testifies to me; for, as Tonton says it isn't for my beautiful eyes.*

Those reflections were interrupted by the arrival of the little fellow, whom the governess brought to wish his little sister good day. After having kissed her hand he wanted to kiss her on the cheek, but Nabotine blushed and stopped him.

"What!" said the beautiful child. "Can't one be kissed by one's little brother? Is there any harm in that?"

"Not that I know," replied the little girl, embarrassed. "I don't really know why I don't want to…wait, pardon me, pardon me, it's true that one can kiss one's brother, but you're a boy…no, that's not what I want to say… Oh, well, look, it's necessary to ask my godmother; I can't decide that all my own."

The little conversation did not go any further; they were both taken to see the princess, who was greatly amused all day long.

Nabotine went on loving her little brother more and more. One morning, when she woke up earlier than usual, it occurred to her to reproach herself because she no longer thought about Finfin. She wondered so much about the reason that she came to perceive that it was since she had taken her little brother in amity.

What if I'm going to love him more that I loved Finfin? she said to herself. *Perhaps it will be necessary to renounce him for the princess. No, it's necessary not to love him as much as that. Alas, if the fay is going to tell me that it's neces-*

275

sary to abandon him to prove my amity to my godmother, what will become of me? Let's see whether it's possible that I'll come to love him as much as I loved my dog. Does he have eyes as beautiful as Finfin's? A fine comparison, no doubt, a dog's eyes and those of a little brother! Finfin had the prettiest muzzle! Yes, but what's a muzzle in comparison to a face? Finfin was colored rose and silver; well, doesn't he have silvery hair and rosy cheeks? Finfin's paws were fine, but hands are much prettier. Come on, come on; it's necessary that I think about not loving him as much; perhaps if I love him less he'll stay here forever. Forever! Alas, what if his parents come to ask for his return? Oh, if only they couldn't amass anything…!

It was thus that our poor child summoned amour, in wanting to flee amity, so true is it that nothing is as dangerous as a scruple pushed too far.

Nabotine did not last long without feeling alarms, and they were so strong that she dared not look at her little brother all day. The princess feared that jealousy might be the cause of that, and in order to assure herself of it she told the little girl that she planned to keep the little boy with her permanently, even if his parents came to ask for his return.

Nabotine replied with such a great embarrassment that it confirmed the princess's suspicions. The fay arrived at that moment, her friend having begged her to sound out her god-daughter's sentiments. She took her into her room and asked her why she did not seem content with the resolution the princess had made to keep her little brother.

"Madame," said Nabotine, "dispense me, please, from telling you the reasons; I'm too ashamed."

"It's rather a jealousy," the fay interjected. "You want to have the sole honor of pleasing the princess and you take in aversion all those..."

""In aversion!" cried Nabotine. "In aversion! I wish to Heaven that I hated him..."

"Go on," said the fay.

276

"Oh Madame, if you'd be so kind as to spare me the shame; you could divine what I have to say to you, you who divine everything..."

"What!" the fay interrupted. "Do you fear loving him too much?"

"I don't know how to explain that to you, " Nabotine replied, weeping and throwing herself at her feet, "but Madame, I don't know if I'd have the courage to lose him as I lost Finfin, in case I come to love him..."

The fay uttered a loud burst of laughter at the child's naivety; she lifted her up, embracing her.

"You're laughing, Madame," she said, interrupting. "Oh, rather ask my godmother for that poor little child; take him to your beautiful castle, so that he'll be happy there, and only permit me to ask you for news of him sometimes."

"No, no," said the fay, "things will turn out better than that. Come here, my dear friend; that's enough of testing Aglaé, it's necessary to make her happy. Her gratitude is at the highest point, since it resists amour. Come, my little cousin, give your hand to Nabotine and receive her for your wife."

"What's this?" said the princess, entering. "Your little cousin!"

"Yes," replied the fay, "and this little cousin, such as you see him, has already played one role here; you've already seen him here in the form of Finfin."

"Oh, my poor Finfin," cried Nabotine, "let me embrace you...but no," she said, "it's no longer the same..."

The princess could not help laughing, as did the fay, who, after having told her friend about her goddaughter's latest stroke, wanted to conclude the marriage; but Nabotine excused herself on the grounds that she was too ugly to be the wife of such a handsome little gentleman, saying that she had difficulty finding herself supportable as a sister.

"You can't think so," said the good fay, presenting her with a little mirror garnished with diamonds. "Look at yourself."

Who had a big surprise? It was our little heroine. She saw that she was the prettiest girl in the world, and her first impulse was to cry to the handsome child: "Oh, look at me, my little brother!"

"He won't be astonished to see you," the fay interjected. "I had charmed his eyes."

The princess was less surprised than her goddaughter by that change; she had too much intelligence and knew the history of the fays too well not to have foreseen that her friend would do that. It is not difficult to imagine that Nabotine, who was given the name Brillante, gave the fay the most touching thanks in the world. She responded to them with these lines, which she improvised on the spot:

Brillante, for all your charms
Don't give the honor to faerie;
Remember this, I beg you;
Nothing embellishes like sentiments.

Charles Duclos: *Acajou and Zirphile*

Intellect is not always worth as much as one assumes, amour is a good teacher, and providence does well what it does; that is the moral of this tale—it is as well to inform the reader of that, for fear that he might misunderstand it. Limited minds never suspect the intention of an author and those that are too vivid exaggerate it, but neither of them like reflecting; that it why I mention the matter.

There was once, in a land situated between the realm of the Acajous and that of Minutia, a race of maleficent genii who were the shame of their species and the bane of human-kind. Heaven was touched by the prayers made against that accursed race; the majority perished tragically, none remained but the genius Podagrambo and the fay Harpagine, but it seemed that those last two were the inheritors of all the malevolence of their ancestors.

They were both unintelligent; the quality of genius or fay only gives power, and malevolence is more often associated with stupidity that with intelligence. Podagrambo, although a very noble, very highly-placed and very powerful lord, was still very stupid. Harpagine was reputed to have more intelligence because she was more malevolent—the two qualities are still confused today—although that proves that she had very little; that is because she was annoying, although malicious. As for the genius, he was wicked enough only to desire evil and imbecilic enough that if anyone had done him a favor he would not have perceived it. He had a gigantic stature, with all possible ill grace. Harpagine was even more frightful: tall, stiff and dark; her hair resembled serpents, and when she transformed herself it was usually into a spider, a bat or an insect.

Those two monsters had no less presumption. Harpagine prided herself on her charms and Podagrambo his good fortune; they had a small, elegantly furnished house, in which one could see ugly Chinese figurines, Martin varnishes,[16] chaises longues and cushions; it was there that they went to annoy one another; they finally threatened the public with marrying, in order to perpetuate their names. Posteromania is the common eccentricity of the great; they love their posterity but do not like their children at all. The proposition of the genius and the fay was received as a declaration of war.

The great Council of Faerie thought the affair sufficiently important to warrant a general assembly. The matter was exposed, agitated and discussed; there was a great deal of talk and deliberation, but something was nevertheless resolved. It was decided that Podagrambo and Harpagine could never marry unless they made themselves loved; that sentence seemed to condemn both to celibacy; or, if they were able to become lovable, it would be necessary for them to change character, and that was all that was desired.

Immediately, they searched their Colombat[17] for some house they could honor with their choice; but it was not sufficient to find a party, it was necessary that they make themselves loved; they understood that they would never succeed in that without a singular artifice. However blind self-esteem may be, one soon discovers one's faults when interest becomes involved.

Harpagine, more inventive than the genius, said to him something like this: "My plan is to take children so young that they don't have any ideas as yet. We'll bring them up ourselves; they'll never see anyone else, and we'll form their hearts to our liking; the prejudices of childhood are almost invincible. My party," she added, "is already chosen. The

---

[16] "Martin varnish," named for its French popularizer, who imported the idea from the Far East in the early eighteenth century, involved the addition of powdered gold or bronze to the varnish in order to give it a metallic sheen.

[17] One of several popular Almanacs issued annually in France was published in Paris by the Veuve Colombat.

King of the Acajous only has one son, who is about two years old; I'll ask for his education to be confided to me. He wouldn't dare refuse me; he'd fear my resentment, and one does more for those one fears than those one esteems. I'll do the same for you with regard to the first little princess that is born."

Podagrambo approved of a plan so well-conceived and the fay departed on her great moustached dragon; she arrived at the home of the King of the Acajous and made her request, which the poor prince dared not refuse.

Delighted to have the little Prince Acajou in her hands, Harpagine left again, and thought of nothing thereafter but carrying out her project. With a stroke of her wand she built him an enchanted palace, which I beg the readers to imagine according to their taste, and of which I will spare them the description for fear of boring them. What I am obliged to tell them, however, because they are not obliged to divine it, is that Harpagine, is designing the garden of the palace to serve as a promenade for the little prince, attached a talisman to it, which prevented him from leaving it unless he fell in love; and as she was the only woman he could see, she did not doubt that her sex alone would take the place of beauty and that the desires of adolescence would give birth to amour in Acajou's heart.

An accident that Harpagine had not foreseen undermined her design from the outset and obliged her to amend her plan. Acajou had received at birth the gift of beauty, he was to be the best looking prince of his time; that flattered the fay's hopes marvelously, who knew in addition that the first fruits of the most lovable young men belong by right to the old, but what caused her chagrin was that the child had also been endowed with all the qualities of intelligence. Harpagine sensed that they would only make him more difficult to seduce. She resolved immediately to correct by art what her pupil had received from nature and to spoil his intelligence, being unable to deprive him of it.

She went into her laboratory, where she composed her drugs; the most efficacious words and the most powerful charms were employed; she composed two bowls of magic sugar; in one there were pastilles whose virtue was to inspire bad taste and falsify the intellect; the other contained bonbons of presumption and stubbornness; the person who ate them always judged falsely and seasoned mistakenly, sustained his sentiment obstinately and gave himself to everything ridiculous—with the result that the malign fay had every reason to hope that if the prince ate them, he would feel a passion for her all the more powerful because it would be more extravagant.

She went immediately to give the bonbons to the child, but as she engaged him by her caresses to eat some, she tried to adopt a jovial expression, which caused her to make such a frightful grimace that he child was scared and threw the bowls in her face. A so-called reasonable person would have been easier to seduce, but enlightened nature gives those who have not yet delivered themselves to reason a surer instinct, which warn them of what is contrary to them.

The bonbons of presumption were those that the fay regretted the least; she had no doubt that Acajou's birth would always give him enough, but she could never get him to swallow any of them. She gave them to a traveler as a precious curiosity, adding to them the virtue of multiplying themselves. The man who received them brought them to Europe, where they had a brilliant success. Everyone wanted to have them; they were sent as presents; everyone carried them in a pocket in little boxes; they were offered as gallantries, and that custom is still conserved today. They do not all have the same virtue, but the old ones are not completely lost.

Meanwhile, Harpagine imagined giving Prince Acajou such a bad education that it would be more effective than all the bonbons in the world.

The news spread then that the Queen of Minutia was about to have a child, and all the fays were invited to witness the birth. Harpagine went along with the others. The queen gave birth to a girl who was, as one might suppose, a miracle of beauty, who was named Zirphile. Harpagine was counting on asking the queen to confide her education to her, but the fay Ninette had already anticipated her, and was charged with bringing up the princess.

Ninette was the declared protectress of the realm of Minutia. She was no more than two and a half feet tall, but her small figure brought together all the charm and grace imaginable. She could only be reproached for an extreme vivacity; it seemed that her mind was too restricted in such a small body; always thinking and always in action, her penetration often carried her beyond objects and prevented her from discerning more precisely those she could not reach. Her piercing sight and lively step were the reflection of her mental qualities.

In order to remedy that excess of vivacity, which fools strove to imitate, and which they called hare-brained in order to console themselves for not succeeding, the Council of the Fays had made Ninette a present of a pair of spectacles and an enchanted crutch.

The virtue of the spectacles was to weaken the eyesight and temper the vivacity of the intelligence in relation to the soul and the body. That was the first invention of spectacles; they have since been employed for an entirely opposite purpose; that is how everything is abused. What proves, however, how harmful spectacles are to the intelligence is seeing how aged supervisors are deceived every day by inexperienced young lovers, which can only be blamed on spectacles. As for the crutch, it served to render the stride more reliable by slowing it down.

Ninette only made use of the fays' presents when it was a matter of conducting a delicate affair; she was, in any case, the best creature one could see: an open soul, a tender heart and a scatterbrained mind rendered her an adorable woman.

The fays who witnessed the birth of the princess thought of endowing her, as was customary, and, being true women, were commencing with gifts of beauty, grace and all the external seductions, when Harpagine, whose malice was more

283

enlightened than the benevolence of the others, said, muttering between her teeth: "Yes, yes, you'll have all that, but you'll never have anything but a stupid beauty, I'll answer for that, for I endow you with the most complete stupidity."

Having spoken, she left. The fays did not take long to perceive their negligence. But Ninette, having put on her spectacles, said that she would substitute by means of education for what the child lacked in the matter of intelligence. The other fays added that in order to remedy in part the harm that they could not destroy totally, the imbecility of the princess would cease as soon as she fell in love. A woman who only has need of that remedy is not completely without resource.

Having taken Zirphile in her arms, Ninette transported her to her palace in spite of the traps of the wicked fay.

On the other hand, Harpagine was no longer occupied with anything but giving her pupil the worst education she could imagine, in order to stifle his intelligence by bad cultivation. As she hoped that stupidity would render all the cares that were taken on Zirphile futile, she ordered the governors of the little prince only to talk to him about ghosts, phantoms and the Great Beast, and to read him tales of fays in order to full his head with a thousand nonsensical ideas. We have conserved in our day, out of stupidity, what the fay invented out of malice.

When the prince was a little older, the fay summoned masters from all directions, and as, in making mischief, she never settled for the mediocre, she changed all the objects of those matters. She invited a famous philosopher, the Descartes or Newton of his era, to teach the prince to ride a horse and use weapons. She charged a musician, a dancing mater and a lyric poet with teaching him logic. The others were distributed in accordance with the same pattern, and they made much less difficulty because they were all particularly smitten with what was not their profession. How many people there are who encourage the belief that the same care has been taken of their education!

With so many precautions, Harpagine did not doubt the success of her project. However, in spite of the lessons of all his masters, Acajou succeeded in all his exercises; he did not acquire, in truth, any useful knowledge, but errors did not obtain any purchase on his mind. A fortunate compensation! After good lessons, the most instructive are ridiculous ones, and those of Acajou's masters put him on guard against their precepts.

He became as handsome as Amour; he was made for painting; all his graces developed. Harpagine pretended that all that was growing for her; it is necessary to let her pretend, and see what happens.

While Harpagine was striving with all her might to make an idiot of Acajou, the fay Ninette was losing her mind trying to give one to Zirphile. The little fay's court assembled al the amiable people here were in the realm of Minutia. On the days when she received in her apartment nothing was more brilliant than the conversation.

There was no discourse in which there was only common sense; there was a torrent of sallies; everyone questioned; no one responded accurately and everyone understood marvelously, or did not understand at all, which comes to the same thing for brilliant minds; exaggeration was the favorite figure and very much in fashion; without having keen sentiments, without being occupied with useful objects, they always talked the language. People were "furious" about a change in the weather; a ribbon or a pompom was "the only thing in the world they loved;" between the shades of a color they found "a world of difference;" there was nothing by which they were not "overwhelmed" or "confounded."

In sum, they exhausted excessive expressions on trivia, with the result that if, by chance, they came to experience violent passions, they could not make themselves understood and were reduced to remaining silent, which gave rise to the proverb that great passions are mute.

Ninette did not doubt that the education Zirphile received in her court would eventually triumph over her stupidity, but the charm was very powerful. Zirphile became more beautiful every day, and the most stupid child that one could ever see. She dreamed instead of thinking and only opened her mouth to say something silly. Although men are not hard to please in the matter of a pretty girl, and always find that she speaks like an angel, they could only praise her beauty. The poor child, always shamed, received their eulogies as a favor and responded to them that it was a great honor. That was not what they wanted, however, and they laughed at her naivety and sought to seduce her innocence.

It is necessary to know a little about vice to fear its traps. Zirphile was candor itself, and candor is no safeguard for virtue, but Ninette watched over her dear pupil carefully. She put her among her maids of honor, where there were often vacant places; the majority left before their time was finished; there was no corps in the court more difficult to recruit.

Zirphile was not spoiled by the example; it was in vain that the young courtiers gathered around her. Too great a desire to appear lovable prevented them from being so. Zirphile was untouched by their homage; all their discourse seemed to her to be insipid or fatuous. In addition, men are governed by their senses before knowing their heart, but the majority of women need to love and are rarely seduced by pleasures if they are not led astray by example. At any rate, no accident befell Zirphile because, for safety's sake, she did not allow any man to approach too closely for her honor, or even certain women too closely for her innocence.

While she lived thus at Ninette's court, Acajou was becoming bored in Harpagine's home. He was already fifteen; his intelligence only served to inform him that he was not made for living with all that surrounded him. He began to sense the nascent desires of nature, which, without having any determined object, sought one everywhere. He had already perceived that he had a heart, of which the senses were only the interpreter. He experienced the melancholy that one could place in the rank of the pleasures, although it makes one desire more intense ones. He sighed after someone who could dissipate that disturbance, but sought solitude nevertheless. He withdrew to the most distant regions of the park; it was there that, in seeking to clarify his ideas, he sometimes made a rather stupid figure.

Harpagine, who knew Acajou's trouble, flattered herself that she would soon be the remedy for it; but she saw with chagrin that all the caresses she tried to give him only served to revolt him and put him in a bad mood. Offered caresses rarely succeed, and it is even rarer that they are offered when they merit being sought.

Harpagine was in despair. The council of fays had pronounced that he would only remain in her hands until he was seventeen, after which she would not have any power over him.

The kings of the Acajous and Minutia were waiting for that happy moment impatiently, in order to unite their kingdoms by the marriage of their children. The genius had no sooner learned about that project than he swore that it would not come to fruition.. He prepared a superb equipage and went to Ninette's court. He was received with the species of politeness that one has for all powerful people, which does not oblige any esteem.

In order not to waste time with superfluous compliments, he declared his sentiments—which is to say, the desires she inspired in him—to Zirphile right away. The little princess, who had not learned to dissimulate, did not let him languish, and declared naively all the repugnance she felt for him. He was quite astonished by that, but instead of being put off, he attempted to touch her heart in order to obtain her hand. He thus tormented himself in search of all the means of pleasing. Unfortunately, the more one searches for them, the fewer one finds.

He tried to imitate the agreeable men of the court, but everything that did not render him merely ridiculous made him appear more sullen. There are ridiculous things that do not affect all sorts of faces, and even a few compatible with grace, but Podagrambo did not shine in that regard; the more he tried to play the fop, the more he proved that he was only a fool.

Finally—for I do not like long stories—after having wearied the court with his idiocies and fatigued Zirphile even more with his insipidities, he was no further forward than on the first day. He was considered the most tedious genius that had ever been seen; that was a discourse repeated from the apartments all the way to the outbuildings.

Podagrambo suspected that he was the joke of the court; that was not by virtue of his penetration, but an eccentricity common among fools is to think more highly of themselves while believing that others are speaking ill of them. In his chagrin, he returned home in order to meditate some spectacular vengeance and to discuss with Harpagine means of abducting the princess.

Ninette, having anticipated the enterprises that might be formed against her dear Zirphile, had given her a scarf, the charm of which was such that it wearer need have no fear of any violence.

Meanwhile, the innocent Acajou could not emerge from the melancholy that was consuming him, and Zirphile was harassed by the same trouble. They often went for solitary walks, and when hazard conducted each of them separately to the palisade that separated Ninette's and Harpagine's gardens—for as I have said, or should have said, they were neighbors—they felt drawn by an unknown force and halted by a secret charm; each of them reflected separately on the pleasure they savored in that place, the most neglected in the park; they returned to it every day, and night had difficulty tearing them away from it.

One day, when the prince was plunged in his meditations next to that palisade, he let out a sigh. The young princess who was on the other side, in the same state, heard it. She was moved by it; she concentrated all her attention; she listened.

Acajou sighed again. Zirphile, who had never understood what anyone said to her, understood that sigh with an admirable penetration; she responded immediately with a similar sigh.

The two lovers—for they were lovers, from that moment on—understood one another reciprocally. The language of the heart is universal; it only requires sensibility to understand it and to speak it. Amour sent at that instant a flaming arrow into their hearts and a ray of light into their minds.

After having heard one another, the young lovers sought to see one another, in order to understand one another better. Curiosity is the fruit of the first knowledge. They advanced; they searched; they parted the branches; they saw one another. Gods, what transports! Their age, the vivacity of their desires, the tumult of their ideas, the fire that animated their senses, and perhaps even their ignorance, are necessary to understand their situation.

They remained motionless for some time; they were gripped by the tremor that the novelty of pleasure bears into new senses. They touched one another; they maintained silence. However, they let a few poorly articulated words escape. Soon, they were talking with vivacity; they asked one another a thousand questions; they did not make any accurate responses, but they were satisfied with what they said and found themselves enlightened regarding their doubts. They understood, at least, that the desired one another without knowing one another, that they had found what they were looking for.

Acajou, who had only ever seen Harpagine, found himself transported into a new world; and Zirphile who had never paid the slightest attention to the men of the court, thought she was seeing a new being. Acajou kissed Zirphile's hand. The poor child, who did not believe that she was according a favor, even less committing a sin, let him do it. Acajou, whose intentions were too good for him to imagine that caresses could offend anyone, redoubled his, and Zirphile returned them naively; having not the slightest idea of vice, she could not have any of modesty.

They sat down on the grass; it was there that they embraced. They clasped one another narrowly. Zirphile delivered herself to all the transports of her lover; she received him in her arms. Acajou raised his hands to his dear Zirphile's nascent breasts; he pressed his mouth to hers; their souls flew to their lips; they were confounded; they were plunged into a divine intoxication; they floated in pleasures and were borne away by a torrent of delights; their desires were inflamed and they did not understand how they could be so happy and yet desire more. They enjoyed all the beauties that they saw and did not imagine that there were hidden ones on which the final phase of happiness depended. It seems to me, however, that they did not profit badly from a first lesson.

Those amiable children were so intoxicated by their felicity that they forgot all Nature and gave no thought to separating. But as they were much later than usual in returning from their walk, Harpagine and Ninette came to look for them, and each of them called to her ward from her own side. Our lovers were frightened by their voices, and, separating regretfully, they feared that their union might be troubled if it were suspected. Amour is confident in its desires and timid in its pleasures.

The image of Zirphile that was engraved in the depths of Acajou's heart enabled him to see Harpagine more horrible than ever. As for Zirphile, although she was obliged to suspend the pleasure of seeing Acajou, what she had just savored gave a new shine to her beauty and spread an air of satisfaction throughout her person. Pleasure embellishes and amour brightens.

Nothing equals the surprise that Zirphile's intelligence caused the entire court; that same evening in Ninette's apartment someone made one of those bad jokes so familiar to mediocre individuals who think they have some superiority over others a little more stupid; poor Zirphile was often the object of them; she replied this time with so much accuracy and finesse, and so little bitterness, that the bad jokers—who were women—were astonished by the sagacity of her replies and humiliated by the manner in which she made them; the men were charmed, and applauded.

Ninette wept with joy and the women blushed with chagrin. Until then they had been able, albeit with difficulty, to pardon Zirphile for her beauty because of her stupidity, but there was no longer any means of doing that; they had no other resource but malevolence. That last quality, in causing hatred, often creates respect, but the little princess was too well-born to make use of that vulgar means.

Our two young lovers had found Amour's first lesson too good not to return to his school. What a joy it is to be instructed by pleasures!

To begin with, lovers, like thieves, take superfluous precautions; by degrees thy neglect them; they forget the necessary ones too, and are caught. That is exactly what happened to our imprudent young couple, and it was the genius who surprised them. Fools only live on the faults of the intelligent. One evening, he saw the young lovers retiring; he was beside himself with rage, but as he had a maxim of never doing anything without asking for advice, although he carried on regardless afterwards, he resolved to consult Harpagine.

On learning the news, the malevolent fay conceived the most violent chagrin. The genius told her that there was no other means of avenging herself than abducting the princess. Although the fay was as furious as him, she preferred to get rid of her rival rather than seeing her in the same place as her lover; she therefore concealed her anxiety and told the genius that it was necessary for him to take charge of that endeavor, flattering herself that he would never have the intelligence to succeed in it.

The next morning Podagrambo hid behind a tree near the palisade where the lovers came in search of one another. Acajou's masters had orders to prolong their lessons so that he could not reach the rendezvous before the princess.

Acajou, so mild in character, showed ill humor for the first time; even temper does not subsist with passion. While he became impatient, the tender Zirphile came to the palisade; she was anxious on not finding her lover there; he had the habit of preceding her. She looked everywhere, and finally dared to enter Harpagine's park and passed close to the genius. At the sight of him, fear seized her and she tried to flee, but it as with so little precaution that her scarf remained hooked on a branch. Instantly, the genius seized her by the dress.

"Aha!" he said. "You come here in search of a marmoset, innocent beauty, and it's for him that you spurn me!"

Poor Zirphile, seeing herself betrayed by fear itself, which had caused her to lose her scarf, had recourse to dissimulation. Before having loved she would not have been so clever. A first adventure, which inspires conceit in a young man, renders the falsity necessary to women; one sex is obliged to blush at what makes the glory of the other.

Although Zirphile was candor itself, she attempted to deceive the genius. "I am astonished," she said, "that you impute to amour a pure effect of my curiosity, which is what made me enter this place. I am no less surprised that you make use of violence, you who can expect everything of your birth, and even more of your amour."

The genius was mollified somewhat by that flattering speech, but although the princess was advising him to hope for everything of his merit, and he was quite convinced of it, he did not want to let her escape.

"If your heart is so sensible for me," he said, "You should not make difficulties about coming to my palace. All these petty concerns of vulgar lovers are frivolous formalities that only delay pleasure without rendering it more intense."

"Well," Zirphile replied, "I'm ready to go with you, and to prove my sincerity, return my scarf to me, so that no evidence will remain here of my escape and your violence."

The genius thought he might swoon with pleasure and admiration for Zirphile's presence of mind.

"Oh, certainly!" he cried. "It's necessary to confess that amour gives women intelligence, for I would never have thought of that, and would have gone away like a fool."

Immediately, he detached the scarf and handed it to the princess, kissing her hand. But she, no longer having anything to fear, pushed him away scornfully.

"Go away, traitor," she said, "or fear the wrath of the fays; that scarf is the pledge of their protection for me."

As she finished speaking she drew away, leaving the genius confounded, arrested by a force to which his own power was obliged to cede. He could only admire Zirphile's presence of mind more than he had before.

That reflection was doubtless not the one that occupied him most. After having remained motionless for some time, he went back to find Harpagine, confused and desperate, and told her by what charm his power had been rendered futile.

Although the fay learned with chagrin the virtue of the enchanted scarf, she was somewhat consoled by the failure of the enterprise of the genius. She hid the different interest that she took in it, however, and, as consolers are never more eloquent than when they are afflicted themselves, she calmed him down by promising to destroy he enchantment of the scarf and render him master of the princess.

The fay was unaware of the misfortune that menaced her. While she was deliberating with the genius as to the means of reestablishing their power, Acajou ran to the palisade. After waiting for some time for Zirphile, impatience made him enter Ninette's park, and, torn between fear and desire, he gradually progressed as far as the palace.

The news of his arrival soon spread there. Ninette came to meet him, followed by her entire court. Acajou advanced respectfully toward the little fay and kissed the hem of her dress. As soon as he and Zirphile saw one another they ran to one another, and the presence of the entre court did not prevent them from giving one another the most vivid evidence of the pleasure they had in seeing one another again.

Zirphile recounted naively the danger she had run; the prince had become even dearer to her in consequence. The more women have risked, the readier they are to sacrifice more. Ninette, naturally indulgent, did not pause to examine whether there might have been anything irregular in the conduct of the young lovers; it was sufficient that fortune had arranged everything for the best.

Having learned about the flight of Acajou, Harpagine entered into the most horrible anger, and came to demand his return, but, fortunately for him, he had reached his seventeenth year that very day and the fays' decree freed him then from the power of Harpagine. She conceived so much rage in consequence that she lost her amour for him, which had only ever been a sentiment foreign to her heart, and, no longer meditating anything but projects of vengeance, she left in order to invite the fay Envious to form an alliance with her.

The celebrations that followed Acajou's arrival did not permit anyone to occupy themselves with Harpagine's resentment.

The men who had tried to please Zirphile lost all their pretentions on seeing Acajou. The women never wearied of admiring his beauty, and they all became secret rivals of his lover. Acajou was so full of his amour that he did not even perceive the enticements of which he was the object. They came from all directions, but when it was admitted that the hearts of the two lovers were closed to any other sentiment than their own amour, it was generally decided that Zirphile had become even more stupid since she had fallen in love than she had been before; that Acajou's beauty was devoid of physiognomy and had nothing piquant about it; that their amour was as ridiculous was it as new to the court; and that it did not constitute a society.

People paid no further attention to them, therefore, and they were so occupied with one another that they did not perceive the desertion of the court any more than they had perceived its urgency. Ninette, who had previously protected Zirphile's conduct with so much care against the temerity of the court fops, left her with Acajou without anxiety; she believed that true love is always respectful, and that the more a lover desires the less he dares to attempt.

The maxim is delicate, but I do not believe it to be absolutely reliable; however, it was not belied in this instance.

They were only waiting for the kings of Acajou and Minutia in order to celebrate the mirage; their ambassadors had arrived and had already settled everything; the liveries were made; the garments were being finished; they only lacked a pompom; the latest fashions had been ordered from Paris, from Chez Chapt, modeled on dolls of the same size as Ninette. In brief, everything essential was ready; it only remained to negotiate matters regarding the laws of the two states and the interest of the peoples.

The two lovers did not quit one another for an instant. Often, in order to escape the tumult of the court, they spent days in the most remote boscage of the park. They gave one another a thousand innocent caresses; they continually said the trivial things so interesting to lovers, which are repeated incessantly without ever being exhausted, and which are always new.

One day, while they were enjoying one of those delightful conversations, the heat obliged Zirphile to take off her scarf in order to talk with more liberty. Harpagine, who had rendered herself invisible in order to surprise them, appeared to their eyes escorted by the fay Envious, mounted on a chariot drawn by snakes and surrounded by a prodigious quantity of hearts pierced by arrows; they were as many talismans representing all those who rendered homage to envy, and the arrows were the image of the merit that caused the greatest torture to the envious.

Harpagine immediately struck Zirphile with her wand and carried her away in the midst of a cloud at the very moment when Acajou was kissing her hand.

The unfortunate prince prostrated himself before the fay, begging her only to make the weight of her vengeance fall on him and to spare the princess. He said everything that love and generosity inspired, in vain. The cruel fay looked at him with blazing eyes.

"Do you dare to hope for any mercy?" she said. "My heart is no longer sensible to anything but hatred. I want to exercise my vengeance at a single stroke on you and your lover; she will pass into the hands of your rival, who is odious to her."

With those words, the chariot flew away, and left Acajou plunged in the utmost despair.

Ninette was soon instructed by her art of faerie of what had happened, but the misfortune of people who know everything is that they never foresee anything. She came to look for the prince. He was beside Zirphile's scarf, which he was moistening with his tears. The little fay neglected nothing to console him, without being able to make herself heard. After having taken him back to the palace almost in spite of himself, she shut him in her cabinet, put on her spectacles and consulted her large books in order to discover what action she could take in that misfortune.

The court reasoned variously; some talked about it a great deal but scarcely cared about it; others, without saying anything, took more interest in it. The women, above all, were untouched by the loss of Zirphile; several flattered themselves that they might console the prince.

They were still in the first phase of court news, in which everyone talks without knowing anything, and recounts the circumstances while waiting to know the facts, when so much is said about so little, when they saw Ninette appear, who announced with vivacity the Zirphile could easily be extracted from the hands of the genius. Everyone hastened to discover what means would be employed.

"Listen to me," said the little fay. "I've just discovered that all the power of Podagrambo and Harpagine depends on an enchanted vase that they possess in a secret place in their castle; it's guarded by a subaltern genius who is transformed into a Chartreuse cat. It's unnecessary to employ great efforts to take possession of it; it's sufficient for the adventure to be undertaken by a woman of irreproachable honor, something that ought not to be rare at the court. She will not find any obstacle, but for any other person to attempt the adventure would be futile."

"That's a fortunate discovery!" said a fop. "I'm most eager to compliment Prince Acajou."

"Shut up," said the fay. "If it required a reasonable man, no one would choose you."

"I'm not joking," relied the young fop, in an ironic tone. "I really dread that a competition in virtue here that might degenerate into a civil war."

"I've anticipated that inconvenience," retorted Ninette, "So I want lots to be drawn in order to prevent any reason for jealousy."

The tickets were made immediately, and the name that appeared was that of Amine. That was a young woman who was pretty rather than beautiful, lively, scatterbrained and exceedingly coquettish, free in speech, circumspect in conduct, continually making enticements and always afflicted by a troop of young men.

Hearing herself proclaimed, Amine was neither prouder nor more embarrassed than usual, but a certain murmur went up that did not seem to be a very definite applause. Ninette took that as a bad augury for success; that is why she nominated Zobeide to accompany Amine, because two virtues are better than one. Zobeide was a little older and more beautiful than her companion; she was in addition a prodigy of virtue and slander; it was even claimed that she was so severe in her sagacity as to have the right to tear apart all the other women pitilessly. A fine privilege of virtue!

At any rate, the two of them departed, and went, following their instructions, to a small building separate from Harpagine's palace. Amine, still lively, marched in the lead. They did not find any obstacle; they went through several doors that opened of their own accord. They finally reached a chamber where they perceived a vase on a marble table, the form of which was not commendable; it closely resembled a chamber pot. I am sorry not to have a nobler term or image.

They would never have imagined that it was the treasure for which they were searching if Ninette had not described it.

If the form of the vase was vulgar, its virtue was admirable; it rendered oracles, and reasoned about everything like a philosopher; it was then a great eulogy to be compared to one for reasoning.

Amine and Zobeide also found the cat that had been mentioned to them; they tried to stroke it, but it scratched Zobeide, although it allowed Amine to caress it, gave her the velvet paw, arched its spine and fluffed up its tail in the most elegant fashion.

Amine, charmed by such a fortune beginning, took the vase and was already lifting it up when Zobeide tried to touch it with her hand. Immediately, a thick smoke emerged from it, which filled the room. A frightful noise was heard. Fear gripped Amine; she dropped the vase on the table from which she had taken it, and the genius appeared instantly with Harpagine. They seized Amine and Zobeide and only spared their lives in order to lock them up in a dark tower.

Ninette was soon informed, as usual, of the failure of the enterprise; she sought the reason and learned from the whole court that Amine was as sage as she was coquettish, whereas Zobeide savored the pleasures of a secret commerce with an obscure lover while she fatigued everyone by the display of her false virtue.

Ninette immediately declared that, the vase having cracked when Amine had dropped it on the table, the power of the genius, without being completely destroyed, had at least been weakened by that accident.

Acajou, no longer listening to anything but his despair, made a vow, in order to avenge himself on the genius's enchanted pot, to destroy all the chamber pots that he encountered, and from that moment on he executed his oath on all those he found in the palace. There was a frightful disorder; the scandal was so great that Ninette tried to make him listen to reason with regard to so many innocent vases, but she was never able to calm him down.

In that embarrassment she had recourse to the Council of Fays. The affair seemed very important, and it was decided that, the power of the genius being weakened, he could no longer keep all of Zirphile's person; that, without losing her life, her head would be separated from her body and transported to the Land of Ideas until it was reunited with her body by the person who could reach that land and disenchant her.

Ninette proposed that it would be more appropriate to leave the head than the body in the power of the genius, for fear that he might make her fall in love with him while she had lost her head, and marry her immediately. The fays paid attention to that difficulty, and ordered that the body would be permanent wrapped in a living flame that would not allow anyone to approach it except the master of the head.

The fays' sentence was carried out as soon as it was pronounced. The genius wanted to attempt the adventure, without ever being able to approach the Land of Ideas. The mad can easily reach it, but the stupid can never land there. As for Acajou, who was madly in love, he had no difficulty in getting there.

The Land of Ideas is very singular, and the form of its government does not resemble any other. There are no subjects; everyone there is a king and reigns as sovereign over the entire State without usurping anything from the others, whose power is no less absolute. Among so many kings, jealousy is unknown; they merely wear their crowns in a different fashion. Their ambition is to offer it to everyone and to want to divide it; that is how they make conquests.

The limits of so many realms contained within a single one are not fixed; everyone extends or narrows them according to his caprice.

Acajou recognized that he was in the realm of Ideas by the multitude of heads that he encountered in his passage; they hastened toward him and all spoke to him at the same time in all sorts of languages and in different tones. He searched for the head of Zirphile but could not see it.

Sometimes he encountered heads that, having resisted misfortune, had been lost in prosperity, some by fortune, others by dignities. He found the heads of wastrels, a multitude of misers, and a quantity lost in war, the heads of authors lost by virtue of success, others by failure, several by appearances of success, and a host by envy and chagrin at the success of their rivals. Acajou found an infinite number of heads lost incognito, which he never wanted to name and I do not want to guess. There were many heads of philosophers, mystics, orators, chemists, etc. He saw many lost by caprice, by putting on airs, by indiscretion, and, in turn, by libertinage and superstition. Some excited his compassion; he drew apart from others as importunate, and trampled underfoot all those that envy had doomed.

In order to find Zirphile, Acajou searched for heads that were said to have been lost for amour, but when he examined them closely he only found the heads of coquettes or those jealous without amour. Fatigued by so much research, in despair because of his lack of success, stunned by all the stupidities he heard, the prince retired into a clump of trees in order to get away from the multitude of crazy heads by which he was assailed. He lay down on the grass and started reflecting on his misfortune.

As he looked around he saw a few trees laden with fruits. He was so exhausted that he had a yen to eat a pear. He picked it, but scarcely had he put his knife to it than a head emerged from it, which he recognized as that of his dear Zirphile. Nothing can express the astonishment and pleasure of the prince. He got up in haste in order to embrace such a dear head, when it moved way a few paces and placed itself on a rose-bush in order to make a body of sorts.

"Stop, Prince," she said to him. "Remain tranquil, and listen to me. All the efforts you make to grasp me will be futile. I would throw myself into your arms if destiny permitted it, but as I am enchanted, I can only be picked up by hands that are also enchanted. Alas, I sigh after my body, and I don't know whether it is still worthy of me; it is still in the hands of the genius and I dare not think about that without shuddering; my head spins."

"Reassure yourself," said Acajou. "The fays, touched by your misfortunes, have taken your body under their protection."

"How you tranquilize me!" said Zirphile. "In any case, dear prince, you know that all my tenderness is for you, and you would be too generous to reproach me for a misfortune of which I am innocent."

"That is well said," replied the delicate Acajou, "but inform me promptly where I can find the enchanted hands you mentioned to me."

"You will find them," said Zirphile, "in the park where they are fluttering; they are those of fay Nonchalante, who was deprived of them because she did not know what do with them. I'll tell you the story. There was once..."

"Oh, damn it," Acajou interrupted, impatiently, "I don't have time to listen to tales; as long as I have the hands I don't care about their story. I'll go to look for them right away."

"Go," said the princess, "and deliver me from the cruel enchantment in which I'm languishing. You might have noticed that all the lost heads that are in this abode only seek to show themselves, without blushing at their estate; there's only me who is obliged to hide myself in fruits; as I'm the only head lost by amour, I'm an object of scorn for the others..."

The head continued to talk but the prince had already gone. He had realized that the princess, since she was no longer anything but a head, had become rather fond of talking.

He had not taken a hundred steps through the park when he encountered the enchanted hands that were fluttering in the air. He tried to approach them in order to catch them, but as soon as he tried to touch them he received flicks, which appeared, to begin with, to be very insolent. However, as his happiness depended on grasping them, he employed all his skill in trying to catch the fatal hands. Every time he thought he had them they escaped him, giving him a slap, or knocking his hat to the ground. The more ardor he put into pursuing them, the more they fled him.

That pursuit went on so long that poor Acajou was completely out of breath. He stopped for a moment, and, finding himself next to a trellis he plucked a cluster of grapes in order to refresh himself. Scarcely had he tasted one, however, than he felt an extraordinary revolution within him. His mind's vivacity was augmented and his heart became more tranquil. His imagination was increasingly inflamed; all the objects therein were painted with fire, passing with rapidity and effacing one another, in such a fashion that, not having the time to compare them, he was absolutely incapable of judging them.

In a word, he went mad.

The fruits of that garden, by virtue of an intimate rapport with the heads that inhabited it, had the virtue of causing the loss of reason, and, unfortunately, they had no effect on intellect. Acajou found himself, in an instant, the most mentally active and most insane of princes

The first effect of such a sudden change was the cooling of the heart. Acajou lost all his amour. Veritable amour can only subsist with reason. Instead of the tender and respectful urgency that he had previously had for Zirphile, he only conserved a sight memory of her. He did not even feel compassion for the misfortune of the princess. The fact of having lost her head appeared to him to be a hilarious thing. It is often from that point of view that a mind devoid of judgment envisages the misfortune of others.

Conceit succeeded modesty in Acajou's mind, and replaced very amply with pretentions the real merit that he had lost.

"I must have been quite mad to run after a head," he cried, "when I could turn those of all the women of the court of Minutia. Let's go; it's necessary to fulfill my destiny, which is to be generally loved and admired without engaging my liberty."

Having said that, he left.

Seeing Acajou arrive, Ninette ran to met him and asked him about the fate of Zirphile. The prince told her that she was only a head, which could not be grasped; that all his cares had been futile, that he had made his decision; and that constancy without happiness was the virtue of a fool.

He proffered a quantity of other fine maxims, which soon enabled Ninette to understand that he prince's character had changed considerably, but that he had an infinite amount of wit. In the beginning, she was sorry that he had not bought the princess back; however, as the present object always prevails over the absent one in lively minds, she consoled herself for the loss of Zirphile by means of the pleasure of seeing Acajou again.

The entire court hastened around him, more out of curiosity than interest. They expected only to find a sage and modest prince, who would give them, as usual, all the ridiculous things imaginable, but they soon conceived a more advantageous idea of him. The conversation became lively and brilliant.

The attentive reader will doubtless recall that the fay's spectacles served to shorten the sight; she had taken them off in order to see the prince arrive from further away, and as she had not put them back on, she formulated arguments at the limit of vision.

Acajou did not stop talking; he said in a moment a thousand extravagant things that delighted the entire court with admiration and rendered all the women mad for him. They listened avidly, and cried: "Oh, how witty he is!" In the end, they gave him so many eulogies that he was obliged to blush, even by conceit. It seemed that the greatest good fortune that could happen to a prince was to lose his reason; all those who encountered him complimented him on it, and the others wrote it down.

Acajou no longer having any amour, became the declared lover of all the women, the fury of good fortunes combining easily with madness. He began with a fairly pretty woman, a free spirit liberated from prejudices, who made the reputation of all the young men since she had lost her own. As it was not necessary to have her to be scornful of her, and sufficient to have had her to be disgusted with her, he quit her two days later. He took another with a charming face, a tender heart and a mild character, who only needed, in order to merit being loved, to receive fewer lovers.

Acajou disdained fixing her, and soon gave her several rivals. He was only occupied in extending the list, and they all hastened to be inscribed there, only having found him lovable since he had been incapable of love.

After having had a large enough number of celebrated women to put to his credit, he resolved to seduce a few uniquely to make them lose the reputation for virtue that they had. If he learned that there was a woman loved tenderly by a cherished husband she immediately became the object of his cares, and such was the latitude that the title of fashionable man inspires that he succeeded in everything in which he should have failed.

The affairs that the prince had at court did not prevent him from descending into the bourgeoisie, where his successes were even more rapid because those who submitted thought they were associating themselves with women in society in sharing their stupidities. Even the men, instead of hating him, envied him and sought him out, admiring him without esteeming him.

Although those who employ their time very badly are those who have the least remaining, the prince had plenty of empty moments by virtue of the lightness with which he treated his good fortune. In any case, fashion required one sometimes to appear bored. He therefore sought a new dissipation in intellectualism, which was then in fashion. It is true that, in order to avoid a certain pedantry that study often gives, the secret had been found of being a scholar without studying. Every woman had her geometer or her intellectual, as she had once had her spaniel.

Acajou, following that plan, gave himself body and soul to all the areas of science and literature. He talked physics and geometry. He made metaphysical dissertations, verses, tales, comedies and operas. The prince excited general admiration. It was claimed that professional authors could not come close to him. Everyone knows that that is only men "of a certain fashion," who have what is called "class," that are superior to the genius of the world and quite "without pretention."

Nothing was comparable to Acajou's lot; a collection of his witty sayings was published, which became everyone's favorite reading; it was entitled *Perfect Persiflage*—a very useful work at court, appropriate to render a young man brilliant and insupportable.

In the end, Acajou fund himself fatigued by his own success; he had never put anything but pleasure in place of amour; posing had succeeded pleasure, and distaste had almost the effect of reason and rendered life insupportable; an honest man would be unfortunate to be condemned to it. Without becoming more reasonable, he became sad. In any case, the property of intellect alone is to excite admiration at first and then to weary its own admirers. The majority of the women who had had the ambition to please him began to blush at finding themselves on an exceedingly numerous list, and disfavored him; he was even accused of being wicked, under the pretext that he made up songs and jokes that mocked his best friends and held up everyone to ridicule. However, he had no evil intention; he only wanted to divert himself by amusing others; but people are always unjust.

Ninette, not understanding how her dear Acajou could cease to be fashionable, put on her spectacles in order to judge the matter without prejudice, and after having examined it thoroughly, recognized that he did indeed have a great deal of wit, but that he was no less mad for that. She engaged him to recount everything that he had done in the realm of Ideas.

Acajou, not knowing what she wanted to get to, gave her a very detailed account, because he loved talking about himself. When he reached the cluster of grapes that he had eaten, Ninette cried: "Ah! I'm no longer astonished that you have so much intellect!"

"Oh, why?" said Acajou.

"It's because you have no common sense," the fay replied.

"A fine conclusion!" said Acajou.

"I know," said Ninette, "that you have too much intellect to be easy to convince, especially when someone talks reason to you, but that's because you've lost yours. The fruits of the realm of Ideas are a deadly poison to it. Fortunately, we have the remedy; I have a trellis whose virtue is to cause the loss of intellect; it's only known to me. I sometimes give the grapes to members of my court who have too vivid an imagination; I want you to taste some."

"I can see people here who have certainly eaten them to excess," relied Acajou, "but I swear to you that I'm not tempted to make use of them. Look elsewhere for the secret of becoming reasonable that of losing intellect."

"There's no surer one," the fay interjected, "and you're no longer in a state to sacrifice any."

With that, Ninette said a great many flattering things to the prince. She knew that the intellect allows itself to be seduced by self-esteem more readily than persuaded by reason."

Acajou, however, in spite of all Ninette's eloquence, was mad enough not to want to lose intellect; that had to be the work of amour.

The young prince had never savored true pleasures, because his desires had always been anticipated; his whims only clung to the novelty of objects, and vivacity uses them up so quickly. He had fallen into a languor, from which caprice extracted him occasionally, only to plunge him back into it again. The amour of which Zirphile had made him feel the initial effects reawakened as soon as the intoxication of the senses had dissipated and vanity was no longer nourished. He sensed a void in his heart that only amour could fill. The misfortune of those who have loved is to find nothing that can replace amour.

Acajou confided his situation to Ninette and begged her to enable him to see Zirphile again, since he would also lose his intellect if he were deprived of her any longer. The fay then took her crutch and led Acajou into a garden that only she knew. That place was garnished with trees laden with the most beautiful fruits in the world, which all had a particular virtue.

Some caused the loss of the passion for gambling, which is so deadly; others the passion for contradiction, so inconvenient in society; these the passion for domination, so insupportable; those the passion for affairs, so useful to those who possess it and so exhausting to others; and several others: the satirical spirit, so amusing and so detested; its even more dangerous opposite, the spirit of complaisance and flattery. One does not see those excellent fruits in our desserts. It is a great pity that that excellent garden is not open to all evil spirits; they would come back more amiable, without being any more stupid than they were before. First I would send there…,

[*A sheaf of pages is missing here more considerable than the rest of the work; any readers who regret that can substitute names, beginning with their own.*]

Having made Acajou approach the trellis whose grapes caused the loss of the spirit of presumption, posing and conceit, Ninette ordered him to pick a cluster. Then, having put on her spectacles, and taking Zirphile's scarf, she said: "Prince, take this scarf; where you go into the Land of Ideas you will only have to wave it in the air, holding it at one end. The enchanted hands that you pursued in vain will come to seize it, and you will be able to catch them. You will then be able to take possession of the head of the princess. When you need to eat or drink you have only to take a few grapes; they will be sufficient for you. Also give some to Zirphile in order to calm the vapors that must have altered her head somewhat; without that precaution you'll find her so different from herself that after having been inconstant by virtue of madness you might well become so by virtue of reason. When you have the head we shall soon be in possession of the body by the attraction that affects women whose head caries away the body. It's appropriate, before your departure, that you eat some of these grapes."

Acajou hesitated slightly, but, animated by the desire to see Zirphile again, and perhaps believing that his intellect was proof against anything, he put a few grapes in his mouth. The effect was sudden; it seemed that he had previously been enveloped by a cloud that had just dissipated and that a veil had been lifted from before his eyes. Objects all appeared different to him. He blushed instantly, and no longer dared speak except to express his gratitude to the fay.

When he went back into the palace he found a collection of his works on his table; he wanted to scan it, in order to verify his condition. He could not imagine then that he had been stupid enough to write them; he yawned on reading his romances and his comedies, and that same evening he hissed one of his operas.

Having wearied the court with is extravagances, and annoying it again by virtue of the return of his reason, Acajou departed the next day before dawn and returned to the Land of Ideas, guided as promptly by amour as he had been by madness.

He found the same objects that he had encountered the first time and followed Ninette's advice exactly. With the aid of the scarf he rendered himself the master of the enchanted hands. He immediately went in search of Zirphile's head, and to that effect he opened a prodigious quantity of pears without finding it. From there he passed on to peaches and melons, and was making a frightful devastation of fruits when he heard a loud burst of laughter. He looked to see where it was coming from and perceived the head of the princess, which, instead of coming to him, mocked his research and his urgency.

As amour is weakened by absence and madness spreads by contagion, Zirphile's head had lost much of the vivacity of its passion and was beginning to adapt to the new country that it inhabited. Acajou sighed, but, remembering the marvelous grapes, of which he had a cluster, he threw a few of them to the head of the princess, which swallowed them, while bantering.

Her blindness was immediately dissipated. She flew toward the enchanted hands, with which the prince received her. Nothing can express the transports by which he was seized. He let the hands go where they wished, and no longer occupied himself with anything but the precious head of his dear Zirphile. He covered it with kisses, which she could not avoid.

She was completely red with modesty, although, in the state in which she found herself, her lover's caresses could not have very dangerous consequences. In any case, it is not always necessary to listen to the plaints of modesty; that which is born of amour easily pardons the transports that it is obliged to forbid.

Acajou wrapped the princess's head in her scarf and resumed the road to Ninette's palace. Night having surprised him, a terrible storm blew up, which obliged the prince to seek shelter. As one can imagine, it was not for him. Lovers fear nothing, but he wanted to put Zirphile under cover, in addition to which he feared bumping the princess's head or his own against some tree.

In that embarrassment he perceived a light in the distance toward which he directed his footsteps. After having walked, at the risk of breaking the dearest head—which is to say, that of the princess—he arrived at the foot of a pavilion that terminated a garden; he knocked on the door.

A moment later he saw an old woman appear who was holding a candle in her hand, and who asked him, grumbling, who he was and what he wanted. Acajou did not want to identify himself in a condition so unworthy of his rank. He hesitated momentarily over the quality he ought to adopt, and as he had a head full of his principal misfortunes and all the pottery he had broken at one time, he replied, without really knowing what he was saying, that he was a poor man who repaired broken faience and that he was asking for shelter for the night.

At those words the old woman's face softened slightly. "Come in," she said, "be welcome. You can render me a service; I have a cracked chamber pot that you can repair."

The old woman immediately went to fetch that precious item of furniture and put it in Acajou's hands in order that he could get to work. The prince, as ashamed of the profession that he had just adopted as of the first usage that he had to make of it, took the old woman's pot. Then, recalling the terrible oath he had made never to spare any chamber pot until he had disenchanted the princess, he was uncertain for some time between the dread of perjury and that of violating hospitality.

Scruple finally prevailed, and he threw the pot against the wall, breaking it into a thousand pieces.

I do not know whether the reader, indignant at Acajou's lack of politeness, will be astonished by what followed, or whether, by virtue of a singular sagacity, he has already anticipated it. At any rate, those who do not have much penetration will be very glad to learn that the chamber pot in question was the fatal vase to which the power of the genius and the fay was attached, and the custody of which they had confided to the old witch. Scarcely had he broken it than there was a sound like thunder, and frightful howling. The castle was destroyed; the palace collapsed. The genius and the fay, delivered to their impotent rage, fled into the desert, where they perished miserably.

Acajou, without being moved by all that upheaval, marched toward the terrible place where the body of the princess was enchanted. The flames that defended it divided as he approached, and, at the moment when he presented the head to it, the body advanced to meet it and was reunited with it.

The fay Ninette appeared instantly, followed by her entire count; her first thought was to deliver the unfortunate. The fluttering hands were disenchanted and returned to the fay Nonchalante, on condition that she was laborious. She devoted herself absolutely to toil, and invented the art of tying knots.

Amine and Zobeide were taken out of prison. From that time on Amine had the privilege of doing anything without anyone having anything to say about it; apparently, she was sensate enough to take advantage of it. As for Zobeide, she doubtless continued to live as usual, but ceased to spread slander.

Ninette, after having given her first cares to the unfortunate, was only occupied thereafter with the marriage of the two lovers. It was celebrated with all possible magnificence. They lived happily and had a large number of children, all of whom were prodigies of intelligence, because they were born with an extreme penchant for amour.

Carl Gustaf Tessin: *Faunillane; or, The Yellow Child*

The Prince of Percebourse having lost his father and his mother in his youth, followed the penchant that he had for traveling. He roamed several lands, spending a great deal there, and returned to his homeland augmented in merit and diminished in money.

He lived in a country held in affection by the fays, and among the various beauties with which they had ornamented a place that pleased them, none equaled the Avenue of Ideas. The trunks of the tress were an alabaster of their natural color, the leaves emerald, and the fruits that only came once every thousand years ripened in the blink of an eye and formed diamonds, at first as big as water-melons, but which then shrank by degrees, becoming tiny in an instant, just like the foam that suddenly spreads over champagne and disappears similarly; only the Sancy of the French crown has been plucked therefrom, and that in the fullness of its decline, its comrades having disappeared before it was picked.[18]

The sun is unable to penetrate that lovely place to the extent that it is necessary to see clearly without being dazzled, and at night, five hundred and eighteen million lamps render a

---

[18] The Sancy diamond, named for its one-time possessor Nicolas de Harlay, Seigneur de Sancy (1546-1629), had a very colorful history. After being borrowed by Henri II and Henri IV, it was sold to James I of England, but returned to France with the exiled Stuart king James II, who sold it to Cardinal Mazarin, who bequeathed it to Louis XIV when he died. Tessin had no way of knowing that it would be plundered after the 1789 Revolution and follow a tortuous route via Russia, India and America to arrive back in the Louvre in 1978.

glare well above that of the sun; it is then that most people stroll.

Percebourse was there one day, carefully exploring all the corners and coverts of the admirable place, when he suddenly found himself in a garden filled with the largest and most marvelous fruits in the world.

First of all, near the entrance, there were two currant bushes that bore redcurrants of a prodigious size; the prince had a desire to eat one. As soon as he had bitten into it, the redcurrant opened up and a lovely woman emerged, so young that she still seemed to be a child, but leaning on a staff with a pair of spectacles on her nose.

"Well, by all the fays!" cried Percebourse. "Where have you come from, my little maid? And why do you disfigure your pretty face with those nasty spectacles?"

"Alas, Sire," replied the Queen with the Golden Scarves—for it was her—"it is for having disobeyed the One-Eyed Giant, the mortal enemy of the Enchanter Bushy-Eyebrows, my uncle, and filling myself up with redcurrants in spite of his prohibition, that I find my eyesight so weak that, if it were necessary to sew my chemises myself, I'd go naked for want of being able to thread a needle.

"That's quite an appetite you had," said the prince, smiling. "But why does a child who ought to be jumping and turning somersaults need that nasty crutch?"

"Alas, Sire," replied the child, "it's that vile giant again who endowed me with it. Piqued by his prohibition of a paltry redcurrant, I ran afterwards to powder his beard gray and show that I laughed at his orders and rules. He took my intentions badly, and by sneezing, damaged my knee-joints so badly that my weakness hasn't permitted me to walk without a stick since."

"That's a hard-hearted colossus. But why were you stuffed into that redcurrant?" asked Percebourse.

"Alas, Sire," replied the Queen with the Golden Scarf, "it's for having had a kingdom full of gardens and gardeners without ever planting anything there but cabbages and currants. But what do all these details matter to you? You appear to me to be full of other cares; I only want to limp back home to spin gold in order to maintain my poor subjects."

"Go, my charmer," said the prince, obligingly, kissing her little hand with a force that made her squeal loudly. "Go eat cherries, peaches and melons, and don't amuse yourselves with your boxes of powder; go have pavilions built, order flower-beds, fountains and orchards; in a word, as in a thousand, go obey and please the giant, for fear that he might crush you."

The queen made a very gracious reverence, and went her own way, while the prince, without pausing for long over the extraordinary nature of that adventure, reached out to pick another redcurrant, choosing a smaller one in order not to risk biting into an imprisoned queen.

Scarcely had he touched it than it split, and he saw two small white hands emerge, the fingers interlaced, twiddling the two thumbs around one another at an incredible speed.

"Oho!" he said. "I haven't seen anything similar in my travels." And as the hands approached his nose very closely, he wafted them away with the back of his hand, as one tries to waft away a puff of smoke; but the two hands persisted and accelerated their movement.

"Little hands, which don't belong to anyone," he said, becoming impatient again, "although you're nice and plump, people like me don't like anyone playing with their nose. At least go to join your body, in order that I can see whether it's pretty enough to permit you such a liberty, for I've seen beautiful arms with hideous faces."

The hands did not say a word, but, as if offended by such a suspicion, their rapidity became incomprehensible—which did not prevent the prince from remarking that the left one lacked a finger. As he was quick, he caught them, wrapped them in a strawberry leaf and put it in his pocket.

"Am I not going to eat a wretched redcurrant" he said, as he picked another one. This one, borne to his mouth, split like the others, and a plump little finger appeared, the color of snow, proportioned like the most beautiful finger in the world; its movement was to flick in a precipitate but measured fashion, which disturbed Percebourse's well-powdered wig so forcefully that, without further ado, he seized the finger rapidly and shut it in his toothpick-case. Then, drawing away from the fatal currant bush, he went forward, thinking about the Queen of Scarves, the two mutinous hands and the flicking finger.

He perceived an apricot tree bearing fruits so large that it was impossible to eat one without slicing it. He picked one, took out his knife, sat down under the tree, laid out a white handkerchief and started to slice the apricot.

"Hey! Hey!" cried a head, bounding over the grass.

What became of the prince at that sight! It was a perfect female head, with long black curly hair; two large eyes, similarly dark but not curly; eyebrows like jet ached like rainbows, fashioned so that no poor little hair surpassed another; a small turned-up nose; and a vermilion mouth so small that it would have been necessary to slice the apricot into thirty thousand morsels in order to enable it to taste one. But that head was always tilted toward the right shoulder, and no matter how the prince tried to straighten it, it always fell over, with a meditative expression that augmented its charms and interested him in its favor.

"Beautiful bust or wig-head," said the prince, anxiously, "where is your body?"

"Look in the trunk of the tree," replied the tilted head, looking at him with a gaze that burned his heart so deeply that it spread an odor of charred flesh throughout the garden.

"Alas," he exclaimed, "how can I cleave that tree, having neither an ax not a saw?" He stuck his knife into it, but his knife shattered like glass; he scratched it with his fingernails, and, having ripped them all out he took out the two hands that he had put in his pocket and started scratching again, so forcefully that the nail of the right thumb stayed there. He wrapped it very quickly in black taffeta, and was in despair at having spoiled the beautiful hand without having made any progress in his task or being able to reach the beautiful body.

He was about to abandon a labor that seemed futile when his good genius suddenly inspired him to approach the eyes of the tilted head to the root of the tree. It caught fire so suddenly and so violently that his greatest anxiety was that it would consume the body as well. What was his joy when he saw it leap through the flames! The body was so proportionate, so well made, that all it lacked to be a model was two hands and a head.

He picked up the one that was on the ground, which fit it marvelously. He took the finger out of the case, which joined the hand, and the two hands the two arms, to form the most beautiful woman in the world, with a tilted head, and who only ceased twiddling her thumbs long enough to give her finger time to flick the roots of her hair—which, as we have said, was black.

"Admirable or divine goddess, fay, queen or princess, what put you there?" said the prince, swooning.

"The slaps I gave the giant," said the charming stranger.

They were about to take the conversation further, and doubtless to declare the most urgent things, when they were interrupted by the hissing of a thousand snakes, which were drawing a chariot composed of chopped hearts traversed by darts. A woman with a wrathful expression was in that horrible vehicle; her dress was black, streaked with bright flames; the snakes that she had instead of hair were tied up with a dead-leaf-colored ribbon, and behind her there was a Fury who was curling her snaky locks with a hot iron, which made the crawling population hiss in a manner as terrible as it was singular.

"I am the fay Envious," she cried, as soon as she was within range to be heard, "the Queen of the Land of Desires. What do you want, prince, for having liberated the most useful of my works, and a princess who causes envy and chagrin to Greek and Roman beauties?"

"I desire the princess," he said.

"Take her, the fay interrupted, "on condition that the daughter to whom she will give birth a year from now is put under my protection and confided to my care; and I swear by my snakes, by my darts, by my fire, my corroded hearts and my tresses, that I will render her so perfect that she will be no less envied than her mother."

The prince and the princess lowered their eyes, the prince with joy and gratitude, and the princess by virtue of modesty and decency, at hearing herself named as a maker of daughters when she had not yet consented to marriage, But the fays know everything, so that one knew that the marriage would take place, that a daughter would be born of it, and that she would have her under her protection, so she disappeared without even waiting for their consent.

"Well," said the prince, as soon as Envious had disappeared, "your story, Madame?"

"Alas," said the princess—for enchanted princesses are rich in *alas*es, so this one said *alas*—"I am Pensive, dissimulative and curious..."

"Pensive, dissimulative and curious!" repeated the prince, shaking his head three times. "Hmm! If we weren't already married before the fay...but it doesn't matter. Go on, if you please, and begin with your name, as everyone else begins."

"My name is Princess Pensive," she continued, "and I shall receive an inheritance of faerie when my grandmother, the fay Matador, dies, for in our family there has always been a fay, and that power usually skips the daughter to pass to the granddaughter..."

"By the way," said the prince, "it appears to me, beautiful princess, that it's necessary to conclude our marriage, and afterwards, you'll have plenty of time to tell me all these things, which already reek of the marvelous and the admirable. It's sufficient, for the present, for me to know that I'm marrying a lovely and well born princess."

Pensive, who knew society too well to show any urgency, but who was nevertheless not sorry to change estate, which came back to her characteristics of dissimulation and curiosity, gave her hand to Percebourse, who led her out of the garden into the Avenue of Ideas, and from the Avenue of Ideas to the Temple, and from the Temple to the bed.

The possession, far from diminishing the charm and felicity of that union, augmented them, which was a manifest proof of the protection of the fay and gave desire to the happiest of husbands.

The prince, solely occupied with his satisfaction, had passed six months without remembering the story when, eventually, at midday one fine morning—for Pensive's mornings only commenced at midday—he begged her to finish it.

"Sire," she said, this time without the *alas*, "I am Pensive, dissimulative and curious..."

"By our daughter to come," cried Percebourse, "you've told me that, and I know it. Go on."

"I've always liked going for walks," she continued. "One day when I was taking that pleasure, I encountered the One-eyed Giant on a river bank. I was about to run away on seeing him when he grabbed my dress and stopped me. 'I'll bet my beard and my height,' he said to me, 'that you're thinking about some absent individual who has rendered homage to you, and who doesn't displease you.'

"I didn't think that question merited a reply, and I kept quiet. 'You're pensive, my beauty,' he added, 'you're thinking about a defeat.'

"That reproach irritated me, and earned the giant a slap, for I'm prompt Prince, just so you know," she said, raising her voice.

"And I'm quick, Princess, just so you're not unaware of it," Percebourse replied, taking what she had just said as a threat.

Pensive, calming down, took up the thread of her discourse.

"'If you had a tender and reasonable heart,' said the giant, 'one could talk business with you.'

318

"'Me, a tender heart, Sire!' I said, 'I've never been in love, and I don't intend ever to fall in love.'

"'You're dissimulative,' the monster interrupted. That impoliteness earned him a second slap, but without being disconcerted, and not feeling, I believe, any great pain, he cried: 'I have a step-brother. Oh, little brute, if only you knew him!'

"'And what is he like?' I said.

"'You're curious,' he replied.

"That misplaced curiosity guided my hand to his cheek again, this time with a force such that the giant, who had seemed immovable after the first two slaps, went as red as Gobelins scarlet and, sneezing, because a part of his enchantments were at the tip of his nose, he separated my finger from my hand, my hands from my arms and my head from my neck, and shut each part in the place where you found them. 'Stay there, slapper,' he said 'until a young prince comes into the garden, pensive with regard to a princess, dissimulative with regard to the choice of his chagrins, and curious to taste these fruits; for, as reverie, dissimulation and curiosity have put you there, only revere, dissimulation and curiosity can get you out.'

"You know the rest, Sire, having succeeded in accordance with my desires and fulfilled my wishes."

Percebourse did not stop short, and was able to see that, if the princess really loved him, he loved the princess.

At the predicted time, Pensive gave birth to a girl whom she called Faunillane, after the Isle of Fauns, which belonged to her father, but as she has worn a golden robe lined with black ever since, she is more commonly known as the yellow child.

Scarcely had she opened her eyes to the light of day than a mite was seen to enter the room where she was, which soon became an ant, and then a spider, and then a cockchafer, and then a silkworm, and then a lizard, and then a frog, and then a toad, and then a viper, and then a grass snake, and then a rattlesnake, and then a crocodile, and then a winged dragon carrying the fay Envious on its back.

"Where's the child?" she asked.

"Here she is," said the princess, who did not know what it was to break a promise.

Envious disappeared with her prey and put her in an apartment hollowed out in a single diamond. To nourish her she gave her two white balls to suck, which rendered her so beautiful, gracious, perfect and lovable that there was no talk of anything but her beauty and the good fortune of the man who would be able to possess her. Her mildness aided her greatly in making herself desired, and it is said in the journal of her life that she only ever cried or wept at the end of eighteen months, when those balls were metamorphosed into grouse wings, chicken thighs and cocks' crests.

Near the place where Faunillane spent her early years thus was the famous Isle of Woods, where a Temple had been built of a structure more Gothic and venerable than new and magnificent. It contained the ashes of a long race of our kings, prodigies of their centuries and the love of their subjects. Next to that Temple dwelt Princess White Dove, who found on her bed one night a little boy as beautiful as the daylight. Her ambition told her that it was the son of Jupiter, but her reason said no, and even the public claimed that her reason was right.

As no one could imagine where the prodigy came from, while awaiting a favorable revelation he was confided to the care of the fay Tease, called thus not because of her teasing, which had nothing extraordinary about it, but because of an ogre named Bull's-Eye, whom she married, who was hairy and played the lute admirably well. She had known Princess Pensive for a long time, so well that she had made her a present of her portrait to ornament the hall where the ogre played at the head of is musicians. She also carried a sketch of her face made in haste, with a crushed nose, and was linked in amity with the enchanter Bushy-Eyebrows, who had a reputation for great power and little credit.

The Prince of Elbows, as the foundling was named, was raised with admirable care regarding external appearance, but in such a school his interior was scarcely purified, with the result that the innocence of his nature and the malice of his guardians chose him as the battlefield on which a hundred conflicts a day took place, under the conduct of Luxury, Pleasures and Sensuality.

It seemed that his happiness lacked nothing but being linked forever to Princess Faunillane, so the enchanter worked to that end so forcefully, and by means of the composition of a liquor so infernal, that his wife, named Fatty with the Triple Chin, was suffocated by it.

For her part, the fay Envious, who knew how the destiny of the princess would suffer from it, put everything to work to prevent such an ill-matched marriage, and as her power alone was insufficient for that, she went to find the fay Spigot, who joined forces with her; together they plotted the doom of Tease and Bushy-Eyebrows.

Spigot, full of courage, went to find them in the form of a young hunter and engaged them to come into a tent erected in a agreeable wood, filled with game. As soon as they were inside, the tent changed into the fay's Steel Palace, and, by means of her grimoire, she imprisoned that enemy couple in a glass filled with a liquid the color of capillary syrup,[19] placed on the sill of a window, the crystal panes of which were misted by the exhalations of the liquid.

That prison appeared to be eternal, and might have been, but for a visit that Princess Pensive made to Spigot. As soon as the bottled pair saw her they started dancing the passepied with such rapidity that the glass fell over, which attracted the gaze and animated the natural curiosity of the princess, who opened the jar and put her nose inside in order to see such a marvel at closer range.

Scarcely had the enchanter and the fay sensed the approach of liberty than they took advantage of it, and since that time they have desolated the universe more than ever.

---

[19] "Capillary syrup" was a supposedly-medicinal compound made by boiling maidenhair fern, *Adiantum capillus-veneris*, with sugar.

"My beautiful little Prudent, who don't know what you're doing," said Spigot, "you merit being put in that liquid, with your impertinent curiosity."

Pensive, who agreed in her heart that she had merited that reproach, withdrew shamefacedly, imploring the fay not to abandon her, and not to permit the marriage of the Yellow Child and the Prince of Elbows.

"Good," said the irritated fay, "you merit being changed into a pigeon and delivered to the power of your father."

At that point, Envious came in, accompanied by Prince Percebourse.

"Not the glass and the liquid!" she cried. "No, fay, friend, you mustn't do her any harm." Then, turning to the prince, she added: "I know that you've lost considerable treasures in foreign lands, and your daughter will only be given to a prince who will try to discover them, will succeed in doing so, and will bring them back, in order that your estate will know a perfect envy."

As soon as that edict was published, all the young princes started running like lunatics, some to the Paris Opéra, others to the Mercantile Palace, others to the public games, others to the homes of traitors, others to friends who borrowed money, others to the homes of a thousand beauties, and yet others who had no idea where Percebourse had been, started digging in the earth and searching it, to see where his wealth was buried.

All those treasure-hunters were accompanied by a little dog named Joke, who knew all the mysteries of Percebourse and Pensive.

Their return is awaited, in order to learn to whom Faunillane, who is becoming more lovable and more charming every day, is destined. Meanwhile, one cannot doubt the happiness of her fate under the protection of such a powerful and redoubtable fay.

Jean-Jacques Rousseau: *Queen Fantasque*

"There was once a king who loved his people..."

"This is beginning like a tale of fays," the Druid interrupted.

"It is one," replied Jalamir.

So, there was a king who loved his people, and in consequence, was adored by them. He had made every effort to find ministers as well-intentioned as himself, but, having finally recognized the folly of such research, he had made the decision to do by himself all the things that he wanted to preserve from their maleficent activity. As he was very stubborn in the bizarre project of rendering his subjects happy, he acted in consequence, and such unusual conduct made him ineffably ridiculous to the aristocracy. The people blessed him, but in the court he was considered to be a madman. Except for that he did not lack merit; so he was named Phoenix.

If that prince was extraordinary, he had a wife who was less so. Lively, irresponsible, capricious, foolish in the head, sage in the heart, nice by temperament, nasty by caprice: there, in a few words, is the portrait of the queen. Her name was Fantasque: a celebrated name that she had received from her ancestors in the female line, and the honor of which she sustained worthily. That person, so illustrious and so reasonable, was the charm and the torture of her dear husband, for he also loved her very sincerely, perhaps because of the facility she had in tormenting him.

In spite of the reciprocal amour that reigned between them, they spent several years without being able to obtain any fruit of their union. The king was penetrated by chagrin by that, and the queen suffered an impatience whose effects the good prince was not the only one to feel. She held it against everyone that she had no children, and there was no courtier whom she did not ask thoughtlessly for some secret in order to have one, and whom she did not render responsible for its lack of success.

The physicians were not forgotten, for the queen had an uncommon docility in their regard, and they did not prescribe a single drug that she did not have prepared very carefully, in order to have the pleasure of throwing it in their faces the moment it failed to take effect.

The dervishes had their turn; it was necessary to have recourse to novenas, prayers, and above all to offerings, and woe betide the servants of Temples to which Her Majesty went in pilgrimage; she rummaged everywhere, and under the pretext of going to breathe a purified air she never failed to turn the monks' cells upside-down. She also wore their relics and decked herself out alternately in all their different equipages. Sometimes it was a white cord, sometimes a leather belt, sometimes a hood, sometimes a scapular. There was no sort of monastic masquerade that her devotion did not adopt, and as she had an alert appearance that rendered her charming in all her disguises, she did not quit any without having taken care to have herself painted in it.

Finally, by virtue of devotions so well executed and medicines so sagely employed, Heaven and earth granted the queen's wishes; she became pregnant at the moment when she was beginning to despair of it. I leave the joy of the king and the people to be divined; as for her own, as in all her passions, it went as far as extravagance; in her transports she broke everything; she embraced all those she encountered indifferently—men, women, courtiers and valets—and to find oneself in her passage was to risk being stifled. She did not know, she said, any delight similar to that of having a child, to whom she could apply the whip entirely at her ease in her moments of ill-humor.

As the queen's pregnancy had been awaited in vain for a long time, it passed for one of those extraordinary events of which everyone wanted to have the honor. The physicians attributed it to their drugs, the monks to their relics, the people to their prayers and the king to his amour. Everyone was interested in the child that was to be born, as if it were their own, and everyone made sincere wishes for the fortunate birth of a prince, for they all wanted one, and the people, the aristocracy and the king united their desires on that point.

The queen took it amiss that everyone wanted to prescribe to her to whom she ought to give birth, and declared that she intended to have a girl, adding that it appeared rather singular to her that anyone dared to dispute the right to dispose of an item of property that belonged incontestably to her alone.

Phoenix tried in vain to make her listen to reason; she told him frankly that it was none of his business, and shut herself in her cabinet in order to sulk—a cherished occupation to which she routinely devoted six months of the year. I say six months, but not consecutively; that would have been as much repose for her husband; it was taken instead at intervals appropriate to cause him chagrin.

The king understood very well that the caprices of the mother do not determine the sex of a child, but he was in despair that she was giving the spectacle of her opposition to the entire court. He would have sacrificed anything in the world for universal esteem to have justified the love that he had for her, and the fuss that he made, inappropriately, and this occasion was not the only folly that the ridiculous hope of rendering his wife reasonable had made him commit.

No longer knowing to what saint to pray, he had recourse to the fay Discreet, his friend and the protectress of his realm. The fay advised him to adopt the policy of mildness—which is to say, to apologize to the queen. "The sole objective of all women's fantasies," she told him, "is to disorientate masculine arrogance slightly and accustom men to the obedience appropriate to them. The best means you have of curing your wife's extravagances is to be extravagant with her. As soon as you cease to constrain her caprices, be assured that she will cease to have any, and will only wait to become sage until you have been rendered completely mad. Take things with a good grace, then, and try to give in on this occasion in order to obtain everything you want on another."

The king believed the fay, and in order to conform to her advice in the queen's circle he made the decision to tell her quietly that he was sorry that he had contested with her so inappropriately, and that he would try to compensate her in future, by his complaisance, for the ill-humor in which he appeared to have put her by his discourse and by arguing impolitely against her.

Fantasque, who feared that Phoenix's mildness might cover her alone with all the ridicule of the affair, hastened to respond to him that beneath that ironic apology she saw even more pride than in the preceding disputes, but that, since the wrongs of a husband do not authorize those of a wife, she would yield on this occasion, as she had always done.

"My prince and my husband," she added, loudly, "orders me to give birth to a son, and I know my duty too well to fail to obey him. I am not unaware that when His Majesty honors me with marks of his tenderness, it is less for love of me than that of his people, whose interests occupy him scarcely less by night than by day. I ought to imitate such a noble disinterest, and I will request from the Divan an instructive memoir regarding the number and sex of children befitting the royal family: a memoir important to the good of the State, on which every queen ought to learn to regulate her conduct during the night."

That fine soliloquy was heard by the entire circle with a great deal of attention, and I leave it to you to estimate how many bursts of laughter were rather maladroitly stifled. "Ah!" said the king, sadly, as he left, shrugging his shoulders. "I can see clearly that when one has a mad wife one cannot avoid being a fool."

The fay Discreet, whose sex and name sometimes contrasted humorously in her character, found that quarrel so enjoyable that she resolved to amuse herself thoroughly. She told the king publicly that she had consulted the comets that predict the birth of princes, and that she could guarantee that the child to be born would be a boy, but she assured the queen secretly that she would have a girl.

That advice suddenly rendered Fantasque as reasonable as she had previously been capricious. It was with an infinite mildness and complaisance that she took all possible measures to desolate the king and the entre court. She hastened to have the most superb layette made, affecting to render it so appropriate to a boy that it became ridiculous for a girl; it was necessary that the design in question change several fashions, but all that cost her nothing. She had a beautiful necklace of that order prepared, brilliant with stones, and insisted that the king appoint the young prince's governor and tutor in advance.

As soon as she was sure of having a girl she talked about nothing but her son, and did not omit any of the futile precautions that might enable those which ought to have been taken to be neglected. She laughed in bursts when imagining the astonished and stupid expressions of the noblemen and magistrates who were to honor her childbirth with their presence.

"I seem to see," she said to the fay," on the one hand, our venerable Chancellor putting on his spectacles in order to verify the sex of the child, and on the other, His Sacred Majesty lowering his eyes and stammering: 'I thought...but the fay told me...it's not my fault, Messieurs,' and other equally witty apothegms collected by the scholars of the court and soon relayed all the way to the farthest reaches of India."

She pictured with malign pleasure the disorder and confusion into which the marvelous event would throw the entire assembly. She imagined in advance the disputes and the agitation of all the ladies of the palace to protest, adjust and conciliate at that unexpected moment the rights of their important responsibilities, and all the court astir for a bonnet.

It was also for that occasion that she invented the decent and spiritual custom of having the new-born prince harangued by magistrates in robes.

Phoenix tried to suggest to her that it was to debase the magistracy for no reason and to cast an extravagant comicality over all court ceremonial to go in grand apparel to display to

Phoebus a little brat before he could understand, or at least respond.

"So much the better!" said the queen, briskly. "So much the better for your son! Will he not be very fortunate if all the stupid things they have to say to him are exhausted before he can understand them; would you like to save for him until the age of reason speeches liable to render him mad? For God's sake, let them harangue him at their ease while we can be sure that he doesn't understand anything and has less ennui in consequence. You ought to know that one doesn't always get away so cheaply."

It was necessary to do it, and on the express order of His Majesty, the Presidents of the Senate and the Academies began to compose, study, cross out, and riffle through their Vaumorière[20] and their Demosthenes in order to learn to speak to an embryo.

Finally, the critical moment arrived. The queen felt the first labor pains with transports of joy that are rarely observed on such occasions. She complained with such a good grace and wept so cheerfully that one might have thought that the greatest of her pleasures was giving birth.

Immediately, there was a frightful rumor throughout the palace. Some ran to find the king, others the princes, others the ministers, others the senate and the greatest number went to roll their barrel, as Diogenes always had, in order to look busy. In the haste to assemble so many necessary people, the last person anyone thought about was the obstetrician, and the king, who was beside himself with anxiety, having mistakenly asked for a midwife, that inadvertence excited immoderate laughter among the ladies of the palace, making the childbirth the most hilarious of which anyone had ever heard mention.

Although Fantasque had kept the fay's secret as best she could, it had nevertheless leaked out to the women of her

---

[20] Pierre d'Ortigue de Vaumorière (1610-1693), author of the oft-reprinted *L'Art de plaire dans la conversation* [The Art of Pleasing in Conversation] (1692).

household, and they had guarded it so carefully themselves that the rumor took three days to spread throughout the city, with the result that, for a long time, the king had been the only person who did not know it. Everyone was therefore very attentive to the scene that was in preparation; public interest furnishing a pretext to all the curious to amuse themselves at the expense of the royal family, they made a fête out of watching the countenances of Their Majesties and seeing how, with two contradictory promises, they fay could get herself out of the affair and conserve her credit.

"Oh, Milord," Jalamir said to the Druid, interrupting himself, "agree that it is my prerogative to make you impatient, within the regulations. For you sense clearly that this is the moment for digressions, portraits, and the multitude of beautiful things that every intelligent author never fails to employ appropriately at the most interesting point, in order to amuse his readers!"

"How, by God," said the Druid, "do you imagine that that there are enough idiots to read all that intelligence? Learn that one always has enough to skip it, and that in spite of Monsieur the Author, one has soon covered his display of the pages of his book. And do you, who are playing the quibbler here, think that your words are worth more than the intelligence of others, and that to avoid the imputation of a stupidity it's sufficient to say that it's your prerogative to do it? Truly, it isn't worth saying it in order to prove it. And unfortunately, I don't have the resource of turning the pages."

"Console yourself," said Jalamir mildly, "others will turn them for you, if this is ever written down. However, consider that, with the whole court assembled in the queen's chamber, it's the finest opportunity I shall ever have to depict so many illustrious eccentrics for you, and perhaps the only one that you will ever have to know then."

"May God hear you," retorted the Druid, in jest. "I shall know them only too well by their actions, so make them act if your story has need of them and don't tell me about them if it doesn't. I don't want any other portraits than the facts."

"Since there's no means," said Jalamir, "of enlivening my story with a little metaphysics, I'll stupidly pick up the thread, but telling tales for the sake of telling tales is tedious; you don't know how many good things you're going to miss! Help me, I beg you, to find my place, for the essential has carried me away to the extent that I no longer know where I was up to in the tale."

"To the queen," said the Druid, impatiently, "that you have had so much trouble bringing to childbed, and with whom you've been holding me in suspense for an hour."

"Uh oh!" said Jalamir. "Do you think that the children of kings are laid like a thrush's eggs? You're going to see whether it wasn't worth the trouble of perorating."

So, the queen, after many cries and much laughter, finally extracted the curious from anxiety and the fay from intrigue by giving birth to a girl and a boy more beautiful than the moon and the sun, who resembled one another so strongly that people had difficulty telling them apart. That was because in their infancy they were dressed alike.

In that moment so desired, the king, emerging from majesty to render himself to nature, made extravagances that at any other time he would have left to the queen, and the pleasure of having children rendered him so childish himself that he ran on to his balcony and shouted at the top of his voice: "My friends, all of you rejoice; to me a son has just been born, to you a father, and to my wife a daughter."

The queen, who found herself at such a fête for the first time in her life, did not perceive all the work that she had done, and the fay, who knew her capricious spirit, contented her, in conformity with what she desired, by first announcing to her a daughter. The queen had her brought to her, and what surprised the spectators greatly was that, although she embraced her tenderly, in truth, she had tears in her eyes and an

330

expression of sadness that was ill matched with the one she had previously had.

I have already said that she loved her husband sincerely; she had been touched by anxiety and moved by what she had read in his eyes during her suffering. She had made, at a time singularly chosen, admittedly, reflections on the cruelty there was in desolating such a good husband, and when her daughter was presented to her she only thought about the regret that the king would have in not having a son.

Discreet, whom the intelligence of her sex and the gift of faerie enabled to read hearts easily, immediately penetrated what was happening in the queen's, and no longer having any reason to hide the truth, she had the young prince brought.

The queen, having recovered from her surprise, found the expedient so hilarious that she uttered bursts of laughter dangerous in the state she was in. She fainted. They had a great deal of difficulty bringing her round, and if the fay had not answered for her life, the sharpest dolor would have succeeded the transports of joy in the heart of the king and the faces of the courtiers.

But what was most singular about the whole adventure was that the sincere regret that the queen had for tormenting her husband caused her to be gripped by a more intense affection for the young prince than for his sister, while the king—who, for his part, adored the queen—marked a similar preference for the daughter that she had desired. The indirect caresses that those two unique spouses gave one another thus soon became a very marked fondness, and the queen could no more do without her son than the king could his daughter.

That double event gave a great pleasure to all the people, and reassured them at least for a time with regard to the fear of lacking masters. The strong minds who had mocked the fay's promises were mocked in their turn; but they did not admit themselves beaten, saying they did not even accord to the fay the infallibility of the deception, nor to her predictions the virtue of rendering impossible the things she announced. Others, founded on the predilection that was beginning to declare itself, pushed impudence so far as to sustain that in giving the queen a son and the king a daughter, the event had completely belied the prophecy.

While everything was disposed for the pomp of the baptism of the two newborns, and human pride prepared to shine humbly at the altars of the gods...

"One moment," the Druid interjected. "You're confusing me in a terrible fashion. Tell me, I beg you, in what place we are. To begin with, to render the queen pregnant, you paraded her among relics and monks. After that you suddenly passed on to India. Now you're talking to me about baptisms, and then the altars of the gods. By the great Thalamis, I no longer know whether, in the ceremony you're preparing we're going to worship Jupiter, the holy Virgin or Mahomet. It's not that it matters much to me, as a Druid, whether the two babies are baptized or circumcised, but it's still necessary to observe the costume, and not to expose me to mistaking a bishop for the Mufti and a missal for the Koran."

"The great misfortune," Jalamir said to him, "of being as subtle as you, is being easily mistaken. May God preserve from evil all the prelates who have seraglios and mistake the Latin of the breviary for Arabic; may God give peace to all the honest lunatics who follow the intolerance of the prophet of Mecca, ever ready to massacre the human race sanctimoniously for the greater good of the Creator. But you ought to remember that we're in a land of fays, in which no one is sent to Hell for the good of his soul, in which no one regards the foreskin of a man as grounds for damning or salving him, and in which the miter and the green turban cover sacred heads equally, to serve as signals to the eyes of sages and ornaments to those of fools. I know full well that the laws of geography, which regulate all the religions of the world, want the two newborns to be Muslims, but only the males are circumcised, and I need my twins both to be administered, so find it good that I baptize them."

"Do it, do it," said the Druid. "That, faith of a priest, is the best motivated choice I've ever heard in my life."

The queen, who took pleasure in overturning all etiquette, wanted to get up after six days and go out on the seventh, under the pretext that she felt quite well. In fact, she was nursing her children: an odious example of which all the women represented the consequences to her very forcefully. But Fantasque, who feared the ravages of spoiled milk, sustained that there was no time more wasted for the pleasure of life than that which comes after death, that the breast of a dead woman withers no less than that of a nurse, adding in the tone of a duenna that there is no cleavage so beautiful in the eyes of a husband than that of a mother nursing her children.

That intervention of husbands in concerns that regard them so scantly made the ladies laugh abundantly, and the queen, who was too pretty to be one with impunity, appeared from then on, in spite of her caprices, almost as ridiculous as her husband, whom they called derisively the Bourgeois of Vaugirard.

"I can see you coming," the Druid said immediately. "You want to give me, insensibly, the role of Schah-Baham[21] and make me ask where there is also a Vaugirard in India, like a Madrid in the Bois de Boulogne, an Opera in Paris and a Philosopher at court. But continue your rhapsody and don't extend any more traps for me, for, not being married or a Sultan, it's not worth the trouble of being an idiot."

Jalamir continued without replying to the Druid.

Finally, everything being ready, the day arrived for opening the gates of Heaven to the two newborns. The fay went to the palace early in the morning and declared to the august

---

[21] Schah-Baham is a character in the notorious libertine fantasy *Le Sopha, conte moral* (1737) by Crébillon *fils*.

spouses that she was going to give each of their children a present worthy of their birth and her power.

"I want," she said, "before the magic water removes them from my protection, to enrich them with my gifts, and give them names more efficacious than those of all the flat-feet in the Calendar, since they will express the perfections that I shall be careful to give them at the same time; but as you ought to know better than I do the qualities that suit the happiness of your family and your people, choose them yourself, and thus exert one single act of will over each of your two children, which twenty years of education rarely achieve in youth, and reason no longer contrives at an advanced age."

Immediately, there was a great altercation between the two spouses. The queen wanted to regulate the character of her entire family to her whim alone, while the good prince, who sensed all the importance of such a choice, did not care to abandon it to the caprice of a wife whose follies he adored without sharing them. Phoenix wanted the children to become reasonable people one day; Fantasque preferred to have pretty children, and provided that they shone at the age of six, she did not care much whether they might be stupid at thirty. The fay strove in vain to bring Their Majesties into accord; soon the character of the newborns was no longer anything but a pretext for dispute, and it was not a question of being right, but of reckoning with one another.

Finally, Discreet thought of a means of settling everything without putting anyone in the wrong, which was that each of them would dispose as they pleased with the child of their own sex.

The king approved of an expedient that provided the essential by shielding the heir presumptive of the crown from the bizarre wishes of the queen; and, seeing the two children on the knees of their governess, he hastened to take possession of the prince, not without gazing at his sister with an expression of commiseration. But Fantasque, all the more mutinous because she had less reason to be, ran like a madwoman to the young princess and took her in her arms.

"You've united everything in order to exasperate me," she said, "but in order that the king's caprices should turn in spite of him to the profit of one of his children, I declare that I demand for the one I have the exact opposite of what he demands for the other. Choose now," she said to the king, with an air of triumph, "And since you find so many charms in directing everything, decide with a single word the fate of your entire family."

The fay and the king tried in vain to dissuade her from a resolution that put the prince in a strange embarrassment; she did not ever want to let go, and said that she congratulated herself greatly on an expedient that would cause to reflect upon her daughter all the merit that the king was unable to give his son.

"Oh," said that prince, exceeded by chagrin, "you've never had anything but aversion for our daughter, and you're proving it in the most important occasion of her life. But," he added, in a fit of anger of which he was not the master, "in order for her to be perfect in spite of you, I demand that this child resemble you."

"So much the better for you and for him," retorted the queen, hotly, "but I'll be avenged and your daughter will resemble you."

Scarcely had those words been uttered on either part with an unequaled impetuosity that the king, in despair at his recklessness, would have liked to take them back, but it was done, and the two children were endowed without return with the characteristics demanded.

The boy received the name of Prince Caprice ad the girl was called Princess Reason, a bizarre name that she made so illustrious that no woman has dared to wear it since. Thus, the future heir to the throne was endowed with all the perfections of a pretty woman, and his sister the princess was destined one day to possess all the virtues of an honest man and the qualities of a good king: a division that did not appear to be the best intended, but on which there was no going back.

The joke was that the mutual amour of the two spouses acted at that instant with all the force that is always rendered, but often too late, in essential occasions. Predilection not ceasing to act, each of them found that the child that ought to resemble them had the poorer share, and thought less of congratulating themselves than of complaining.

The king took his daughter in his arms and hugged her tenderly. "Alas," he said to her, "What use will your mother's beauty without her talent to make the most of it? You'll be too reasonable to turn anyone's head!"

Fantasque, more circumspect about her own verities, did not say all she thought about the sagacity of the future king, but it was easy to suspect, by the sad manner in which she caressed him that in the depths of her heart she had a high opinion of her share.

Meanwhile, the king, gazing at her with a sort of confusion, made her a few reproaches with regard to what had happened. "I sense my errors," he said, "but they are your work. Our children might have had much more value than us; you are the cause of the fact that they will only resemble us."

"At least," she said, immediately, throwing her arms around her husband's neck, "I'm sure that they will love one another as much as is possible."

Touched by the tenderness in that sally, Phoenix consoled himself with the reflection that he had so often had occasion to make, that in fact, the natural goodness of a sensible heart suffices to repair everything.

"I can divine all the rest so well," said the Druid to Jalamir, interrupting him, "that I can finish the tale for you. Prince Caprice will turn everyone's head and will be too much the imitator of his mother not to be their torment. He will turn the kingdom upside down trying to reform it. To render his subjects happy he will put them in despair, always blaming others for his own mistakes, unjust for having been imprudent, regret for his faults will cause him to commit new ones. As sagacity will never guide him, the good that he would like to do will augment the harm that he will actually have done. In a word, although, fundamentally, he is good, sensitive and generous, his very virtues will be prejudicial to him, and his stupidity alone, combined with all his power, will make him more hated than a reasoned malevolence would have done.

"On the other hand, your Princess Reason, a new heroine of the land of the fays, will become a prodigy of wisdom and prudence, and without having adorers will make herself so adored by the people, that everyone will wish to be governed by her; her good conduct, advantageous to everyone and to herself, will only do harm because her brother will incessantly oppose obstacles to her virtues, to which public prejudice will attribute all the faults that she does not have, even though it does not have them itself.

"There will be question of inverting the order of succession to the throne in order to make the fool's bauble subservient to the distaff, and fortune to reason. The Doctors will expose with emphasis the consequences of such an example, and will prove that it is better that people blindly obey the madmen that hazard has given them than to choose reasonable leaders for themselves; that although a madman is forbidden to govern his own property, it is good to leave him the supreme disposition of our property and our lives; that the most insensate of men is preferable to the wisest of women, and that if the male or the first-born is an ape of a wolf, it is necessarily good politics that a heroine or an angel born after him should obey his will.

"Objections and replies will follow on the part of the seditious, in which God knows how your sophistic eloquence will burn. For I know you, it is above all in speaking ill of what is that your bile is exhaled voluptuously, and your bitter frankness seems to rejoice in the wickedness of man because of the pleasure that it obtains from reproaching them."

"My God, Father Druid, how you go on," said Jalamir, very surprised. "What a flood of words! Where the Devil do you get such fine tirades? You'll never preach as well in the sacred wood, although you'll never speaker truer. If I let you go, you'd soon change a tale of fays into a treaty on politics, and it would be found every day in the cabinets of the Princes Bluebeard or Donkeyskin instead of Machiavelli. But don't go to so much trouble to divine the end of my tale. To show you that denouements are not lacking when necessary, I'll expedite one briefly that isn't as scholarly as yours, but is perhaps as natural and surely more unexpected."

You know, then, that the two twin children were, as I've remarked, very similar in their features and dressed in the same way. The king, believing that he was holding his son, was holding his daughter in his arms at the moment of the influence, and the queen, deceived by her husband's choice, having mistaken her son for her daughter, the fay took advantage of that error to endow the two children in the manner that suited them best. Caprice was therefore the name of the princess, and Reason that of the prince, her brother, and in spite of the eccentricities of the queen, everything was found in the natural order.

Having succeeded to the throne after his father's death, Reason did a great deal of good with very little fuss; seeking to fulfill his duties rather than to acquire a reputation, he did not make war on foreigners or do violence to his subjects, and received more blessings than eulogies. All the projects formed under the previous reign were executed under his, and, in passing from the domination of the father to that of the son, the twice fortunate people believed that they had not changed master.

Princess Caprice, after having caused multitudes of tender and admirable lovers to lose their lives or their reason, was finally married to a neighboring king, whom she preferred because he had the longest moustache and leapt best at hopscotch.

As for Fantasque, she died of an indigestion of grouse-legs in a stew, which she wanted to eat before going to the bed where the king was getting bored waiting for her, one night

338

when, by dint of enticements, she had engaged him to come and sleep with her.

François-Augustin de Paradis de Moncrif: *The Gifts of the Fays; Or The Power of Education*

Among the various sovereigns who reigned in Arabia in remote times, Princess Zoraide was celebrated for the amity that she had contracted with two fays. She was well worthy of pleasing those intelligences, who only exercised their superiority over mortals in those days with a view to rendering them happy. A short time after the death of her husband, to which she was extremely sensible, that princess became the mother of two sons, and, sensing the end of her life approaching, which all the art of the fays could not hold back, she spoke to them thus:

"I am leaving two children in the cradle, both destined by our laws to reign at the same time. You know better than us the virtues or faults that sovereigns distribute as benefits or evils over their subjects. You have loved me too much to refuse me, in my last moments, the sweetness of flattering myself that my children will make the happiness of the estates that I am leaving them. You will endow both of them with the qualities that render men worthy of supreme authority."

One of the fays, whose name was Zulmane, approached the cradle, and, touching the elder of the two princes with her wand, she said: "Child born to reign, a powerful fay is endowing you; she gives you intelligence, valor and probity." With those worlds she flew to the empire of the fays. There, on the emerald tablet where the gifts they make to sovereigns are inscribed, she engraved those with which Alcimedor—that was the prince's name—had just been favored.

The second fay, whose name was Alsime, remained silent, directing her gaze alternately between the two princes.

"What!" said Zoraide. "Will my second son obtain nothing from your power? While his brother shines with all the qualities that make true monarchs, will this one only show common virtues. Is it at this moment, perhaps the only one that remains to me, that I must cease to be dear to the most helpful of fays, the generous Alsime?"

"How you are in error!" replied the fay. "My silence presages nothing catastrophic for Prince Asaid, your second son. I was seeking to divine in the future what the destiny will be of his brother. It seems that Zulmane has endowed him with everything that ought to render a prince accomplished. All those gifts will have their effect; but will they be sufficient? May she not be abused regarding the success for which she hopes! I shall employ my science better in favor of Asaid. At this moment, when he has only just been born, it would perhaps be in vain that I would endow him with the most fortunate qualities. In the impressions that he will receive subsequently from the objects by which he will be surrounded, a thousand different obstacles, might alter the effect of my gifts if I abandoned him to himself."

She took the child in her arms then. "O precious child of the mortal that I cherish the most," she said, "I will pour into your soul those imperceptible philters that develop the virtues and stifle the seeds of the vices, until the time when you are worthy to reign."

At that interesting promise, Zoraide sensed a transport of joy, which, in terminating her life, rendered her last moments delectable. The fay, whom she was holding embraced, saw her soul rising up on its immortal wings, to return to the center of light from which it had descended.

Alsime took the reins of government during the childhood of the two princes, and, respecting the work of Zulmane, she only occupied herself with regard to the elder in watching over the conservation of his life, and reserved for the second all the secrets of her art that served to embellish souls.

The two sovereigns advanced insensibly in age. Alcimedor soon manifested a scorn for dangers, or, rather, he appeared to expose himself to them without being aware of them. He always showed more intelligence than would naturally be expected at the various ages through which he passed successively, but it was detectable in him that intelligence was like a talent by which he was dominated, not an enlightenment of which he made use at the behest of reason. In sum, it was recognized that he did not lack any of the gifts that Zulmane had given him, but that those gifts did not necessarily fulfill the idea that had been conceived of them. However, no one dared give him advice, out of respect for the fay who had endowed him.

With regard to Asaid, his mind only developed by an ordinary gradation, but in his various kinds of progress he acquired an amiable character. It was not what superiority has of the dazzling that burst forth within him; one discovered what an enlightened reason, equilibrated and seasoned by charm, characterizes much better. That fortunate assemblage was the fruit of the first impressions that the fay had given him, and which she had taken care to perfect.

Alsime had given that prince two presents of inestimable price. One was a mirror of which the marvelous property was that, as soon as one had acquired the habit of looking into it, it was only necessary to look at it fixedly and one saw at the same time both that which one was and that which one believed oneself to be. The other was a sort of microscope, which enabled one to distinguish in the most attractive objects what they had of the deceptive and the chimerical. It seems that in making habitual use of that secret, as almost all pleasures are mingled with illusions, one would soon fall into an insipid indifference; but the microscope only magnified illusions dangerous to society; it left the care of perceiving those which only harm ourselves to reason alone. Those precious gifts have remained on earth; it is a pity that the manner of making use of them has been almost entirely reversed.

When the two princes reached the age of eighteen, the fay declared that from that moment on they would both be charged with the redoubtable weight of government. "It is no longer permissible for me," she said to Asaid, "to remain with you. But I shall often descend from the luminous region from

which the fays consider in the blink of an eye all the events of
the earth; I shall come to enjoy with the prince that I have
formed, and whom I love, the felicity that he will maintain in
this empire." With those words she rose up into the air, borne
by an azure cloud, and disappeared.

Sovereign power was thus divided equally between
Alcimedor and Asaid. They had a tender amity for one another; both of them desired to reign with equity; both acted with
the same objective; but their character had no resemblance,
and it often happens that with common principles, and even
with equal enlightenment, the difference in the character of
men creates a great difference in their conduct.

Alcimedor, unshakable in his projects, as soon as they
seemed equitable, never examined sufficiently the inconveniences that might arise therefrom. If his ambition turned him
toward glory, his courage would only allow him to envisage it
as that of conquerors. His probity would not have permitted
him to use unjust means to succeed in that same glory, but
everything that might be a subject of legitimate war appeared
to him to be a necessary enterprise. Everywhere that force
could be employed without injustice, he preferred it to gentle
means, which would have led to the same success with more
time.

Accustomed since childhood only to consider in the pre-
rogatives of the throne the virtues that they gave the sovereign
scope to exercise, Asaid only permitted himself ideas of glory
that were compatible with the wellbeing of his subjects. He
thought that veritable power ought to impose limits on itself.
He regarded as so many triumphs the favorable effects that
prudence and time spared authority. The court and the people
benefited from his conduct, all the more so as they saw that of
his brother with trouble and anxiety.

It was difficult for sovereigns so different in character to
live for long in the perfect union that is necessary for the good
of government. In fact, a subject of division soon rose between
them. Alcimedor learned that they had ancient rights over a

neighboring kingdom, then possessed by King Mutalib; he proposed to take up arms to assert them.

Asaid refused that project. "My brother," he said, "the most glorious ambition for us is not to become more powerful; we are powerful enough, being superior to the other princes of Arabia. What use would new promises and further wealth be to us? They would not give us new virtues. Why expose subjects whom we love in order to subjugate others who would only regard us as tyrants? No one dares trouble our tranquility; we are respected; is it wise to demonstrate that we are redoubtable unnecessarily?"

Asaid spoke in vain, and, seeing that his brother was persisting in his designs, he proposed to separate their state into two different sovereignties. That division having been accepted, scarcely was it terminated that Alcimedor launched the war. It was unfortunate. Vanquished instead of conquering, he had recourse to Asaid; he asked for troops in order to avenge his defeat. Asaid preferred to procure him a more salutary aid. He made an alliance with the prince that Alcimedor had attacked, and became for the future a guarantor against the attempts of his brother when the peace was concluded.

The seal of that peace was a double marriage. Mutalib having two daughters it as agreed that the elder would marry Alcimedor and that Asaid would be united with the younger. Soon, the marriage celebrations succeeded the troubles of war, and the presence of Alsime completed giving the ceremony all the splendor that could embellish it.

The two princesses, although both ornamented with rare qualities, did not resemble one another either physically or mentally. The one who married Alcimedor had for her part all the singular features whose assemblage forms what is conventionally called beauty, but once one had said that she was extremely beautiful there was nothing more to add to the eulogy of her face. What was much more remarkable is that she had exactly the same character that was discovered in Alcimedor, and that conformity made people at their court think that the spouses would have a very happy life together.

In the event, it was entirely to the contrary. Both of them, only wanting to be strictly just and equitable, were devoid of complaisance as soon as they thought their designs reasonable. Both of them, with a great deal of intelligence, found in their conversations subjects for distaste, distance and inimity. Neither of them, for love of sincerity, spared the vanity of the other when they saw a just motive for mortifying it, and by that conduct they were soon reduced to a simple commerce of convention and representation.

The destiny of Asaid was very different, and that was his work. The princess with whom marriage united him, by whom he was always loved madly, had everything that could fill the heart and exercise the reason of a spouse. Her face did not give the idea of what is commonly regarded as beauty, but even women admitted, on seeing her, that to be sure of pleasing, it was necessary to be made like her. In addition, by the graces of intelligence and character, charming for people who were indifferent to her, she became in regard to the man she loved, spiky and difficult in her commerce.

Born sincere and with an extremely sensitive heart; seriousness or joy, regards, duties, and reason itself took on all the impetuosity of passions in her. Penetrating with regard to what was happening in a soul that was dear to her, if she did not discover in the complaisance that was shown to her then what she manifested so naturally at little cost; if she did not find in amity and confidence the delicacy and unreserved extent that characterized her own, she passed from reproaches to dolor to despair. Her society, in sum, was alternately delightful and insupportable.

Asaid, charmed by the virtues, intelligence and tenderness that he found in the princess, forgave the imperfections of her character. Far from ever opposing impatience or bitterness to them, it was that condescension and that mildness which gave birth to a veritable amity, sustained by reason, which had no weakness, Convinced that one cannot take too much on oneself in order to put an end to the wrongs and chagrins of the person one loves, he yielded, soon restoring calm, and gradually, the impetuosity of hr humor being vanquished, nothing remained but the tenderness—and what tenderness! Asaid did not discover anything that did not serve to render him happy.

Their court only respired pleasure, decency and zeal. Everyone around them sensed an eagerness to please them that did not depend on interest or servitude: an inestimably happiness, almost always unknown to sovereigns. They could sometimes forget that they had courtiers and think that they were surrounded by amiable and sincere friends. Talents and arts cherished and protected by them had for their principal ambition the glory of collaborating with the pleasures of the life of two such respectable masters.

Meanwhile, at Alcimedor's court, the desire to please was merely a fear of disgrace, and everything, even amusements and pleasures, was put at the rank of austere duties. Thus, Zulmane's gifts had produced in Alcimedor no other fortune than seeing himself a sovereign, without having the love of his subjects, and an unhappy husband, without having any reason to complain of the princess.

One might have thought that with conduct so different, those princes should never have experienced a common destiny. Suddenly, however, a warrior people emerged from the depths of Tartary who came to inundate Arabia. In vain the other sovereigns combined their forces with those of Alcimedor and Asaid. Those unknown men were brave, disciplined, and so formidable in numbers that they overwhelmed everything that opposed heir passage. Their king, named Aterganor, added further to their strength and valor by the high opinion that he had of the elevation of his soul.

That conqueror having rendered himself master of the capital city to which Asaid and his brother had withdrawn, assembled the most considerable men of the two nations and spoke to them thus:

"I have not set out to conquer you in order to put you in slavery. I know what your virtues are; they have increased the ambition I had to reign in Arabia. Men like you only ought to obey the greatest king on earth, the monarch of Tartary. Peoples that I have subjugated, I have not come to carry away your riches or force your will. Conserve your customs, your mores, and choose yourselves the new master who, under my authority, will be charged with the care of rendering you happy. I establish at this moment the entire equality of condition. For twelve suns let there be no other distinctions between you, and no other regards, than those made voluntarily. Employ those days of a liberty so pure to elect a sovereign. Even if he is drawn from the most obscure blood, on the strength of your choice, he will appear to me to be worthy to reign."

The conqueror then told the two princes that he would leave them free in their palaces and go to camp in the middle of the redoubtable army that surrounded the city.

The ordered equality of condition gave birth to a sudden revolution. All those for whom servitude, duties and respect had been a burden no longer thought of supporting them. Among the persons accustomed to be foremost, to make the law in accordance with their will, some scarcely conserved authority in their family.

Alcimedor's guards and officers all deserted his palace, and a deserted palace is sadder than an inhabited cabin; his courtiers abandoned him, no longer occupying themselves with anything but the part they had to play in electing a new master. Alcimedor and the princess, his wife, accustomed to the arrogance and confidence to which a long prosperity had given birth, were unacquainted with the elevation of soul that ennobles in adversity; they remained alone and humiliated.

Aterganor wanted to enjoy the spectacle of those changes; he liked to see the dejection or the dignity with which great reverses were sustained. He remarked in the different estates, with pleasure, men whose consideration had disappeared entirely with their credit and their titles, and who, from a rank that elevated them, reduced to their own merit, fell into the crowd, confounded and scorned.

But what was the excess of his astonishment when, on arriving at Asaid's palace, he sought in vain for evidence of the evolution that he expected to recognize there?

He saw the guards at their posts and the courtiers all the more occupied in showing their fidelity to their master because that homage was a pledge of their virtues. He found the prince and the princess in a state of soul equally far from fatuous firmness and humiliating sadness; they were only talking about the desire to see a sovereign crowned who rendered his subjects happy, and whose respect and love they experienced in such an admirable manner.

Aterganor thought he was being abused by a dream. "O fortunate Asaid," he cried, "and you, respectable princess, how superior your glory is to mine! You have taught me that I have not yet reigned. I only envisaged the domination that is born of force and was only maintained by fear, and which only seeks to extend itself. You have made me know that veritable authority over men has its source n heir heart."

Then the delegates of the two nations presented themselves in order to propose the king they had chosen; all of them proclaimed Asaid. Nothing was seen anywhere but tears of zeal, amour and joy; nothing could be heard but the name of Asaid.

At that spectacle, Aterganor descended from his throne; he deposited his scepter in the hands of Asaid, and, placing his own crown on the head of the princess, he said to them: "Reign, since all hearts summon you. Would I dare to subjugate those whose example I admire and whose virtues instruct me? I render sovereignty to all the peoples I have vanquished; I shall only exercise here a single right of empire. Let Alcimedor cease to be sovereign; I reunite for you alone the estates that you shared with him."

As Aterangor finished speaking, a clap of thunder was heard. Zulmane appeared on a chariot, and to hide from the eyes of mortals the prince for whom her gifts had been so unprofitable, she took Alcimedor away, as well as the princess, and was lost in the immensity of the skies.

Alsime appeared then on a throne shining with the most vivid colors of light; she confirmed the law that the just Aterganor had just made, and which assured the happiness of the peoples that Zoraide had recommended to her, She recognized with transport in the new glory with which Asaid was surrounded the fortunate fruits of her education. And it is since that new reign of Asaid that that part of Arabia has been named Fortunate Arabia.

Marianne-Agnès Falques: *Durboulour; Or, The Benevolent Lioness*

There was once a king who was a great servant of God and his Prophet; he was the father of three sons, whose mothers, whom he loved very much, gave birth to them on the same day. The more he was the master of placing the crown on one of their heads, the more he wanted to know which of them as the most worthy of it, and would render his subjects happy. He resolved, therefore, to test them, and said to them: "The one who is the most courageous and the most robust, and who can render the best account of his travels, can be assured of having preference and being my successor. Then he ordered them to go hunting, in order for them to commence applying themselves.

Each of them chose a horse from the stables, took provisions, and set forth. Their names were Gulbidar, Scandarbi and Durboulour. They hunted without having found anything, and returned very sadly to their father's palace, consoled after a fashion by seeing their common misfortune.

Durboulour remained behind for a few moments in order to examine something bright that he perceived in the sky, albeit very high. It was a feather that descended spinning, and which cast a great light. As soon as it reached the ground he picked it up, with all the care it merited; it was made of gold garnished with diamonds and precious stones. Beautiful as it was, it was only a feather, and a hunter would have been ashamed to boast about such a hunt, so he did not mention it to his brothers, much less to the king, his father.

That prince embraced his children and consoled them, saying that the poor success of their hunt proved that it was necessary to arm themselves with patience in the world, and that events did not always respond either to desire or will. Then he told them to go to bed.

Meanwhile, Durboulour found the means to place the beautiful feather in a secret place in the palace, where only the king ordinarily went. By night the latter perceived a bright light through the door; he did not doubt that a fire had started in his apartment; he ran there, and recognized with surprise the effect of the beautiful feather, the examination and the property of which charmed him. No one but one of his sons could have entered that place, so he sent for them and said: "My sons, to which of you do I owe the most beautiful of feathers?"

Scandarbi and Gulbidar cried simultaneously: "It's to me."

The king turned to Durboulour. "You aren't saying anything?"

"What do you expect me to say, Sire? It's only a feather, and the two of them are disputing it. But ask them how it is made, and Your Majesty will soon see whether the truth is in their mouth. That's the means of recognizing which of them has been fortunate enough to render that feeble homage to Your Majesty."

The competitors for a kingdom do not usually love one another, and that affair, of which Durboulour had all the honor, united the hatred of his two brothers against him. The king had no suspicion of it, and paternal love made him excuse those who had done wrong.

A few days later he said to them: "I've reflected a good deal, my children; this feather presents an object of a voyage worthy of princes like you. It's necessary to bring me the marvelous bird that bears these feathers. Depart, take the money you will need, but each depart alone. The one who brings me the beautiful bird will be my successor."

They set forth, and when they had ridden for a fortnight they found a great forest, at the entrance to which they saw a superb white marble fountain; it was facing three roads, and bore inscriptions that indicated the nature of each of the roads in question: *The man that goes to the right burns; the man that goes to the left drowns; the man who takes the middle course never returns.* They were embarrassed by that reading.

Scandarbi and Gulbidar were of the opinion to go elsewhere, but Durboulour said that he was resolved to make the proof of the three roads alone. After much argument they agreed to draw lots, but his brothers cheated Durboulour and made the road from which no one returned fall to him. They agreed the time when they would meet up again and promised that they would wait by the fountain for a determined time, in order to return to their father together.

Scandarbi found water in the route that he followed, but he did not risk drowning. Gulbidar did in fact, find fire in the one that had fallen to him, but as it was very hot he did not think that it was a good idea to approach it. They returned promptly to the fountain, therefore; they bought tents and settled down under the finest shade, savored the fresh air and spent the days in delights, content to have one competitor fewer, for the verity that they had found in the inscriptions convinced them that Durboulour would not be able to escape the danger to which he had exposed himself. They hunted for their pleasure, but in truth, they scarcely launched any arrows except at birds.

"Who knows," they said, "whether we might be fortunate enough to find the one we're seeking, and which the king has the folly of desiring. What tells us that it's there rather than here?" But that is not the way that one pursues virtue and makes a celebrated name for oneself. Hazard rarely presents difficult things.

Meanwhile, Durboulour, resolved not to neglect anything to belie the inscription, and at least to sell his life dearly, was less sorry to perish in thinking about the hatred of his brothers, which presented the prospect of an unhappy life if he did not merit the generosity of his father. He therefore wanted, at any price, to obtain it by rendering himself worthy of it.

After riding for some time, occupied with those ideas, he perceived a lioness ahead of him, the physiognomy of which was beautiful and majestic.

They looked at one another for some time, and then the lioness said: "Have you no fear, young man, in following such a dangerous road?"

"Far from being afraid," the prince replied, "everything ought to tremble before me."

"That's very proud," she said, "But I won't answer for your not having another opinion in a little while. If you take another few steps you'll be devoured, and I feel sorry for you; your physiognomy and your courage interest me. Believe me, return whence you came, for you'll find in these parts a huge snake that devours everything."

"Anyone who allows himself to be eaten," said the prince.

"I swear to you," said the lioness, "that I'm no more timid than anyone else, and that it has eaten all the lions I've made. I had two in my last litter, which are already grown and give rise to the finest hopes; I keep them carefully hidden, but I live in continual fear."

"I hope to tranquilize you soon," said the prince.

"You reassure me slightly," said the lioness, "but I dare not guide you to the place where you will find the monster."

Eventually, the prince's words having inspired the confidence that true courage always gives, she called her children and told them to look after and take good care of the Durboulour's horse. To him she said: "Mount me, if you please; I cover more ground in an hour than the best horse in twenty-four. Don't be astonished by my movements or the diligence with which I carry you through the woods and mountains."

In fact, she stopped shortly thereafter and said to the prince: "You'll find the monster in that little valley a short distance away. Go look at it, you who fear nothing; I'll wait for you here."

The prince set forth, and did not take long to encounter the monster—or rather, to see it coming toward him. Durboulour was not astonished, and cut off its head; but another one grew, just as strong. The same thing happened several times; the combat was beginning to become unequal, but the prince decided to strike a blow at the tail; it was so terrible that it separated it from the body. Then it fell, its strength failing, and the prince found himself master of the terrain.

He got his breath back, cut the tongues out of all the heads, even those that were still in the body, and made a parcel of them, which he carried away. He came to find the lioness, who was so delighted that she said: "Dispose of me and I'll do anything you wish; I'll carry you wherever you want to go."

"Madame," the prince said to her, "permit me to mount you, and that I take you first of all to see the state in which I put your enemy.

They found it dead, in great putrefaction, but the lioness, in order to satisfy a desire for vengeance quite natural in females, gave it a few bites with her teeth and scratches with her claws. They quit that place of horror in order to and take some rest near a spring that the lioness knew; she renewed her assurances of attachment to the prince so eagerly that he told her his story and the motive for which he had undertaken his journey.

After shaking her head several times during his story, the lioness said: "The marvelous bird is a long way from here, if I can believe what I've heard said about it. Your horse wouldn't take you there in twenty years, but I've told you that I'm at your orders. I'm going to take you to see a fay, a friend of mine, whose dwelling is more than thirty days' journey from here by ordinary means of transport. She might be able to give you more reliable information about what you're seeking. Come on, mount me; I'll take you at a rapid pace, traveling day and night. Hold on tight and don't sleep any more than I do."

After several days the lioness stopped and said to the prince: "You see that tree on that little arid mountain? That's where the fay I mentioned to you makes her abode. Go to her house, salute her and say to her: 'Good day and good evening, beautiful and great lady, admired and beloved by all those who know her.' That isn't true, but she'll be flattered by it, and you'll see that she'll receive you kindly."

What the lioness had said happened. The fay found the young prince as beautiful as a sun, and was touched by his compliment and the polite boldness that he testified to her.

"I hate all men," she told him. "I do them as much harm as possible, but I want to give you pleasure; perhaps it will cause others pain. In any case, it requires a great interest to have determined you to come into this desert, where no man has ever appeared."

The prince confided his designs and his adventures to her. The fay was astonished that he had defeated the monster of the forest.

"Here are its tongues, Madame," he said.

The fay admired his modesty and mildness, for virtues also touch the wicked; she could not even help saying: "The dear child! What risks he has run! Come let me embrace you; you merit people taking an interest in you, my good friend. Oh, if I were younger…the misfortune of being old is that it's necessary to be sage. Listen; I don't know exactly where the bird you're asking about is, but I have an older sister who can tell you. Take this box of mastic to her on my behalf; she'll know what that means. She lives on the fifth mountain after this one."

The prince thanked her, took his leave of her and went to find the lioness, to whom he rendered an account of his visit,. The lioness immediately put him on her back, and, traversing all the mountains while the prince counted them carefully, they arrived at the home of the second fay.

Durboulour was very well received by her, but she told him that she was very sorry not to be able to instruct him

"Don't worry," she said, "my other sister, even older than I am, can give you news of it." She told him where she lived, and gave him half the box of mastic to give to her.

The lioness, still meek and grateful, undertook that journey as cheerfully and as promptly as the others. The last fay lived in an old ruined castle. The prince went into it, and the fay looked at him with an expression to make anyone tremble, but he did not. She softened at the sight of the mastic and the pleasure the prince gave her by virtue of the grace with which he spoke to her and talked to her about her sisters.

When it came to questions regarding the marvelous bird, however, she said: "I have absolutely no idea where it lives, and, in consequence, where you might find it." Seeing how that discourse afflicted the prince, however, she added: "Don't worry; my son knows; he'll be back soon, and I'll engage him to instruct you and prevent him from devouring you, for he's an ogre by taste and temperament; it's a fault I've never been able to correct in him."

A few moments later the son arrived. The fay had the prince hide, and the ogre said, as they all do: "I smell fresh flesh."

"You're right, my son," said the fay, "but it's a man recommended to me by your aunts, and I beg you to inform him of the place where he can find the marvelous bird; he's come a long way."

"Since you and my aunts are interested in him," the ogre said. "I want to be of service to him."

The prince appeared and approached, proudly but nobly, and the ogre, who had never shown or been shown any politeness, was so flattered to receive some that he said to the prince: "I want to oblige you; in addition, I'm at war with those to whom the bird belongs. This is what I advise you to do in order to take possession of it. Go straight through the verdant valley that you can see down there, and then pass nineteen mountains; go up to the summit of the nineteenth and you'll see the shining garden of the palace in which the bird is contained, in a cage worthy of it. Don't allow yourself to be dazzled by anything you see or distracted by anything you hear.

"When you've arrived at the door of the place where the thing you desire is confined, you'll find a broad staircase that descends underground. It has nineteen steps; only go down eighteen and you'll be able to see whether the bird's guardians are asleep or awake. Those guardians are eighteen giants condemned to conserve the garden, the bird and the cage against all those who come, like you, to take possession of it, but they don't have the power to climb the nineteenth step. If you find them awake, turn back; if they're asleep, take the bird very quickly, and leave the same way."

The fay thanked her son for his kindness and his good advice, but she said to Durboulour: "That's only advice; I can give you something more essential. Take my ring of princely metal; kiss it as soon as you find yourself in a difficult situation; it will help you, either by means of the ideas it gives your enemies or the expedients it presents to you. Go, my son; come back this way, and don't forget to bring back my ring, if you can escape all the dangers you're about to run.

After having thanked them and bid them adieu, the prince followed the ogre's advice. He traversed the garden; after having found the staircase and seen the giants asleep, he took the bird and the cage, and was half way across the garden, when the trees there, from which the prince had almost emerged, spoke to him on seeing him go past. The most beautiful was their spokesman. "What! You're taking away our bird! At least take a few leaves and fruits in order to conserve that masterpiece of nature and art, that marvel of marvels."

Those trees were gold and silver, the leaves emerald and the fruits diamonds, rubies and pearls, Durboulour could not help admiring them, and although he had been told in the fay's house—and the lioness had repeated it to him a hundred times on the way—not to respond to anyone and not to take anything from the garden, the prince did not think he was risking anything in collecting one of those branches laden with flowers and fruits, in order to shelter the beautiful bird from the insults of time during the journey.

He had no sooner broken one than the tree started shouting; "Help Help! He's cutting our branches!" The other trees repeated the same plaints. Those cries woke the giants and gave them the power to emerge from the subterrain built in gold and large diamonds and come to the aid of the trees.

They seized the prince, who had no doubt that he was doomed, but he did not forget to kiss the princely metal ring; it alone could extract him from such great danger.

A council was held, and the giants, struck by the courage and resolution that the prince had shown thus far, agreed that it was necessary to let him live, on condition that he went in search for the saber of the Sufi Salomon for them, which they could not acquire by themselves, and which was necessary for them to obtain their liberty.

They put that proposition to the prince, who promised them to go in search of it, even if it was in Hell. They indicated the mountain to him in the hollow core of which it was guarded by a blind giant who was condemned to grind gold in a huge mill. That saber had great virtues, and any king who possessed it would be able to regard himself as the master of the world.

The prince set forth to execute that great design and came to find the lioness, whose great reproaches he endured. She told him that if he no longer had any desire to be king and to succeed his father, she had a great desire to return home in order to be in the bosom of her family. She calmed down, however and told him that if he failed in anything that had been prescribed for him in future, she would abandon him without taking the trouble to enquire as to how he would be able to return home.

The prince promised her everything, and begged her insistently to take him to the place indicated to him. She consented to do that, and set forth with her customary diligence.

They arrived at a huge cavern excavated in a mountain of multicolored marble. He approached it quietly, and saw the giant, who was asleep—or rather, pretending to be asleep. He also saw the saber suspended from a large golden nail above his head. He took it, but as he was leaving the cavern the giant seized him, for the blind have very keen hearing

"Aha!" he said. "You can't escape me."

The prince kissed his ring, and said: "Don't hold me so tightly."

The giant relaxed his grip and said: "Before I decide how to kill you, I want you to tell me what your design was in taking the saber confided to me. I also want to know who told you where to find my retreat."

The prince, who could not tell a lie, told him truthfully everything that had happened to him.

"Is all that true?" said the giant

"I can't assure you anymore," said Durboulour, "but if you want a witness, I'll go to fetch the lioness who bought me."

"Call her," he said, "but I'll keep hold of you."

It was necessary to endure that mistrust. The lioness came, very vexed by everything she saw. The prince said to the giant: "I haven't had time to warn her; let her tell you what she knows about my adventures."

The lioness gave an account in conformity with what he had just said.

"I'm utterly sick of being blind," said the giant. "My brethren give me the desire to imitate them and trust you; you have courage and skill, for you needed a lot in nearly carrying away the blade. There's one means of returning my sight; if you can succeed in that, I swear that I'll render you master of the saber."

The prince and the lioness promised to attempt anything.

"Well," said the blind giant, "I'll give you your life; I'll do more, I'll let you go; on condition that you bring me the chemise of Matchin-Paticha, the daughter of a great king, whose estates are thirty days' journey from here."

The prince engaged himself by oath to bring it to him and left, very annoyed by the further enterprise that he was obliged to undertake and very afflicted by the fatigue that he was about to cause his good friend the lioness. He assured her very strongly that the blind giant had been much wilier than him.

"I can see that," said the lioness, "but I have an obligation to you that I shall never forget. Mount up, mount up, and let's make this further expedition quickly."

They arrived, without knowing their way, on the bank of a very wide river. Seeing that he could not pass over it, Durboulour kissed his ring. Immediately, a ship appeared in which everything was gold, including the slightest equipment, except for the heads of the nails, which were brilliant diamonds.

After having admired the superb machine, the prince boarded it, and did not find anyone there. He examined everything carefully and read an inscription attached to the mainmast; it told him that by turning the lever below the inscription to the right, the vessel would go wherever he wanted.

"What!" he said. "Take me to the palace of Matchin-Paticha right away!"

And right away, the ship set sail.

The astonished prince continued reading and saw that by turning the lever to the left and saying: "Let the ship return to the place from which it set forth," it would immediately turn back. Those words, accompanied by a gesture, made the vessel return to its original location.

The prince found that conveyance were comfortable, and came to render an account to the lioness of what he had seen.

"Depart, Prince," she said to him, "and conduct yourself in a fashion to be able to take possession of the chemise you're seeking. In the meantime, I'm going to rest, and you'll find me here."

The prince embraced her, boarded the ship, turned the lever, set forth more rapidly than the wind, and found himself facing the king's palace.

The ship's cannons saluted of their own accord; the flag, a gold and silver oriflamme of embroidered with pearls and gems, was deployed. The king, the queen and the princess ran to the windows of the palace; the entire port resounded with cries of joy and admiration.

The king descended to the shore himself in order to see such a marvelous thing at closer range. Durboulour distinguished him easily by means of the honors that were rendered to him. He disembarked, and proved to him that he knew how to behave with crowned heads.

"Where have you come from?" the king asked. "Where are you going?"

"I'm the son of a king," said the prince, "I'm traveling in the interests of the family, and I'd like to see the great Tchin-Matchin, father of the beautiful Paticha."

The king embraced him and invited him to come to his palace. The prince accepted that honor and thanked him for the guard that he offered to put around his ship during his absence. "It guards itself," he told him. "One can't board it without a ticket, and I can't receive more than one person at a time there."

That discourse was confirmed by what happened to a few curious individuals or marauders; they wanted all the more to board the ship because they perceived that no one was guarding it, but after having received the equivalent of a hundred blows with a rod, they were thrown into the water with such great vivacity that some of them perished there.

The queen and the princess received the prince equally well; his politeness, and above all, curiosity, eventually determined the king to visit the beautiful ship, in spite of the danger that the courtiers found in leaving his sacred person exposed to the will of a stranger; but he was brave.

The prince went aboard for a few moments beforehand, under the pretext of receiving him, but in fact to cover up the inscription on the main-mast and to hide the lever. The king was charmed and surprised by everything he saw. The queen and a few viziers were equally well received, but always alone.

Finally, what the prince had anticipated arrived; the princess had so much desire to see the marvel that the king, who loved her, could not refuse her that satisfaction. He was reassured by so many examples that she was finally given that permission, on condition, however, that in order to preserve the delicacy of the court and the decency of her estate as a marriageable daughter and princess, Durboulour allowed her to explore the ship on her own, and that he would always remain in view of everyone next to the main-mast.

The princess was no sooner aboard the ship than the prince turned the lever and departed with the greatest rapidity, in the midst of the cries and regrets of the people and the court.

The prince was with the lioness in a trice. They were delighted to see one another again. He embraced her, and presented the princess to her. The princess was slightly alarmed by the presentation, but the mildness, the politeness and the behavior of the lioness soon reassured her. She had them both climb on to her back, and she returned to the marble cavern where the blind giant lived.

When they had arrived, the prince asked the princess very politely to give him her chemise.

"In verity, Monsieur, that proposition is never made; I would never consent to it."

"Don't think," said the prince, "that I can dispense with it; I swear to you that I only came in search of you for that. I would give you my life; you ought to give me your chemise."

"But what about my rank? What about modesty? What about decency?"

"Your rank is not offended, for no one can know what happens in this desert; with regard to your modesty, I ought to preserve it; I'll go away; Madame"—he indicated the lioness—"will help you to undress."

He did, in fact, retire. The lioness persuaded her to put on her garments without a chemise; she consented to that, all the more so because it was a matter of the interests of the prince, and she was beginning to love him.

When the giant heard someone approaching he asked: "Is that the desired chemise?"

"Yes," said the prince, "But you're too cunning for me. Put your hands behind your back, let me tie them; you can smell the chemise and you'll see by its odor that it can't belong to anyone else."

The giant obeyed. What would one not do in order to recover one's sight?

"Ah, that's it!" he said. "I know the fine odor of roses and plantain. How obliged I am to you, my dear friend! Give it to me so that I can rub my eyes with it."

But the prince had already taken a step back and said from a distance: "Fair exchange. The chemise is well worth the saber. Take your saber with your teeth, being it to me and I'll put the chemise under your arm."

"Oh, the blind are very unfortunate!" said the giant. "They bear all the expense of confidence."

Everything was executed in accordance with the prince's proposition, although the giant would dearly have liked to keep both; Douboulour, once he was master of the saber, was astride the lioness in a moment, with the princess behind him.

Durboulour was obliged to propose to the beautiful Paticha, however, to take her home.

"What!" she said. "Take me back to my father without a chemise! Oh, Prince," she added, "that wouldn't be becoming to you or to me." That was a pretext to hide the desire that she had to go with him. In fact, when one has given one's chemise, liking and attachment are well proven.

When they had arrived at the brilliant palace, the prince only went down the eighteen steps, and showed the giants who were guarding the marvelous bird the saber of the Sufi Salomon. They prostrated themselves at the sight of it, and handed over the cage and the bird scrupulously, which the prince took away without looking back. He heard all the trees in the garden uttering cries of joy, and saying: "Saber, great saber, beautiful saber, by the virtue of the saber we're going to recover our original state."[22]

The prince, the princess and the bird returned to the lioness, who was, in truth, a benevolent animal, whose manners were charming. She took them very swiftly to the house of the old fay, the mother of the ogre. The Prince presented Paticha to her, returned her ring, testified his gratitude to her, and returned with the lioness to the place where she made her ordinary dwelling.

She found her children in good health; she shed tears of joy, for they had been very good and had behaved in accordance with the advice they had received in their infancy from such a good mother. She found them grown and embellished; she caressed the all the more because they had taken very good care of the horse; they had taken it to the best pasturage, where they had guarded it with all possible care. In sum, Durboulour found it as fat as a dervish,

After the most tender adieux, and reiterated embraces, the prince and the princess separated from the lioness, not without tender protestations of gratitude and amity. The prince visited her several times in the course of his life, and he bore lions in his standards in order to render such a solid and essential friend illustrious.

The prince's horse did not carry them as comfortable or as swiftly as their good friend. Durboulour was often obliged to go on foot and lead it by the bridle, but they finally arrived at the white marble fountain just as his two brothers were about to leave.

They were as sorry as they were astonished to see Durboulour again, but they did not give him any evidence of it; on the contrary, they heaped him with amities and questions, to which he replied with the frankness of a worthy man.

---

[22] Author's note: "All Oriental books are full of the prodigies of Solomon's sword and ring, so no one ought to be surprised by this event."

They took the road to the parental home together, but the two brothers agreed between themselves that, Durboulour being the only obstacle to their good fortune, it was necessary to render themselves masters of the marvelous bird and the beautiful Paticha.

"Since he has told us his adventures, we can do it," they said, "and, in sum, the one who doesn't succeed the king can marry a princess, heiress to a great kingdom."

Those ideas occupied them, and they resolved to execute them at the first opportunity. It did not take long for them to find one.

Durboulour was dying of thirst; the caravan well had neither a pulley nor a rope; travelers ordinarily carried them with them. Scandarbi and Gulbidar had them, but they refused them to their brother; they only offered to give him a hand to descend into the well. Thirst sometimes causes the most enlightened man to lose intelligence. He accepted their offer, and when he was at the bottom they were preparing to fill it with stones when they thought they heard a caravan approaching, for crime blurs the senses.

They drew away promptly, abandoning their unfortunate brother and threatening to kill the beautiful Paticha if she continued her tears and groans. Not content with that ill-treatment, they told her that if she dared to mention Durboulour, and if she contradicted anything they said, she was assured of dying.

Full of hope, and no longer seeing any obstacle to their project, they arrived at the court of the king, their father, who embraced them and asked them for news of Durboulour. But they told him that, always having been reckless, he had wanted to take the road from which no one returned and had doubtless perished, since they had waited for him at the white marble fountain for a lot longer than they has agreed.

"But Sire, here is the marvelous bird. It's true that neither of us can boast of having made its conquest alone, for if one of us killed the snake, the other had the courage to obtain the saber of Solomon and to carry away Princess Paticha, who will be able to console him for the loss of your estates, assuming that the marriage is to your liking,"

The king, ever prudent, said that he would consult his Council, and occupied himself with the marvelous bird, which he admired all the more the more he gazed at it; but that did not prevent him from preparing a house for the princess and treating her in a manner appropriate to her rank, particularly in giving her numerous chemises.

Meanwhile, the unfortunate Durboulour was in despair in the well. To have surmounted so many difficulties, to have succeeded in his projects, to have carried away a princess who was worth all treasures, to be loved by her, and to lose everything in a moment by virtue of such a cruel perfidy, of which his brothers were the authors, no longer having the ring of princely metal, was to experience all misfortunes at the moment of coming into port; and although his courage sustained him, he spent a very bad night.

But he had always been lucky, and he was again. Firstly, he found a stone on which he could sit down. The next day, a caravan did, in fact, arrive, and everyone knows that they stop at every well. He asked for help; it was given to him with ropes, and he was pulled out.

He was recognized as the son of the king, for the caravan was composed of subjects returning to the capital. He was given the best horse and all the help they could offer him. In the end, he arrived the following day, when the king was at table with other two princes.

They were a little confused on seeing him appear, but the rumor caused by the arrival of Dourboulour, who was believed to be lost, served to hide their trouble.

The king had Durboulour advance and embraced him, saying: "You have need of consolation, my poor child; your voyage has not been fortunate.

"Oh, Sire, I do not see the beautiful Paticha."

"You'll see her soon and in good health," replied the king.

"My voyage has been fortunate, then," the prince went on, with vivacity. "You must have been given the marvelous bird."

"It's in my cabinet," said the king, "and I owe it to the valor and cares of your brothers."

"Oh, Sire," said Durboulour, "how hard it is to be obliged to accuse persons so close and who were so dear to me of such great crimes!"

"What tale are you telling?" said Scandarbi, insolently. "Do you want to cast suspicion on our conduct?"

"I don't want anything," said Durboulour, "But you have apparently killed the great snake?"

"Undoubtedly," he said.

"How many times did the head grow again?"

"Five times," he said.

"And how many remained?"

"Four," replied the brother.

"That isn't true, for here are the tongues of the eleven that I cut off, or that I left in the body."

The king, who knew very well the tongue of a snake—a knowledge that all kings need to have—examined them and said: "He's right; they're the snake's."

"Good," said Scandarbi. "When I killed the beast, I didn't bother with them."

"But Sire," said Durboulour, addressing the king, "it's apparently Gulbidar who carried off the beautiful Paticha?"

"I told the king that," he said.

Then, putting himself on his knees before his father, Durboulour begged him to summon her and interrogate her himself.

The beauty arrived, delighted to see Durboulour. She threw her arms around him, in spite of the modesty that still reigned in her person. She related everything that had happened, agreed with pleasure that she had sacrificed her chemise, and did not disguise the barbarity with which Scandarbi and Gulbidar had treated Durboulour by leaving him in the well, where the entire caravan certified that they had found him.

The king made the two princes leave the table and sent them to prison under strong guard. "Come, my children," he said to Durboulour and Paticha, "take the places of which courage and virtue have rendered you so worthy of filling. The realm is legitimately yours," he said to Durboulour. "The difficulties, the dangers and the success have acquired it for you veritably. It seems to me that more fortunate still is the amour given to you by a princess worthy of all prayers, but it requires the consent of the king, her father."

Ambassadors were sent forth immediately; they came back with those of Tchin-Matchin, charged with full powers, and the marriage was celebrated.

Gulbidar and Scandarbi could not sustain the good fortune of their brother and died of languor and chagrin. Old age carried away the king a short time later, and Durboulour was happy on the throne with the beautiful Paticha.

Courage brings everything to a conclusion.

CLASSIC FRENCH FANTASY

Honoré de Balzac. *The Last Fay*
Gabrielle-Suzanne Barbot de Villeneuve. *The Naiads   Beauty and The Beast*
Chevalier de Béthune. *The World of Mercury*
Jean Carrère. *The End of Atlantis*
Charlotte-Rose Caumont de La Force. *The Land of Delights*
Comte de Caylus. *The Impossible Enchantment*
Félicien Champsaur. *Pharaoh's Wife*
Jacques Collin de Plancy. *Voyage to the Center of the Earth*
Gaston Danville. *The Perfume of Lust*
Comtesse D.L. *The Tyranny of the Fays Abolished*
Paul Féval. *Anne of the Isles*
Charles de Fieux. *Lamékis*
Judith Gautier. *Isoline and the Serpent-Flower*
Nathalie Henneberg. *The Green Gods*
Gustave Kahn. *The Tale of Gold and Silence*
Edmond Haraucourrt. *Dieudonat*
Françoise Le Marchand. *Florine and Boca*
Marie-Jeanne L'Héritier de Villandon. *The Robe of Sincerity*
André Lichtenberger. *The Centaurs; The Children of the Crab*
J-M. & Randy Lofficier. *The French Fantasy Treasury 1-3*
Charles Lomon & P.-B. Gheuzi. *The Last Days of Atlantis*
Maurice Magre. *The Marvelous Story of Claire d'Amour; The Call of the Beast; Priscilla of Alexandria; The Angel of Lust; The Mystery of the Tiger; The Poison of Goa; Lucifer; The Blood of Toulouse; The Albigensian Treasure; Jean de Fodoas; Melusine; The Brothers of the Virgin Gold*
Marie-Madeleine de Lubert. *Princess Camion.*
Camille Mauclair. *The Virgin Orient*
Hippolyte Mettais. *Paris Before the Deluge*
Victor-Emile Michelet. *Superhuman Tales*
Henriette-Julie de Murat. *The Palace of Vengeance*

Charles Nodier. *Trilby   The Crumb Fairy*
Edgar Quinet. *The Enchanter Merlin*
Henri de Régnier. *A Surfeit of Mirrors*
Restif de la Bretonne. *The Fay Ouroucoucou* (2 vols.)
J.-H. Rosny Aîné. *Pan's Flute*
Marie-Anne de Roumier-Robert. *The Voyage of Lord Seaton
to the Seven Planets*
Nicolas Ségur. *Penelope's Secret*
Brian Stableford (ed.). *Funestine; The Queen of the Fays*
Kurt Steiner. *Ortog*
C.-F. Tiphaigne de La Roche. *Amilec   Giphantia*
Simon Tyssot de Patot. *The Strange Voyages of Jacques
Massé and Pierre de Mésange*